Rabbits and Moons

A Novel

L. Wendell Vaughan

Grosbeak Books
New Bedford, MA
USA

Praise for Rabbits and Moons

"A viewpoint and perspective seldom encountered, at times brutal, gritty, and yet eloquent..." **Dwayne Almeda, SF writer**

"A warm, inviting story infused with romance, rainforest intrigue, and Central American Flare..." **Kirkus Review**

"Vaughan has a unique writing style that kept me engaged throughout the story..." **Rated 4 stars out of 4, Onlinebookclub.org**

"Rabbits and Moons is a complete journey. Eleanor is a flawed but sympathetic character, and the supporting cast is vividly drawn. Set in a Central American orphanage that is a Ship of Fools of international volunteers, Eleanor is drawn into drama both mundane and life-threatening. The author has a real penchant for rendering the grotesque with vivid charm..." **Paull Goodchild, author of The Case of the Indian Pale Ale**

"Rabbits and Moons is so well written that you get to escape into the book. You feel like you are with the characters experiencing every event. This book is a must read." **Ford**

"A fantastic trip for the mind. Vaughan's descriptive ability and attention to detail creates a vibrant landscape. A startling vision of a third world country through the eyes of the main character who takes it all in stride. A marvelous and captivating read. Highly recommended..." **Stonefly, Country Western song writer.**

"Could not put it down. There is a psychology to this book that is gripping..." **Thurten Ogly, writer (The Epic)**

"Thank you..." **Annabell M, retired analyst**

BOOKS BY
L. WENDELL VAUGHAN

Rabbits and Moons (Book 1)

Betting on Paradise (Book 2)

Library of Congress Control Number: 2020909825
Library of Congress Cataloging-in-Publication Data
Vaughan, L. Wendell
Rabbits and Moons: a novel/L.Wendell Vaughan 2nd ed.

Rabbits and Moons may be purchased for educational, business, or sales promotional use. For information please email: grosbeakbooks@gmail.com

Book cover design
Photograph by Hisbeth-Rodriguez
Altered by Grosbeak Books

ISBN 978-0-9702979-5-2 paperback
ISBN 978-0-9702979-3-8 digital ebook
ISBN 978-0-9702979-4-5 Hardcover

With love,
To my grandmother,
Louise Beachamp Vaughan,
Who hated the phrase —
I can't

"If I advance, follow me.
If I stop, urge me on. If I retreat, kill me."
— Henri de la Rochejaquelein

Chapter 1

The Bus Ride

Three children with gooey noses and small bright faces stood and faced me backwards over their seats, heads just above the rim, staring at me. With each sway and bump of the bus, their bodies jiggled. Wide-eyed and toothy, they disappeared and popped back up again, laughing.

"What's so funny?" I asked them in Spanish, which caused them to disappear. When they bounced back up, giggling, front teeth missing and pink tongues exposed, I thought, *this is going to be a long bus ride.* But eventually they grew tired and sat back down for good. I watched them pee into plastic bags which the mother threw out the window and munch on torn pieces of corn tortillas. The mother was young with a button nose, her dark cheeks dappled with freckles. She turned several times toward me and smiled. She even asked me if I wanted some food. I thought she was kind. She had children to feed. I pointed to the orange and jicama I had brought and said that I was fine. Once she touched the white untanned skin of my lower arm and said, "*Suerte.*" My response was to sweep my eyes over her family and say, "Why, you have luck!" Not that I really thought that; I didn't want children; too constant, too permanent.

Five of them, the father silent and pensive by the aisle, were crammed tightly into one small seat. I imagined them living in a generic thatched hut made with corn stalks, smelling of corn while they ate corn, and everyone else in the village living in similar houses with smoke peeling from their thatched roofs in unrefined swirls scented with corn. Then there were the beans and rice, day after day after day after day. The constant cleaning to keep the dirt floor pristine—understandable, but redundant. It never ceased to surprise me how neat and pressed their clothing appeared—even their oily hair, coiffed and colorful with bows and ribbons yet smelling like corn, but a sour corn, as though it had been picked and peeled and thrown into a bag for far too long. Lives constantly threatened by cold, heat, humidity, vermin, another child being born, a goat dying, a drunken husband, the unexpected arrival of the military. I was perfectly content just being me and fumbled around my bag for chewing gum.

The bus I was on was a yellow Blue Bird school bus built for elementary-aged kids. I sat on a seat by myself with my knees bent sideways. The unforgiving chassis caused every ditch, pothole, and ravine to send me jolting into the air, which made it impossible to read. The windows were shut to keep out the dust, and the air was clogged with sweat, sour corn, and too many breathing mouths. My only solace was the drifting thoughts about whatever came into my head, which were random and obsessive at times. We had already been on the road for hours, and there were hours left to go. I had already undergone and overcome the duplicity of my family back home, churned over words I wished I had said to an unfit ex-boss, and yearned for the touch of a past lover's hands—but not the complications those hands brought.

For an entire year, I'd kept myself chaste due to the need to not be attached to another. The freedom from entanglements and commitments was enlightening. My only responsibility was to myself. My happiness, my desires, my wants and needs. It may sound selfish, but I was a traveler, which was the title I gave myself whenever someone asked.

First there was Mexico, and now Central America. So far, I'd made friends but never a commitment. Lately I'd been thinking about stability. There was also a visceral gnawing—or, should I say, a craving to take a lover. But then I reminded myself of the simplicity of my life and shied away, though I was beginning to rethink my decision.

For instance, across the aisle form me sat a lanky Swiss fellow. Like me, he had an entire seat to himself because he was too long to sit properly otherwise. He was trying to read the newspaper *Las Noticias*, a regional paper filled with stories of car crashes, murders, bribery, and now and then the odd story about witchcraft. Every time the bus hit a ditch or swerved, the paper smacked him in the face. It made me laugh, a haughty laugh that caught his attention. He stood, braced himself using the backs of the seats for support, and came over to my seat to join me. The legroom was still too small, so he maneuvered his body halfway out into the aisle. I could tell he was one of those travelers who didn't use deodorant, which I found very offensive. I also knew from conversations with the locals that they weren't fond of the smell either. A strong stench of used kitty litter emanated from his hairy, drippy pits. When he casually put his arm up over the back of the seat, I couldn't help but cough and wave my hand in front of my nose.

The Swiss wore faux Central American clothing, the kind no one wore except hippy types, gringos who wanted to seem cool, but weren't because they tried too hard. He had a weak jaw and pouty lips, the lower one wet from him licking it. I was thirty and placed him in his early twenties. With his questionable hygiene, I was surprised to see clean, white teeth when he smiled. But he didn't like Americans and stated, "Americans think they're better than everyone else." As though he wanted to teach me a lesson before even knowing me. "So, what," I snapped, slightly irritated, then added, "I bet you watch a lot of American television." This remark caused him to fiddle with his chin and reply, "Maybe." And proceeded to try and guess my name. "Sue? Janet? Linda?"

"Eleanor," I finally said, which made him laugh and ask, "Where are your glasses? I think of Eleanors as wearing glasses." *What an exasperating fellow*, I thought. But then, for some irrational reason, I imagined what it would be like to have sex with him. As he stretched sideways, he slanted his back and leaned against my shoulder. His wispy, blond air fluffed next to my right cheek while sweat beaded on his forehead, and his lips were puckered. It would have been very natural to kiss. But when he yawned his overly wide mouth without covering it, the food encrusted between his back molars was disgusting. It was obvious to me that sex with him would be smelly and quick, but there would be great pleasure in telling him that Americans were much better at satisfying their partners than the Swiss. I asked him to move back to his seat. "Too hot to sit together," I said. He told me he didn't mind the heat, but he understood and moved anyway. Before leaving, he gave me the paper he had been trying to read. I thanked him and stuffed it into my daypack for later. After he'd returned to his original seat nearer to the front of the bus, he kept turning around to give me little waves with his hand, and I'd wave back. But after the third time, I ignored him.

It wasn't long after my episode with the Swiss that the bus began to crawl up into the mountains. The ubiquitous soldiers with their maroon berets and AK-47s stopped the bus every fifteen minutes. It was nothing terrible, just maddening because the same men were told to get out each time. It was also very time-consuming, which put me on edge. To arrive in El Puente in the middle of the night was not a pleasant thought. I'd been told the town was more like an outpost where few people lived and there weren't any hotels. I knew that most remote towns in the country were quiet and shut down by nine. With the streets empty and everyone asleep, how would I get a water taxi to the orphanage, my final destination? My heart and gut tightened. I sipped some water and ate an orange. There was nothing I could do about it.

I was to be a *niñera* at the orphanage, helping take care of the three- and four-year-old children. The place was located on a river in the middle of a rainforest, and the main access to the compound

4

was by boat. The idea to volunteer at such a place came to me after griping to a fellow language student in Antigua, Guatemala that I was tired of attending Spanish-language classes. She suggested I volunteer somewhere, and that a different venue to learn the language could help with learning the heart of a language—idiomatic expressions. She also told me about her sister, who had worked in an orphanage in Nicaragua and had become fluent in the Spanish language. The orphanage idea piqued my interest, since it was my goal to become fluent.

Yes, I know that I said I didn't want children, but working with them and having them are completely different. If I didn't like it, I could leave. I was good at it—that is, leaving a situation when it became boring or distasteful. It had become part of my journey. With my learned travel habits in mind, I soon found an orphanage that would take me and signed up. I had few expectations but hoped for the best. Yet at the moment, all I could think about was my arrival to a town that would almost surely be dark and unwelcoming.

When the bus stopped for the twentieth time, I peered out the cloudy window at the military police. They looked like a bunch of kids playing hooligan cops. Some even looked like they were ten or twelve, keeping their small index fingers on the triggers of their assault rifles. Their night goggles flapped in front of them, and cigarettes dangled from their mouths. They talked to each other about women's boobs and made bad jokes about the clothing of the men they were harassing—men who wore vaquero attire, loose jeans on thin bodies, torn slacks, cowboy boots, and hats; thick leather belts with big metal buckles fitted with rhinestones, heralding bucking horses and the lone star. Others wore traditional indigenous clothing: striped chinos tied on with ropes knotted at the waist and loose-fitting cotton shirts. A few more had on T-shirts with bad jokes in English like, "I don't need a hairstylist, my pillow sets my hair" and "If people are talking behind your back, fart"—American T-shirts sold on the street and in open-air markets. I had a few. They were cheap. Sometimes charities gave them away for free too.

The men being patted down by the boys all had one thing

in common: they looked indigenous, poor, and scared. At these inconvenient stops, the men, except for the lanky Swiss because they weren't looking for foreign white people but only their own kind, had to get out of the bus. Yet the Swiss always got out too. He was the only one that seemed to enjoy the harassment. He even giggled whenever the *niños militares* bumped the noses of their blunt guns into his back or arms. Often, he looked around and grinned. I think he wanted someone to take his picture.

Sometimes the whole shakedown took so long that the men relieved themselves like patient burros onto the grasses below. The first one would lower his hand and take his penis out, then another. Their urination would cause a swooshing, splattering noise as their piss hit the sod and dirt below. The relief was always followed by a mild shake and a zip back up. The boys with their guns pointed at crotches snickered as they commented on dick sizes. The Swiss, who had no chin, would pee too, but when he peed, he let out a big sigh which caused everyone to look at him. No one commented on his penis, even though I saw many of the men look at it. I imagined it small, like the pink lobes of his ears, or long and thin like the fingers he kept combing through his hair.

At each checkpoint, I too got out of the bus, but it wasn't to stand with the men, since I was a female. The jostling bus wreaked havoc on my bladder. Hidden behind a thicket of bushes, I would pee and watch the ridiculous trumpery of military searching for bad guys (guerrillas, terrorists), which was ridiculous, since most of the bad guys were actually the police. I did feel lucky that no one ever bothered me or even looked at me while I squatted off to the side. Being a gringa, I was a nonentity. Not part of the dance, just a mere apparition on these buses, like a bundle of generic clothing or a bag of garbage. In a different place or situation, being invisible wasn't so easy. I liked the lack of attention. It made riding buses in the country tolerable, along with the scenery. The scenery was often very pretty.

Once we were out of the mountains, the military disappeared and twilight crept in. We drove without a hitch along a smoothly paved road with a dry, cracking desert on both sides. Somehow on this wonderful pavement, a tire went flat right in the only village I'd seen in hours. It did occur to me the villagers may have booby-trapped the road for business, but then why think negatively? I had to go to the bathroom, and I was positive the village had one somewhere. Yet it was another delay. It rattled me more than all the other delays because it seemed like it would take the longest. Since there wasn't a spare tire, the driver and his assistant went off to find one. If the Swiss had still been on the bus, I would have complained to him about my situation, but he'd gotten off a while back by a sign that had the international picture of rocks falling. I had no idea where he was going and didn't care.

When I got off the bus, a foreigner, possibly European or American, stood to my right by an embankment near the back of the bus. He was tall and ruddy-white with a sinewy body, wearing a beige felt fedora that dipped over his left eye. He was nibbling on a piece of hay like a hungry rabbit. This chewing and biting made him appear either very bored or nervous. A good-looking man, his square chin and flattened cheekbones made him handsome the way an oddly shaped rock can be striking. I placed his age to be somewhere around fifty and figured he would be much better in bed than the Swiss due to experience, but I wasn't in the mood for imagining sex with strangers anymore. Stress and the call of Mother Nature's urgencies had gotten rid of my foolishness. I went up the short hill to the village.

Once in the center of the village, I looked around for a restaurant or sign that said *banos*. It was a dusty place with unpainted cement buildings, rebar sprouting like rogue hairs from unfinished second stories. Most of the side roads were dirt pathways, and in the middle of the square was a small, stucco church with Christmas decorations and lights surrounding the door, even though it wasn't Christmas. There were also multi-colored bulbs blinking, hanging off of fences and poles throughout the place. The lights were festive, and for a few brief moments I stood taking it all in.

Moving on, I found a *tienda* with an outhouse in the back. The owner of the store let me use it for the equivalent of a penny. It was neat and clean with a deep hole. Unfortunately, the minute I bent over to pee, a swarm of black flies matted themselves to my bottom, making the ordeal still more uncomfortable. I fussed and swished my hand over my butt, but it was pointless.

When I returned to the bus, the foreigner was still milling around, chewing on hay. From afar, I looked at him more closely. His clothing looked rich. He wore pressed blue jeans, a collared long-sleeve shirt, and had a leather jacket slung over his right arm. I assumed he was the type of fellow who shopped at fancy stores for wealthy people who wanted to appear casual. I thought it odd that he was waiting for the bus, since it was a third-class bus. He glanced at the sky and kicked the dirt. He then began to circle as though he didn't know if he should stay or go.

I walked over to him to say hello, curious to know if he was going to the same place I was heading to. He must have sensed my intentions because he immediately glanced over at me with coral blue eyes, barbed and flecked, that gave me a look that said *Stop, or I might bite you*. In mid-step, I stopped and stood frozen in place. I wondered what could be wrong, or if he possibly was a madman. When his circling turned into frantic pacing, he threw his hands in the air and took off up into the village. I was happy to see him leave and hoped he wasn't coming back because who needs crazy? Hungry, I went over to a vendor stirring a big steel barrel of steamy water. I bought a waterlogged tamale and a tepid Coca-Cola from him and sat on a hefty boulder by the bus to eat. I then pulled the newspaper out of my daypack that the Swiss had given me and began to read.

After going over the comics section, I read a terrible story about a car crash, then an opinion piece about the United States invading Kuwait and the upcoming election between George Bush and Bill Clinton. The article favored Bill Clinton; I hadn't thought much about the elections back home, but thought Bill seemed a bit cooler than George. Flipping to the front page, the headline was about a corrupt government official. The Ministry of the Interior had been caught falsifying land deeds, but the government wasn't filing charges because the Minister of the Interior was the president's cousin. Below the story, was another headline: *Assesinato en el rio.* A picture of a man wearing a fedora was the suspected killer. He looked a lot like the man who'd just run off.

Holding the paper toward what was now an orange, disappearing sun, I realized the picture had to be him. The penetrating eyes were a dead giveaway. I looked around to see if the man had come back, but he hadn't, so I began to read the article. It wasn't good. He had recently been acquitted of murder, even though all the evidence indicated that he'd committed the crime. His acquittal was due to him bribing the judge in charge. This admission of corruption met with such impunity had me shaking my head. The article also stated that the murder victim was a fifteen-year-old boy, the grandson of a Doña Yenara Pinola Alvares. Doña Alvares lived in El Puente—the town I was heading for. *Creepy,* was my first thought. Reading further, it appeared that Doña Alvares' brother, Don Edmund Poco Pinola, had been framed by the man wearing the fedora for the boy's murder and had been sentenced to life in prison and had died trying to escape. The story then went into the gruesome details of how the boy had been shot and dumped in the river with cement blocks attached to his feet. The paper noted that cement blocks float in Central America, and he floated into a patch of mangroves. His bloated, decomposing body had been discovered by a young orphan who resided at the orphanage where I was to be a volunteer. *Poor thing, what a horrible sight to see,* I grumbled in my head. Then made an *umph* noise, *what am I getting myself into?* I looked around to see if the driver and his assistant had returned.

To my great joy they'd come back, and the tire repair was all set. I got back on the bus and opened a window to look at the desert. It was flat for miles until it ran into a long mountain range. The evening sun had left traces of copper and gray in the sky. The scene was beautiful, breathtaking; remote and mysterious as the earth submissively rolled into darkness. We had a good six hours to go. My estimated arrival time in El Puente would be somewhere between midnight and one in the morning. It chilled my core and turned the fading earth cold and bleak.

Chapter 2

The Arrival

The town was pitch black when I stepped off the bus. There were no lights on anywhere, and the sky was without stars, which punched another hole in my fragile psyche. I could taste the dampness in the air. The disheartening idea that it might rain swept over me, then scolded myself for getting off the bus; I should have stayed on until the last stop, which was only an hour away. I could have slept on the bus until morning and then jumped on another at daylight and come back, but I hadn't, so here I was: a solitary, vulnerable human set adrift in a lightless town without an umbrella or a bench to sit on. I kicked a pebble out of frustration and listened to it echo as it bounced down the potholed road, but then quickly regretted it because what if I'd disturbed something bad? What if I awoke or caught the attention of some ill-minded people? I held my breath, then let out a chuckle. What good was fear?

Then the clouds moved away, exposing the sky. It was the darkest blue and full of sparkling stars, bringing me a sense of joy, but it was one of those moonless nights. The thought of the night without a moon was troubling, like when a light switch in a room doesn't work. But then there was the Milky Way, dotting the sky with green and orange and clustered strips of white. It was so bright that it turned the rooftops of the only three buildings in the town the color of ash, highlighting the dirt road that broke off at the jungle's edge.

A cement bridge to my left crossed over a rushing river with cascading white foam. It also made sucking noises as though slurping up the mud from the bottom. Below the bridge, a dock was lined with several canoes with outboard motors. A dog with white spots sniffed at an overflowing trash bin. I listened in earnest over the churning river for a human voice or some laughter, but all I heard was the dog crunching on something hard and brittle.

I walked over to the three cement buildings and peeked behind them. A light was on the first floor of the middle building. I smiled at the possibility of good fortune. I went up to the door and knocked. Nothing. Not one sound could be heard from within. I knocked several times again, and each time my knock grew louder. Finally, something shuffled from within, followed by footsteps that came right up to the door. "*¿Quién es?*" asked a woman with a hoarse voice.

"*Me llamo Eleanor*," I said, telling her my name. My throat was raspy, too. I was tired and hoped the woman would have a room for me to sleep in. "*Necesito alquilar una habitación por la noche.*" I wanted to know if she would rent me a room.

Silence.

I cleared the phlegm from my throat. "*Yo pagaré mucho.*"

The woman fiddled with the lock and opened the door, but only enough to expose small, squinting eyes. A dank odor of rotten corn and animal wafted into the late-night air. The putrid smell knocked me a step back, but the woman grabbed my arm and clenched it with gnarly fingers. The idea of making money seemed to make her bold. I tried to twist away, but where was I to go? I let her pull me inside, and as she did, she stretched her head out the door and looked around as if to check for others.

She stood approximately a foot shorter than my five feet and seven inches; I looked down at her, wishing once again I'd stayed on the bus. Her face, shadowed by the backdrop of a dull, yellow light, was that of a withered old lady coupled with the bad stench, my gut told me to leave. Yet, again, where to? When she moved closer and smiled, she displayed high, rosy cheeks and calculating eyes that sized me up. A woman of many faces, I thought, and thrifty. Her black-and-white hair was in a loose bun. I had woken her up. When our eyes met, hers narrowed. "*Cinco dólar*," she said.

"*No problemo*." The money exchange rate would make my stay less than a dollar. But before paying, I asked about a boat to the orphanage and if there was someone who could take me tonight. She shook her head 'no' while holding out her hand to be paid. I paused once again to look around the room. The floor was tiled and swept clean. The only furniture were two blue plastic chairs next to a lopsided wooden table. I had hoped for a couch but would be fine sleeping in a chair with my head on the table. I was content and relieved to be inside a building with a door.

I dug in my pocket for the money, but just then a tattered, diminutive man burst through the door. He pushed my body against the doorjamb as he passed. The woman grabbed me and held me against her body; I could see in her eyes that she was afraid I was going to leave. Her small, round frame felt like mealy down, and I quickly re-pocketed the money and pulled myself away. The man reeked of garbage, and his breath was bitter and tangy on my cheek, soiled no doubt by the rotgut he had been drinking.

He took a bottle of clear liquor from his pocket and sat down at the table, mumbling incoherently and drinking. This threw the woman into hysterics. She ran over to him and took hold of his oversized coat with both hands. She shook him from side to side and tossed him to the floor. She was strong. I watched her berate the drunkard, bent over, her face inches from his. She spoke rapidly in a language that sounded like upside-down French. It was filled with shushing words and ticks that swallowed each other. The man barked back in the same tongue, only his speech was sloppy and slow. He finally crawled away into a back room.

"Christ," I mumbled. All I wanted to do was sit at their table and go to sleep, but I couldn't stay here. I wanted nothing to do with their domestic squabbles. I quickly turned and left. The cool, damp air was refreshing as I hurried down the path, my destiny unknown. But before I could make it around the corner and back out into the road, there was a shout from behind. The woman's silhouette squatted in her doorway and a skinny boy came toward me. The boy walked lazily with twisted, knobby knees while rubbing his eyes. "I take you," he said in heavily accented English. "*Orfanato.*" He gave me a price. I knew it was high, but I would have gladly paid ten times what he was asking to get out of this town. Waiving him over, he smiled. What luck: it appeared the family was in the water taxi business.

The boy gave me a toothy grin, took my backpack off my shoulders, and slung it over his skinny body. He wasn't much bigger than the bag, and for a moment I thought to take it back but dismissed the urge so as not to offend. He beckoned me to follow him with his hand. We went down to the dock by the row of canoes. When a twig snapped, I turned around and looked back at the village. The woman was only yards away. She had waddled after us, looking like an obstinate rat. She hummed an off-key tune that I found unnerving. I wished she would just go away.

Seated on the middle bench of a canoe, I watched her approach the boat. It was the first time I had noticed her clothing. It was indigenous, but different from what I was used to seeing in this country. Instead of a *huipil* and a heavy black, wool skirt, she had on a cloth skirt and blouse and a vest with decorations in the middle. I turned to the boy and asked if they were *Mam* or *Q'eqchi'*. He said, "No, *Mapuche.*"

"Mapuche?" I repeated and shrugged. I'd never heard of the Mapuche people before and wondered if they were transplants from the north, like many of the other groups in the area, but asking more questions seemed too tiring, so I let my curiosity slide.

The woman looked down at me, her nostrils flaring from the walk. She huffed, smacked her lips, and said in stilted English, "Tell Cleef to see me. Yena."

"Yena?" I questioned.

"*Me llamo* Yenara. Yena to friends."

The name Yenara sounded familiar. I'd seen or heard the name recently, but where? Before I could ask any questions or acknowledge her request, the boy slammed the boat into gear and we shot backward, then forward into the rushing river. I glanced back at the woman called Yenara, Yena to friends, and watched her grow smaller and smaller as we pushed with haste up the river, a river painted white with hints of orange and yellow lit by the silver streaks of the stars. On each side, I could sense more than see the jungle and the foreboding awe it inspired. It was moments like these—the ugliness of the town contrasted with the beauty of nature, discomfort overshadowed by rapture, fear replaced by glory—that filled me with exultation for life.

In no time at all we reached the orphanage's dock. I paid the fare and threw in an extra *quetzal* for the boy. I thanked him, and he sped off behind a corner of mangroves. The high-pitched whine of the canoe's engine dissipated, and I was left with silence before me. I yawned loudly and shook my limbs. It was cold, so I took my sweatshirt out of my pack and put it on, then followed the path lit by a floodlight up a dirt ascent laden with clumps of sparse grass. At the top, the floodlight revealed a white cottage and a long building that looked like a dining hall. Another well-sized building was next to it, and another large building faced them. In the middle, there was a play area with sand with upside-down canoes on one side. I glanced at the buildings again, wondering which one I should go to. Made of wood, they looked soggy, like they were sinking into the ground. In the building that sat alone away from the others, a light on in its screened-in porch. Two white fellows in faux ethnic balloon pants were sitting on the floor of a sparse, cavernous room, leaning up against a wall, legs straight out and drinking what appeared to be rum and Cokes; a half-empty rum bottle and an empty liter of Coca-Cola were tipped over on their sides on the floor. Happy to see there were people awake, I walked in through the squeaky screen door, put my backpack down, went over to the fellows, and said, "Hello."

"*Shh.* No noise," said the frizzy blond with a clipped British accent.

"Orphanage, right?" I asked in a low tone.

"Who are you?" the Brit asked with a suspicious look, a mischievous half-smile like he'd made a joke, only he hadn't. His hairdo was so absurd it made me smile. He had two ribbons tied into bows on his head, which created two well-formed ponytails out of his kinky hair. When I read his ratty T-shirt, I chuckled silently. In cursive were the words *It's my hair that makes me sexy.* I took him to be around twenty-five in years and twelve in maturity.

"My name is Eleanor. I'm to be a *niñera.*"

"Jolly good. Did you hear that, Alex? We've got help." They clinked their half-full glasses together and took long, loud slurps. It was tempting to ask them for a drink, but another night. Tonight, all I wanted was to sleep in a bed, if there was one, but as noted earlier, a chair and table or even the floor would do.

"Where's the bathroom?" I asked.

"We go outside in the bushes," said Alex in a thick German accent. It was then that I realized I knew him. His dyed China-red dreads were tied up in knots on his head atop a moon face with a long, crooked nose. His grin was puckish, and his small, black eyes looked like marker dots. He still had the same three purple pimples on his soft chin and the same piercings running up and down his ears, but the nose ring that resembled the kind pigs wear to keep them from rooting was new. The whole quirky mess gave him an unusual appearance. Artistic, as if he were a Cubist painting. However, he was saddled with a personality prone to theft and severe jealousy. He could be hard to be around. We met in Puerto Escondido months ago, where he stole my Spanish verb book. He also never cleaned his dishes in the communal kitchen at the rooming house. He constantly insulted everyone. By the time I left, no one would talk to him except his girlfriend, Milla. And no one understood what she saw in him. I didn't like him there, and I was sure I wouldn't like him here. I pretended not to recognize him, and he seemed to do the same with me.

"The bushes are the bathroom?" I asked.

"The boys use the bushes; the girls use the mud," Alex explained with a serious air.

I wasn't amused and said nothing back.

"The bathroom is through those doors and to the right," the Brit interjected. "The water isn't working. You can't flush."

"Thanks. Is there a place I can sleep?" I said, believing I was finally making some headway.

"Right on my lap, sweets," Alex said, kissing the air.

"Bloody hell, Alex, don't be a wanker," the Brit said, then looked at me. "We're babysitting."

"Yes, babysitting," Alex repeated. "And you need to be quiet." He put his finger up to his lips and looked toward the inner room. "The children are sleeping. *Shh.*"

I rolled my eyes and groaned and went off to the bathroom. The toilets didn't have seats. Filled with piss and shit, the stench was overwhelming, but I peed anyway. The toilet wouldn't flush, but then the Brit told me they wouldn't—no running water. There weren't any doors on the bathroom stalls, and the three showers didn't have any curtains. Bare-bone accommodations, I thought, not particularly bothered. I went back into the porch and asked if there was drinking water somewhere.

"Drinking water is outside. Two tanks. Drink from the right one," said the Brit.

"No, it's the left tank," Alex interjected.

"Right."

"Left."

I went outside and over to the tanks. I tasted the water from both. The right tasted better, so I filled my bottle from the right and went back in. I didn't want to talk to the boys anymore. I was too tired for their obnoxious behaviors, so I began to rearrange several of the throw pillows to make a bed by the door to what I presumed to be the kid's bedroom.

"What are you doing?" Alex asked. I didn't answer.

"You can't crash our party," Alex said, sitting upright. I ignored him.

"There is a room," said the Brit. "Go up to the second floor. Go through a door on the left of the hall to the third floor. The room is up there. It has the only free hammock." He then smiled. Alex smiled too. I didn't smile back. There was something not right about the room or they wouldn't be smiling, but I went anyway. Without another word, I picked up my pack and went up the stairs.

On the second floor, there was a distinctive thick cedar smell, and I heard the rhythmic inhale and exhale of heavy breathing from down the hall. The place reminded me of every flophouse, hostel, and cheap hotel I had been living in over the past year. As I gazed down the hall, I hoped the rest of the crew was not like the two downstairs. If so, I'd leave.

I took the creaky steps to the third floor. Once at the top, I placed my pack down and took my flashlight out because I couldn't find any light switches. The room was small and lined with boxes on one side, which made it even smaller. The walls were the slanted mahogany rafters of the roof, which made it hard to stand up straight. Because the rafters had gaps, the starlight streaked and created stripes on the walls. Cobwebs entangled with clumps of dead bugs were everywhere; even the hammock had a web. I hated hammocks because when I slept, I liked to move around, and the hammock I was looking at appeared more for a child than an adult, and I didn't even think I could fit in it. The room also had a dusty, baked feeling to it and a fetor that resembled a complex mixture of decomposing organic matter and urine.

Fully dressed in jeans, shirt, sweatshirt, socks, and sneakers to keep crawly things from nibbling at my toes, I delicately crawled into the hammock. It was very unstable and swung back and forth unmanageably. I soon fell out onto the slimy floor and made a loud clunking noise. I stood up and wiped my hands on my pants, then gave it another shot. I fell out again. Below someone shouted, "What!?!"

I tried once more, but whether the contraption was poorly built, too small, or it was just my lousy hammock skills, I fell out again. Dumbfounded, I sat on one of the cardboard boxes to think. It sunk to half its size and almost dropped me to the floor. With my knees bent up to my chin and my butt pressed against something pointy in the box, I reached down and felt the polyester, stringy hair of a Barbie doll and pulled it out. Her jointless arms and legs twisted at the hip and shoulders, as if pointing at me. I let it drop back into the box as a well of frustration, heat, and fury crested my neck and brow. I was so miserably tired that my brain felt like lead, and my eyeballs were hard, dry marbles.

Sitting like a poorly made pretzel, I slumped over and fell asleep until a mosquito dive-bombed my right ear and another bit my hand. I jolted forward and swatted the air, drool matted to my chin and left cheek, and I wiped it with the back of my hand. Heaving myself up, I stood and slapped a few more mosquitoes dead. When a few more buzzed my head, I mumbled, while paddling the air with my hands, muttering *"Pendejos"* and my favorite, *"Me cago en todo lo que se menea"*— I shit on everything that moves. Then I picked up my water bottle, tripped over a box full of Legos, and knocked it into a box of Matchbox cars. Everything scattered to the floor. From somewhere in the building someone yelled, "Shut up!"

Fed up, I descended back down to the first floor. The porch lamp was still on, but the idiots were asleep. Great babysitters, I thought. They had their heads tilted to the side and their mouths wide open. It was tempting to be very immature and stuff my grungy, two-day-old socks I had on into their mouths, but I took the high road and kept going. I went out the screen door and down to the river's edge. The cool, damp air bathed my face and lungs. The freshness of my surroundings and the vastness of the river before me were joyful and life-giving. I breathed in deeply and calmed myself. It would all be fine. I'd experienced plenty of "first bad days" in my travels. I had also found that the worse the beginning of the trip, the better the destination often was.

I washed my hands in the river water and used the sand to scrub off the grime. Then I walked around in circles before sitting down on a large rock by the dock to stare off across the broad span of water. I would wait for morning. Once the sun was up and the birds were singing, I would reintroduce myself to the place, all wrongs corrected by a new day. I just needed to be patient.

A ghostly fog crawled over the dark, cobalt blue gulf. The silence was eerie and deafening, inspiring a visceral fear in me of what might lurk in the woods or even within the cool hues of the river. A knocking sound came from the dock pilings, and I froze, then quickly got up and walked over. "Who's there?" I asked. It was nothing; just flotsam from the river. This made me laugh. Giddy with exhaustion, I may have even wept a bit. With a sigh, I went back to the rock and sat down again feeling more exhausted than I'd ever felt before. Even if I had wanted to go back up to the building, the walk seemed too taxing. The air, chilled and scented with the earth's decomposing matter and water, had me hugging myself to stay warm. I slapped a mosquito flat against my cheek. I unclipped my hair to let it dangle around my neck and face to head off the bugs. I hadn't been back to the States for almost a year. It was probably snowing there—that is, if I had my months correct and it was early March. Sinking down onto the ground, I fell asleep.

Chapter 3

Daylight

The world was boiling, and I was right smack in the middle of the combustion, bubbling like a plastic top in the heat, unable to swim but somehow buoyant. Surfacing, the tiny whispers of ethereal air resounded as the wind rose and fell, being played on a piano of clouds. When I reached out to grab one of the notes, I couldn't. Grunting, I tried again, but the notes were quick. I laughed. Such a typical dream—teasing me, not letting me do what I wanted.

I opened my eyes in sudden fright and abruptly sat up. The action threw my torso against a wall of bodies, soft, gushy flesh that smelled like beans and paste. Kids. Little kids, and lots of them. A couple of them had fallen onto their bottoms and looked stunned for a moment, only to scramble up and run. Most scattered like squealing balloons, zigzagging in exaggerated fright. They bumped into each other as though not sure where to hide. Others charged into the water and began splashing each other. For a brief moment, I thought I might still be in a dream. But then I realized through a surreal haze of being still half-asleep and the unrecognizable surroundings that I was at the orphanage. The sun was bright and hot, so I removed my sweatshirt. The birds singing out of sync made everything seem like madness, but then blocking the rays of the sun with his pom poms was the silhouette of the Brit.

"When you sat up, you should have growled," he said, adding, "Gosh, I would have loved to have seen them spin and trip all the way back to the *dormitorio*, the little rascals."

"Maybe next time. What's the *dormitorio*?" I asked, picking twigs and leaves out of my hair. I also wished a different adult was talking to me instead of the pom pom jerk. I felt all beaten up and was still so tired that standing felt like running a marathon.

"It's the building you walked into last night. It's where the little kids and us sleep."

"Do you ever take out the pom poms?" I asked for no reason except they were his most prominent feature.

"What?"

"Never mind." I threw my legs straight out to touch my toes. The stretch was difficult to do, and I gave up and leaned back on my hands. I hadn't eaten a real meal in twenty-four hours and wondered if there was food somewhere, but since my muscles seemed too tired to carry me anywhere, I just stretched again.

The Brit watched me and said, "Try the doggy down yoga pose. Terrific for the hamstrings. The kids will do it too. *Vengan, niños.*" He then bent over and made his body into a V, but his hands weren't far enough from his legs, which caused his bottom to rise too far up in the air. It was such a ludicrous position to see that it made me laugh. It felt good to laugh. It was like the feeling the sun gives off after it has been raining for weeks.

"What's your name?" I asked.

"Gunther. And if my memory serves me correctly, you're Eleanor. Now, Eleanor, it's not right for you to laugh. This yoga stuff is good for you," he said, still upside down. His voice strained, he added, "*Miren, niños.*"

Several of the little kids came over and tried to copy what he was doing. Their attempts were preposterous and resembled nothing like the downward dog position. One little boy wearing yellow rubber boots and blue-jean overalls with a Gucci label across his chest had his bottom on the sand and his legs kicking in the air. Another little boy who looked to be only a foot-and-a-half tall, thin with delicate, refined features, lay face down on the sand and stayed there, not moving. He was wearing Brooks Brothers plaid shorts and an Izod dark blue shirt, and on his feet was a pair of Doc Martens. How odd, I thought, but as I looked more closely at what the other children were wearing, their outfits also boasted big names like Burberry, Rodini, Lacoste, and Guess. I had imagined orphans to wear tattered clothing, especially in Central America, but here the children wore clothing explicitly for those with money. Coupled with the beautiful blue river in the background, the yoga group almost looked like they were at an exclusive lakeside country club.

"What's with the clothing?" I asked. "It's all designer."

Still in his pathetic downward dog pose, Gunther grunted, "Nothing but the best for our little tykes."

"But?"

"Donations from the riches of the USA. You are American, aren't you? Or Canadian?" he asked as he stood upright, his upper lip wet with drool.

"American."

"Which state?"

"Massachusetts," I answered.

"Massachusetts. That's Boston?"

"Yes."

23

"I went there with my parents years ago. Nice enough. I'm taking my gap year now. Anyway, been to New York too. Loved it," he said, shaking out his arms. He then burst out laughing because the children were still trying to copy him. "*Bueno, niños.* Haha—A bit gormless, aren't they?" Then he turned to look at me again. "You still knackered? I know I am. Babysitting is rough on a person." Then he changed the subject. "You need to get up. On a bit of a schedule here. We need to wash their faces." With a burst of energy, he clapped his hands together as though signaling me to stand up and wash faces.

I reluctantly got up with the help of a big rock, but instead of kicking my shoes off and rolling up my pant legs to help wash faces, I went over to two girls wearing bright floral Marimekko sundresses. They were impressive. They were the only two who understood how to do the downward dog pose correctly. "*Magnifica, niñas,*" I said and joined them. The stretch felt marvelous. Standing up, my gaze fell upon a house that jutted out into the water. "What's that building?" I asked. I knew I wasn't being very helpful. I wasn't sure why I was being so obstinate, but it probably had something to do with his annoying behavior last night.

"Little kids' schoolhouse," Gunther answered in a flat tone. His pant legs now rolled up, he waded into the water.

A canoe with a person at the bow and a man sitting slouched in the stern with his hand on the outboard motor's tiller buzzed by close to the shore. "People go up and down this river all day long," Gunther said, staring after it. "You know why they have motors on their canoes?

"To go fast."

"Funny. Yes and no. Some Yamaha sales guy showed up one day and sold the locals engines. Now they're all in debt. They'd rather fish, the locals, that is, but fishing doesn't pay for the motor. Driving a taxi does. Did you see the scowl on the man's face driving the boat?" He frowned and pointed his index finger at me. "Now quit waffling around and help."

The sun over the treetops had begun baking the air. Jumping fully clothed into the water was tempting, but my tired head seemed too heavy, and I felt I might sink. Hunger was still harassing me, my teeth felt rough with sludge, and the taste in my mouth was tinny and sour. I thought of the last place I had lived, a mountainous town called Corriente with old Maria in her cement, earthquake-cracked house. The shower only dribbled water, and the toilet didn't have a seat, but the idea of eating her hearty oatmeal breakfast with vanilla twists and cinnamon sticks made my mouth water.

"How many *niñeros* are there?" I asked, picking a washcloth up off the ground, then asked another question before he answered the first. "Do you have oatmeal here?"

"No to the oatmeal. As for the *niñeros*, they're ten of us foreigners here, but two are teachers, Hamit and Harry, and one is a doctor, so seven *niñeros*, but then didn't you say you're a *niñera*? So that makes eight of us. Eight. Such a nice, even number."

"All foreigners here?"

"No, there's local staff. Mind you, we don't normally wash the kids' faces in the river. We don't have any running water right now. This morning we used buckets of water and gave them sponge baths in the showers. Now are you going to help me or not?"

"What about the water tanks?"

"Just the pipe to the bathroom broke."

Squatting down to eye level with the girls in Marimekko, I asked them their names, but they remained silent, just looked at me with their big brown eyes and dimples. "Gunther, what are their names?"

"Bernarda is the one with the short, dark, curly hair, and the other with light brown hair is Charlotte. Two little gems. Usually they wear shorts, but today they wanted to wear dresses. They must have known we had company." Gunther spoke from the shallows of the water. He was standing ankle-deep with a cloth in his hand, beckoning to the little boy with the yellow rubber boots to join him.

"You know, you're much better when you're not drinking," I said.

"Aren't most people?"

"Yeah." I sat back down because squatting was too tiring. Gunther directed a huffing noise at me. When I looked over at him, his mouth was agape, and he was staring at me.

"Yes, I will help. It's just that I feel like a truck ran over me last night. I just need a moment."

"By the way," Gunther said, "I wasn't that pissed last night. Alex was the legless ass. A raspberry tart. Hell, I told you the right water tank to drink out of, didn't I?"

"Which one?"

"Left."

"I thought you said right."

"Maybe it is the right. Anyway. Why'd you sleep on the beach?"

"Small hammock."

"True." He finished washing two other little boys and whistled for Bernarda and Charlotte to join him.

They ignored him and leaned their bodies against me to pick the rest of the leaves and twigs out of my hair. Bernarda had sparkly eyes, a devil's chin, and round cheeks that bunched up when she smiled, exposing little, white Chiclet teeth. She was chunky in the way a baby is plump but not fat, whereas Charlotte was wiry and strong-looking for a youngster. Her small, wide nose sniffed a lot, and her two soft, brown eyes appeared to see more than the obvious. Both girls had bean goo stuck to their cheeks, and a few sticky breakfast remnants clung to their clothing too. I asked them in my most precise, simple Spanish if they had just eaten; Charlotte opened her mouth but said nothing, and Bernarda whispered that my hair was soft. I stood and took hold of a hand each and led them into the water to wash their faces.

"Gunther, none of these kids look indigenous. All mestizos."

"I've been told the Mayas don't give their kids up, but a fellow, a priest that came by here, said they were starting to. Too many kids, not enough food. That's why most of them are here to begin with. It's like a boarding school for the poor. Most aren't adoptable. They go home for the holidays. Well, not the little ones, but the older kids."

"That's what Rosario told me when she interviewed me for the position."

"Yes, Rosario. We don't see much of her here," he quipped.

"Back home I have friends that went to boarding school. Odd ducks, most of them. They have a hard time understanding the average Joe. It's like the masses have cooties or something like that." I was finding it hard to wipe the bean smudges off Charlotte's face. The stuff was like glue.

"Now that's not right. I went to boarding school, and I'm about as good a chap that you'll find," he said and looked over at me with a stupid, dumbfounded expression on his face.

"I think you just proved my point," I remarked and lightly laughed, then changed the subject. "This stuff sticks."

"We just ate. Imagine if we left it on." Then he paused, stood straight up, and scratched his head. "Now I wouldn't go sleeping on the beach tonight. There's crocs and manatees out there. I know people say manatees are friendly, but I don't trust the buggers. I think they're mean. You sleep on the beach again, they may crawl up and bite you." As he spoke, he washed the face of a tough-looking square box of a boy. He had a small mouth that Gunther stretched from side to side like Play-Doh.

"This is Frankie; the other little boy with the rubber boots is Raymond. We think Raymond is something like two-and-a-half, not quite three. You know, too small, needs more help than most." He gave Frankie one last wipe. "There we go. All nice and clean." Frankie sloshed his way out of the water with a determined grin while swinging his arms, making bear sounds. Next Gunther beckoned for the tiny boy with the plaid Brooks Brothers shorts to come to him. The youngster had been waiting patiently on the river's edge watching Frankie's face being washed. His name was Henrik, and Gunther directed him to take his sandals off before walking into the water, but he didn't want to, so he walked away to go play with Raymond by a drooping avocado tree.

"Oh, come on, Henrik. Don't be like that," Gunther pleaded, then gave up and said, "*Venga*, Bernarda." She walked out to him. Without looking at me, he said, "Charlotte, whose face you have been washing while I've cleaned several, doesn't speak. According to Doc, she was found in a shack sitting by the body of her dead grandmother. They think she'd been there for days. Doc says her vocal cords are healthy and that not speaking is a choice."

"How sad. Although, it doesn't sound like a choice. I mean, I'm sure she'd like to talk," I replied. Then I asked, "Do you think I'll be able to get some food?"

"You're not very helpful."

"I'll come back after I change my clothes, brush my teeth, maybe get a bite to eat."

He looked up and smiled. "No problem. Here comes help." Glancing up the ascent toward the *dormitorio*, I could see a cluster of scrappy, bedraggled people coming our way.

"Get the bucket by the dock," Gunther said to me in a commanding voice. "Fill it and use it to flush the toilet. Leave the bucket in the bathroom. Yup... Someone forgot, and that's why the bucket is down here where it shouldn't be." He looked at the others on the hill and shouted, "It's about time. Lots of faces to wash!" Turning to me, he continued, "And so few hands. Just jesting with you, Eleanor. My first night here, I babysat with Alex. I drank so much I threw up. Spent the night in the kindergarten house and pissed on myself. Useless the next day."

"What's the word for 'kindergarten' in Spanish?"

"Kindergarten, only with a Spanish accent."

"That's easy... Does everyone drink a lot here?" I was trying to cut down on my drinking.

"No, only when babysitting. And sometimes when we're not. Okay, most nights, or is that every night?"

Then a thought occurred to me. "Which one of the kids found the dead body in the mangroves? That must've been awful."

"You heard?" Gunther stopped washing and looked at me.

"It was in La Noticia."

"Albert found the body." He then pointed to a little boy with short, cropped hair by the dock. He was picking yellow and white flowers. "He's our little poet."

I walked over to the dock to retrieve the bucket and stopped to say hello. Albert handed me a flower and said, "*Bonita.*" I thanked him. He had a soft oval face and dreamy brown eyes. I could see why Gunther saw him as a poet; he had a quiet ethereal nature that was endearing. I felt a pang of sadness at the thought of him seeing a dead body. After I filled the bucket with river water, I passed by him again. He'd stuffed his nose into a bouquet of picked flowers. He smelled them and sighed.

"He's a bit of loner," Gunther observed.

A heaviness greater than the tiredness I already felt swept over my body, and I fell into thoughts about my own life. I wondered what I had done to myself this time. Although daylight had brought on a new and better perspective of the place, I felt a nagging compulsion to leave. As an only child, with my father dead and my mother in a mental institution, family wasn't an obstacle to my travels; no one was clamoring for me to come home. There was no one to worry about me or criticize my lack of ambition—which I wasn't sure if I lacked or not; it was still in an incubation period.

But at thirty, most of my peers were married, getting married, or serious about a career. My aspirations were simple. Learn enough Spanish to pass the University language exam back home in order to receive my college diploma. Very, very simple yet I questioned my sanity coming to this place, then let my doubts slide because hungry has a way of muddling thinking and most decisions.

Switching the bucket handle from one hand to another, I huffed up the hill. Yes, I'd give this place a chance, I said to myself. I'd never met an orphan, let alone worked at an orphanage. Then it occurred to me: Was I an orphan? Unanchored, adrift in the world. I chuckled; I suppose I was. I put the bucket down and wiped my brow. The birds sang and squawked above, and the children's giggles echoed from behind. The place was small and compact, almost like being swaddled. The idea of being swaddled made me feel good.

In mid-thought, the incoming *niñeros* walked over to me. We exchanged a few introductions. They all seemed friendly except for Alex, who refused to even look at me or say hello, but then I didn't say anything to him either. None of us lingered too long because they were in a hurry to help Gunther. I assessed each one as best I could while wondering if any of them would turn into a friend. It would be no big deal if no one did, just another thought.

There were two girls from England, Molly and Golly. They were hefty with large, fleshy arms and heavy, pendulous breasts and mentioned something about snoring at night and hoped they wouldn't keep me awake. They both had brassy red hair pinned back with plastic butterflies. They were hard to tell from the back, but luckily their faces were very different. Molly had a thin, sharp nose and glossy, gray eyes surrounded by thick, dark red lashes, and pretty clear facial skin considering her heavily freckled arms. Golly had a piggish-looking nose and tiny eyes made even smaller by her large cheeks, which were covered in pin-pricked freckles. I wasn't sure about either one as a friend. They both had incomprehensible Cockney accents. Their hello sounded like Ay-O, like they'd dropped something and were in trouble. Like Gunther, they were enjoying a gap year.

When a fellow with a long, pointy nose introduced himself as Jack, I immediately thought, *He's a peculiar man*. Not that I have anything against being peculiar; in fact, I fancy myself a bit that way. He asked me if I had been making noises in the attic last night. I said, "No." He then grabbed hold of a demure woman's hand and introduced her as his wife, Sarah. She wouldn't look me in the eye at first, but when she did, she told me that if I were a bug, I'd be a wasp.

"But they're mean bugs," I protested.

"They just protect themselves, that's all. Why, they help keep the bug population down, and act as an aphrodisiac for birds. And wasps are pollinators." Then she stopped talking and smiled at me as though I should be proud. I gave a nervous chuckle but then conceded that the wasp might be a much better bug than I'd thought.

Everyone seemed to be more or less around my age except for a very tall, regal-looking woman named Catarina. I put her age at fifty-something. She was thin, with a youthful appearance and expressive wrinkles around her mouth and eyes. She wore a long, fluffy cotton skirt that swished when she walked. She also told me never to call her Cat. I wasn't sure what to make of her. She seemed very no-nonsense and possibly might find me too immature to hang out with.

I made my way into the compound. It was a much different animal during the day than night. Sunny and bright, small and compact. A one-room house painted white with a gray porch had a sign that said OFICINA. I was happy to see there was an office, which I took to be the place to find the head of the orphanage or at least some information, but the door was locked, and no one seemed to be around. To my left a few kids, possibly aged six to their mid-teens, were mingling around a doorway. I smiled and said, "*Buenos días.*" They nodded back the way people nod when suspicious of someone, slow and emotionless. I was glad my assignment was the little ones.

In the middle of the buildings was something one might call a quad. As I had noted the night before, there were several overturned canoes surrounding sand, dirt, and some craggy grasses. The canoes were placed on top of cement blocks, and someone had built a fort with sticks and piled rocks to look like a pyramid in a corner. Beyond the buildings was the jungle, with a pathway going left and another going directly into the forest. The left path had a light blue sign with lettering painted with bold, purple handwriting saying, "CLÍNICA." The other sign was painted in the same color and read "ESCUELA y BIBLIOTECA." It pointed directly into a thicket of brush.

Looking past the shrubs, by the second sign there was a muddy path with boards placed over a stream. The path itself was riddled with dips, roots, and rocks, and twisted its way to a grassy knoll with a cement pigsty. The pigs were poking their pink noses over the fencing, and one was trying to crawl out. The blue sky above held fragile clouds that hovered over the knoll, casting shadows over the earth. It reminded me of a painting one would see of a New England farm back home in *Yankee* magazine. I let my eyes tread down the hill and saw a white building that resembled a giant box, and next to it was a building with a steeple. I assumed the buildings to be the school and the library, but why a steeple when the orphanage was secular?

During my interview with Rosario in her office back in the city, she told me she wanted nothing to do with churches and 'their castrating religion.' Rosario was from Honduras and had been brought up Catholic. She felt the whole shebang of God, obeying and praying. "Was for the birds, but then the birds are too smart to fall for all that jargon," she had said, adding, "What good does it do for these kids to think God will save them?" Then she paused for dramatic effect. Looking directly into my eyes, she continued, "They need to learn to save themselves. We all do."

A husky woman with thick, curly, black hair and dark eyes that smiled more than her mouth, Rosario liked to go out at night to the discos. She wore a Versace dress that at the time I had thought was a knock-off, but now I knew better. She must have retrieved it from a donation bin from the United States. It didn't fit well. She had lots of lumps, rolls, and bulges, even a small tear under her armpit.

She was sitting behind a sparse desk with an old, pink rotary phone by her left elbow and a Smith-Corona electric typewriter by her right. She asked me questions, and I was a little intimidated by her because she was the boss. Rosario had done something with her life that seemed worthy and was still young, possibly forty. She had an intelligence unique to people who are doers. I wanted to tell her one day that I too would do something, but I just wasn't ready yet. When she asked me if I liked children, I answered, "Why, of course," as though it were a silly question, but I could tell she could see right through me. Her eyes tightened as if she'd detected a flaw, then looked off at the wall. It seemed she had discovered what she was looking for and no longer needed to ask me anything more. The truth was, I didn't know if I liked children or not, since I'd never been around them. Most of my friends back home were just starting to get married and didn't have any babies yet, so maybe I did like them. It wasn't a lie, just an unschooled thought.

But it didn't matter. My position was voluntary. I was to receive room and board for my efforts. Either I would work out and stay, or I would leave. Or I would do both because everyone did both. When I left her office, I thanked Rosario, but she neither shook my hand nor thanked me. She had suggested that I stay at the orphanage for at least three months to give consistency to the kids' lives. I didn't get how three months or one month mattered. Rosario sensed my hesitation toward commitments, and she was probably slightly jaded about all the people that showed up to volunteer. All our faces looked alike; mainly white and either North American or European. I was sure that many foreigners stepped into her office to pontificate about the glory of helping others and the honor it was to do so. Possibly she may have wondered why I hadn't done so too. It was very simple; it didn't occur to me. Before I left her office, she handed me a letter of introduction to take to the orphanage.

I still had the letter in my backpack, but it seemed there was no one to give it to. Entering the *dormitorio*, I saw the place was empty of people, tidy and spotless, and made my way to the bathroom.

Chapter 4

Cadmael

Before sitting, I lined the rim of the polished porcelain bowl with the pink crepe paper that was hanging off the tiled wall on a wire. I was used to toilets without seats, but I preferred the dips and curves that a seat provided. However, toilets were expensive, and for many redundant. The bathroom smelled of disinfectant, along with a slight hint of urine, seemed the odor was endemic to the place, whether it be critter or human.

While sitting I stared at the stall walls. White was a ubiquitous color here. The toilets, the sink, the showers, the walls, and all the exterior wood of the buildings were white except for the dining hall. Overall, I liked the bathroom. The gray floor had been swept clean and washed, not a cobweb or bug in sight. Then out of nowhere, the annoying buzz of a fly had me looking around the stall. It was then that two houseflies landed on the pink toilet paper by my left knee and started fornicating. Their beady eyes were glaucomatous and unemotional, the sex stilted as they barely moved, and when they did, it was only to twitch.

Ripping a piece of the toilet paper off, I knocked the fucking houseflies to the floor where they lay by my right foot, still engaged and twitching. Getting up, I took the bucket of water, poured it into the back of the tank, and flushed. It wasn't the first time I'd had to flush a toilet in this manner. I'd been in many a village with unreliable water sources, toilets without piping and basins that drained into the streets.

At the sink, I fiddled with the faucet knobs to see if there was any water, but nothing. There weren't any mirrors either. I knew my face had to be filthy, but I supposed if I couldn't see myself, it wouldn't bother me. I was used to not seeing myself. For the past year, I had barely looked in a mirror. If there was one, it was usually warped, making a person's chin too long and their eyes too big.

Suddenly, there were unexpected grunting noises and the heavy clomp of two booted workmen shuffling into the bathroom. "Hola," I said, standing up straight, almost at attention, baffled by their presence. They threw me a quick glance and nodded a silent greeting. Their cowboy attire was splattered with mud, and their dark faces looked greasy and hot. I shrugged; apparently anyone could walk into this bathroom.

The men seemed fascinated by a pipe that ran the length of the far wall. They poked at it while the older fellow mumbled something in the same language I'd heard last night; French-sounding and filled with shushes and upticks. I left.

The adjacent room was long with a clean, maroon cement floor and white walls. There were several plastic baskets full of clothing, blankets, and towels, and under a bench were a couple of pairs of shoes. Curious, I went over to a basket filled with dresses and picked out a few. They were doll-like, and the labels on the back displayed Saks Fifth Avenue and Dolce Gabbana. There was also a half-deflated rubber ball on the floor, three very worn, beige beanbag chairs, and several neatly stacked books placed against a solid wall. The room was lit by windows on both sides, which allowed a breeze to come in.

The kids slept in the next room. Several cribs lined the walls beneath expansive windows. Another workman was standing outside by the water tanks with a wrench in his hand, looking in at me. I waved, and he waved back with his wrench.

I ran my fingers over the row of cribs. They had thick mattresses covered with colorful wool blankets. Everything was neat and tidy and clean. The crib room had a brown cement floor, which also had been swept spotless. When I looked up, the maintenance man by the tanks was staring at me. I waved again, and he waved back. I waited for him to return to his work, but instead he waved me to come over. Then with his wrench, he banged down hard on the rusty spigot attached to the left water tank and broke it. Water gushed onto the tall grasses. I was thirsty, so thirsty that my tongue felt rough. I rushed outside to nab a few drops before it was all gone.

Kneeling, I cupped my hands to bring the water up to my lips. It was sweet and refreshing, and I gulped it down. I splashed it all over my face, scrubbed my cheeks, mouth, and forehead. The coolness and the act of washing the crust of sleep away was exhilarating. I then stopped and stood up because it occurred to me that my actions might look peculiar, almost crazy to the workman.

With water running down my chin, I smiled at the man and wiped my mouth with the back of my hand. He looked at me critically, squinted and bit his lower lip. Unlike the other workmen, he was young with clear, dark eyes and distinct Mayan features, high cheekbones and a firm chin and a slender, sensitive face. Flushed with heat and sweat, his muscles seemed tense and full of energy. He winked at me. I winked back because why not? It seemed to puzzle him.

I introduced myself and shook his hand.

"I'm Cadmael," he said.

When I asked him what was wrong with the tank, he replied with a glint in his eye and in basic Spanish, obviously his second language, which got me thinking that if the locals all spoke Spanish the same or worse than me, how was I going to improve? But then shrugged to myself with a come-what-may attitude. Cadmael told me that the tank needed cleaning due to too many dead things in it. Seeing my worried look, he laughed, adding in English, "A joke." But I didn't think it was one.

The water flowing out had leaves and spiders in it. Cadmael explained he was draining the tank to fix it. Barely listening to him and disgusted by what I may have ingested, I stared at the tank then over to the tree beside it. There was a maroon backpack hanging on a low branch. The flap was turned back, and an abundance of the country's bright colorful money was bursting from its top. He saw my surprised expression. His eyes followed mine, and he moved in front of the bag blocking my ability to see it. He stood staring at me and when I met his gaze, his eyes had dimmed, his all his jovial nature gone. An awkward situation. I shook my head to indicate I hadn't seen anything, smiled, laughed, then told him I was hungry and walked away. I was here to learn Spanish, or so I hoped, and not get involved in local shenanigans.

Chapter 5

Harry

There were three of them. They stood behind the buffet counter, looking at me with perplexed eyes and tight, disgruntled mouths. My stance solemn but hopeful, I stared back. One woman was short, thin, and young, another was pregnant and a little older, and the third was a middle-aged, humorless woman with broad, set-back shoulders and a chest that reminded me of a puffed hen. She was chewing bubblegum in a hapless, bovine manner. It made her funny to watch, but I didn't dare smile because I was under the impression she wasn't trying to be amusing. They all were wearing thick Mayan skirts and cotton T-shirts with writing I couldn't read due to their white, stained bibs.

Behind the three women pots and pans were piled neatly on top of a counter, a six-burner cast-iron stove, and a shiny, empty metal sink. It seemed they had cleaned up breakfast, but not everything was put away. There was still a small pot of beans on the stove and a basket of tortillas on a counter by the back door. On the brink of collapsing from hunger, I wasn't going to budge. Besides, I figured if I played it right, the goods could be mine, but my only play was to be stubborn, and by their expressions, I felt they might be better at this game.

Then luck stepped in. The hefty, ill-humored woman blew an enormous bubble. When it popped, it stuck to her straight, firm nose. This made the pregnant woman next to her laugh. When she laughed her bib drooped down, and I saw that her T-shirt had dark lettering that said, "What Part of 'No' Didn't You Understand?" I chuckled, which possibly caused the young, thin one to burst out laughing. She was covering her mouth with a dishrag. The dishrag had a bug on it, and when she saw the bug, a large beetle with hideous horns, she threw the rag and the bug onto the floor and stomped on both, making a loud crunching noise. We all cringed, which made the pregnant woman laugh even more. The young one was now in uncontrollable laughing hysteria too. It was all I could do not to plunge into rib-splitting, crying laughter because both tears and hilarity were welling up inside of me, but I wanted food most of all, and the bubblegum lady wasn't even smiling. She looked downright mean, but the standoff had been broken. A glint of amusement shone in the woman's stern eyes.

The two younger ones, having peeled away to continue their chores, had left me alone with the hefty woman with bubblegum stuck to her nose. She was trying her best to pry it off while keeping her eyes on me, eyes narrowed and serious with a glint of mirth, but I didn't dare smile or say anything. The battle was still being played as she seemed to be trying her best to appear angry. Then she huffed a loud, lazy, exaggerated huff, put her left hand on her hip, cleared her throat, got the gum from her nose, and popped it back into her mouth. She then sauntered over to the stove, took a plate from a pile, filled it with a ladle of beans, and threw a tortilla the size of a Frisbee on top along with a fork. When she handed me the plate, she winked. Her T-shirt read, "My people skills are fine." I thanked them and took my plate of food to find a seat.

The dining hall was a huge space, filled with long, wooden tables lined with benches. Above it all there was a vaulted, thatched ceiling with animals flitting around the mahogany rafters, possibly birds or bats, I thought. Scrutinizing the tabletops and floor, I saw there weren't any droppings and settled down at a table near the entrance to eat. Then from somewhere in the back of the room a person shouted, "You're back!" I looked around but couldn't figure out where the voice came from.

"Behind you!"

In the shadowed lighting toward the right back corner was the silhouette of a man waving a fork in the air. "Join me!" he yelled buoyantly. I walked over, carrying my food.

"Amazing! You got food."

"You have food?" I replied, sitting down.

"They always give me food. Esmeralda loves me."

"The bubblegum lady?"

"Yes. Bubblegum is her favorite. I always bring her gifts when I return from the city," he said, spooning rice and beans into his mouth. Looking at his rice and the lack of it on my plate, I felt like I'd been shortchanged.

"What's your name?" I asked.

"You know who I am."

I didn't say anything and remained silent while scanning his face. I had been to so many places and met so many people, I might have known him. He was near my age or a few years older, and he was gorgeous. Not that I wanted sex anymore. Too tired. Besides, I blamed the boredom of the bus to have me fantasizing about it. I stopped filing through my memory banks because the more I studied the features of the man sitting in front of me, the more I was sure I wouldn't have forgotten his face. His features were uniquely fitted, the way a brilliant thought or song or taste amazes a person by its sheer inventiveness— his nose was prominent but not hooked. His eyes were dark and nearly black, only they were blue. His cheeks and chin perfectly formed into masculine strength. I could tell he had just shaved, as his pale skin that was slightly tanned and smooth, had a nick. It was by his right ear that had a little piece of pink toilet paper covering it. Even his hair was beautiful—thick, dark brown tufts piled on top of his head that fell just below his ears, giving him a messy but endearing quality. His hair also seemed in need of constant attention. Within the few minutes we had been together, he had pushed it away from his forehead twice, and after the second time he said, "Since you left, I've had no one to cut my hair." His voice was deep with an accent touched by Oxford English, along with hints of something much more foreign.

"I think you've mistaken me for someone else," I said, taking a bite of food. It was a tasteless, bland clump of beans, and the tortilla resembled soft, slightly undercooked plastic corn.

He had stopped eating to rub his chin. Then he licked his well-formed upper lip as though thinking and said, "You're Maddy. I'd know you anywhere."

"My name's Eleanor."

"No. That can't be right."

"I think I know my name," I said, putting my fork down.

"Come to think of it, Maddy has blonde hair." He then paused and looked over at a tree. "Or was that Phoebe? Anyway, it doesn't matter."

But apparently it did. After tapping his fork several times on the table, he eyed me critically and asked, "Are you sure you're not Maddy?"

"Yes!"

"Okay, well, I don't suppose you cut hair?"

"I can, but I doubt you'll like the results."

This made him laugh, a deep baritone guffaw. When he finally stopped, we continued eating in silence. It seemed everything was all messed up now because I wasn't who he thought I was, which made me feel awkward, but I didn't want to get up and leave, as that would have been stranger still. Staying put, I ate my food, filling but tasteless, and very unsatisfying. When I looked at his plate for no particular reason, I noticed red flecks all over his food.

"Do you have salsa?" I inquired. When he hesitated to answer, I got up. "I gather it's in the kitchen?"

"Stay. No. Now you know better than that; you have to bring your own," he scolded.

Settling back down, I said, "I don't know better about anything. I'm new."

"You didn't say you were new."

"Well, I am. Now I don't have any salsa, but I bet you do."

He leaned back, cleared his throat, and eyed me suspiciously. "You don't ask people to share their salsa here—it's rude." His dark blue eyes, the color of a New England ocean on a clear, crisp day, danced about in the morning light with such mischief that he had to be joking.

"Rude?" I asked with a smile. But when he didn't smile back, I grew suspicious of him.

"Rude," he repeated without looking at me, head bent, shoveling food into his mouth. This odd behavior caused his handsome face to turn, well, somewhat unattractive.

After a few moments I said with irritation, "So you're not sharing?"

"No. Not sharing," he said and looked at me with a pigheaded stare, then averted his eyes to chow down.

"Does sharing only apply to salsa or is there a 'no sharing' rule for everything? Like, oh, I don't know—let's say I wanted to use the pencil you have by your book?" I asked, my tone tight, my actions knowingly pushy, because it was so peculiar not to share salsa.

He had a book by his plate with the title *Historia de Central America* across the cover, and beside the book was a notepad and a pencil. He'd stopped eating to stare at them as though pondering which item he liked least. Finally, he looked at me and said, "I might let you borrow this book. Can you read Spanish?"

"Working on it."

"Okay, you can borrow the book."

"But I want the pencil."

"No, only the book," he said, and furrowed his eyebrows to punctuate the "no."

"Let's go back to the salsa. That's what I really want."

"We don't share condiments," he said in a flat, penetrating voice and pushed the book toward me.

"Keep your book," I said, still thinking this must all be just a preposterous joke.

"Are you sure?" he said, pushing the book toward me again.

"I don't want it," I said and pushed it back toward him. "I want the salsa."

"Seems someone is on a rude jag." He pursed his lips, lips I no longer found enticing. Smacking them, he opened his mouth and smiled. "You must be American."

"Whatever," I said, suddenly feeling tired. "And what frosty European country do you come from?"

He laughed again, another great, big, hearty laugh. When he stopped, he placed both hands on the table and leaned forward as though he wanted to tell me a secret. Then, in a hushed voice, he said,

"Salsa and other stuff like ketchup, mustard, are sacred, but then who wants to put mustard on beans?"

"Or ketchup," I said, taking a bland bite of food, and changed my mind, "I'd put mustard or ketchup on these beans in a second."

"Yes, could be tasty," he said, smiling. "Now, how do I explain? Put it this way. If you left money lying on the ground, and next to it a bottle of—." He took out a small bottle of red salsa picante from his pants pocket, shook it briefly near my face, then snapped it away out of sight. "—The money would be left, and the bottle would be gone." He then threw me a look as though what he had said made perfect sense. I said nothing back; I wasn't going to agree with such nonsense, even if it was true.

"Gobs and gobs of bland food," he rambled on, his voice becoming more and more lively. "Too much salt added to overcome the blandness. But you won't puff up. You'll sweat the salt off by midday, just in time for your next infusion at lunch. The food here never changes." Then he abruptly stopped talking. Something over at the water tanks seemed to have caught his attention. "There's no water right now. The fellows know what it is, but they need to go into town, someone needs to drive them. But it won't be today. Look at them just sweating and standing around. Lots of sweating and standing around." I looked over at the workmen; they were standing beside the water tanks, chatting.

"I met Cadmael." I wanted to ask him why a young man who worked at an orphanage would have a bag of money, but that would be getting involved with something I was sure I shouldn't know about. So instead, I asked, "Who are the other two?"

"Aapo is the boxy square one. Eadrich is the older fellow. Remember to drink out of the left tank. The right is river water," he said, leaning in again.

"Are you sure?"

"No."

45

Sitting back, he continued, "We always have eggs in the morning, but they run out, which is why we aren't eating any now. Sometimes we have cabbage. They even put some sort of sweet, creamy stuff on it. I think it's the powdered milk combined with sugar. And occasionally we have a pig. In fact, I think we're due for a pig. But then maybe not. Speaking of pigs, you have mud on your face. Around your nose and eyes. Green—your eyes. Green's a pretty color."

Instead of thanking him for the compliment—the reference to looking like a pig bothersome—I changed the subject. "Who runs this place? I mean, who do I talk to about sleeping arrangements because I won't sleep in the attic room, and I heard the beach isn't too safe either—crocs, possibly nasty manatee?"

"Manatee? I suppose there could be a mean one. Well, Rosario runs the place, rarely visits. but sometimes her niece shows up. Her nickname is Blue Eyes. She helps out, or I think she does. Not sure."

"Is she here?"

"No, she's never here. What's your job?"

"Niñera," I said.

"Most new people are. Maadddy—"

"Eleanor," I corrected him.

"Eleanor. You could drive the workmen into town tomorrow and buy some salsa," he said with a smile.

"I could use some today," I said, knowing the answer.

He ignored me and said, "I'm the history teacher here. I'm Dutch. So, yes, I do come from a frosty European country." He then stopped talking to look at me skeptically. I could tell something was churning in his mind. "The People's Republic of *Dormitorio*," he finally said. "They figure out who sleeps where. It's more like what's available. Those who've been here the longest get the better sleeping arrangements. Jack and Sarah have a room to themselves, but then they've been here almost as long as I have."

"Which is?"

"A little over a year. Then again. has it been that long?" He counted months on his fingers, stopped, shook his head, and said, "Less than a year, I think. So you don't smell like this all the time. Or do you?"

"It's been a rough couple of days. Slept on the beach last night."

"That was you? Interesting. Do you have a sleeping bag?"

"No."

"Mosquito net?"

"No."

"Blow-up raft?"

"No."

"Change of underwear?"

"Yes, well, I need to do laundry," I said, laughing.

"Have you been traveling around?"

"Yes, but not camping."

"Yeah, I know what you mean. Okay, my roommate just left, and well..."

"What was your roommate's name?" I asked, curious.

He paused for a reflective moment, then said, "Maddy, or maybe it was Phoebe, but I won't call you Maddy or Phoebe. I'll call you by your real name."

"That would be nice. It's Eleanor."

"Yes, Eleanor. I have a huge room, and I'm not always there because I have a fiancé." He paused and looked at me with those penetrating, deep blue eyes as though wondering if I was listening intently.

"I'm practicing abstinence."

We sat in silence for a few minutes. I stuffed my mouth with beans while he watched me with a peculiar expression.

"Why would anybody practice abstinence? Odd, but, well, good," he said, then rubbed his chin and continued in a troubled tone. "Alex has been wanting to sleep in my room, but I don't want him as a roommate. He's nice enough, but I, well, I like it when there's another person in the room, but not Alex. Nothing wrong with him. No, I take that back. There's plenty wrong with him, but then there's usually something wrong with people." He paused here to raise an eyebrow at me, then continued. "Look, I like having another person in the room because, well, it's comforting."

"Comforting?"

"Yes, comforting. Like having a pet."

"A pet?"

"Why, yes, but I don't expect you to be waiting for me. That would be horrible. I go away most weekends, and I'm out a lot." He paused to fiddle with his history book as though not knowing how to phrase what he wanted to say, but then finally managed to just say it. "So, if you want?" He leaned in, latching his eyes onto mine. "I'll give you a corner of my room." And then he smiled, adding, "Seems I can share."

"Not bad. And you don't have to worry. I won't be waiting for you."

"Good."

What a strange fellow, and, *If I had salsa, would he kill me in my sleep to get it?* was all I could think, but then again, the arrangement couldn't be better. He said he would rarely be there. After a few moments of readjusting my attitude, I added, "Excellent. We're roommates. How wonderful. But I have a question."

Either he didn't hear me or decided to ignore me. He ripped a piece of paper from his notepad and said, "Tomorrow, drive the workmen into town. Buy yourself a sleeping bag, et cetera, et cetera." On the paper, he wrote down a list of things I needed to buy and handed it to me. "I don't think I forgot anything. And while you're there, have a nice meal." It was as though all the nonsense from before had disappeared.

"Thank you." I meant it. He was kind. Then I asked my question. "What's your name?"

"Harry. Harry Van Cleef," he said, and stood up.

"Van Cleef? I've heard that name before."

"It's a famous name. I like it." A very unusual response to one's last name, I thought.

"The movie *The Good, the Bad, and the Ugly*. Lee Van Cleef was the bad."

He laughed, gathered his book, pad, and pencil, and brought his empty plate over to a bucket. His sandaled feet slapped along the cement. Before walking out, he turned and said, "You should swim. It's the best bathtub we have."

"Yes. But stop." I remembered where I'd recently heard his name. "Yenara. Or is it Yena? Wants to see you."

Harry's face darkened and his eyes steeled, then flattened, as though his mind had wandered off someplace to a thought he'd misplaced or didn't want to remember. I kept my gaze locked on his unfocused stare. His transformation from joyful to worried baffled me.

It took a few moments, but he finally wandered back to the man I had first met, jovial and somewhat bizarre. Smiling, he said, "Great, how nice. How do you know her?"

"I met her last night, briefly."

Silence. The expression on his face had stilled. "Good," he finally said, and stepped into the doorway that didn't have a door. He stretched his arms up over his head and exposed a flat, slightly tanned tummy, yawned, then glanced over the quad, possibly to regain a sense of equilibrium. With a shrug, he gripped his book, pencil, and notepad against his chest, and with his free hand, he fished around the front pockets of his khakis and pulled out a pair of sunglasses. He placed them on his face and breathed in deeply. Then as though struck by a burst of energy, he took off. Shoulders rolled forward and took brisk strides toward the sign reading LA CLÍNICA. His light green Izod shirt was all I could see until he disappeared into the jungle.

Then a loud bang of metal on metal caught my attention. The workmen by the tanks had the big steel barrels turned upside down. I questioned the sanity and safety of driving them into town. I didn't know them. But then, I didn't know anybody here, but here I was. I sighed, got up, and bused my plate.

Chapter 6

Hamit

Still my first day and not even noon, I thought, standing at the end of the dock in my bathing suit. It occurred to me that time stood still here. I'd read somewhere that jungle life could be like that; something to do with lack of sleep and the heavy heat and humidity. I still hadn't helped out much, except for washing a few faces. But then again, after eating, I went into the dormitorio and saw Jack. He was counting cubbyholes and told me to take a bath. "Sure thing," I replied.

Directly across from the orphanage was a fancy boat club. Through the binoculars I'd found hanging from a hook at the end of the dock, I could clearly see the place, a one-story building on pilings jutting out over the river, its roof thatched and brightly lit by the sun, with an open-air dining area with waist-high, wooden railings. Attached to the front of the dock in large black lettering was the club's markedly unimaginative name: "Club de Bote."

The place exuded an esoteric, wealthy atmosphere that piqued my interest. Not that I cared for or sought opulence; it was more that it looked comfortable, and I had slept on a beach last night.

Scoping out the boats, I counted ten Bertrams lined neatly along a dock that hugged the shore. Next to their behemoth bloated bellies, resembling errant sidekicks, were several smaller motorboats with glinting outboards. In the lagoon to the right of the building, windless and dark, stood sleek sailboats. Their hulls were mainly white, but some displayed blue, green, and red bottoms. Possibly, I thought, their owners drank more than most and needed something besides the odd throw pillow to know which boat was theirs. These boats embedded in the windless cove were silent and picturesque, sails down and booms draped with drying towels and clothes, whereas farther out on the river, a small schooner and a sloop were fighting the currents, twisting and bucking like snared, giant, angry birds, and their dinghies jerking and floundering at the sterns.

The whole shebang—the club and the canopy of paurotis palms, giant kapoks, and corkwood trees looming in the background with birds gliding in and out—was fascinating to look at. The echoing of laughter and clinking of glasses, a flaunting of a fairytale world beyond the hopes and dreams of many—it was also oxymoronic, I thought, thinking of the orphanage and its well-worn wooden buildings. I imagined the patrons ate Waldorf salads with sweet apples, walnuts, and cherries. or burgers piled high with fresh lettuce and juicy tomatoes. Although my breakfast was still digesting, the thought of eggs Benedict garnished with a slice of melon and a cup of brewed coffee was glorious. Sighing, I laughed at my self-imposed poverty. It wasn't so bad, except I itched and my pits stunk.

Putting the binoculars back, I jumped off the low end of the dock into the shallow waters. The water was cool and languid. Yes, the best bathtub, as Harry had put it. In fact, I couldn't get Harry out of my head. There was just something about him, an offensive yet playful tug. I found myself wanting to argue with him again about sharing salsa and pencils. I also wanted to ask him about Yenara the Mapuche woman. I wanted to know where the group came from. No particular reason, just curiosity.

I twisted and rolled in the water like a seal. Kids nearby sang a nursery rhyme inside the kindergarten building, off-tune with clapping and lots of laughter.

The river lay flat in our little nook, which allowed for safe swimming, but just beyond the dock toward the middle of the river, it had a tremendous surge going north. It imparted an unnerving quality. It was the push from the lake, Lago de Cho, to the hungry, salty Caribbean Sea that caused the pounding rush and ripples.

"A couple of weeks ago, they found a guy with ceeement tied to his feet, clunking around the mangrove roots up by the schoolhouse," said a voice with a southern drawl. "Cost only one dollar to kill someone here. They forget that the damn cement is porous, makes the corpses float." He then chuckled, a deep, phlegm-filled sound that prefaced a wheeze and cough.

I turned to see a stout man with a bulging belly standing on the beach by the dock. His cotton, short-sleeve shirt was wrinkled, and he had sweat stains on his belly. His shirt was half-tucked into extra-large orange cargo shorts. He had the face of a duck with a nose that protruded out and up, and thick lips that seemed to be reaching for his nose. His white, thinning hair looked matted down with some sort of grease but was unkempt in the back, causing white strands to form a cowlick. His skin was paper-white with blotches of red. Unattractive at first glance, there was something about him that seemed untamed and very humorous, which added a hint of desirability, but not much. He held in both fat hands a mug with a neon pink picture of a naked lady sitting under a black umbrella. When he took a sip from the mug, he slurped. I smelled the enticing aroma of coffee and wondered if he had more. He wasn't looking at me but gazing out over the water.

"We're on the wrong side of the pond," he said after a moment of silence. Slurping again, he looked over at me, his eyes folded into the fat of his brows, and asked, "Do you have the time?"

"No."

"They're supposed to be coming today, but maybe it's tomorra."

"Who?"

"Why, my wife 'n' kid," he said, taking another loud slurp, his gaze perusing the river. He looked over at me again. "You new?"

"Yup."

Looking back over the river, he said, "The president flies in on weekends. He swoops down behind the club. His house is there. He has a Bell 212 helicopter. I knows my aircrafts 'cause I was stationed in Da Nang during 'Nam. You know that war was never declared a war, just a confleet. Hell—lost half my skull over there for that confleet. Got a titanium plate in its place." He coughed and wheezed; his spasms caused him to spill his coffee on his right hand. He shook it dry and said, "Guess what my head can do now?"

"What?"

"I receive radio transmissions. Want to know the weather?"

"Hot," I said.

"Sunny and hot. Real hot. Hotter than a witch's brass tit in a desert—" He then looked back over toward me and down at the water. "Anything nibbling at your toes?"

"No."

"I don't like swimming. Grew up in Alabama by a swamp. Lost an earlobe to a snapper." He gazed back over to the club and scratched his heavy middle. Then he huffed, "That man is bad. Full of maleficence."

For a moment I had to think about who he was talking about. "The president?"

"Yup."

Months ago, I had read an article in La Noticias that had shed light on how the president thought of the people he governed. During a balcony speech in the capitol, he had expressed his displeasure of being a leader of a country full of "Indians." He apparently felt he was better than that. "If he doesn't like the indigenous people, why does he live here?" I asked.

"Enough of his own kind here." He then paused, shushing me. "Do you hear a boat?"

A water taxi whizzed by carrying a load of boxes, followed by a sailboat with a red hull. A man wearing a fedora stood at the helm. "What country to you think that guy's from?" I asked, pointing to the sailboat.

"Ummm, I think I knows that guy." He burped. "Oh, well. Guess the family go'in to be late. By the way, I'm Hamit."

"Eleanor." The sailboat went around the curve of the river and disappeared, then turned back around again. When the boat glided past us again, I tried my best to get a look at the man's face, but all I could see was an angled chin. Tall and thin, something about him looked familiar, but that seemed foolish at the moment. I don't know why it seemed foolish; it just did.

"Well, Eleanor," Hamit's voice refocused my attention. "If that man comes over here..."

"What man?"

"Why, the president. I'll make it a point to step on his arches and will enjoy the sound of their crunch." He took another long, loud slurp from his mug, then snorted while turning his entire body toward me. He was wide and boxy. "Now, my wife is small and pretty; my son takes after me. If they show up, I'll be at the steeple schoolhouse."

He walked away up the embankment by kicking one foot out in front of the other with his body leaning backward. his flat, orange bottom almost neon. Another interesting character. I chuckled to myself.

Splashing water on my arms and legs, I used the sandy bottom to scrub the muck and grime off my skin. The river smelled like wet wood, its texture soft and cleansing. Mangrove thickets hugged the sides of the beach and were filled with birds. Inside the mangrove's spidery roots were hairy, brown coconuts bouncing rhythmically back and forth. I imagined a body with cement blocks attached to its feet being caught up in the entangled roots and felt ill.

To wipe the image from my mind, I walked deeper into the water, then dove headfirst down to the bottom and back up, swimming into the darker blue areas, a glorious serenity sweeping over me. The celebratory act of being filthy is becoming clean again, I thought, lying on my back looking up at the blue sky, its depths limitless, its blueness sublime. Suspended and feeling weightless, I rolled back onto my stomach and took a few more strong pulls toward the current, then stopped. The water gurgled in front of me, its grab inches away. I rolled back onto my stomach and kicked with lazy, frog-like strokes along its periphery.

"Eleanor!"

It was Gunther. He was standing on the beach, waving me in. A bunch of little kids stood by his side, and they started waving too. "You can't drown; we need help! The children need you!"

"I can swim," I said.

"Good for you." He placed his hands on his hips. "Now come on back. It's snack time."

I splashed back onto solid ground. "I don't have a towel. Everything I have smells like bat piss from that damn attic," I said, dripping wet.

"I hope you're not a whiner," he said. "Are those lilies on your suit or petunias?"

"Roses."

"Lovely. After snack time, I'll show you where the washbasin is located. To wash your clothes."

Over by the school, Catarina and Alex were marching the children up into the quad. The little girls, Charlotte and Bernarda, whom I had met earlier came over to me, along with another named, Penelope.

Penelope put her soft, small hand into mine and then stood without moving. She had big, round, light brown eyes lined with thick, black lashes, a small nose, and a little mouth that she pressed down on with her upper lip as though thinking about something puzzling. She had on purple jellies and a green-and-black striped Benetton shirt and yellow Perry Ellis leggings. With her long, black hair she looked rather chic.

Charlotte and Bernarda fought over my other hand. Not wanting to cause problems, I let Penelope's hand go, ruffled the hair of all three girls, and suggested we walk hands free. It made me realize why Catarina had the kids holding onto her skirt. She was up at the top of the embankment with five kids attached to her. The girls and I walked by Raymond and Henrik, who were quietly sitting on two rocks under a withered tree.

Raymond said he was very, very tired in a tiny voice. I suggested we all walk over to the quad together, but the boys didn't move. Instead, the three girls sat down on the dirt beside the boys. Then the one called Frankie stormed over like he owned the world. His fists were tight, his lips pursed, his arms swaying. He was almost as small as Henrik, only much beefier and bellowing defiance. His eyes sparkled in the sunlight, full of mischief. He told me several times in squeaky Spanish that he wasn't going to spend the rest of the morning in school and would prefer to swim. He wanted to put his bathing suit on, and would I come with him to get it?

"No," I replied. He stormed off and found Molly and Golly. The girls shook their heads at him. This caused him to kick a clump of grass repeatedly until Alex slinked by and tapped him on the shoulder. He stopped, looked at Alex, and smiled, and they walked off together up the short hill. At least Alex was good for something, I thought.

Once everyone was in the sandbox area, we sat on rocks and a few logs and sipped on a beverage called "the green drink." No one knew what was in it, but it seemed to be a kind of horchata—rice, milk, and then a questionable green part, but cacti seemed probable. I found the drink very tasty. The children seemed to as well, all their faces wore green mustaches. Albert came over and sat by me. His button-down shirt was a generic make, with a floral pattern filled with pinks and purples. It clashed with his plaid Brooks Brothers shorts. He gave me one of the yellow flowers he had picked. He then asked me if he could have my bathing suit because he was fond of roses. I was amused that Albert knew they were roses, but Gunther somehow didn't. I pointed this out to Gunther, who pointed out the washbasin behind the dorm. "Wearing a bathing suit, and mind you, a small one, is distracting. Please wash some clothes."

"What about when we shower?" I smirked. "There's no curtains."

"Well, we don't shower together."

"Good to hear."

He walked away. I couldn't tell if he was mad at me or liked me. I decided to go with liking me in a sisterly sort of way because even though I didn't have a brother, if I did have one, he seemed like he would make a good one.

Chapter 7

Sarah and Jack

As the day crawled along at a snail's pace, I washed my clothes. At first, I wondered why they weren't using the water from the basin to wash the kids' faces, but then understood when I had to walk over the spongy, wet ground that sucked at my flip-flops, ripping them off more than once. I was glad to see the cement basin was on top of a mound of dry dirt.

Shaded by a mango tree that littered the surrounding terrain with rotting fruit, I pumped away with one hand while kneading a pair of my soapy shorts with the other. It felt good to be doing this simple task. It was straightforward and relaxing, calling for repetitive motions and no thinking. I watched several salamanders scurry over and around the basin. Frogs and lots of other squiggling things plopped and swished in the mucky puddles.

The mosquitoes that buzzed in never landed on me. I sprayed myself after swimming with the DEET that I found near the screen door. It smelled like creamy caramel, and I delighted in its scent.

After a piece of clothing was washed, I took a few wet steps over to a clothesline that someone had strung between a low-lying juniper tree and an orange blossoming jacaranda, then clipped it secure with the plastic clothespins on the clothesline. I didn't have many clothes, but what I had were disgusting and full of holes. Debating on whether to throw out or wear a pair of socks, I saw Jack standing only a few feet away from me as though he had appeared out of nowhere, and I found his presence peculiar. Putting the socks in the basin, I waited for him to say something. I figured he must have something important to say, or why else would he walk through the slushy, wet grass to see me?

Jack wore knee-length beige shorts, and the skin on his calves was ghostly white, which made the pink bug bites on his legs stand out. He'd scratched his fresh bites, and many had scabbed and were painful to look at. I was glad to see his arms, lightly tanned, were unmarred. His short-sleeved cotton shirt, which was only buttoned halfway up, exposed a very white, pasty, concave chest with a few curly black hairs. He was very thin and slight. His narrow shoulder width and the fact that he was short made his head look too big, but he wasn't unattractive. He had an oddball look to him similar to Hamit's, only different. Jack's attractiveness depended on his personality, which could be enticing or a huge turnoff. Presently, he was somewhat ugly.

He was staring at my breast with his large, pointy nose and his two small eyes. He also had an unhinged drool to his lower lip that made him grotesquely infantile, like a big-headed rat waiting to be fed. I couldn't help but wonder if his mother had given him breast milk or just threw him a bottle and shut the door. I would have just shut the door.

However, I knew that I had nice tits. Round, cheery, not too big or too small, I recognized them as my best feature. They made up for other structural deficits not worth talking about. I also liked to play up their seductive abilities and had picked up a bad provocative habit while washing my clothes in front of a male housemate back in Corriente, Mexico. When kneading my clothing in the sudsy basin in the household's courtyard, a young French boy who lived in the house

liked to come out and sit in a chair in front of me to chat. I would de-
liberately press my breasts together with my arms and pop them out
the top of my V-neck T-shirt, then drop them back in with each re-
lease. It took some dexterity to keep the nipples from being exposed,
but sometimes I would let them jump out just to see his eyes grow bigger.

Looking at Jack's hungry expression, I realized I was most likely
washing my clothes in such a manner. I was also still wearing my bathing suit, which was loose and droopy around my breasts. Jack must
have seen my bouncing boobs from afar, and like the sirens they are,
they compelled him to come over to get a closer look. Standing up
straight, I picked up the miserable pair of white ankle socks I had been
debating on whether to wash, stained with holes in the heels and big
toes, and brought them up to my chest to cover my naughty breasts. I
didn't know Jack and teasing him was probably not a good idea.

A dense silence thickened the already soupy air, and we both
watched a leaf flutter down between us. I waited for Jack to explain his
presence, but he seemed tongue-tied, or maybe I just assumed he was.
Then something else piqued my interest. On the high ground behind
Jack was Sarah on all fours, looking like a cat stretching out its front
legs while digging around in the earth. Jack followed my line of vision
and turned to look at his wife. He paused for a moment, then turned
back, his expression somber.

"Sarah's an entomologist," he said, his tone hinting at regret. He
then made a noise through his long nose, then proceeded in a crisp
monotone to tell me about himself and his wife. His eyes now looked
at my forehead or the tree behind me, but never my chest. He also
turned from appearing vermin-like to someone I imagined read lots of
books, preferring them to people. Possibly people were too annoying.
It had something to do with his energy level, which seemed somewhat
frenetic and at the same time subdued, or maybe it was an inability to
smile.

Sarah and Jack were from Wisconsin. They had been working at the orphanage for nearly a year. He was working on getting a doctorate in child psychology, and Sarah was studying the bug life of the rainforest. Jack's doctoral dissertation was on "children with or without parents, coupled with commune living."

"Commune living?" I asked.

"Why, yes, I lived in one once. This place reminds me of it. Only we don't have to do dishes here." I'd never lived in a commune before, but thought he possibly had a point.

"This orphanage is a perfect setting for gathering corroborating evidence," he continued while picking a black caterpillar from his leg. Tossing it a few feet away, he continued, "My hypothesis? To prove that this place, right here, these kids, are a model for how a child should be raised. One size can fit all. Most parental units or individuals are ill-equipped to raise humans properly. Overwhelmed, self-indulgent creatures that either overshadow a child's growth with their own insecurities or don't bother with being around at all. It's the actual cause of socioeconomic injustice, and it's just not fair. Children would be better off raised by others who know better." His tone was pedantic and snooty, and full of academic condescension.

"What's unfair?" I asked, scrubbing a pair of shorts, disgusted by the hole near the crotch.

"What?"

"Seems unnatural. People like having parents. Come to think of it, I think parents like their children more than the kids like their parents," I said, inspecting a pair of chinos with a stuck zipper. "I don't think it would work—that is, not allowing parents to raise their kids. I don't think the point is fairness."

"Then what is the point?" he snapped.

"I have no idea," I said, suddenly confused because all my clothes had become unwearable. When did that happen?

"Then you shouldn't be voicing an opinion if you have no ideas.

Leave it to the experts."

"I suppose that's you?" I said, not thinking Jack was an actual e pert, but a wannabe expert, then added, "If I were writing a disserta tion on kids, the title would be 'Looking for Approval Ruins People's Lives.'"

"People who don't seek approval are poor employees," he fumed. His expression was sour. His shoulders stooped so low that he looked like a question mark, indicating a possible malfunctioning spine.

"Are you going to have religion in your commune?" I asked while pulling a shirt out of my pile of rags in nearly perfect condition. "I can't believe it, one good shirt," I mumbled.

"Religion? There will be no religion!" he snapped.

Looking up at him, I smiled. "What if one of the little kids comes up with one? I've heard little kids are good at creating imaginary characters. I had a friend who had one, took up half the back seat when we carpooled to elementary school. Yup, three of us had to push over, almost sit on each other's laps so this made-up friend had enough space."

"Odd. Please don't answer or say anything else. Anyway, I am the go-to guy here," he said, and flicked another insect off his arm. We both watched in silence as the bug sailed over to Sarah and landed on her bottom. She didn't notice. She seemed to be too preoccupied with whatever was lurking in the grass.

"Go-to guy?" I asked, bringing my attention back to Jack.

"Yes. If you need anything, let me know."

"Nothing, but I'm going into town tomorrow and—"

"I know. Gunther's going too."

"How did you know?"

"How could I not know? Now listen, we have meetings every night. We talk about what worked and what didn't during the day. We

63

have different chores that we divvy up each evening for the next day, so no one gets stuck doing the same thing all the time. We get up at five o'clock; breakfast is at six-thirty; school is at nine; recess is at ten; lunch is at noon; playtime, which is clean-up and free time too, is the entire afternoon. Dinner is at six o'clock. Nothing changes. It's perfect. Structure and consistency to help them develop properly."

"Define 'properly'," I asked, curious.

"Why don't you?" he said with one raised eyebrow. "I think it would be amusing to see what you'd say. I might even put it in my dissertation."

Stumped, I folded my arms across my chest, then quickly unfolded them because I realized I'd pushed my breasts up. "I have no idea how to raise a kid properly," I muttered.

"So why did you bring it up?"

"I didn't; you did. Anyway, when's bedtime?" I did think I would have enjoyed growing up in a rainforest with a river to swim in, but I didn't think I would have liked Jack as one of my fathers. He was too uptight, not much fun, and a giant pissant.

"Bedtime. Bedtime. We're working on it. Should be early, but it's always late."

A bird chirped while another sang an upward-down tune. I slapped a mosquito that had been resting on my ankle, sucking blood. Even the DEET had issues here. Most likely watered down by the humidity. The bite started itching immediately.

In silence, we both looked over at Sarah again. She was sitting on her calves. Her sundress bunched around her thighs and exposed smooth, white skin. Her knees were smudged with grass and dirt. She was watching a bug run around in circles in the palm of her hand.

"There are over six hundred thousand species of ants in a rainforest," she said, her voice ethereal and shaky, as though she were about to cry. "But that number is being whittled down." Then she looked over at us with two large, glassy blue eyes that seemed too big for her very white oval face, and added, "Their habitat is shrinking. Before we know it, poof... Gone." And then she began to cry. She looked and sounded very, very sad, with tears dripping down her cheeks into her mouth and off her chin. She made me sad too, and tears started to well up in my eyes, but just then a mosquito bit the top of my head. Irritated, I caught the blood-sucking jerk and with angry vengeance smashed it between my fingers and wiped its shattered carcass on the cement basin. Sarah, still occupied by her weeping, didn't notice.

Jack, who'd seemed lost in thought, awoke from whatever he was thinking about and walked over to Sarah. He gently helped her up off the ground, brushed the insect out of her hand, squeezed her waist lovingly, and wiped her tears away. "Don't cry, honey; we have plenty of bugs here," he said, his voice soft and cooing. Holding Sarah against his body, he turned toward me and said, "Lunch is in about twenty."

They walked away arm in arm, Sarah resting her head on Jack's shoulder, Jack's head resting down upon hers like puzzle pieces that fit perfectly.

Jack was right about one thing: I was a terrible employee. Before heading off to go traveling, I had been a secretary who took too many coffee breaks and often let my boss answer the phone. Hell, it was always for him anyway. A job and not a career. Humph. I wondered if I hadn't been an only child, and if my father hadn't died when I was ten, and if my mother wasn't in a mental institution, delusional and paranoid, I might have more thoughts on how to be a better person. I wondered if maybe Jack was on to something, too, and that possibly having more than two parents or parents that weren't parents, but people schooled in raising kids was a good idea. But then again, his theory was organically wrong. It also occurred to me that Jack would like my mother, and she him. I think she would have enjoyed raising a child with a group of parents, instead of shouldering all the pressures and responsibilities alone.

Across the quad, the older kids were coming back from school.

There were a lot of them, and not one had a backpack or even a pencil or pad in their hands. Did they not have homework? They raised
a dust storm with their shuffling feet, grabbing and pushing. They
poked and pulled at each other's hair. A scuffle between two boys
broke out. They looked like mad dogs fighting.

Back in the city, while talking with Rosario, her voice sultry, lipstick a flashy red, boobs lifting and resting with every breath on her
gray metal desk, she told me that the kids needed to leave the orphanage once they turned fifteen.

"A wonderful age to get a job," she had said, then added stuff
about their duty to help their families out if they had one. "We aren't
in the business of making babies. We're in the business of saving babies. Teenagers and idle time are a terrible mix."

While I watched the kids kick and punch each other, I thought
that anything above four seemed terrible. Unclipping a light cotton
shift from the clothesline, I slipped it on over my bathing suit. It hung
like a sack of potatoes, which was perfect. Driblets of sweat beaded
under my eyes and fogged my vision. I wiped the sweat away with the
back of my hand and walked over the waterlogged ground to the *dormitorio*. It was almost time for lunch. I was also glad to see that the
boys had stopped fighting, held back by two adults I hadn't met yet.

Chapter 8

Harry and Cadmael

We had a few more minutes until lunch, and I went over to Bernarda, Charlotte, Penelope, and two other girls named Annabelle and Rosamond. The girls were building a fort out of cardboard. The five of them were pensive and quiet in their deliberations, their serenity a bastion of peace. I helped them angle the cardboard into a giant box big enough for all six of us to crawl into. We sat knee-to-knee and played patty-cake. Only Penelope knew the words. Bernarda shouted out the words she knew the best like, "PATTY! BAKER! OVEN!" Charlotte just grinned, and Annabelle and Rosamond hummed.

From across the way, one of the kitchen ladies banged on a pot and shouted, "¡A comer!" Lunch time. The kids wanted to keep playing.

I was surprised by their lack of desire to eat. Helter-skelter, they ran from us and hid behind doors. "Playing is just too much fun," Catarina said to me as she pulled a kid named Otto out from under the throw pillows.

"Lunch is an issue," Jack said, standing next to me and holding on to the three girls so they wouldn't run away. He then asked me to do him a favor. "I think I saw three kids, maybe four down to the water. Could you get them?"

As I dashed out the door, Jack shouted, "Tell them they can swim later after lunch."

"Don't they always swim after lunch?"

"Yes, yes, yes, but they forget—and then again, they never forget."

As I crested the hill, I spotted all four. Frankie, the only one I knew, was kicking a mound of dirt like a ruffian, grunting with each kick. He was concentrating too hard to pay any attention to me. Sweat ran down his cheeks, his arms swinging and his right leg kicking and kicking while puffs of dirt exploded into the air. Since I figured he wasn't going anywhere, I went to get the others.

They were walking around the kindergarten building's narrow porch with no railing. Young children in the States would have already jumped, fallen, and drowned, or so the public led one to believe. The kids seemed sure-footed and chatted amongst each other. When I walked up to the water's edge, they looked over at me, but then went back to talking about something they saw in the water.

"*Muchos peces*," I said, assuming they were looking at fish.

A kid with spiky black hair glanced over at me and nodded.

"Lunch!" I said in Spanish. Weren't the kids hungry? Didn't they want lunch?

Nothing. They didn't even look at me.

Behind the boys, a pelican on a post flapped and stretched its wings. A smaller, very thin boy with a rectangular face and a crew cut blurted out, "Pelícano." They were looking at the prehistoric bird just as it stretched its broad, bat-like wings and bobbed its cuplike beak up and down. They giggled at it, but nothing more.

"It's time for lunch," I said in Spanish. I didn't blame them for not wanting to leave, as there was nothing interesting about black beans and rice, again. They turned back around to look at me. I could hear their breathy sighs over the lapping of the water and Frankie's kicking and grunting.

I imagined going onto the dock to make my presence known more forcefully. And then I imagined them running away, falling into the water, splashing around, and possibly drowning because I was too tired and slow to fetch them out in time. It could happen. I picked up a stone and threw it into the water. The splash set the pelican to flight, up over the mangroves and soaring low, skimming the river. When the bird flew up and back down, diving deep into the water, the kids looked spellbound as they watched it appear back on the surface with a fish in its beak, then throw its head back to gobble the food down.

"*Como el pelícano.*" The pelican is eating, didn't they want to eat too?

They moved off the dock. "*Que bueno,*" I said as they nonchalantly walked down the narrow wooden plank to solid ground. We stood for a few minutes looking at each other. They wore Gucci shorts and shirts, and I whistled, thinking how nicely dressed they were. They tried to whistle back. It was comical. Then I pointed to the cafeteria, and they walked away with little enthusiasm up the incline.

"Frankie, *¡venga!*" He was still kicking even though the mound was gone. Then suddenly he stopped, jumped up three times in the air, and charged up the hill, taking bold, muscled steps, stopping two or three times to kick something or tug on a piece of grass.

"Now, that wasn't too hard was it, Eleanor?" I said to myself, watching the little fellows melt into the rest of the kids on their way into the cafeteria.

"It's a mere two-minute walk from the dormitorio to the cafeteria on a good day," Jack huffed as he joined the group.

"I think we'll beat our fifteen-minute handicap," Gunther bragged. Turning to me he then said, "Yup, we need to get into the caf before the big kids, or, well, what a mess. Hard to get them to focus once the big kids get in line." He then poked my arm gently. "You're not going to leave us now? They're really a good lot."

"No reason to leave yet," I said, smiling.

"What does that mean?"

"I'm not leaving."

"Everything's a test, isn't it?" Gunther said, lightly nudging my shoulder.

"I suppose," I replied, lightly laughing, and nudged his shoulder back.

"They were on the school dock, weren't they?" Jack asked as we moved the children into the buffet line. "Some of these kids were shining shoes before they arrived. Others sold Chiclets on the streets. All by themselves! They'd never fall into the water."

"They could slip. Anyone could slip," Sarah said in her melancholy voice. "I could slip."

"But you're not going to, honey," Jack said kindly. He threw his hand out to touch her but missed.

"A bit of bollocks, them acting this way, but don't worry. Once they start eating, they're perfect." Gunther's tone, solid and knowledgeable. Yet I was only half listening. By the dormitorio's door, Harry and Cadmael were discussing something. Cadmael had the maroon backpack and was clutching it to his chest. Harry had his hand on the backpack. The expression on his face went from taut to amused and back again, and then he laughed. It was a light, airy laugh, like he was amazed or angry at something but didn't want to show it. Cadmael gave him the bag. Harry opened the bag up and gave Cadmael a stack of money. They shook hands, and Cadmael smiled and walk down to the dock. Harry turned to look at us all waiting to go into the cafeteria.

I caught his eye, dark and light at the same time. His expression was relaxed. For a few brief moments, we just stared at each other. Then he waved and yelled, "Hello, roomie," and walked into the dormitorio. The whole scene seemed strange, and I looked around to see if anyone else had noticed. Gunther was still babbling about the kids, Jack and Sarah were holding hands and nudging the children along, and everyone else was in the cafeteria, so no. Odd, odd, odd, was all I could think. In a country where a person can be killed for a dollar, and where most of the people earn a dollar or less a day, a bag full of thousands is very suspicious. Once again, I had no desire to get involved in something that was potentially dangerous, but for entertainment purposes, I would keep my eye on Cadmael and my new 'roomie.'

Chapter 9

Lunch

Getting the kids to line up by the buffet counter in an orderly fashion took another ridiculous five minutes. Absurdly distracted by the enormity of the room, some sought out dents on the cement floor, chased little bugs, and wandered around in circles while others just stared, possibly moping about something in their heads. It occurred to me that having children was a lot of work, and right now it was very irritating. Then poof! All spastic outbursts gone, and they stood in the buffet line like little angels. So, that's what it is, the angel and the devil syndrome; drawn in with smiles, then brutalized by irrational behaviors. And worst of all, they seemed to have the upper hand.

Esmeralda was especially gentle with the kids. She even smiled, showing three gold teeth. The kids would peer up at her from below the counter, eyes wide with wonder. But when she looked at us volunteers, she frowned, clamping her mouth shut. I wondered if she really disliked us or if it was just some game she played.

Before we arrived in the dining room, Catarina had placed the children's forks on the tables along with plates and filled all their cups with milk. "The more organized we are, the more organized they are," Jack said. "And don't do anything for them that they can't do for themselves." I nodded in agreement. These little kids were very chaotic. They also asked me to either carry their plates or carry them. Strangely, I didn't mind, but I held back from carrying a child or a plate.

Besides, they were good at it. The kids would tiptoe or shuffle along with their food, eyes on the prize to make sure not to spill a drop. They were dexterous at dodging the older kids who came piling in like a swarm of vermin. Only Henrik and Raymond had trouble, so I took their plates to the table for them. Jack nodded approval. "Those two are very young."

The benches were low and the tables high. Henrik and Raymond stood or kneeled when they ate, as did many others. The children were slow, distracted eaters, and put little bits of food on their forks or picked a bean up with their fingers and placed it in their mouths, then forgot they were even eating and looked oddly surprised when they swallowed. Several made nasal sounds like they had stuffy noses and "nom-nom" sounds. The entire ordeal was exhausting to watch.

"What time is it?" I asked Catarina, who was the only one wearing a watch.

"Noon. It's always noon when we eat."

"Right. I just feel like I've lived a lifetime already today. Time seems to stand still here."

"It's comforting, especially when you're my age. At home, I get up, eat breakfast, and then it's dinnertime." She laughed and said, "You'll get used to it."

Lunch revealed to me what appeared to be everyone at the orphanage, an eclectic assembly of orphans, toilers, and wayfarers. There were the workmen, laundry ladies, and maids eating at a long table in the back of the kitchen. There were our twenty-four youngsters, toddlers, and those a touch older, and over a hundred or more other children ranging in ages from five to fifteen, along with the five people looking after them.

The older kids sat toward the back of the cafeteria while our little band sat in the front by the kitchen. I was glad the big kids didn't sit with us because they were unnerving. Upright and loud, they exuded an undisciplined air like they were up to no good, as though at any moment they might throw milk on me or kick my shins. They tossed the Frisbee-size tortillas back and forth, twirling them on their fingers like pizza dough. A group of boys had smashed black beans all over each other's faces. A girl with her hair pulled neatly back with a pink ribbon was using her fork as a catapult to lob food over the tables. She randomly hit unsuspecting kids. Everyone was talking at once, and no one seemed to be listening. When I tried to listen to their cacophony, it gave me the feeling of drowning in a noisy pool.

Feral, I thought while helping Henrik off the table. "Where are you going, Henrik?" But he wouldn't answer, just wandering off. As I watched him, he went to see Esmeralda. She gave him something from her pocket. When he came back, he had a piece of soft candy in his hand. I helped him back up onto the bench, and he stood beside me, popped the piece into his mouth, and began chewing and chewing and chewing. I thought how cute he was and how little, and how much I preferred our three tables of youngsters to the wild-eyed youth behind us.

I also noticed that the grown-ups with the robust older bunch seemed indifferent to the barbaric mayhem. There were two men and three women, non-indigenous, but mestizos, mixed. One of the men was tall with a pencil-thin build and a massive head of black hair, standing and making theatrical gestures at a group of boys who had put something down his back.

The three women, all under thirty, were slim-limbed with thick middles. Their jawlines constantly moved like spastic pistons because they too were talking, which meant they couldn't possibly be listening. They also laughed a lot. One of them with big, round ghost eyes and fat squirrel cheeks caught me staring at them. She locked her eyes on mine and projected mean little rays of hostility at me. I waved. Her reaction was to point at me with her chin while babbling out of the corner of her mouth to the other women. It was obvious she was talking about me, especially when they all looked my way like curious cows in a field. I gave another limp wave; they nodded back with nostrils flared.

I looked away, lazily spooned rice and beans into my mouth, and said to Gunther, who was sitting across from me, "The women over there are giving me foul looks."

Gunther laughed and rolled his eyes.

"Why's that funny?"

"Nothing. Well, they don't like us, that's all," he replied.

"And why's that?"

"Rosario, a very shrewd woman, mind you, gave paying jobs away to non-paid foreigners—us." He then clarified his remarks by saying, "Rosario wanted foreigners—Europeans, Americans, Canadians—raising the little tikes. She can get them for free. She also prefers how we raise kids. Teaching them, instead of doing everything for them." His lilting voice was delicate and pleasant.

"So, what are we teaching these kids?" I asked, thinking I hadn't seen us teach a thing.

"I don't know."

"They carry their own plates. But according to Jack and what I've seen in the country, they had jobs before coming here. Compared to shining shoes, carrying your own plate is a day off."

He laughed and continued explaining who the local help were. "Now Luis and Umberto," Gunther said, pointing them out to me. "Look after the boys." Umberto was the black-haired, tall man who now sat laughing with a group of kids. Louis, who was much shorter and stockier, was by the milk barrel trying to get a congregation of children to sit back down. "They're super," Gunther said. "But the only person they talk to is Harry. Harry pays them to be his substitute, now and then. The women are good with the girls. Don't know them at all, though. They leave us alone. I'm also not going to call it envy, even dislike for us, but I think it's more of an angry sadness they feel, for themselves. You know, we're working for free to help the kids. They are grateful. But these were jobs. Paying jobs." Gunther took a bite of his meal and chewed slowly. He seemed caught up in a thought he wasn't sure how to express. Two twins, very thin and dainty looking, were standing on the bench next to him. They were eating by using Gunther as a crutch. Each had one hand on Gunther's shoulder and a fork in the other. With each scoop of food, they leaned into Gunther and spilled more of their food than they ate on to his lap.

Gunther then abruptly waved his spoon at me and almost knocked the boys off the bench. Their eyes went wide and black beans flew through the air. "Luck, it's all about luck, not being hit by a stray bullet," he blurted out.

"That's random," I replied.

"Luck certainly is," he adamantly said.

"What about common sense?" I asked.

"Well, if you don't have luck, common sense won't help you."

"With common sense, a person would know not to walk into a dark cave that says, 'Caution, monsters live here,' making luck obsolete."

"But if you don't have any luck, it's most likely the creatures aren't in the cave. They're at your house, eating your flatmates, who had the common sense to stay home. And because you don't have any luck, you go home before they're finished, and they eat you too." We both laughed, a lighthearted peal that felt refreshing.

Settling down to concentrate on eating, I noticed the kids were on the move. Wooter, a very gruff kid sitting by the twins, took his cup and scrambled down off the bench. He ambled over to one of the older kids who was standing by the milk barrel and pulled on the kid's shorts to get his attention. Something passed between them, and the older boy picked up the milk ladle and gave Wooter a generous pour. Bernarda and two other little girls in lovely Lilly Pulitzer dresses were over by the milk barrel with cups in their hands. They also pulled on the older kid's shorts. He ladled more milk out for the girls. Over by the buffet, Albert and a kid named Mouse got seconds from Esmeralda.

Mouse came over with his full plate, shoved it on top of the table, and climbed up next to Alex, who to my chagrin, was sitting next to Wooter who had returned. I don't think he meant to sit with me; he was preoccupied with the children when he sat down. When he finally noticed me, he frowned and so did I. Mouse put a mouthful of beans in his mouth, swished them around, then opened his mouth wide to show us the partially masticated food. When we made faces, he fake-laughed loudly and shut his mouth. But when we turned away, he puffed up his cheeks and popped them, food splattering all over the table and everyone's plates.

Then Alex then did something that astonished me because it seemed out of character. He gently placed his hand on Mouse's back, and in Spanish with a thick German accent he said, "Now, now... food is to be eaten, not spit out." He wiped Mouse's face off using his own spit on the stubborn, sticky bean goo. Once his face was clean, Alex ruffled his hair, and firmly but with care took Mouse's fork from him. Mouse leaned into Alex and remained quietly at his side as Alex ate what remained of his own meal. It was an endearing sight to see. It was the second time I'd seen Alex act like a caring human being, but this kind temperament seemed to be reserved only for children. Alex must have noticed I was watching him because he looked over at me and said, "I know you're from Escondido."

"Right."

"You knew my girlfriend, Milla. She's coming tomorrow." His expression had changed into a wooden, flat, hard-to-read stance. In Escondido, at the rooming house on the beach, I watched Alex trip people when they walked by; I saw him take their items when they weren't looking, like shirts, books, and sunglasses. He was rude and not funny, although I believe he thought he was funny. I had been puzzled at the time why Milla, who seemed so good-natured, someone who laughed easily and never said anything mean about anything or anybody, even the rats that plagued the communal kitchen, liked someone as twisted as Alex. But then what did I know? As I thought of the past men in my life, some were wonderful, while some were drug dealers, drunks, womanizers, and narcissists. All in good fun, though—most of the time.

Alex licked his puckish lips and in a haughty tone said, "I need Harry's room."

I remained silent, astounded at how fast information circulated in this place.

"Now be a good girl, let Milla and me move in."

"It's not my room to give," I replied.

"*Dummer Arsch*." It was one of his favorite insults and meant "stupid ass".

Mouse, who had snuggled in against Alex's stomach, had fallen asleep. Alex had his arm around him. It was a sweet sight. So what if he was kind to children (although a very good attribute to have at an orphanage)? Overall, he was a jerk. His face was repugnant and currently gloating with smugness. I said, "I don't want to talk to you." I picked up my plate and moved over to the table behind us.

"*Verdammter Narr*," he said. Another one of his snide remarks. Milla told me it meant *fucking fool*.

"Yup, there always has to be one rotten apple in the pack," I mumbled, sitting next to Jack.

"You mean 'barrel,'" Jack corrected me.

"Right. Enjoying your meal?" I noticed there were red dots on the side of his plate.

"Why not?" he replied.

I looked around to see if there were any more red dots on the other plates. Sarah's plate had green dots. Molly and Golly had wiped their plates clean, leaving no colored dots. Catarina, Hamit, and Harry were sitting at the third table. I knew Harry had salsa but wondered about the other two. Chuckling, I thought, *Of course they do*, then proceeded to remove Mouse's spit pieces from my food and noshed down a bland pile of rice and beans.

Jack stuffed the last of his tortilla into his mouth. "Gotta go," he said and stood up. Before leaving, he put a hand on my shoulder. "We like the kids to bus their own plates, but they need guidance. They're bad at it." This caused me to wonder if the previously paid staff had made the children bus their plates. Then I thought most likely not if they did everything for them, and certainly not, if the kids were "bad at it"—so much easier to just do it for them. "So we are teaching them something." But Jack had already left.

The high-carb meal had me feeling weighted down, and it occurred to me that I had a room, but not a bed. Not even a blanket. The thought of not sleeping well again caused me to feel even heavier. I put my fork down to ponder my not-so-ideal circumstances. With a sigh, I looked at Sarah. She was sitting across from me, mewing and fidgeting while looking around the room as though she'd lost something. I began to look around the room to see what it might be. Both our eyes fell on Jack at the exit. I watched Sarah jump up, clear her plate, and run after him.

"Them two—sex addicts," Golly said. She looked at me with an amused but judgmental expression. She then picked at a molar, and added, "Awright geeezzaa! I hope one day I 'ave a relationship like 'em. Sorted, mate."

"What?" I asked. Her accent confused me.

"They've got a nice relationship," she replied, slowly enunciating each word. Golly and I watched Sarah and Jack walk hand-in-hand to the *dormitorio*.

Chapter 10

Molly and Golly

After lunch, I discovered a game that the *nineras* liked to play during afternoon playtime. The beetles were buzzing, and white moths danced in the sun's rays. Some of the kids wanted to hang out in the quad, Bernarda, Charlotte, and Penelope being three of them, and two others were the twins, Earl and Greggo. Then Raymond and Henrik and a hefty, square-backed boy with a wide middle and who was tall for his age joined us. I wanted to go to sleep. I thought of pretending I was sick or something, although this wasn't too far from the truth, since needing sleep can make a person feel ill, but I didn't have anywhere to sleep, so why bother?

I flopped down by a log, and Golly and Molly sat next to me on the same log. The kids didn't have any modern or conventional toys. They played with sticks and stones, made dirt rivers and leaf boats, and built mountains with brambles and castles with pebbles and mud. They were content playing with each other and the earth. It was all very symbiotic. Henrik dug a small ditch. Charlotte made it bigger. Penelope pushed a leaf boat through the ditch, and Bernarda constructed a stick house along its banks. Albert, who came up from the river with a handful of flowers, smelling and caressing them, gave Molly, Golly, and me each one before tucking the rest into his Jam'n Bermuda pockets. He had changed out of his previous shorts. No one knew why he had done this; he just did it. Albert picked up a piece of bark and made farting motor noises with his mouth while pushing the bark through the ditch. At one point, he found a bigger piece of bark and left us to see how it would float in the river.

The kids were quiet and diligent, and for the most part solved their dilemmas by adjusting the method or tool. They had time to think. The creations were their own, which wasn't to say I didn't want to play with them, but it didn't seem necessary. Besides, the tranquil serenity of the afternoon had my body folding in and head nodding. The humidity was at its height, and puddles of sweat pooled below my eyes. Slumping over like a Raggedy Ann doll, I dozed a languid, dreamy sleep, only to be snapped awake by Molly and Golly's high-pitched laughter.

"What? Who?" I said, stumbling to sit up. Catching sight of their legs, I saw they had oodles of bug bites.

"The bugs like you," I said, looking up at them, my head heavy and sluggish.

"*Fuck'n* bugs love me legs. Given me pizza legs," Molly said, scratching a raw-looking lump of flesh just above her ankle.

"*Don'* scratch, you'll make it worse," Golly remarked, tugging on Molly's arm.

And then the game began. It was a manifestation of the environment that stories would be created with the appearance of being real. It was gossip pulled out of the air, imagination searching for something fun. It cut through the boredom of sitting and watching the same scene over and over again. It put excitement in the tasteless food and added to the passiveness of repeating the same chores day in and day out. Although I'd been at the orphanage for less than 24 hours, I imagined the days were all pretty much the same. So, my thinking at the time was, What harm could any of it cause? Where could any of it go?

"You know, the dustbin lid over there," Molly said, and pointed at a child. "And his twin." She pointed at another. "They're Rosario's *Li'l Tom tits.*"

"What?" I mumbled. Their Cockney accents were so thick it made me want to go back to sleep. Their lack of consonants was too much, and the "Aaa" sound was excruciating to the ear. I wished I'd stayed down by the river with the rest of the crew. But then I asked, "What are Tom tits?"

"Babies. Rosario's kids, dustbin lids," Molly clarified. "And the faaat one." She pointed at the square-backed boy. He used his weight to push his fellow orphans around. Motoring his leaf boat up the canals with a bullying, clumsy manner, he stepped on everyone's boat, including Charlotte's twig-boat, which made her frown. Charlotte, unable to talk, had a quiet, hidden personality. Without fussing, she went over to an unused area and made another river. Penelope and Bernarda followed her, leaving the large boy to play by himself. I felt bad for him. His body was too big for his age.

"*Oi*, the big guy. We can never teach 'im a thing," Molly continued, then whispered, "He's Hamit's kid. His name's El Gordo." Molly then laughed a horrible-sounding laugh, like a sound a poodle might make if it were a deranged human.

"El Gordo?" I said and then asked, "What's his real name?" El Gordo meant "the fat one." Who would name their kid that? By saying his name, his head popped up, and I quickly replied, "Nothing." He was wearing navy-blue baggy gym shorts and a T-shirt with a growling tiger on it.

"Hamit named him," Molly giggled. "Looks like 'm too."

"Did you just say he's Hamit's kid?" I asked. "And the twins are Rosario's?"

"What do yah think?" Golly piped in. Her deadpan expression gave nothing away.

"I don't know," I said, leaning back against the log and shutting my eyes again. A deep wave of paralyzing sleep enwrapped my brain. The heat was like a sedative, the girls' game confusing, their accents were too difficult to understand. Golly nudged me awake and said, "Bernarda. She's a real pistol, innit." She scratched a puss-filled sore on her fleshy calf. "Why she's... she's Jeje's kid."

"Who's Jeje?" I asked, stretching my limbs to help ward off sleep, then sat up straight.

"Young kitchen girl."

I chuckled while moving away from Golly's gross legs. Their accents were becoming normal to me as the ebb and flow of rarely using K's, swallowing their L's, inflaming A's, never using H's, and replacing the 'th' sound with an F somehow made sense. Feeling peppier, I wanted to hear more about their odd matchmaking, I said, "Go on, who else?"

The two of them began looking around, their minds churning. Then Golly squealed, causing all the kids' heads to pop up. Hushing her voice, she said, "Raymond and Henrik."

"And?" I was fascinated.

"Manolo. You know, the launch driver. They're his kids." She thought this disclosure to be very funny. Covering her mouth, she rocked back and forth on the log, laughing, and Molly joined her. Once again, the kids' heads popped up.

Molly and Golly's flaming copper hair, cinched with butterfly clips, made them look as juvenile as they were acting, but I liked them and their silliness. Matching the kids with the adults added intrigue to our afternoon. But I was curious about Molly and Golly and asked, "How did you two end up here?"

"In England we travel before becoming serious," Molly yapped, then added, "We not twins, you know."

"I didn't think you were," I said, wondering why she thought I thought they were twins.

"Wee best friends," Golly clarified.

Then Molly randomly said, changing the subject, "Wee don't have any nappies."

"Could use a sheet," Golly remarked.

"The kids don't look like they need diapers," I said.

"Some do when they sleep," Golly continued.

"That kid needs a giant nappy," Molly squealed while pointing at a small boy.

"Yes, yes, a giant nappy," Golly said excitedly, repeating the word "nappy" again and again.

"Nappy" had an annoying sound due to the emphasis on the A. They also seemed to love saying the word; possibly the A sound had a favorable ring to them, like the sound of an uncontrollable chihuahua they once had. Or the screech of metal on metal as a train went around a bend when they were traveling somewhere. Or maybe it just had them thinking of their mothers, fathers, and friends at an amusement park, riding a rollercoaster.

Charlotte and Bernarda, who were to my left, perked up and smiled every time they heard the word "nappy." Their heads would cock to the side, and I was certain their ears moved. Penelope, standing with her boat stick in her hand and her face punched up into a snarl, pointed her stick at Molly and Golly and said, "Stop."

"What?" Molly said. She gave Penelope a sour look.

"STOP," Penelope repeated, her tiny voice angry.

"Cheeky, aren't you," Molly said.

"She knows some English," I said, amused.

"She's annoying. She's Alex's kid," Golly said, looking grumpy, her shoulders pulled in and her jaw slack. So, she finds Alex irritating too, I surmised.

Shut down by Penelope, Molly and Golly didn't want to talk anymore. They sat in silence and dug their sandaled toes into the dirt.

Awake and energized by the matchmaking, I crawled over to Henrik and Raymond. They had piled small stones into a pyramid. I tossed a rock on top of it, and they took it off. Henrik handed it back to me. Their rock placement was very methodical, and I gathered I'd disturbed their organization.

It was then that I noticed the afternoon had a fervor to it, as though the world around us was chaotic and humming, but unable to touch us. The river with its motors, shouts, and surging waters was another world, far away from this nano slab of dirt and sand. A colorful red-and-blue macaw perched in a linden tree by one of the upside-down canoes, fluttered its wings and squawked. I watched it until it flew away, then let my gaze roam. I caught the eye of the workman, Aapo. He'd been asleep underneath the shadows of the middle canoe while Eadrich, the oldest workman, had the canoe to the left, and Cadmael, the youngest, was to the right. How odd they take naps there, I thought.

Aapo, middle-aged with creased, hard features, was staring at me. His face was muddy and streaked with sweat, and the whites of his eyes shone. He looked menacing. He wasn't blinking, so I thought he might still be asleep, dreaming with his eyes open. But then he turned his head away to look up into the belly of the canoe. There had been something about Aapo's stare. His eyes and expression reminded me of the women who had been sneering at me earlier at lunch. Gunther had called it "an angry sadness, not a dislike." I felt it was both a festering bitterness and self-pity. I'd seen the same discordant expressions on a few of my Spanish teachers back in the city, in Corriente in Mexico. The teachers had become bandy and argumentative over my ability to travel in their country, but they couldn't travel in mine. The exchange rate was unequal. Their rambling discourse often brought up the issues of failing monetary systems in countries that borrowed too heavily and forfeited their bill-paying by cheating their citizens. Their index fingers pointed at me, at the unscrupulous foreign companies that refused to pay taxes and stole their land. The multitude of abuses, unconscionable. I never thought to apologize or defend. Our worlds were as different as the moon and the sun, yet were somehow in the same galaxy. I knew we wanted the same things from life: to eat well, have warm shelter, live in peace, to keep children safe, to travel, see and do different things. In their view, I had it and they did not. And on the surface, they were right.

Leaning back against the log, I watched Golly and Molly pull themselves out of their pout by pushing each other back and forth until they laughed.

Then Golly turned to me and said, "I have an idea. Why don't you babysit tonight? Ya don't have a bed, so why not? Nuff said, yeah?"

"Babysit, sure." What a great idea. I imagined the throw pillows and what a nice bed they would make. Then Raymond came over and sat in my lap. I laughed and said in English, "What are you going to be like when you grow up?"

Golly giggled, "Why, he'll be president of the country. Won't you, Raymond?"

The funny kid nodded yes.

Chapter 11

Catarina

Just as Jack had told me earlier in the day, a nightly meeting took place after dinner with all the *nineras*. It had been amusing, until it lagged and we all grew bored. It started with everyone sitting in the great room on throw pillows in a circle. Jack stood in the middle of all. The kids, nestled behind us, were quietly reading to themselves, although most weren't really reading, just looking at pictures.

Jack, bent and pointy, was doing a huffing thing that made his nostrils flare while twisting his hips one way, then another. It made his question-mark stance look goofier, as though he was a contortionist who didn't know what he was doing. Catarina whispered into my ear, "It's Jack's method of loosening up before diving into a lecture."

Once ready, he orated on the hazards of putting clothing in the wrong bins because it made dressing the children frustrating and time-consuming, and something about causing cross-dressing by the children since they picked out their own clothes. "If the dresses are mixed with the shorts and pants, well, what kind of message is that sending?" he asked. People snickered.

He then went into playtime.

"I like playtime," Alex said. Alex was lying on his back, spitting foam into the air, and when it fell back down, he would catch it with his tongue, or it would land directly back into his mouth. It was disgusting to watch.

"Of course you do, Alex," Jack said, cringing at the foam-eating. "Now I have an experiment. We have boxes of toys up in the attic. Let's bring them down."

"Toys? I don't think they've ever played with conventional toys," Gunther remarked.

"That's why it's an experiment," Jack said.

"What are you going to call this one in your dissertation?" Gunther blurted out.

"The title to the chapter will come to me when we see their reactions," Jack replied.

"We? What do you mean by 'we'?" asked Gunther.

"I meant me," Jack corrected himself.

"Why not 'we'?" Gunther asked.

"Because the dissertation is about me and my thoughts."

"So you finally admit you're a madman using all of us as your guinea pigs—and you're taking all our good thoughts to be yours," Gunther said, proud of himself.

Jack huffed, paused, stared at the floor, shook his index finger at Gunther and said, "Not a madman, Gunther. An intellectual." This made us all giggle, which caused Jack to huff again, and then he continued with his diatribe. Disturbed over the shabby condition of the clothes, he held up a lovely, turquoise Donna Karan dress with a frayed hem. He gritted his teeth and threw the tattered frock onto the floor, making an "ugh" noise. Catarina picked the dress up and tossed it at

Alex, who wrapped it around his dreads as a headdress. Most thought the color complimented his red hair. I kept quiet. If I was going to speak to Alex, it wouldn't be with a compliment.

Jack then shifted from pessimist to optimist about the children's wardrobe. He liked the fact that we probably had the best-dressed orphans in the world. I liked that idea too. We all did, and there were a lot of "hip, hip, hoorays" over dressing well. Enlivened by our nonsense, Jack became more animated and threw his right arm into the air. He pointed at the ceiling as though whoever lived above in the rafters or the sky should be listening to him and broke into a sermon. "If the clothing was washed on the gentle cycle or even on 'normal' in a modern-day washing machine, it would last, keep its color, never get a hole." He shouted the last few words, which caused the kids to glance up from their books.

"The clothes!" he continued, both arms stretching up. "Could be hand-me-downs for generations. But that's not the case here. Here, the cement washboard rules. Here, these busty, thick-armed women scrub the threads into indiscernible, infinitesimal dust."

"Could we call it thread-barren instead?" Gunther interjected.

"What? Sure," Jack mumbled, then added, "Yes, thread-barren, Christ! Threadbare spots and a lot of discoloration."

"My pants used to be white," Gunther again interjected. It was obvious he was making fun of Jack, but Jack either didn't notice or didn't care. Gunther's balloon pants were red and brown, and always had been red and brown. Looking around the room to see if anyone else thought this meeting was odd, I noticed Catarina was busy picking crud out from under her nails. Molly and Golly were asleep, lumped together like chunks of lard. Alex was playing with Frankie. Gunther and I were the only ones paying attention.

"Rosario should be visiting soon," Jack continued, then with his mouth open, a word on the tip of his tongue, he abruptly stopped talking to concentrate on something outside the window by the cafeteria.

"She's bringing more clothing, I assume," Catarina asked, looking at Jack.

"More what?" Jack mumbled as he walked over to the window.

"Clothing," Catarina stated.

"Why?" Jack said. He scratched his chin, troubled by something outside. I stood up to see what had caught his attention. Sarah was by the cafeteria entrance, trying to catch the bugs and moths that were swarming around the floodlight above her. She had an open mason jar and was sweeping it through the air.

"Don't bring any of those things into the dorm! We have enough creepy things crawling around in here!" Jack shouted at her. The little kids looked up again. Raymond and Henrik took the opportunity to become very vocal. The little boys were not only making up a story to go with the pictures but were adding words such as "goo-goo, boo-boo, eek," and "wee-kee." Curious to see what book they were reading, I crawled over. It was *Green Eggs and Ham*.

When the screen door opened, Jack walked out. The meeting had ended. Catarina rose, straightened out her skirt, and said, "I have stuff to do." She walked out of the room. Her sandaled feet slapped along the cement floor all the way to the bathroom. Then Molly and Golly woke up. They looked sweaty and disheveled and rolled their bodies over to a group of kids that were reading the book *Are You My Mother?* Molly pointed to something in the book that made Golly and her burst into a high-pitched giggle. The kids laughed. Gunther went over to a group of boys and tossed a pillow back and forth with them. Jack came back into the room with Sarah. He took the bottle from her hand and placed it back outside the door. He folded Sarah into his arms, and they headed up the stairs. Molly and Golly once again commented on them being sex addicts. Then, someone, I don't know who, put a cassette in the boombox. All the kids dropped what they were doing and jumped up to dance. Downtime had also ended.

The cassette tape was ranchero music. The lyrics weaved a twisted tale of sweaty love-making. The tune was eerie and seemingly inappropriate for kids, but I doubted they listened or even heard the words. It was the rhythm, the beat of the bass that drew them in, their eyes lighting up as they danced. The young ladies from the kitchen and a few of the older children came bounding through the screen door to join the rumble too. It was an unexpected sight, but welcome, their hips gyrating, their faces glowing in the dull twenty-watt bulb.

Instead of dancing, I made my way down to the water with a bucket. The evening cool air felt good to breathe in. The quad and path to the river were partially lit by the compound's two floodlights. I was in no rush and took slow, short strides. I felt the thumping beat of the music under my feet and heard the words as I walked. With each step, the sound faded, like the motorboats making their way north or south on the water.

Descending the grassy embankment, I heard rustling coming from a bush to my right. My mind raced to thoughts of danger. *What evil lurks?* I wondered. When I walked over to the bush, swinging the bucket by my side and snapping twigs under my feet, the rustling stopped. The only sounds were the waves on the shore and the distant melody of the music. Suddenly two people scrambled out from under the bush, giggling. Their abrupt appearance gave me a fright, and I dropped my bucket. Then I laughed, seeing nothing but two naughty kids, a boy and a girl. They were around fourteen years old. They ran holding hands to the big kids' dorm. Their clothing was in disarray, and the girl's hair was full of brambles. Having regained my composure, I thought about what Rosario had said: "We're not in the business of making babies—we're in the business of saving them." Easier said than done.

Once at the river's edge, I sat down on a rock and put my bucket on the ground. The bugs were noisy and bit my ankles. I picked up a fallen branch with thick leaves and began swatting my legs and head. The flow of the river was felt more than seen. It occurred to me that I had been at the same spot this morning sitting on the same rock, the water having the same tug. It rumbled beneath my feet, as though at any moment it would grab up a foot or an arm and drag me in. The morning was light-years away, and yet only hours had passed, slow measured hours filled with seconds and minutes that took their time. Sighing, I smiled. One could live a long time here and still be young.

Now at the river's edge, self-flagellating with a branch clustered with leaves, I breathed in the cool air, coupled with a feeling of contentment. Away from the need to talk and be part of something bigger than myself, I enjoyed the alone time. As my eyes adjusted to the dark, I could see the outline of the trees on the other side of the river and the single bulbs from the various houses. They looked like fireflies permanently it. The club's yellow and multicolored Christmas lights were soothing and nostalgic. I had spent Christmas on a beach in La Playa, Mexico with friends from language school. It rained as we sat on swinging seats at a bar drinking margaritas. There were green blinking lights there too, and Rubin the bartender wore a Santa Claus hat. I remembered laughing a lot and then smashing open a piñata filled with McDonald's Happy Meal toys.

"Fancy seeing you down here." It was Catarina. She had a bucket with her, the leaky black bucket with a crack in the bottom. She put her bucket down and pulled on my shirt to follow her to the dock. "I think he's here," she said.

"Who?"

"Him."

Slapping a mosquito, she dug into her skirt pocket and pulled out a pack of cigarettes and quickly lit one. Taking a long drag, she blew the smoke out all around us, then offered me one. I took it, lighting it off hers. I wasn't a regular smoker. More like a social smoker, or someone who smoked when the need for smoking was necessary for, say, to stave off bugs. They were Gitanes, short, stumpy French cigarettes, and made me lightheaded. They did the trick because the bugs disappeared.

"You must have brought them from Montreal," I said, tossing my branch aside while exhaling smoke all over my arms and legs.

"Yeah, I only have a few packs left," she said, peering out over the water. "Do you see the sailboat?" she asked.

"Where?"

"There," she said and pointed to a boat sitting around a hundred yards out. The mast light flickered as the boat rocked, blending in with the Christmas lights. But as we studied the outline, the whole boat slowly appeared. Then the light flicked on, illuminating the boat's sails and the outline of a person sitting in the cockpit. Whoever it was stood up, fiddled with something, and then sat back down.

"I think it's him," she mumbled.

"Who?" I asked again.

"Harry's friend."

"Dutch?" I don't know why I said that. Harry was friends with Umberto, and he wasn't Dutch.

"Not sure. Why did you say Dutch?"

"Harry's Dutch."

"No, he's not."

"He told me he's Dutch."

"He likes Dutch people, or no, it's the licorice he likes. I don't know how he gets it here. It's sent to him, maybe. It's sweet and strong-flavored."

"Yum."

"He doesn't like sharing it." She then began to look around and asked, "Where are those binoculars?"

"At the end of the dock."

I followed Catarina as she walked down the dock. I wasn't fond of licorice, but sweet sounded good. I imagined Harry munching on it in the room and not sharing, and me not giving a damn except that maybe I would want to lick off the sweetness.

Catarina placed the binoculars up to her face and narrated to me what the man was doing: "He's going down below." I could see he had left because the light in the cabin allowed for the detection of movement, but I didn't tell her that because it would spoil her narration.

"Now he's coming back up. He has coffee or something in a mug. He's pouring from a glass bottle into it. I bet it's booze. He's sitting back down. He's lighting a pipe." When he lit a match, it illuminated his face briefly, but not long enough to show what he looked like. I saw he had a white face and maybe a long nose. Could it be the same sailor as earlier? I said nothing because I had nothing but speculation. Besides, there were a fair number of gringos sailing around these parts, especially with the boat club across the bay.

"So, where's he from?" I said, standing off to the side to let Catarina position herself better. Fish were jumping in our cove, which briefly drew my attention away.

"I don't know, I think America."

"I meant Harry," I said, looking back at her. "If he's not Dutch, where's he from?"

"I don't know. Come to think of it, his mother may have Dutch ties. Oh, my—I love the way he puffs on his pipe. The smell is dreamy."

A fish popped up and swam around in circles, making a whirlpool. The sliver of moon made it hard to see, but there seemed to be some phosphorescence in the water that caused the combustion to sparkle. I wished I had the binoculars so I could see the fish better, but I supposed her man was more important than my fish. Taking a drag from the cigarette, I blew more billowing puffs around us.

"He's sitting, drinking, and smoking. I saw him with Harry a month back. He's handsome, dreamy handsome." I stared at her face, half-hidden behind the binoculars; in the blue darkness, she looked younger. It took her wrinkles away and made her thick, strawberry-blonde hair the color of fall corn. Standing there, she had an energy about her that felt wild and possessed due to the man on the boat, I said, "You should get Harry to introduce you."

She laughed, then sighed as though my idea was silly. Resting the binoculars on her chest, she gazed back out over the river and said, "Now my sailor man, if it's him, he's an American." She said "American" in a John Wayne accent. I laughed.

"American," I repeated, using the same vernacular. Taking a quick drag, I once again blew the smoke around us, then asked, "Can I have a look?" She handed me the binoculars.

I saw that he was hunched over and reading a book by the light of a small hand lantern. "He could be cute. It's hard to tell, but his face looks—well, I think he's older," I remarked, forgetting that Catarina was much older than me.

"He looks like the Marlboro Man. You remember that commercial." She then giggled and asked, "Do you think I could swim out there?"

"Now?"

"Tomorrow, if he's still here—or the next day." She rubbed her chin and continued. "At lunch, Harry told me you're driving into town in the morning."

"People don't keep much to themselves here."

"Why would they? This place is the size of my pinky. Anyway, he thought I might want to ask you to get me something. And I do. See if you can get me a bathing cap." Then she laughed. "I hate the idea of climbing out of the water looking like a drowned rat."

"I've a better idea. Why don't we shout to him? Have him come over." His boat was anchored in the heaviest part of the currents.

"And ruin the surprise?" She then laughed again, a deep throaty guffaw.

"Those currents hit right around where his boat is anchored," I said, trying to discourage her.

"I'm a fantastic swimmer." Taking the binoculars from me, she took one last look before placing them back on the dock's hook. We stubbed out our spent cigarettes, and Catarina stuffed the butts into her pack so as to not litter. We then dashed off the dock because the mosquitoes were flying in from all angles. Remembering the buckets, we filled them and headed back to the *dormitorio*. With every step, we sloshed a little water on the ground. They were only half full when we arrived at the door. It didn't really matter, since the toilets would be a mess by morning anyway.

The party was still going strong when we walked in. The one sultry ranchero song was played over and over again until ten, or maybe it was eleven when someone finally realized we should put the kids to bed. It was easy getting them to brush their teeth—they liked it. They used Crest bubblegum-flavored toothpaste, which I tried because I had the region's chalky, only slightly peppermint-flavored toothpaste in my bag. The Crest was overly sweet, though, so I opted to continue with the bland chalk.

Once the children were in their cribs, they fell right to sleep. I was the babysitter and rearranged a pile of throw pillows outside the crib room in the dressing area. Lying back against the pillows, it felt good to be on something soft. There was a small lamp by my elbow and I turned it on, opened the book that I had gotten from a Spaniard at the bus station before coming to the orphanage. I had traded him Hemingway's *Old Man in The Sea* in English for a book written in Spanish with no title and a writer I'd never heard of. But I needed practice, so I took it.

Chapter 12

The letter

I read while listening to the soft breathing of the children. The lumens from the plastic lamp were dull and strained my tired eyes. The whole compound was strangely quiet as the birds, the bugs, and even the river slept. It left me wanting company. I needed something other than the taxing prose of the book to keep me awake. As it was my first real night with the group, the idea of knocking off one of the kids because I didn't hear them choking or crying would be a giant screw-up, not to mention, tragic. Periodically, I crept into the crib room to inspect my charges. Their sleep was peaceful and rhythmic, and I found myself envious.

'*Siempre he econtrado que el amor no es Seguro. Las personas, nada más que animales esponjosos, piensan que están por encima de sus instintos básicos, lo que causa víctimas—¿Quién es su víctima.*' I was having trouble understanding what the psychiatrist in the book was trying to say. Although the Spanish words were simple, the concept was not, and because it seemed to be a revealing statement about the main character's personality, I was keen on interpreting the text correctly. My mind was slow, and the sentence reminded me of a word jumble.

I realized the issue I had with difficult Spanish structures was my thought process. I was literally translating the words, but what I needed to do was think of what it all meant. My beginner Spanish teacher in the mountains of Mexico had taught us all a bunch of *maldiciones*, bad words and phrases, to keep us interested in the language. *Maldiciones para los calles*, street language, it was called: *pinche pendejo*, fucking idiot; *cabrón*, asshole; *no me jodas*, don't fuck with me; *chingar*, fuck; and one of my favorites, although I enjoyed using them all, *me cago en todo lo que se menea*, I shit on everything that moves. While attending the school, my fellow students and I would swear at each other during the morning breaks while other students in more advanced classes chatted about what their host families were like, or conjugated verbs. Now my grammar and ability to translate a poetic verse suffered shortcomings, although I'm very capable of telling off a street thug.

"*Pinche pendejo*," I mumbled to the book. Then speaking out loud, but low, I read the translation I had written down, "love and victim." Needing more words in the sentence, I scribbled, "I have always loved, and then I became a victim." Whoa, not right. My head started to hurt with too much thinking. Speaking out loud again, I whispered, "I am loved, but too many victims." Possibly?

Stumped, I put the book down and leaned back to rest, only to pick it back up again to write in the margins the *presente de indicativo* Spanish verb conjugations for love: amo, amas, ama, amamos, aman. Yet most Spanish-speaking couples didn't say, "*te amo*"; they said, "*te quiero*" — I want you, not I love you. It seemed that '*te amo*' was used by families, not by lovers, although lovers could use the word "love" if they wanted to, according to the soap operas.

As the hours very slowly ticked by, I fell asleep periodically, only to be jolted awake due to the book falling to the floor or my lower back sliding onto the cold cement. It was like a brainwashing torture, and it made me miserable and grumbly. The night continued in this manner until, blasting into the silent night, El Gordo began screaming like a blaring car horn. The abrupt noise bounced me to my feet.

El Gordo was sleeping on a cot across from me in a corner by the clothing bins because he was too big for a crib. He slept with his eyes open. Although his corner was dark, all night long I could see him staring at me as the lamplight reflected off his glassy eyeballs. It was eerie. I tried my best not to look at him. He reminded me of some nocturnal, creepy carnivore. But whenever I looked up from my reading, I couldn't help but glance his way.

The sound he made was horrible, and I didn't understand what was causing him to scream. It chilled my blood, and the need to resolve his craziness made me frantic. I went over to him and touched his shoulder. His body was hot and damp, and he was prone on his cot with his mouth wide open, honking. I leaned in and whispered, "El Gordo, El Gordo, wake up." But it did nothing. He needed to stop, but he was stuck in some terrifying world in his head and the noise, the noise, had to stop. I looked into the crib room. Luckily, no one seemed to be moving or up—yet.

"El Gordo!" I said louder and with more insistence and shook him, but he didn't respond. Retrieving the flashlight from over by a shelf, I went back and stood by his side. "For Christ's sake! What is wrong with you?" I cringed. A small cry broke out from the crib room, and something fell to the floor from above. He was waking everyone up. I turned the flashlight on and shone the light in his face to get a better look. Then he stopped as abruptly as he had started.

His mouth was open, and the light exposed his back molars, throat, and tonsils. I wondered if his tonsils were causing him to make the odd honking noise. He didn't brush well; there were still black bean bits stuck along the rim of his upper teeth. His wet cheeks revealed that he'd been crying. The stillness of his body unnerved me as his chest ceased to move up and down. Again, I touched his arm, and he breathed which caused me to gasp for air as though I too had been holding my breath.

I wondered whether he was having a psychotic breakdown. My

only dealings with psychosis had been with my mother. When her paranoia and imagination got the best of her, I would just run out the door to a friend's house, but I couldn't do that here. When El Gordo exhaled, a deflating, squeaky balloon sound, his eyes finally shut after so many hours of being open. But was he asleep? I kept the flashlight beam directed on his face and stood staring down at him for what seemed like a long time.

Eventually, I went back over to my pillows. I sat down and shut the flashlight off. He immediately began to *honk... honk...honk* once again. And once again the jarring sound caused me to jump up frantically. I once again grabbed the flashlight and turned it back on. With the light shining on his face, he stopped honking, and his eyes shut again. His dark hair framed his sweaty face, and his chubby body was calm. Under my breath, I cursed my fellow volunteers for not telling me about El Gordo's sleep issues.

Not daring to take the light off him, I rearranged my pillows so that I directly faced him. Sitting back down, we looked at each other. El Gordo eyes were open, and he was staring at me with dark, ghoulish pupils that had little yellow dots due to the flashlight. But at least he wasn't screaming anymore. I glanced out the window at the sky and saw the moon, a thin crescent band just above the tree line. A sense of relief swept over me as daylight would be arriving soon.

Exhausted and feeling crusty, I waited. Maybe a minute or two had passed before footsteps came down the stairs. It was Catarina. She padded into the room wearing a nightshirt and flattened slippers. She looked like she was sleepwalking, but when she stopped at El Gordo's cot and said in a hushed voice, "Damn kid wakes me up all the time," I knew she was awake.

"Is it time to get up?" I asked.

"No."

She went into the bathroom and came out minutes later. "You know, without the running water, we don't flush at night."

"Of course." The toilets were a mess and smelled.

She looked at the flashlight and El Gordo. "What's with the flashlight?"

"He likes it."

"That's new."

I watched her shuffle back up the stairs.

A few minutes later, Jack came into the room. His presence woke me up because I had fallen into a semi-unconscious state. Not wanting to talk to him, I kept my eyes half-shut and watched him slink by. He was wearing boxers and no shirt. His chest was hairy, indented, and thin. He looked sickly. He also seemed to be still asleep. Walking in a rhythmic downward trod, he neither looked left nor right. He went into the bathroom where he was loud and splashy. When nearing completion, he belched the names 'Raaaaaalph' and 'Aaaaaart.' Then he whistled like he had made a big mess and was astounded by it. When he came back into the room, he paused and looked at El Gordo and said, "Odd kid," then left.

Sarah passed Jack as he was going up and she was coming down. In the light of the starry night, I saw him rub her stomach and then continue up the stairs. Sarah came into the room. She had on a pair of boxers and no top. She was flat-chested and looked like a teenage boy, her hair cropped, her long bangs dangling in front of her face. I was amazed at how she walked, loud like her feet were ten feet long and pigeon-toed. Unlike her husband, her peeing was silent. She came back out and left without saying a word.

Then Molly and Golly came into the room. I clamped my eyes shut so tight that they were quivering. They had no conception of an indoor voice and if they spoke, I knew all the kids would wake up. But of course, they were talking to each other and were exceptionally galling. With my eyes still shut, I leveled my breathing so that I definitely seemed asleep. I could feel them standing in front of me. "She asleep?" Golly said, or was it Molly? This caused me to press my eyes even tighter.

"*Ew*, her eyes are twitching."

"Ook, Golly, El Gordo's *lookin'* at us. His eyes are yellow."

"*Ew*."

"*Ew*."

They went into the bathroom and made all sorts of noises and sounds to indicate the bathroom grossed them out. Then they started talking about a boy back home who had perpetual snot dripping out of his nose. *What the hell?* I thought. When they went to leave, they stopped in front of me again and stared at me for a good minute. Then, sounding like elephants with all left feet, they lumbered up the stairs. I couldn't believe the little kids were still asleep.

A few minutes after they left, Harry stormed in.

"Christ! Grand Central Station," I mumbled to myself.

"What?" Harry asked and walked over to me.

"The children are sleeping—Shhhh." I was in a panic.

"It's around five. They get up. You get up, the whole lot of you get up at five. I'm going to bed."

"Why do you get to go to bed?" I asked.

"Because I can." Harry seemed out of sorts, almost furious over something. His clothing was wet, and his boots were thick with mud.

"What happened?" I asked, sitting up.

"Nothing. Nothing I can't fix—I think?" He breathed in to let out a sigh, then asked. "What's with the flashlight?" He was speaking loudly, almost shouting. El Gordo sat up, put his hands over his eyes to shield them from the light. He then looked under the cot. He pulled out a worn, beaten-up teddy bear and hugged it, laid back to bed with it tucked into his arms, and fell asleep with his eyes shut.

"A bear. All he needed was his bear."

"That kid. He always sleeps with a bear. Everyone knows it," Harry said, as he made big puddles on the floor. "I have a list of stuff I want you to get for me in town." I shined the light on Harry; his eyes were dark and deep-seated with something burning inside him. The intensity was fascinating to see. His emotions swung from trying to be in control to sad to happy within seconds. He was a lot more mercurial and affecting than he'd been in the cafeteria. What an interesting fellow, I thought.

"You better write it down," I said. Everyone had asked me to buy them something. Jack wanted more salsa; Sara wanted a small net for catching bugs; Molly and Golly wanted candy; Catarina a bathing cap; Alex wasn't talking to me, so I didn't have to get him anything, and Gunther was coming with me.

He left and went upstairs. A few minutes later he came back down with just a towel wrapped around his waist and an envelope in his hand. He seemed calmer. His feet were bare, and he stood in the puddle he had just made. His body looked stronger than it did when clothed. My gaze roved around his midriff which caused him to look at me with a puzzled expression. Nonchalantly, I looked up to meet his eyes and grumbled silently that it was such a shame he was in love with another. But then what a mess casual sex would cause with my new living situation, and I thanked my lucky stars he was with another. Besides, I also had him marked as a possible criminal.

He handed me an envelope with a piece of paper inside of it. Then with his other hand, he gave me a wad of money. "Give it to the owner of the hardware store. The money is a down payment. Get a receipt."

I stuffed it all into my pants pocket and said, "Will you help me with something? A brief translation." I picked up the book and flipped through the pages until I spotted where I had left off. "*'Siempre he econtrado que el amor no es Seguro. Las personas, nada más que animals esponjosos, piensan que están por encima de sus instintos básicos, lo que causa víctimas—quién es su víctima?'* Could you repeat it back in

English? Verbatim, if possible?"

Without hesitation, he said, "I have always found love to be un-safe. People, nothing but fluffed up animals, think they are above their basic instincts. This causes victims—Who are your victims?" And then he began to laugh, a big, loud, boisterous laugh that I found obnoxious, because who could sleep through boisterous, even if it was time to get up? And to think, hysterical El Gordo had just fallen asleep with his bear. I also felt he hadn't translated the words correctly, because "fluffed up animals" sounded wrong to me.

Stifling his laughter but still full of mirth, he looked down at me, his intense stare unsettling, and asked, "Who are your victims, Eleanor?"

"No one. I don't believe in victims."

"I don't believe your book agrees with you," he said in a very low voice, keeping his gaze tightly locked on mine.

He then stormed off into the bathroom and made an "ugh" sound, and then stormed back out and stopped in front of me again. "I forgot to tell you. I noticed your clothes hanging on the line. Rather worn—like squirrels have gotten to them, don't you think? Well, while in town you might want to buy a few things, something nice. The owners of the Club de Bote told me they're thinking of throwing us a thank-you party soon for helping the orphans. They're good that way. Oodles of tasty food."

"Now who's being rude?" I said, irritated about the clothing comment, but he ignored it or didn't hear it. He was staring out the window at the sky and said, "I believe the party will be during the Rabbit Moon phase—how unfortunate."

"What's a Rabbit Moon?" I asked, but he had dashed off out the screen door that slammed behind him. I wondered where he would be going with just a towel in the wee hours of the morning and went back to my first impression of him, odd and irritating.

From the crib room a child coughed, and another stirred. Then little voices began to speak back and forth. The children were awake. I lazily got up and went into the room; my head and bones felt heavy, and there was a distinctive urine odor. Most of the children were standing with their hands on the top rail. They looked like lemmings searching for danger, only cuter with big, round faces and big, round eyes.

A little confused at what I should do with them, I began saying the same things I say to the neighborhood dogs back home. "Nice, nice, Looky, big boys and girls. I bet you're hungry!" Only I said it in Spanish.

Directly above me, while I was steeped in this saccharine behavior, the adults upstairs were fumbling with their garments and shoes. Swear words were floating in and out of their rumblings, a glass broke, and someone stubbed their toe and jumped around, shaking the ceiling.

Thinking I should do more than just mumble stupidities, I took Charlotte out of her crib because she was the closest to me. Charlotte was heavier than I thought she would be; a solid child. She wrapped her arms around my neck and snuggled. When I went to put her down, she clung, but everyone wanted out. I apologized and put her on the floor, ruffling her hair. She followed me around the room.

As I took each kid out of their cribs, I noticed the scent of urine on them. Wooter, whom I held away from me, had underwear full of poop, and Bernarda wasn't any better. Once on the floor, they all ran into the bathroom except for Charlotte, who stayed glued to my side. Her need for me was precious, and I felt endeared to her. While I walked around the room, I narrated what I was doing. This seemed to make her happy, which made me happy too.

Then someone put a tape into the boombox, a hip-hop Latino song. A nasal, raspy voice sang, "*Muévelo—Bebé.*" The volume was high, the sound chaotic. When Jack and Sarah stepped into the crib room, dressed and looking half-asleep, Jack shouted at me over the music, "We need to take them to the river to wash. But you and Gunther need to leave. I heard the launch pull up to the dock."

"What's with the music?" I shouted back.

"What?"

"Nothing."

Wanting to change into something clean, I ran out through the screen door and over the sloppy backyard to the linden and jacaranda trees. Seeing my clothing, I saw what Harry had meant. The whole lot of it was embarrassing, but so what? I hadn't met a traveler yet whose clothing didn't have holes.

Sensing that someone had followed me, I turned around. It was Charlotte, standing on a mound of dry land. I told her to stay put, but she didn't listen and walked through the soup over to me. She wanted to help. I gave her my shorts to hold. Then I grabbed the rest of the clothes, and we walked back into the dorm. When Catarina appeared with several other children holding onto the folds of her skirt, she told Charlotte to hold on to her skirt, and she did. I watched them head down to the river and thought of Old Mother Hubbard.

Dressing in the fouled bathroom, I tried my best not to breathe. With haste, I grabbed my daypack, water bottle, and burst out onto the quad and ran down to the dock. It was a muted gray dawn. When I passed the *oficina*, I saw a woman I hadn't seen before standing in the doorway. She had a flashlight in her hand and shone its light on me. She asked me who I was in Spanish. I stopped and told her. She had dark skin and light blue eyes. *Blue-eyes*, I thought. Digging into my daypack, I pulled out the letter of introduction that Rosario had given me and handed it to Blue-eyes. She thanked me, and I went on my way.

At the beach, the kids were wading in the water naked. Their faces were being washed as they splashed each other. The sun was still resting below the tree line, its drowsy light weaving golden streaks with orange hues into the indifferent flutes of the rivers flow. The sailboat was still present, dark and solitary. I thought of the man below the deck, asleep in a cozy bed. It was a lovely thought as the morning fog drifted in, like translucent cotton filled with mystery and serenity. Standing on the dock were Gunther, Aapo, Cadmael, Eadrich, and the launch driver, Manolo. They were waiting for me. I picked up my step; I was going into town.

Chapter 13

Manolo

Manolo the launch driver was slick-looking. He wore pressed, navy-blue cotton pants and a white-collared shirt with a tiny Polo emblem over his left breast. His clothes were spotless. His loafers were dark leather, unmarred and buffed, a novelty that lent him the mythical sheen of wealth, something unconscionable for a poor, indigenous boy from the north. He had come down to the river with his humble parents for land, according to Golly and Molly. They told me, "His *fadher* was foreign"—a rich wolf who had seduced his mother while her husband was working in the maize fields in the western part of the country. Undoubtedly, this was another fanciful tale told by the girls to bide their time while watching the kids. But then again, Manolo had the air of an aristocratic hound. Taller than the average local, his light-brown skin glowed with snooty aplomb. A poser who stood relaxed behind the wheel of the launch— a Boston Whaler fit with two seventy-five-horsepower motors providing enough moxie to power us like a spooked gazelle down the river, if desired.

"A lady's man, that one is," Gunther said, leaning into me. "Don't think he can't tell that you think he's cute. My advice is not to look at him. He's the dog's bollocks in these parts. He'll diddle you while fondling another."

I laughed and took a sip of water. I hadn't had time to brush my teeth. The taste in my mouth was stale, but the water was cleansing, and the crisp, morning air tantalized my lips and tongue. Sitting by the stern in front of the giant bobblehead engines were Aapo, Eadrich, and Cadmael. They were huddled together, hunched over with brown jackets wrapped tight, hats pushed down, only chins exposed. I wondered where they had come from; possibly they had houses in the back recesses of the jungle behind the orphanage. Gunther and I sat on a side bench by the gunwale. Leaning against the hard fiberglass siding of the boat, I imagined drinking coffee and thought about how wonderful caffeine would feel.

"And another thing," Gunther said into my ear. His breath smelled of bubblegum toothpaste, sweet and artificial. "Manolo's not only our ticket out of this muddy mound of earth, but more importantly, he buys our booze."

"What do you mean?"

"Give him money, and he delivers the rum. Now remember, in his world, women treat him like a god. So don't get cheeky."

"I'm not cheeky," I said, knowing damn well I was often cheeky. I took another sip of water, and my empty stomach growled. "When we get to town, maybe we should eat first."

"I'm game. Now, everyone has the ability to be cheeky with a pillock like him." He threw his eyes towards Manolo. I wanted to ask him what "pillock" meant but felt I didn't need another English word to hamper my Spanish.

Gunther, being a chatty fellow, continued talking. "Now I need my rum," he said with an alcoholic's sincerity, which made me chuckle.

"You shouldn't laugh; this is serious business."

"Don't worry," I said. "I won't mess with your supply guy."

"Yours too."

The boat puttered past the "no-wake zone" sign. The letters were messily hand-painted in black. Underneath the black print, someone wrote with even sloppier lettering *peligroso* in red. The morning mist floated around the sign and the edges of the river, creating a spooky atmosphere.

"I think of monsters looking at that sign," Gunther said. He pressed his body close to mine for warmth; I didn't mind, since I was also feeling chilly.

"It's beautiful here," I said. The rising sun sharpened the foliage colors, and the flurry of birds was spellbinding.

"The mornings are the best before all the river wankers wake and the duffer clods are still asleep. But we don't normally see it because we're bathing the kids. Then breakfast, which is always an insanity of myopic theatrics. Bloody hell, I could use a big, fat tortilla right about now." He sat back, tucked himself down into his seat, and shut his eyes. "Could be all ruined soon."

"Breakfast?"

"No, the jungle. The river. All of it," he said, keeping his eyes shut.

"How?"

"They discovered oil in *Lago de Cho*." He then opened his eyes and looked directly into mine. I was under the impression he was trying to read my thoughts. His irises were a deep, glassy blue, his pupils enlarged, and his skin puffy around them with darkened shadows beneath.

"You look tired," I said.

"So do you. Hell, I was up all night. What's your excuse?" he muttered.

"So was I." I frowned.

Gunther then let out a big, windy sigh. "Lago de Cho. It's the lake that feeds the river. The banks are blooming with flowers and all sorts of vegetation. Howler monkeys swinging from tree to tree. A damn pity to ruin it. Hell, lots of buggering and destruction going on around here because of that oil."

"That's depressing." The image of the river's waters awash in slimy, black crud and the foliage beat down with machetes, bulldozers, and modernization was heart-wrenching.

"Land grabbing," he whispered, his eyes closed again.

"I think I read something about land deeds being changed or counterfeited by some government guy—The Minister of the Interior. Anyway, I thought the land here had been given to the people that lived in the mountains. When the fighting ended."

"Yeah, some moved here. Come to think of it, a lot did." He paused to think, then continued. "Isn't that the way? The government, the rich and powerful, discover something valuable, and they want it, even if it means going back on their word or counterfeiting land deeds. A real web of deceit and greed creating another sad tale. For instance, that boy that was killed. Harry knew him. First time I ever saw Harry get angry. I mean really angry. Stormed around, broke a few things, went to the big city and came back with a black eye." Gunther cleared his throat, then changed the subject. "You know, the manatees can be nice. I've seen them bobbing along in the water. It's disturbing they'll get all gunked up." Gunther stretched his arms to the sky and bent down to touch his toes.

"Doggy down again?" I questioned with a smile, although saddened by the manatees and their future.

"Gosh, I'm miserable this morning," Gunther grunted and

reached for the sky again. "Golly went on like a bloody codswallop last night, keeping me up. Her snoring could win an award. A cup of coffee would be just right."

"In town?"

"Doubt it. Nothing but the dodgy stuff from the floor. They export the good stuff. I suppose I'll take the dodgy bits, though."

"I'll take the dodgy bits too," I said, repeating his vernacular. "I'll take the dodgy Nescafé." Gunther slid farther down on the bench, his head tilted softly against my arm. Without further notice, he fell asleep.

Looking around for something to entertain me, I shot a glance toward the workmen and saw they, too, were asleep. They had paint stains on their clothing. Cadmael was the best dressed. He wore jeans that looked new, and his coat had fewer smudges. The older men's hands were callused and arthritic and looked too big for their bodies. Even Cadmael had prominent nicks on his supple fingers. I gathered they knew what was taking place on the river and wondered if it bothered them.

I then thought about eating a muffin. I don't know why I was so keen on eating a muffin, especially one with fruit in it, like blueberries or raspberries. The problem was that they didn't make muffins in this country. In the big cities, I'd found bakeries that made cookies and loaves of bread. The baked goods were made with bleached flour and salt, and the bread resembled unsweetened cotton candy. The cookies were an amalgamation of flour, fat, and water. Dense, lard-filled products with little or no sugar. Tooth-breaking crisps. Nevertheless, I sat in the boat with my mouth watering, thinking about eating a muffin, but I would take a cookie if offered one, possibly two, with a cup of café con leche made with powdered milk and Nescafé.

Manolo shifted the throttle forward, which kicked the launch into a faster gear. As we sped along, I gave Gunther a nudge because I wanted to discuss more politics with him. He was out cold and didn't respond, not even a flip of the hand to shoo me away. Exhaust billowed up from the back of the launch, and oil splatters made slimy rainbow trails in our wake. I was sullen about the manatee, the fish, and the birds, and how much I liked to swim. It saddened me to think it might all disappear one day. In its place, foul waters bubbled with oil.

Huffing, I chewed on my lower lip and turned toward Manolo. I wanted to ask him what he thought of the discovery of oil in the lake. The boat had slowed down, and he was concentrating on something on the shore. When I asked him where we were going, he waved my words away with his right hand like I was some kind of pest. Not wanting to be cheeky, I kept quiet but searched the shore, trying to see what he was after.

Then out of a mangrove thicket walked a petite girl in a tight, black cotton skirt, wearing a pink, puffy-sleeved blouse with a low neckline. I threw Manolo an exasperated look; pit stops to flirt with little girls was irritating. I wanted to get to town and eat. Again, I refrained from commenting. His little girl was giggling with her hand over her mouth. Her excitement to see him was infantile although somewhat endearing, yet foolish due to his caddish reputation.

She couldn't have been more than fifteen. She had a round face and wore cherry-red lipstick. Her thick eyebrows made her young years appear exotic. Her small, plump breasts were pushing out of the top of her blouse; possibly she had found a push-up bra somewhere because they seemed much too high. Standing by a twisted patch of thick, green leaves dripping water, she waved to Manolo with a gleeful grin on her face. He waved back, his expression placid, but his eyes churlish and alive. The skiff chugged, and he throttled back the motor, allowing us to drift lazily toward the shore.

"This is going to be a long morning," I grumbled.

The girl, nearing hysteria with anticipation, gave several demanding jumps and shouts for Manolo to come closer. I gathered she wanted to come aboard, but right before the boat slid into a cluster of roots, Manolo kicked the engines into reverse, propelling us gently backward. This caused the girl's face to droop with disappointment. Then an angry expression appeared on her face, eyes beaded together, mouth pursed. Manolo was quick to go into damage control. He told her in florid Spanish that she looked beautiful. She ate it up. When he threw her a kiss, she caught it and placed it on her lips.

Manolo asked her to wait for him, that he would be back after he got rid of his cargo, which was us. She giggled a reply that I couldn't understand. Her Spanish was incomprehensible, high-pitched and mixed with Mayan words. Her incessant giggling was so childish that I wanted to shout at her to go home to her mother—even run. But why bother? I figured the only outcome would be an angry Manolo and a pissed-off Gunther.

Manolo gave her a two-fingered wave goodbye. The little girl waved back with a shake of her head. The mist engulfed her body, and the birds cackled above. I wondered if she would remain standing there until he came back. *How tiring*, I thought while picking at my crusty teeth.

Manolo gunned the outboards, and we charged backward only a foot before jerking to a stop. This flipped into Gunther. He didn't wake up. I looked at the workmen and they were still sound asleep too. Turning my attention back to Manolo and the boat, it was obvious what had happened: the blades had snagged a root. If he were nicer, I would have jumped up to help, although I wasn't sure what I could do. Instead, I sat, unslaked and hunched, studying his face and waiting.

He sucked his teeth and bunched his lips together, then looked at the water around the boat. The birds, small and large in the trees, were chatting up a storm, and the little girl was belly-laughing at our predicament. This made me laugh too—loudly, like stuck air bursting through a funnel. Manolo snapped his eyes around and threw me a very damning glance.

"What a nasty fellow," I mumbled in English. But I found myself smiling again as the little girl had grown bolder with her laughter. It was like hearing peals and peals of tinkling, clanging bells.

Manolo gazed at her with disbelief. Then he slowly turned the idling outboards off and began sifting through boxes underneath the steering wheel. He found a machete and with it in his hands, he moved to the back of the boat, climbed over the sleeping workmen, leaned over the transom, and began hacking at the water and roots, grunting. The splashing was tremendous.

After a few minutes, he stopped and looked up. I mumbled, *"Me cago todo lo que se menea,"* because I was hungry and irritated. It was bad timing. Once again he threw me a mean look and stood with the machete by his side, glaring at me. His shirt, sopping wet, revealed a hairless chest and cold, distracting nipples. I could see his pants had ripped, and he had cut his right hand as it dripped blood. His perfectly coiffed hair was loose and blinding him, and everything was quiet except for the sound of the little girl laughing.

"Manolo," I said, continuing in Spanish, "Can I help? Could I get you a bandage?"

It seems the little girl heard what I said because her face grew grave, and she said something that sounded like, "If you had come to shore and gotten me, this never would have happened," which was silly and cute, and made me smile at her.

"Manolo," I said, looking at him, "why don't you raise the motors?"

I could tell he wasn't happy that I'd said this. It was something he knew and should have done. Jumping over the workmen and back to the wheel, he raised the outboards out of the water, then went back and sliced a vine the size of an adult's arm off the blades and tossed it near the shore. Returning to the wheel, he took off his shirt and neatly placed it on a bench. He then found a small towel and wrapped it around his injured hand. Taking another towel from a box, he wiped down his sweaty face and chest. The girl and I watched him do this, and I believe he was aware he had an audience because I saw a slight grin. He was good-looking and lovely to watch. Finished, he started up the outboards and sped off toward El Puente, leaving the little girl standing alone, a still, silent figure by the mangroves. *Rather gruff*, I thought. *Not even another adieu.*

As we whizzed down the river, my hair flying free, I saw Manolo take a third towel from a box and again wipe his sweaty, wet, taut body. Looking around to see if anyone had woken up, because what a scene Manolo was making with the towels! But they were still asleep. It wasn't until we reached the dock at El Puente that the workmen and Gunther opened their eyes. It was as though an alarm had gone off. Bam! They were all awake.

"Ick, I've been drooling," Gunther said, wiping the spittle from his cheeks. "Why's Manolo half-naked?"

"I don't know," I replied, not wanting to get into it.

"Manolo," Gunther said, as we all got out of the boat, "where'd your shirt go?" But Manolo was not in the mood to talk. Not answering, he looked beyond Gunther to the buildings, as though he didn't exist.

"What did you do?" Gunther asked me while watching Manolo drive off in a fury.

"Nothing," I replied, walking away to scout out the town.

"I know you did something," Gunther said, chasing after me.

"The guy's a bit of an ass."

"No one cares because that's not the point."

Again, not wanting to get into it because it was a long story, and I wasn't sure if the story would incriminate me or not, I walked away to find some food.

El Puente had the same ghostlike appearance it had the night I arrived. In the light of day, the chipped, stucco walls and overflowing garbage were more apparent. Since it was morning, I hoped a store would be open, but no luck—not even a hapless vendor with a bucket of soggy tamales floating in tepid water. Pausing, I couldn't quite figure out which house had been Yena's. Not that it mattered, but I was curious about my whereabouts the night before last. Possibly I had dreamed it all because it seemed so long ago, and unfathomable with the drunk man and such a nutty woman.

I went back over to the men and followed everyone behind a building. The car was parked half on a rutty road and half in a ditch in front of a pink cement structure. This was the place, I thought; the door looked like the same wooden door where I had struggled whether to go in or out.

"Yena's house," I said to Gunther while walking over to the car.

"Yena's place. I don't know her well. Harry's friend. Rich, I've heard. She owns houses here and lots of land in El Pueblito. Harry is helping her do something with the buildings and land. Selling it, I believe. It was her son that was killed," Gunther stated.

"Sad." Then I thought about Cadmael and Harry and the backpack. "Cadmael gave Harry a backpack full of money yesterday."

Squinting, he said, "Well, ummm. Those two are interesting people. Harry pays Cadmael to fix Yena's properties up. I don't know why Cadmael would give Harry money, though. In fact, I don't think they've been getting along very well." Then he laughed, "Harry sometimes pays me to sub as a teacher for him." He then paused to shift gears. His tone became suspicious and condemning. "So, what did you do to Manolo?"

Ignoring Gunther's question and still curious about Harry, Yena, and Cadmael, I said, "The Minister of the Interior. It must be Yena's land he's been fooling with. And Harry, what a funny guy." Then looking at the car, I mumbled, "This car work? It looks like it should be in a junkyard."

"I have a mind not to talk to you anymore unless you tell me what you did," he snapped. Gunther was glaring at me. For a moment I stopped to think about his temperament. It was persnickety but amusing, and his garrulous chatter was easy on the ear because it was easy to filter out; he was like a well-spoken butterfly dashing in between bushes. A new friend, possibly? But one that was upset with me.

"Manolo screwed up; that's all. He was trying to impress some girl and made a mess of it," I finally said, then diverted my attention back to the car. It was a blue Chevy Impala, low to the ground and leaning to the left because it was halfway in a ditch. Parked three feet away from Yena's house, it rested below several windows, and someone had peed on it from above. The hood paint was sparse and chipped, and there was yellow thick glop puddled in the indentations that produced a urine odor.

"Pitiful. Maybe we should take the bus," I said, sniffing the air.

"The car will work. Give it a try," Gunther remarked, still not convinced I was innocent. "If Manolo no longer gets me rum, I will— well, I don't know what I'll do, but something."

I ignored him and gave the driver's side door a couple of hefty tugs. It creaked, lurched, then opened. The whine of the old hinges reverberated throughout the empty streets and beyond. A sleeping dog by a bucket of trash woke up and scratched his ears and licked his sandpaper-dry mouth. A couple of unkempt children appeared from behind a rusty steel barrel. I waved to them, and they ran away squealing only to come back and peek around the corner. They had big, brown eyes and clung to each other, creating one body and three heads. We pretended not to see them. Slowly, they inched their way over and stood by us.

"I sell you car?" The tallest kid said in broken English. He was skinny and looked to be about five years old. "Fifty bucks," he said, grinning.

I held the key up and said back in Spanish, "I already own the car, but thanks."

The two smaller kids ran away.

"Not yours," the tall boy said, standing his ground.

119

"Not yours either," I said back in English, adding, "*Este es del orfanato.*"

He shrugged and walked away to join the two other boys standing behind the rusty barrel and the sleepy dog.

During my quibbling with the kids, Gunther had gotten into the car. He was sitting in the front passenger seat and drummed his fingers impatiently on the dashboard, his mouth relaxed, his eyes distant and intense. The workmen were still milling by Yena's house. They were griping to each other about the back seat; it was full of tears and rogue springs. I was at a loss as to what to do about it, but then Aapo went over to the trash bin and pulled out a couple of cardboard pieces. They lined the seat with the cardboard and got in. I thought it was odd that neither of them was the driver and asked them if they could drive.

"No."

Then to Gunther I said, "When did that ever stop anybody around here from driving? I don't think anyone wants to drive this heap of crap. That's why no one cared that I'm new and driving into town."

"Now, now, don't be like that. I'm here, aren't I?"

"Why?"

"Why not? Okay, I want a tasty meal."

"You'd risk death for a tasty meal?"

"Wouldn't you?" We both laughed because it was true.

The ignition was worn and chipped like someone had been starting it with a screwdriver or a knife. The key drooped loosely from it, making me think a screwdriver or a knife might work better. The shift gizmo was missing, which added to my growing anxiety about driving the car. "Now, how am I going to know what gear we're in?" I complained. The clutch took a lot of muscle to press down, and I had flip-flops on. There was also a powerful mildew smell, and I believed vermin were using the vehicle as their home. I didn't want to touch anything, but if I didn't, how would we get anywhere?

Resigning myself to fate, I turned the key and pumped the gas. After a few gallops and oil-fueled puffs of exhaust into the air, the car started up, purred and hiccupped. Putting my arm over the seat rest, I looked into the back. The workmen had the windows rolled down and were chewing on toothpicks. It seemed risky to be putting such pointy objects in one's mouth. Pressing hard on the clutch, I played with the directionless stick until I figured out where reverse might be and hit the gas pedal.

The car leaped forward, almost ramming us into the cement wall in front of us. Thankfully, I hit the brake in time. Once again, I fiddled with the naked gearshift and bucked us backward into a small ravine. Then I shifted us forward over a few large rocks and knocked over the rusty bin, scaring away the dog and the kids, then drove out onto the main road. The speed was excessive for the terrain, but not because I had a heavy foot; the car just seemed to have a mind of its own.

Jumping in and out of potholes at a dangerously high speed, I could see in the mirror the workmen swinging back and forth, still picking their teeth as though we were on a peaceful Sunday drive.

When we barreled up over a gnarly hill, the leap into the air knocked the key onto the floor. It didn't matter; the car kept going. At one point, I ran over an empty wooden crate in the road that attached itself to the chassis. We dragged it until the car splashed through what appeared to be a gray-colored stream. The stench was overbearing, and we left the box and the stream behind us. Good riddance.

After a good half hour, the road flattened out, and the pavement became more regular. We passed by swaths of banana groves and rows and rows of pineapple plants. The sweet scent was thick and syrupy; the pungent, sugary air made the mold smell even more nauseating. To our right, a fenced-off golf course presented itself. It belonged to the large fruit company that operated in the region.

The golfers, dressed incongruously for the area, were not unlike our orphans; plaid and collared, short-sleeved shirts, and khakis. They glanced over at us as we drove by. We waved. They didn't wave back—most likely because we looked like the help.

El Pueblito was a typical dusty, blight-ridden town, with one-story cement buildings painted half-blue, with the rest white or solid colors of beige, pink, or a dull yellow. Rebar twisted and flayed at the tops of structures, as construction had been halted for whatever reason. I'd seen hundreds of these towns, and it was often hard to tell them apart, but each one had something unique. This town held the headquarters of a profitable fruit company. As we drove into the center, it was obvious that the wealth from the company didn't trickle down into the hands of the average citizen. The few locals we saw were bent-over, tired women wrapped in shawls, their leather sandals twisted and uncomfortable-looking.

"Who works the fields here?"

"Locals. Some migrants. I think it's a dollar-a-day job," Gunther remarked. "When they're not well, some take the bus to go see Doc."

"Doc?"

"Our clinic doctor. It's free."

We rumbled along at a very slow speed, looking for a restaurant. Passing a path to the lake, there were hints of a vast stretch of water. "Lago de Cho," Gunther said.

Driving on, we drove by shops that sold hats and brooms and other sundries. When we passed a hotel called the La Vista, Gunther again commented. "I'd say a lot of hanky-panky goes on in that hotel. Plush. The only place to sleep beside the dollar-night bordello. Harry likes the Vista."

"He stays there?" I asked, wondering where a good restaurant might be.

"That gobsmack has the life, I tell you. He plays golf with the fruit people and eats at their headquarters. He's a nice fellow, too."

I slammed my foot down hard on the brakes so as not to hit a dog sleeping in the middle of the road. The car stalled, sputtered, and died. The key still on the floor, I reinserted it, but before trying to start the car up again, I looked into the back seat at the workmen to check on them. They still looked peaceful and were still chewing on their toothpicks. "*Estan Bien?*" I asked, amazed at their unruffled demeanor. They nodded, yes.

Bringing my attention back to the car, I managed to get it going and pulled it over to the side of the road. "Yeah, better to go on foot," Gunther said.

"So, I gather the oil company is buying the land Harry's selling," I said to Gunther as we walked down the street. I couldn't let the subject go, but my roommate's activities seemed fascinating. Not that I cared what Harry was up to, but it bothered me to think he was helping kill off the local wildlife.

"I don't know. Harry's a...Well, he's private. Hard to get him to tell the whole story about anything." Gunther paused to sigh, then added, "There's something about the land and the family. All screwed up, especially with the death of the kid. I overheard him talking to Doc the other day. You'll meet her soon. Anyway, Yena needs to sell quickly and leave. That is, Yena and her family." Gunther then fell back into a judgmental mood, raised his right eyebrow, and said, "I don't think it was the girl that pissed Manolo off. What did you say to him?"

I gave him a teasing smile and crossed the street. The workmen were walking fast toward a place called Maria y Joaquin's Café, and I wanted to catch up to them.

"No more gossip for you, then!" He shouted at my back from the sidewalk. "Keeping it all to myself now!"

I turned to look at him. His infantile behavior was comical. Joining in, I said, "Yeah, you think? You know what? I'll give you—I'll give you five minutes. And that's generous. We'll see if you can keep gossip to yourself."

He put two fingers up to his mouth and made the imaginary gesture of locking his lips. I laughed and continued walking toward the restaurant. When a car came careening out of a side road almost hitting me, I scrambled out of the way onto the sidewalk. Out of the corner of my eye, I caught sight of the person in the passenger seat. It was Harry. The car was a nondescript black sedan. It disappeared in a cloud of dust around a corner. I shrugged and looked to complain to Gunther, but he had walked off toward a convenience store.

Chapter 14

El Pueblito

There was a payphone right outside the restaurant. It cost a few cents for a local call, but an overseas call was difficult to calculate. I made a point to always call collect, not that it mattered. Since my mother had moved to the mental institution, my uncle Phil was staying at her house. It was a big house with large couches, lots of light, and my father's wonderful paintings on the walls. Uncle Phil felt someone should live in the place to protect it. The truth was, he was going through a divorce. I didn't mind him living in the house. I was glad he was there. He was the only family member I had besides my mother. He didn't even have any children, so no cousins. A couple of times I called him during my travels to give him an update and to receive one, but after our last chat a few months back, he told me not to call anymore because he had decided phones were evil, disruptive, and demanding things, just like his wife, and he wasn't picking up anymore. Uncle Phil was my mother's brother. My mother also refused to receive phone calls at the institution. The one day she had accepted my call, which was before I left, she told me she didn't have any children. They had all died mysterious deaths, and she was glad they had all gotten their comeuppance because they'd ruined her figure. She ended the conversation by telling me, "Beware, parenthood is a scam."

As I stared at the payphone, the heat of the day wrapped its clammy claws around my neck; a bead of sweat ran down in between my breasts. I had a great urge to call someone and tell them about my life, where I was, and what I was doing. I thought it was swell of me to be working with orphans and not just concentrating on myself, although it was still exactly what I was still doing—concentrating on myself. But it didn't sound that way. I thought of calling a friend, but then my friends weren't keen on me calling collect, and the number of coins it took for a conversation was ridiculous. Besides, the receiver looked banged-up, as though someone had been smashing it against the metal parts of the wall, and there was gum stuck to the mouthpiece.

"Calling someone?" Gunther asked, walking up to me, his tone and mood placated by the cigarette he was puffing on. He was also munching on a cookie from a packet he had tucked into the waist of his balloon pants.

"No," I replied. Gunther gnashed and puffed while looking at me. I stared back, then said, "Harry and some friend almost ran me over."

"So, the gobsmack is here. Alex must be teaching for him. Well, watch yourself. The number one cause of death in this country is by car. Or is that Mexico?" He smacked his lips together and opened the door to the restaurant. "Right smart, this restaurant. The carne asada's scrummy."

I walked in through the open door and paused, "Why would Harry give me a list of things to buy for him, if he's here today?"

"You'll have to ask him."

The restaurant had a cheery brightness to it. Lots of windows, white walls, and sizzling smells. A plump woman bundled up in indigenous clothing was sweeping in a far corner, and a gruff, ponderous man with a stained white bib stood staring at us by the kitchen door. We walked over to where the workmen were seated. They had already ordered Coca-Colas and were sipping on them. Gunther ordered Cokes for the both of us by merely pointing at the Coca-Colas on the table and nodding to the man with the bib.

Delighted to be sitting in a restaurant, we all smiled at each other. Gunther then began babbling to the workmen in half-English and half-Spanish about the disgusting smell of Brillo in the room. I didn't like it either, but it wasn't worth making a whole morning's worth of conversation about. Besides, it was good to know the place was clean, even if the cleaning product was overused.

Letting go of the Brillo irritant, Gunther started in on the "deplorable little black flies" that were nibbling at the spilled pieces of rice on the table. Something about their presence was ruining his appetite. His babbling was incessant, and I distracted myself by playing with the two plastic purple flowers in a Mickey Mouse vase that was on the table. Mickey Mouse had his gloved finger up to his lips as though he was telling us to be quiet. I turned Mickey's hushing finger toward Gunther. He looked at Mickey and at first seemed offended, then laughed, saying, "Jolly good, jolly good."

We ordered our food, everyone getting the carne asada. The waiter noticed our attempts to slap away the flies and brought a fan over directing it at the table and turning it on high. It worked; all the flies went away. Relaxed, we waited for our food. Gunther, finally exhausted by all his annoyances, had stopped talking, which got me asking the workmen about their families.

Eadrich was from an indigenous village located in the northern mountains. He had left due to the government's conscription policies to fill up the ranks of their army. Cadmael was his son, and he didn't want him to be forced to join, nor did Cadmael want to either. Eadrich called the government and their cronies criminals and wanted no part of them. His wife was the kitchen lady, Esmeralda. Aapo was his cousin.

"Tidy little family thing they have going on," Gunther remarked.

"Isn't that normal? I mean, tidy little family things," I said.

"Why, yes, England is filled with them."

I told the workmen a story about my time in the northern part of the country. About soaking in the hot springs, and how much I loved the plentiful eucalyptus trees, as their scent was very calming. When I was through, Gunther told me I sounded privileged because he doubted any of them had ever had the free time to soak in the hot springs. He also, while I was speaking, pointed out my grammatical mistakes at every chance he could. He explained to me that even though he didn't speak Spanish beyond a child's ability, he knew his grammar.

"I took French in school, but before coming here, I memorized a Spanish grammar book," he said, adding. "Although I never quite cracked it—the speaking part, that is, but I do know what is right and what is wrong. And I'll tell you one thing: these boys here don't speak Spanish well at all." When he spoke, he was crunching a cookie, flaking bits of it everywhere. He had been trying to sneak pieces from his pants' waistline without anybody noticing.

"I like their Spanish, it's simple—easy to understand," I said back. "Speaking of right and wrong, you should share your cookies. Not nice to eat in front of hungry people."

"What cookies?" he asked without a smirk.

"Never mind. Anyway. Listen—about my ability to speak Spanish. At least I can form sentences. And most of them are correct. But all you do is say one Spanish word and fill in the blanks with English."

"I beg your pardon—" But before he could go on, the food arrived.

Four plates piled with rice, black beans, a long piece of pounded steak, and a vegetable medley of tomatoes and zucchini were put down on the table. Placed in the middle was a large basket with a cloth covering a stack of tortillas. As we all dug in with zeal, the only sounds to be heard were the whirring of the fan, the scraping of plastic knives and forks on ceramic, and melodious ranchero music resonating from a small speaker by the kitchen door.

Just as we were finishing up, another group entered—two fat kids, a stout woman, and a thin, withered man with a cowboy hat on. Locals. The fan was moved to their table, allowing the flies to pour over our empty, food-splattered plates. The flies, unable to distinguish between our flesh and cooked food, flitted with warp speed around our ears and arms too. We slapped the air with no results, quickly paid, and left.

The town seemed dustier and more stripped of color than before. Thin dogs were milling around boarded-up buildings, which added to the decay. I noticed the La Vista Hotel resided next to a cement block structure; its wall facing the road was nothing but metal bars with a locked door and a small window to pass liquor through. Inside was a refrigerator filled with cold beers for sale. The vendor was drunk and dancing to static ranchero, rap music in the cage. He was twisting around and banging into the walls like a real kook. When he saw us walking by, he stuck his tongue out and rubbed his crotch, then licked his lips. No one made eye contact for fear he might spit or call one of us out. On the scruffy sidewalk below the window, were two men asleep against the wall, and a cat was lapping up spilled beer. It was a miserable testament to the degradation of drinking, yet not a complete turn-off. On the list in my pocket of items to buy were several bottles of rum, and one of the bottles was for me.

As we ambled down the dusty street, I saw an unpaved road that led to the fenced-off headquarters of the fruit company. It was a clean building with a solid, white cement fence around it with barbed wire running along the top. Several Mercedes were parked behind a chain-link fence guarded by a well-armed attendant. So much wealth, I thought, and then looked back at the cage and shook my head at the disparity.

"So, are you a rich American?" Gunther asked.

I laughed, "No."

"Yeah, a job for me when I get back. Not sure what, though. Still thinking about it."

Walking down a few more blocks, we found the hardware store, but it wasn't open, which made us all grumble with disappointment. To bide our time, we slogged our stuffed, tired bodies over to the park to wait. The workmen peed by a tree. Lucky them. I went back to the restaurant and used their bathroom, a dingy room with a clean bowl but no toilet seat. The flies were unbearable.

Back at the park, I saw there were several iron benches. The ground was nothing but erratic clumps of grass that were high and short, plus some trampled dirt. The large jacaranda trees were gorgeous and made up for the missing grass. Bristling in the light morning breeze, they sounded like paper being folded repeatedly. I claimed the bench under one of the trees. Gunther took a bench by me, whereas the workmen stretched out on the ground. They placed their cowboy hats over their faces. I put my sweatshirt under my head and wrapped one of the sleeves around my eyes to block out the sun. It didn't take long to fall asleep. It was like falling off a cliff and disappearing.

I woke up twice before getting up. The first time I awoke, my eyes opened like lead levers. It was hard to keep them from shutting again, but after a couple of shuts and opens I was able to keep them focused and peered out from my sleeve to look around. For a brief second, I thought I was back at the orphanage on the beach. I fell back asleep. The second time I woke up, it was because I heard people chatting. Gunther was awake and was sitting with Harry on his bench. The sun was directly behind their backs, and it painted an oddly shadowed picture of their hair genuflecting and prancing like wood nymphs in the morning breeze.

They were talking about someone called The Scott. There was something about him living on a boat and that he was broke and needed money. I wanted to get up and ask if he was the fellow that had anchored his sailboat in front of the orphanage, but I couldn't raise my head and before I knew it, I had fallen back asleep. When I did finally sit up, stretch, and regain my bearings, the sun was tilted towards the west, and the morning scorch had given way to a dimmer afternoon as though the sun would be setting soon. Gunther was on his bench, smoking a cigarette and reading a copy of *Wuthering Heights*.

"Girl book," I said, teasing him while stretching my arms above my head.

"Boy book now," he replied. "Did you sleep well?"

"Yeah, I feel great." And I did. For the first time in days, I felt rested. Noticing the workmen weren't around, I asked, "Where's everyone?"

"Visiting relatives."

"Was that Harry I saw earlier?"

"Yup, the wanker played a round of golf today."

"I need some supplies," I said, getting up. My neck was stiff, and my hand had fallen asleep. Shaking my limbs, I left Gunther on the bench to read and walked down the street to the hardware store. Again, I wondered why Harry had given me a list of stuff to get him when he was planning to be in town. Possibly he just wanted me to earn my keep.

A few cars rumbled by on the road; their lack of catalytic converters caused the exhaust to spew thick, noxious fumes, and I quickly covered my nose and mouth with my hand. I often mused about staying and living somewhere in Mexico or Central America, but then the lack of catalytic converters in the cars always brought me back to reality. Besides, I wasn't sure how I would make a living.

The hardware store was a typical tienda. It had a few straw baskets and brooms along with plastic items out front, coupled with a metal tire rim, oil cans for sale, and a mangled looking weedwhacker. There was no door to the store, so I just walked in, stopped, and looked around. The man behind the counter was counting the money in the cash drawer. He had heavy tufts of thick, gray hair and a face that looked like a folded piece of brown, coffee-stained paper. He also had a very large ball-sized belly. The lettering on his T-shirt, stretched tight, read, 'I'm silently correcting your grammar.' *Great, another one*, I thought.

I went over to the man and read him the list of items that I needed.

"*Muchas cosas*," he said, giving me a burlap bag and indicating it wasn't free by showing me the price. He then pointed to the shelves lining a far wall, suggesting I would find everything there. I nonchalantly walked over and eyed the cookies and Clorets. I nabbed a couple of packets of both and two small bottles of Coca-Cola, which I promised to return for the deposit. The back shelves were dusty and mostly empty. I counted three boxes of laundry detergent and various canned goods, but not one of them was the same. I found the salsa and threw several bottles into the bag. There were four different local rums; I grabbed the biggest and cheapest. A bathing cap with colorful flowers all over it had been randomly placed next to an orange sponge that looked used. I took the bathing cap. Mosquito netting, sheets, a blanket, a pillow, a rubber raft, and a few other knick-knacks like pencils and pens I tucked into my bag too. My list completed, I walked back and gave the man Harry's list, which was still inside the envelope. The man's nubby fingers had a hard time opening it. His brow was sweating, and his damp armpits had made wet splotches down the sides of his body. He smelled of booze. The paper in his hands looked too delicate. He was better suited for counting money, I thought. Squinting, he read Harry's list.

"*No entiendo*," he said, handing me back the paper. The note only had one line written on it and a signature. It was the letter from Rosario that stated I was to be a *niñera* at the orphanage.

I looked in my daypack for the correct envelope, but then remembered I had given it to the woman outside the *oficina* before getting on the launch this morning. She must have wondered about its contents. Embarrassed, I tried to explain the mistake, but he didn't seem interested.

I paid, stuffed as many items as I could into my daypack because I didn't want to buy his bag, but had to buy it anyway, as the daypack was just too small. Turning to leave, I was stopped by the sight of a large, brown rat sniffing and nibbling at the black beans in a bin. I froze, thinking if I moved, it might chase me. The man saw the rat too. He growled the word "*pendejo*" and threw a hammer at it. His aim was too high, and he broke the foggy, smudged window above the bin. The rat, seemingly unfazed, merely looked at the man. *What a cheeky rat*, I thought. The man, angry, charged the rat with all his hefty weight, and the rat jumped off and scurried behind the cans of paint on the floor. The flurry of activity scared me because I can't stand rats. I took several steps backward and knocked over a bunch of buckets. My biggest fear was that the rat would come out of its hiding place and run toward me and climb up my leg. After a few minutes, when the rat didn't come back, the man shrugged and went back to counting his money.

Once again, I turned to leave, but the waft of fresh air filtering into the room from the broken windowpane caught my attention, along with the echoing sounds of someone slapping something. Bending down, I leveled my eyes with the opening and saw a woman sitting on a stool by a smoking fire. She was kneading and patting tortilla dough. She was round and looked very serious about her task. Then she glanced over at the window; she must have sensed someone was peering out. I could tell she saw me. She stopped working and cocked her head to the side and said something to someone hidden behind a tree in front of her. Shifting my position, I saw it was Harry. What a ubiquitous character, I thought. He was chewing on something he had in his hands, a tortilla most likely. Our eyes met briefly, which caused him to flinch and step farther behind the tree and out of sight. Turning back toward the woman, her gaze directed at me, I saw it was Yena. She had the face of a hag and saint all wrapped up in one, I thought, thinking of her getting the boy to bring me to the orphanage.

Averting my eyes, I walked out of the store and turned to go say

hello, but then stopped. It was strange that Harry had stepped out
of sight. Why would he hide from me? I had seen him earlier, so what
was different now? Once again, I thought he was an odd fellow, and
decided to let him be. Continuing my walk back to the park, I stopped
again. I wanted to tell him that I could not give the man the list, and
this way he could go tell the man himself. But my feet knew better and
kept walking toward the park. I mindlessly continued down the street,
ignoring the catcalls from the kook in the cage. But then I stopped
in mid-step again because I truly felt stupid. My mind wouldn't stop
perseverating on how disappointed Harry might be with me. It was
such a simple task to give someone a piece of paper, and because he
gave me a place to sleep, I wanted to do something for him; I wanted
to be grateful, not indifferent. Twiddling my thumbs and sniffing the
air, I thought about how good I was at indifference and how bad I was
at being grateful. I wanted to work on being grateful, I thought. The
Spanish translation, *De corazón bueno*, meaning, of good heart. Then
I laughed at myself and how silly I was acting. "Eh, *pendejo*," I grumbled and began walking back to the hardware store to Harry and Yena.

But then someone tapped me on the shoulder from behind. I
jumped, thinking it was the kook having escaped his cage. To my relief, it was Cadmael. His lips were pursed, his eyes concerned. He told
me we needed to leave immediately because it was dangerous to drive
at night. I knew what he meant. At dusk, it wasn't the banditos that
caused accidents. It was the loose cows and horses. For some reason,
they liked to walk out into the road once the sun set, I supposed to escape under the cloak of darkness.

I followed Cadmael back to the park. His steps were fast and with
purpose, and it was hard to keep pace with him because my flip-flops
were meant for strolling. Still torn about the letter and Harry, I finally
shrugged and let it go. What did it matter? If he came to town a lot, he
could get it another day.

The drive back was the same as the drive there: horrible. When
we arrived in El Puente, the sky was pitch black. Manolo and his little
girl were waiting by a crooked lamppost. The light was on; it illumi-

nated their feet, alluding to the existence of their presence but not fully disclosing them. When they walked out to say hello, Manolo's hair was tousled, and his shirt was untucked on one side. The little girl had lost her bow.

Manolo was also in a good mood. He winked at me. I winked back. All was well.

It was late, so we bought hot dogs from a man with a cart for dinner, and we each drank a beer except for the little girl, who had an orange soda. Standing around eating, Manolo kept poking and playing with the girl's hair, which made us all roll our eyes at each other. When we finally motored back, no one spoke, although we grumbled when Manolo took his time dropping the girl off.

The low gurgle of the motor's slumberous droll had Gunther and me yawning. As we slid into the dock of the orphanage, Gunther and I smiled at the sound of the ranchero song with its singer's raspy voice and the heavy bass bellowing down upon us from the *dormitorio*. We had missed the nightly meeting, and the kids were dancing. Poking Gunther, I grinned, "I've got a bed, and a room to put it in."

"Now don't go bragging," he teased, and we both laughed. It had been a good day.

Before heading up, we stood on the dock, and I looked out at the lights of the sailboat docked off our shore. "Is that The Scott's boat?"

"Believe so," Gunther said.

"Catarina thinks she might like him."

Gunther chuckled, "Harry's friend. Don't know if that's good or bad."

Chapter 15

The Room

The great room was ablaze with music and dancing. I delivered the rum, salsa, and other items to the prospective owners and went upstairs. The hall was dark and musty as if filled with cobwebs, although I didn't see any. At the end of the hall, a light was on in the hammock room. Slanted, oily-looking rafters and loping hammocks made me want to scratch my skin, even though it didn't itch. The silhouettes of Catarina's slim build and Alex's stooped body were milling around and shifting through their backpacks. They were having a conversation. Alex was better with Catarina, I thought. Kinder.

"You're back," Catarina said, looking up. She hurried into the hall. I reached into my bag and pulled out the bathing cap I had bought and tossed it to her, along with her change. She threw me a kiss. I smiled back and waved goodnight. I wanted nothing more than to set up my new bed and luxuriate in it.

Opening the door to Harry's room, now mine too, I flicked the light switch on by the door. The bulb was the same single twenty-watt do-nothing that made everything everywhere a fuzzy, dingy hue. If there was dust, I wouldn't have seen it. But the room was fantastic, big with a swept look to it, and there was a broad window with a screen.

Harry's side, which was to the left, was a setup for a king. I don't know where he found a rubber raft that large because it was two or three of mine put together. His sheets were rumpled, but the bed was made, with mosquito netting tucked around the bed edging. At the foot of his bed against the wall was a small dresser with a mirror. Putting my stuff down, I went over to the mirror. Small and round, it reflected me perfectly because it wasn't warped. I looked like I always looked, I thought: a little disheveled, my hair in need of brushing. On the dresser, Harry had lined up all his toiletries against the wall. There was a comb, nail clippers, a plastic container of toothpicks, and an open gray bag with all his other stuff in it, such as shampoo and a toothbrush. I noticed he wore Old Spice deodorant, which accounted for the frankincense-and-myrrh scent in the room which, mixed with the cedar rafters, gave the air a newly cleaned old-house aroma. Harry was neat. My housekeeping abilities were unarguably poor, but I'd try my best to be tidy.

My first order of business was to give Harry back his money, which I put on his dresser next to his toilet kit. The next task was to inflate the raft I bought. It was blue with colorful fish all over it and came with a built-in pillow. It was going to be a tiresome job, so I took a plastic cup out of my backpack and poured rum and Coca-Cola into it. It was sweet and fizzy which was delightful on my tongue. I gulped half of it down before attempting to blow up the raft. After a few moments, I realized that drinking while blowing was making me drunk and laughed while pouring myself a little more.

Once the raft was nice and firm, I tucked it into my corner. I put a thin wool blanket over the raft and the sheets over the blanket. It had been Harry's idea to make the bed this way in order not to sweat at night because rubber, heat, and skin created puddling.

My new pillow along with the built-in pillow made the incline too high, but great for reading. I secured the mosquito netting around the bed. Luckily, there were nails on the slanted roof, which it could be hooked onto. When I finished, I stood back and examined my work. It wasn't as impressive as Harry's corner, but it had a delectable coziness to it.

Changing into a clean T-shirt and leggings, I took my flashlight out of my pack, turned off the overhead light, and crawled into bed to read more of my book with a newly bought pen to take notes. The raft made a squeaking sound as the rubber muddled against the floor every time I moved and the music from the great room made the floor vibrate, but I didn't care. Delighted to have privacy and to be lying completely flat except for the lift of the pillow, I opened up my book and peeled through the pages until I found where I had left off. Taking another sip of my drink, I read, "*Tenía la cara de valles, montañas y caminos que se cruzaban sin ir a ninguna parte.*" Interpreting it, I wrote in the margins: He had the face of valleys and mountains and pathways that crisscrossed going nowhere. Eadrich's face was worn away with weather and patience, I reflected, and then somewhere between remembering his face and the words, I fell asleep.

It was still dark out when I awoke. The room was shadowed and streaked with the color of tarnished pewter from the low-lying moonlight filtering into the room. Once again, at waking, I was confused about where I might be, but then felt the netting and remembered. As my eyes began to adjust to the dark, I could see my tossed-off clothing folded on the floor by my bag. Next to the clothing was my book and turned-off flashlight. I thought hard about whether I would have done any of those things. No. I glanced over at Harry's bed. He was there.

He slept naked and was curled up into a crescent, his back to the wall and his face turned toward me. His body was ashen, soft, and warm-looking. His dark eyebrows resembled a child's ink drawing. His massive head of hair was dark and cupped his face. I marveled at the serenity he had in sleep and found solace just looking at him. Slinking down into my sheets, I listened to him breathe. It was light and barely audible.

Then out of the blue, a clunking sound came from the hammock room. In the room next to ours, bare feet were walking around. Someone else came down the hall past the door. The moon had slid off somewhere, making the room pitch black. The wee hours of the morning, I thought. When everything shuts down, turned itself off, but not us. It was time to get up.

Throwing the netting to the side, I crawled out and over to my flashlight, turned it on, and set it against the wall.

With little care, I changed my clothes, brushed my hair with a few strokes, and then clipped it up. Taking a sip of water from my water bottle, I swished the liquid around in my mouth, gulped, and drank the rest. Fumbling in my bag for a toothbrush and paste, I slid into my flip-flops and reached down to turn the flashlight off, but before doing so, I glanced momentarily at Harry. He was looking right at me, which caused me to pause. His sheet was pulled up around his body like a cocoon with his face protruding out. I thought of a birthing butterfly and smiled.

"You're awake?" I said, standing up. A feeling of foolishness swept over me. My underwear had two holes, one for each cheek. All my underwear had holes, and Harry knew all my clothing had holes. I had also forgotten to buy anything new, but then why should I listen to him? My clothing, my life. But damn those cement washboards and damn the harsh soaps.

"Do you have any aspirin?" His eyes were steady and unblinking.

Reaching into my toilet kit, I found a bottle of Bayer and threw it to him. He put his hand out through the netting and caught it.

"Water?"

"Gone."

He dry-swallowed the pills. I wanted to ask him when he had come in and what made him want to fold my clothes. But the phrase *de corazón bueno* ran through my head, so I said, "Thank you for folding my clothes." Following up with, "See you later," I reached down once again to turn the flashlight off, but then remembered something important. "I never delivered your list to the man yesterday."

"I know."

"The money you gave me is by your toilet kit." Then, because there was a bigger issue that had been bothering me, I asked, "Why did you hide from me?"

A noticeable silence stiffened the air between us. The question sounded like an accusation, which was not what I intended, but the words were already said. It made me uncomfortable, and I looked down at the floor. "I don't care. It just seemed strange," I said, latching onto my indifference and looking at him. His eyes reflected the light, giving him a mystical appearance.

"I wasn't hiding from you," he said, his tone low and gravelly from sleep. "I didn't want the man in the store to see me." He cleared his throat, then continued. "If you had called out my name, he would have come over, and, well, he wants something from me, and I don't want to give it to him. It's not an issue. I can get the goods in the city. I'm building a garden for the *clinica*."

I took what he said to be the truth, although I did find it strange that all of this secretive business was over a garden. But the explanation seemed plausible. I was neither friend nor foe, so why lie? I shut the flashlight off and walked over to the door and opened it.

"Eleanor?" he said, stopping me from leaving.

I glanced back at him. The hall light allowed me to see Harry, clearly. He had the sheet below his chest and his arms relaxed by his side. He looked boyish and handsome, and I thought, what was I doing with a handsome roommate?

"I won't be here for the next couple of days. I'm going away to the city. You know there's a holiday coming up."

"What holiday?" Good, I thought, pleased I'd have the room to myself.

"Not sure, there just is one. A lot of the older kids will go home for the weekend. No school on Monday."

"What day is it?" I asked.

"Friday. It will be quieter here. But the little kids go to school all the time. What else are they going to do?"

"Does your fiancé live in the city?" The question sounded peculiar to me, like I might be prying. I knew it was all in my head, but at that moment, standing there in the room looking over at him, at his handsome face, I began to feel off-balance—like I was being drawn into a cave to be devoured. I chuckled at myself and shook the feeling away. Although the room full of morning sleep and crumpled sheets did resemble a farewell to a lover, not a roommate.

"Yes, I will be seeing her," he said. His answer brought our world back to where it should be, at least for me. He had a fiancé. He was just my roommate. Nothing more, nothing less.

"What's her name?" I asked, thinking I should know, especially since we, or maybe just Harry, would talk about her.

"Jacquelina."

"Pretty name."

"It is."

"Have a great time." And I meant it and turned to leave once again.

"Sure, it would be a shame not to."

I laughed lightly. Still feeling his gaze upon me, I looked back at him. Once again, I felt girlish and off-kilter. His presence was like a whisper calling in the dark. I wanted to say something witty back, but I didn't have a thing. Then up through the floorboards came the nasal twang of the morning music: "*Muévelo—Bebé—Muévelo—Bebé—*"

"Get used to it," Harry replied over the muffled din. Reaching under his pillow, he retrieved what I believed to be earplugs. Placing one in each ear, he rolled over to face the wall. I walked out the door and shut it. The words of the song translating in my head: *Move it, baby—Move it, baby—Move it fast—*

Chapter 16

Catarina and The Sailor

That morning was the first time I had been a true member of the wash team. The early hour had an opaque blackness to it as we stood on the beach, fumbling with the kids' soiled clothing. The children, still confused as to why they were washing in the river, whined about having to go into the water. Someone mentioned crocodiles, another manatees. Neither comment was helpful. The weak blues and pinks peeked over the distant forest canopy and was followed by a blazing ball of solid yellow. It washed the river in color, like a sight out of a future world. I envisioned Mars and spaceships. The kids fretting and brandishing messy behinds brought the beauty into perspective; we were nannies, and our duties were to clean these sleepy, messy children. Onesies made by Gucci and Gloria Vanderbilt were defiled with urine and poo. We piled the clothing by a budding aloe plant to be brought to the laundry ladies later in the morning. Someone brought up midnight bathroom runs for the kids, but it went nowhere because there were too many of them. Certain children like Wooter and Raymond had large bowel movements stuck to their legs and backsides, along with my darling Bernarda. It was apparent they hadn't digested the black beans well. Beans came out in the same form that they went in—whole. The beans made a mess of the shore. The river wake pushed them onto the sand, creating a suspicious black line.

The adults were still half-asleep, the kids dazed and naked in the cool morning air; we pushed them with irresolute kindness into the water. They pushed our hands away, and we pushed back. They needed to rinse off. Once in, we couldn't get them out.

Once back in the *dormitorio*, the children fussed over clothing because they didn't like rips or stains. Jack had been right; we needed a new infusion of donations. Their shoes mangled, but solid and mainly sandals, were in disarray, having been haphazardly tossed by the bins and under a bench. We lined them up, and the children felt better as they scrambled to pick their footwear out. No one minded sharing clothing, but shoes were sacred and only had one owner. By the time the gong for breakfast sounded like a city crier selling goods, they all had shiny faces, and their designer-labeled attire looked smashing, if a little torn. The same attitudes seen at lunch and dinner about eating were not any better at breakfast. They preferred playing, not eating. It made the time between the gong and sitting down to breakfast long and interminably exhausting.

After breakfast, we once again marched our charges down to the river to clean their faces. When it came time to bring them back up to the *dormitorio* to play before school, Catarina and I stayed by the river's edge with a bucket and a hoe, our task was to clean up the shoreline of undigested black beans. It was still early, but late enough for the sun to have baked the dampness in the air into desolate mugginess. Then came the mosquitoes. We sprayed ourselves with DEET, which made our old bites sting.

"Do we ever spray the kids?" I asked while scraping the hoe along the sand, collecting the beans.

"No, it makes them sick. Doesn't matter anyway. They've been bitten so many times they've grown immune."

"I've read about that. Didn't think it worked," I said, stopping to watch two black beans float out into the shallows.

Catarina wasn't helping. Instead, she was standing on the dock holding the binoculars up to her face and smoking a cigarette. Her strawberry-wheat hair loosely hung around her shoulders, and her white cotton blouse billowed in the fluttering breeze. Above her, on the overhanging branch of a sapodilla tree, a blue parrot preened itself and screeched. Catarina took the cigarette out of her mouth and said, "Tell it to go away. If it poops on me, I'll be mad."

"What do you see?" I asked, looking out at the sailboat.

"He's eating. I think it's toast. I bet he has butter. I bet the toast has gobs of butter and jam on it. Blackberry jam. No, I bet it's marmalade or peach jam; I love peaches." She took a long drag and let the smoke float out gradually. "He's making me hungry."

"For him or the food?" I asked, chuckling while walking up beside her. Even though we had just eaten, I knew what she meant. She was hungry for the taste; that was all. "I believe his name is The Scott," I said, staring off at the boat.

She put the binoculars down on the dock and looked at me, her expression sober, her eyes flecked with a quiet coquetry. "That is his name, The Scott," she said, and smiled.

"How did you know?"

"Talked to Harry last night." She put her cigarette out with her fingers, tucking the extinguished butt into her skirt pocket. "Can't have butts lying around. Bad for kids and the environment." Then she laughed, pulled out the floral bathing cap I had gotten for her from her other pocket, and put it on. She tucked her thick curls up into it, running her hand along her neck so as not to have missed a strand. Facing me, she asked, "How do I look?"

"Unique. Fun. A little like my mother. Well, before she went completely bonkers." The flowers were spectacular but old-fashioned.

"You should have stopped at unique and fun," she said, with a light laugh.

She took off her shirt and skirt. Underneath she wore a turquoise one-piece bathing suit with spaghetti straps. Her arms were thinner than Id thought. She looked older, smaller all around, and I wondered if she had the strength to swim out to the boat?

"You came prepared," I said, keeping my apprehension to myself.

"You bet I did. Now wish me luck."

"Good luck," I reluctantly said. It troubled me that I might be the last person to see her alive.

Without hesitation, she dove in. A solid, straight dive. When she came back up, her stroke was all wrong. There was too much thrashing, which caused her to exert misspent energy. Looking around for anything that might float, I saw the bumpers along the docking side of the pier were lifesaver rings. Untying one, I yelled, "Hey, turn around," and threw it to her. She hadn't gone very far, and it landed on her head. Grabbing it, she used the ring as a kickboard. The going was slow. The man on the sailboat was watching too. He was standing up in the boat with one hand on his hip and the other holding a pipe. He looked tall and wore a fedora. Once again, something about him hit a familiar chord.

Feeling a presence to my right, I glanced over to the shoreline. I don't know when he arrived. It was Harry. He was standing on the beach by my abandoned hoe; solemn and with the intensity of a ship's captain, he watched Catarina swim. He had on a black bathing suit in the style that was often seen on Hollywood actors in the fifties. It was slim-fitting and rested just under his belly button and down a few inches on his thigh. Sean Connery in *Goldfinger* came to mind, along with William Holden in *Sunset Boulevard*, but Harry looked better than either of them. He looked good. Not too fat, not too thin, and in shape. His legs were long and sinewy, his stomach flat. He glanced at me and waved. I waved back, then quickly averted my eyes back to

Catarina. If she went under or was carried away, I wasn't sure what I would do. I was a capable swimmer, but I'd never saved anybody from drowning before.

Just as I had figured, when she reached the deep blue color, the gurgling thrust of the waters snagged her slim body and dragged her north. It gave me a queasy, jumpy feeling. I unhooked another lifesaver, thinking I should go after her. The man on the boat had gone back to sitting, smoking his pipe, and reading a paper. *What a dud*, I thought.

Then I heard Harry clear his throat. Looking over at him, I saw that he was rubbing the top of his head the way someone does when they have resigned themselves to do something they hadn't planned on. He took three or four steps into the water, and without further delay, he dove in. When he reappeared, he was ten feet from his entry. He broke into a crawl, his strokes long and powerful, his kicks unabashed and straightforward. He quickly and easily caught up to Catarina. Surprised at Harry's sudden appearance, she laughed, a high-pitched lilt that resonated across the surface like a bell skidding over ice. Harry took hold of the lifesaver ring and laughed too, a deep guffaw with a light, enchanting fullness that seemed to drag me further into his world. It frightened me. I bit hard on my thumbnail.

With more powerful movements, Harry kicked the two of them over to the boat. I grabbed the binoculars and adjusted the lenses until I saw their smiling faces. They were having fun. The man on the boat, his hat angled down over his left eye, had finally put his pipe down and flung a ladder over the side. Catarina climbed up, and he helped her by taking hold of her rump and giving her a heave into his arms, where she remained longer than seemed necessary. Parting, he handed her a towel. Harry followed close behind. When he was finally on board, the men shook hands and Harry went down below as though he knew the boat well.

Feeling a great sigh of relief that they were safe, I rubbed my eyes, stretched, and then went back to see what they were up to. I was hoping they would be eating bread with jam and to see some coffee being poured. Nothing like living vicariously.

Harry, back on deck, had a towel and began to dry his hair, creating a big mop-like mess. He then sat and leaned against the gunwale to sun himself. Catarina was chatting with the boat owner, The Scott. They weren't even eating. "What a rude man, not offering food," I mumbled.

Before putting the binoculars back down, I went back to get one last look at Harry. He was still lying against the gunwale, talking with his eyes shut and laughing. I could hear him from where I was standing, not the words, but the tone and inflections. Then they all laughed together, which meant he must have said something funny. The more I gazed over at his stomach, arms, and legs, and watched how he held himself with confidence and poise, I realized I had a crush on him. *How awful,* I thought, and removed the binoculars from my eyes. It was very apparent to me that having Harry as a roommate was like a recovering alcoholic living in a liquor store.

I put the binoculars back on their hook while listening to the sounds of their laughter filtering through the air. I then folded Catarina's clothing, since I didn't want to leave the dock just yet. Sighing, I left the clothes in a neat pile on the dock for her return. I went back down to the beach to scour the shore for edible waste while repeating in my head, *One day at a time, one day at a time.* I then remembered Harry's reference to my being his pet. I was something to come home to, to keep him company when his wife-to-be wasn't around. It was fine, we were roommates, platonic roommates, and I was determined to keep it that way, and I was sure he felt the same way too.

Chapter 17

Doc and Albert's Flowers

Feeling woebegone and whimsical, I left the beach with my hoe and a half-full bucket of beans. A woman I hadn't met before ambled toward me over the quad. Each step looked as though it were painful. Swaying, she stopped to take a deep breath. She was tall and full-figured, the color of darkened walnuts. Her clothing was too big for her. Gym pants ripped at the knees, a faded green shirt loose and billowing; her face sublime in the subtle fashion a person without make-up or glitter at first seems plain, then stunning. Her hair was down, a massive, unbrushed tangle, long, wavy, and thick. She wore sunglasses, and her full lips looked nibbled and chafed.

"Yah, the new *gurl*—Eleanor," she said, sitting down. Her long legs wrapped and crisscrossed on the ground.

"Yes," I replied, not sure what to think because she was all mottled with sweat, her energy level cumbersome and ailing. It was like a sick but beautiful animal had just crawled out of the jungle.

"I'm Doc," she said, her voice tired and almost a whisper. Before

I could respond she added, "Harry out in *dah boo't*?" Her accent was Caribe.

"Do you need help?" I asked. Her head was now resting in her hands.

"Yah and no. *Fook'n* malaria. Hell, the walk from dah clinic was too much for me."

"Malaria?" I had been out and about for so long that I didn't even think to take a malaria pill. Malaria, dengue, and a few other insect-borne diseases were never on my mind, but now they were.

Doc must have seen the worried expression on my face. "Don't worry," she said. "I come here *wit* it. But some mosquitoes here do carry it. A low-grade type."

I was about to say, but couldn't we contract the bad type from you? Meaning, a mosquito bites Doc, then me, and, well? But I let it go because I didn't see the point. Besides, no one else seemed to have it. Looking up, I saw Esmeralda by the door near the kitchen's outside wash area. She wore a white apron smeared with the morning's meal. Her expression was flat and unemotional, but that was normal. She waved me over. I walked up to her, and she silently handed me a wet rag while giving me a shove to take it back over to Doc.

"*Tank* you," Doc said when I handed her the rag. She rubbed the cloth all over her face, then rested it on top of her head.

"Can I get you some water?" I asked.

"*Nah*, I just need to sit for a minute."

Over the soft, humid wind, squeals of laughter came from the great room. Glancing towards the *dormitorio* door, I saw Jack and Sarah talking together, standing halfway in the open door. Sarah held the jarful of bugs she had gathered last night in her hands. From the way she was acting, it looked like she wanted to bring it inside, but Jack wouldn't let her. Then the kids came walking out, nonchalant as they chatted and walked to school. Sarah put the bottle down. Jack and Sarah followed the kids.

The children, incapable of walking in a straight line, meandered from one fallen stick to a bush, to a tree, to a piece of grass down the path. Frankie, Raymond, and Henrik were goose-stepping. Mouse had run over to Esmeralda. She took something out of her pocket and gave it to him. He put it in his mouth and ran down to the schoolhouse, skirting the older kids' dorm, around the back of the cafeteria, and through a clump of gnarly bushes.

Doc grunted, and I looked at her. She was trying to get back up. I went to help, but she waved me away. "I'm fine," she said, and wobbled toward the path that had the sign for the clinic. Her legs twisted in, her head giving way to a slight wag. She turned back and shouted, "Eleanor!"

"Yeah!" I said, not having moved.

"Tell Harry I won't be goin' to the city. Tell'm don't forget the medical supplies."

Cadmael, who was working with Aapo and Eadrich by the water tanks, snapped his head up at the sound of Doc's voice. He threw his wrench down and raced over to her. She was taller than him. He grabbed hold of her waist to help her walk and planted his face in her breasts. Doc leaned into him like a crutch and played with his hair, twisting small clumps in her fingers the way lovers might do while strolling in a park. Knowing that Cadmael was Esmeralda's son, I glanced over at Esmeralda to see her reaction. She was smiling, something I didn't expect. The emotion became her. It lit up her face.

I then glanced over at Eadrich and Aapo, as they were family members too. I wondered if their expressions would be as delighted as Esmeralda's, but fixated on their work, hammering away on the piping, they were too busy to notice.

Fluffing my shirt to let some air in, I turned to go down to the school and almost fell over Albert, who was standing by my side. He held mauve and vermilion flowers bunched together in his hands.

"*Flor*," he said to me while smelling them. "*Huele hermoso.*"

"*Sí, huele hermoso,*" I repeated, crouching down to smell them. His eyes were glistening and his cheeks were rosy. It was touching that he had such a fine taste for nature's delicacies.

The scent of the flowers was hypnotic, and I kept going back for more. They contrasted with the foul jungle odors that were so prevalent in the compound, offensive smells that frequently caught me off guard. Decay, not just of wood and leaves, but of animals and waste and mildew. The shadows along the muddy pathways, the grounds around the cement washing area, under the schoolhouse, by the outside walls of the *dormitorio*, at the foot of a tree—harsh odors that were constant reminders that what lives dies, and when it dies, it smells.

I asked Albert where he had found the beautiful flowers. Instead of telling me where, he looked away, sighed, and kicked the dirt with his sandaled feet. He became enthralled by the little clouds of dust he was creating with each kick, but then stopped to pick up a pebble. I didn't think he was really interested in the dirt or the pebble; he was stalling for time. The kids were already entering the schoolhouse and I suggested he go to school, but he pretended not to hear me. So I asked him again about the purple and vermilion beauties because it would be nice to make a bouquet out of them and put them in my room. *It would be pretty,* I thought. *I would set them down by my bed and smell them at my leisure.* But Albert just shrugged and turned his back to me. This made me think he wanted the flowers to be his and only his. I didn't blame him; they were precious, like finding a ruby or sapphire in the middle of a rockpile.

"They're your flowers," I said. I figured I could find my own, the place being small. "Now you need to go to school."

He turned toward me, smiling, his cheeks rosy and dimpled. He wanted me to smell the flowers again, which I gladly did. Then I suggested we go down to the school together and look for flowers later. This confused him because we'd never looked for flowers together. Scrunching up his nose and upper lip, he mumbled something about his flowers not liking school and wanted me to hold them for him. "Thank you," I said. But just when he was about to give them to me, he pulled them away.

"Albert," I said, thinking, *What a wily child.* "Let's you and I walk to school."

As I was looking down, a pair of large, wet, sandy feet appeared by Albert's. "Hello, Harry," I said and looked up with a smile. "Did you have a pleasant swim?"

"Biggest tub we have." The joke was getting old, but I laughed anyway. Harry's hair was slicked back, his body glistening in the sun. He had his sandals and a shirt in his right hand and seemed to be in a very chipper mood. I found myself staring at his handsome face far too long. He had morning stubble on his jaw and chin and held his head at a slight tilt to the left in a relaxed manner as though thinking. On his left cheek was a small mole—a beauty mark, I assumed. Since we were standing in silence, my gaze fixed on him, he turned from looking off into the jungle toward me. For about five seconds, we had a staring contest, even though it wasn't meant to be one. I smiled and averted my eyes toward Albert and his flowers and the dilemma of school. But all I could think of was what Gunther had said about Manolo: "Don't think he doesn't realize you think he's cute." It made me feel foolish because I didn't want Harry to think I thought he was cute. I also wondered why he was still standing in front of me and staring at me. He had a puzzled expression on his face. Needing something to say, I said, "Albert doesn't want to go to school."

"He never does," he answered, then placed his hand on Albert's shoulder. Turning Albert toward him, he tousled his hair, while telling him gently to go to school, which was exactly what Albert did, just like that.

"Seems you have the magic touch," I said, which made me smile because what I said could have been a double entendre.

Harry had a paternal expression on his face as he watched Albert, reluctantly but dutifully walk down the embankment, his flowers held in front of him and smelling them frequently. Satisfied that Albert would make it to the school, Harry looked at me and asked, "What do you think? A poet in the making?" He then paused to make sure once again that Albert went into the school. We both watched him walk into the schoolhouse. "Watch him, he likes to play hooky," Harry said. "Wanders off into the woods, the mangroves. I've caught him roaming over by the pigpen the other day." Sighing, he then smoothed his hair back with his free hand and continued, "Catarina will be back before lunch. The Scott will motor her over."

"Ah—they're getting along." And then, something more important, "I don't suppose those red-and-purple flowers grow up by the pigpen?"

"Never seen them there. Don't know where those grow."

"Doc. I met Doc," I blurted out.

"I thought I saw her talking to you." Immediately his brow knitted together then relaxed into a warm expression, his eyes taking on a curious twinkle.

"Her malaria is back," I said. She won't be going into town with you—but don't forget the medical supplies."

The message caused his brow to knit again and the twinkle to disappear. He then looked at me as though trying to figure out what I had just said. I also had the feeling he wanted to say something, but then thought it best not to, or wasn't sure how to form the words. He put his hand up to his mouth and rubbed. He looked over at the workmen and frowned. "Have you seen Cadmael?" Before I could answer him, he said, "Never mind." With swift movements, he slipped his leather sandals on his messy feet and his shirt on his wet body. Then, with brisk, determined strides I'd seen him take several times before, he dashed off towards the path to the *clinica*, branches flipping up as he barreled his way into the jungle. Another act of chivalry, I thought. Off to save Doc, too. *Who for art thou, Harry?* I whimsically sighed. *A bad boy? Or a good boy?* Glum over the dead-end prospects of my one-way infatuation, I picked up my bucket and hoe. I tossed the black beans into the woods and looked around to see if there were any red-and-purple flowers, but there were only yellow ones. I propped the hoe against the building and walked down to the river to fill the bucket back up with water. The rest of the *nineras* were standing in the river, wetting their toes and talking. We all walked back up together to the *dormitorio*. We had chores to do. As we strolled up the embankment, discussing our children, we told stories about Frankie splashing water on Penelope during morning washup, and Penelope splashing back, only more furiously, and so on and so forth. And, how we all would like to go swimming because the sun's heat was already oppressive, but it would have to wait until the afternoon because the mornings were too busy. We went into the *dormitorio* and began picking up the great room. Scattered on the floor were throw-pillows, books, clothing, and cardboard for building forts. Tidying up was all very cooperative, as there were a lot of hands. I didn't mind cleaning with help; otherwise, I found it very, very boring.

Chapter 18

Peeing Outside

The day continued in a very passive manner. As the afternoon waned, the lack of running water became more of an issue. We were eating a high-fiber diet. I wasn't sure, but it tasted like the tortillas may have even had sand in them. The green drink alone could cause a sudden, giant bowel movement. As a result, we spent most of our time lugging heavy buckets of water from the river to the bathroom for flushing. The beating tropical sun made excessive lifting a torturous, sloppy task. We all complained, and I suspected that anybody who went swimming urinated in the river.

Understandably, the older kids were seen periodically peeing in the woods, the girls squatting and the boys spattering the low-lying leaves. This caused Jack to bristle. "What if our little ones see them?"

So what? I thought. It hadn't even occurred to me to let the kids pee outside, but now that a few were, it seemed a perfect solution to such a tedious situation. Besides, going to the bathroom outside would only be temporary until the workmen fixed the pipe. But then, I knew little about the formation of bad habits and good habits—how easy it was to break a good habit, exchange it for a bad habit, and never be able to retrieve the good one again. It just wasn't something that ever worried me about myself, especially in my peripatetic, nomad life. So, when I said, "Come on, Jack, why not?" I was truly in the dark about why we shouldn't allow the little kids to pee outside.

Gunther, too, thought it was a splendid idea to let the kids pee outside. But Gunther, who I was getting to know better, did not believe in common sense at all, which he pointed out the day before and continued to point out every chance he got. While we stood outside the *dormitorio* door with empty buckets in our hands, he said, "With luck they'll fix the pipes today, not common sense. Having the outside world as our temporary toilet is lucky for us. Which means luck once again rules."

He let Wooter and Albert urinate into a puddle of muddy water by the washbasin. I scolded him for doing so because it wasn't sanitary, and Gunther matter-of-factly snapped back, "Bloody hell, do you not listen? Luck will prevent you from coming down with a disease. Besides, pee is ammonia. You're better off walking through the peed-in puddles than the clean ones." Then he suggested that during my next trip to El Pueblito (because I was now the designated driver for the orphanage, which I didn't mind because it allowed me a tasty meal once a week) that I should look into some pharmaceuticals to "foster a more positive outlook on life."

"Whatever," I remarked, not wanting to argue because his remark was stupid.

But as luck would have it, Jack, who had been leaning against a corner of the *dormitorio* with his chin in his hands, a pose he often took, whether thinking or not, had heard Gunther tell Wooter and Albert to pee in the puddle. Before he could storm over, the boys were finished. I smiled at his wide-eyed look and gaping mouth. Gunther and his lucky outdoor toilet were about to cause Jack to implode.

"Christ! Hell! Shit!" Jack snapped, his sandals slapping on the wet ground.

His outburst prompted me to mumble, *"¡Me cago en todo lo que se menea!"*

"What?" Jack fumed.

"Nothing," I replied, stepping aside. Since it hadn't been my idea to let the boys pee there, I wanted out of the line of fire.

Jack's hyper, angry presence caused Albert and Wooter to start peeing again. Nervous reaction, I thought, but then they were smiling, almost challenging each other to keep peeing. I wondered how they were able to do that—pee on-demand, and with gusto. Gunther told them to stop and tidy up, but they ignored him. Jack's face became pointier; his fists clenched, his knuckles white, his teeth bared, I had the feeling he didn't want to shout again and holding it back had him twisting and bubbling. During breakfast, Jack had been discussing a chapter in his dissertation on the importance of "Parenting Calmly"—which was also the name he gave the chapter. It would have been a shame for him not to follow his own lesson.

"Bloody hell, Jack," Gunther scoffed. "You'd think the sky was falling in."

"Don't say bloody hell in front of the kids."

"*You* just did," Gunther remarked in a smart-aleck tone. "Look here, Jack, it's only natural to pee outside. Porcelain toilets are a modern-day phenomenon. Something to be proud of, but not necessary."

"Are you kidding me!?" Jack said, circling in front of Gunther. He looked like a tailless dog. "The kids now know the freedom of outdoor peeing! They'll never stop!" Then Jack crossed his arms and asked, "Have you ever read Hobbes?"

"Now don't go judging my education," Gunther said, arms down by his side, his shoulders relaxed, taking the chafing in stride. "And, yes, I know Hobbes."

"He was British?" Jack said.

"So are a lot of people," Gunther replied.

"Hobbes was brilliant: 'Life without rules'—people become 'nasty and brutish.' Is that what you want for these kids?"

"A bit excessive, Jack," Gunther said, laughing.

While they talked, the boys apparently had run out of pee and were now searching for rocks and sticks. Finding a bunch, they tossed them into the soiled puddle. Each time a rock or stick plopped into the water, they gave little jumps of glee. If I hadn't been so amused by the scene, I would have taken them away from the area and down to the river to make sandcastles or look for flowers, or so I told myself.

When the sound of peeing into the puddle rose again, we all turned to see that Mouse had joined in the fun. This caused Albert and Wooter to throw down their sticks and rocks and begin to try to pee. Both Jack and Gunther snapped at the boys.

"What happened to 'parenting calmly?'" I asked with a straight face.

"What?" Jack barked at me, adding, "Not now."

I wanted to reply—"Then when?" But let it go.

With controlled tempers, Gunther and Jack demanded the children put their penises back into their shorts. Gunther, seemingly anxious that Jack's Hobbesian words could be right, told the three boys, "There will be no more peeing outdoors. We have rules to follow." Wooter, Albert, and Mouse pretended not to hear, continuing with their fake peeing stance.

"How's luck working out for you now?" I said to Gunther, then added, "I think this is where common sense is needed." He responded by acting like the three boys: He ignored me.

Gunther once again told the boys to zip up. This time, they dismissed his words by chatting with each other. "To think they're only three," I said.

"Could be four; we're not sure," Gunther remarked.

"Experts at getting under one's skin," I said, watching them.

"Damn Hobbes and his damn philosophy," Gunther muttered.

Then Jack and Gunther went into a full-frontal assault, nagging the boys into putting their penises away. They also wanted them to go down to the river and play. Unable to take the demanding barrage of "don'ts" and "no's," the kids finally complied by zipping up and heading off to the beach, but not before throwing a few sticks into the muck.

Mouse followed Wooter and Albert, but being perpetually excited, ran around in circles like a maniac and came back to the puddle. He picked up everything he could get his hands on and tossed sticks, rocks, leaves, and twigs into the muck. The backsplash hit both Jack and Gunther's shins and feet.

"Yuck!" Jack wailed, which made Gunther laugh. Jack, flummoxed and incensed, stared at his shins with almost literal steam coming out of his ears. Then he stormed away, slapping his sandals in swishing motions on the spongy ground. Gunther and I silently watched him head toward the river. Jack, now taking exaggerated strides, resembled a cartoon character with his long legs and short body.

"Seems you've caused a mess," I said, adding, "I think Jack is right. The boys aren't going to stop."

"Now, negativity never helps anyone. Positivity," he remarked and headed off to the beach too.

Since I was by the washbasin, I filled my bucket up with water. While walking back to the *dormitorio*, I skidded in the muck and spilled all of it. *Now the joke's on me*, I thought and chided myself for laughing at Jack and Gunther. But then Jack and Gunther were funny, so I decided I could laugh at them all I wanted, and they could laugh at me, and I wouldn't get mad at all because why should I? And then I thought, *what fun I'm having here. What fun, clownish people I'm sur-*

rounded by. And then I laughed, and laughed again, and then refilled the bucket with water.

Chapter 19

Peeing Faux Pas

By late afternoon, the outdoor peeing situation had taken a more obsessive turn. We, the *niñeros*, began to realize that the boys—Wooter, Albert, and Mouse—had no intention of forsaking the mud puddle for indoor toilets. It didn't matter what they might be doing—swimming in the river, building a sandcastle, or just sitting around. Without so much as a sound, they would just walk off together up the hill from the beach or slip outside the *dormitorio*. They had created a secret society. All it required was a look or a nod of the head to indicate that it was time to go behind the *dormitorio* and pee.

We took turns following them to keep them away from their target, but sometimes we didn't catch their disappearing acts. Once at the puddle, a place they never went alone, they would pull out their penises and either pee or pretend to pee or throw rocks and sticks at the muck.

Catarina, who had come back for lunch, beaming from her visit with The Scott, couldn't stop saying the word "delicious" to describe him. She also felt it was fine that the boys peed outside, but suggested,

"We should steer them toward the woods."

Molly and Golly, seeing Mouse finally having some friends, both commented, "Fuck a duck, why it's not so bad if they're pee'n outside in the muck. An' Mouse, he got friends now." An erratic, impulsive child, Mouse often annoyed the other kids. His jerky movements caused him to ruin sandcastles instead of building them. He twisted cardboard instead of molding it. When he threw rocks, he often hit people in the knees and sometimes their faces. Peeing outdoors was a sport anyone could do. The messier it was, the more fun they seemed to have. It was the perfect activity for Mouse. He was finally accepted by a few of his peers, which made us happy for him, yet confused.

It didn't take long before Albert, Wooter, and Mouse had gathered up more of the boys, including Earl, Otto, Frankie, and even El Gordo to join their secret peeing society. They constantly whispered to each other. They had also grown bored with the puddle by the washbasin and were now peeing everywhere and on everything. There also seemed to be an understanding that the girls weren't capable of standing and peeing. This caused the boys to become arrogant and haughty when they walked by them. They boasted to the girls about being able to move objects. They showed off their new powers by making pebbles and twigs roll fast and sometimes slowly.

Bernarda, Charlotte, and Penelope were puzzled by this urinating turn of events, and their inability to join in the fun with the boys angered them. Their faces twisted and their lower lips pushed out, they stared and frowned at the boys until they came up with a solution. They found plump little sticks and stuffed them into their underwear. Penelope, who had on leggings, looked like some miniature, skinny pervert; the stick was obvious and ran from her crotch to her bellybutton. When the girls wanted to urinate like the boys, they pulled out their sticks and went, "Yeeee," and "Weeee," while pretending to pee. No one knew where they got those sounds from. We tried to tell them it was all right not to have a penis, but our psychology was lacking, and our words only made their pouts more exaggerated, their willfulness to be like the boys more pronounced.

Later in the day, Henrik, Raymond, and Mouse were peeing on a log in the quad, trying to knock a caterpillar off it. When I went over to tell them to leave the poor thing alone, they turned and peed on my foot. This made them laugh. Yes, they had indeed become "brutish and nasty."

And Jack? Jack, who had been angry to the point of near-spontaneous combustion, was now thrilled and walking around whistling "Yankee Doodle Dandy". It was irritating. He was knee-slapping happy because he had been right. He also declared he would dedicate a chapter of his dissertation to what it means when your child will only urinate outdoors, and planned to call this chapter, "The Peeing Faux Pas."

With a notebook in his hand, his nose pointing up toward the trees exposing large, ovular nostrils, he stood on the sandy beach with the sun low in the sky behind him and said, "I want to share a few thoughts with all of you." And he began to read to Gunther, Catarina, and myself. "Once a child discovers the freedom of peeing outside, it becomes one of the first steps of rebellion against adult control. It manifests itself as a pulling away from their primary authority figures (parents or people who act like their parents). Since birth, they have needed the help of adults to be cleaned after the expulsion of waste. It starts with the diaper, then the hand-up to the toilet. Once they accomplish going to the bathroom themselves, they are free from having to ask permission for the rudimentary and frequent task of urination and defecation. It instills a sense of freedom and independence." He then scratched the top of his head and added, "The theory's good. Possibly needs some rewriting."

"Well, I hope you're including me in your acknowledgments," Gunther quipped.

"Possibly," Jack replied.

"Sounds doubtful," I said, wondering if my three girls, Charlotte, Bernarda, and Penelope, would recover from this day.

"Wanker," Gunther snipped at Jack, walking over to a hairy cedar tree to pee.

"So you're advocating for them to pee outside now?" Catarina said.

"No! Not at all. Turn the place into a sewer, if it isn't already," Jack replied with his fists balled. He was the type of fellow whose temper waxed and waned like waves in a choppy ocean.

"All the more reason to build little boxes so they can step on them to sit on the toilet. All by themselves. Independence. I like independence," Catarina declared, smiling.

"We did talk about that a while back, didn't we?" Jack said, calm once again.

"And it was my idea, those boxes," Gunther griped, coming back from the tree. "You wouldn't have come up with the 'peeing faux pas' crap either if it weren't for me. Gosh, I'm just full of ideas, but does anyone acknowledge me? You just can't steal people's ideas."

"No," Jack said.

"No, yes? Or no, no?"

"No."

"No, what?"

"NO."

"Christ, never mind," Gunther said, sitting down to pout.

"A bunch of *wildpinklers*," Alex said, walking over and nodding toward Raymond and Henrik. They were peeing on each other's feet by the schoolhouse. Henrik's urine was spattering all over Raymond's yellow rubber boots, and Raymond's urine was drenching Henrik's Doc Martens. The boys were in hysterics, their bodies jiggling with laughter.

"Wildpinklers," Jack repeated, writing it down.

"Do you even know what the word means?" Alex asked.

"Sounds good," Jack replied.

"*Dudelsack*," Alex said, then continued, "I'm with Gunther. Acknowledgments are nice."

But Jack wasn't listening. He was too busy writing and pausing to think. Alex sat on the ground by Mouse and Frankie who were trying to keep their eyes open. *Too much fun for one day,* I thought.

Jack looked up from his notebook and said, "We have wood and hammers and saws, but we need nails."

"Shouldn't the workmen have nails?" I said, thinking I might have seen one hammering a board.

"They use a lot of glue," Catarina remarked.

"On what?" Jack asked.

"I just see them using glue," she replied.

"There's a box of rusty nails on the shelf in the great room," Gunther said. He then walked away from us toward Henrik and Raymond and told the boys to wash their feet off in the water. They complied without being stubborn. "They must be tired," Catarina remarked. She had been watching too.

It was almost time for dinner, so we counted all the kids in front of us because we didn't want to leave one behind. As it turned out, someone was missing. It was Albert. We all agreed he wasn't going to the bathroom because he never did that alone. No one panicked. Everyone knew Albert was a wanderer.

Catarina was about to leave to go check the pigpen when Albert sauntered out from behind the schoolhouse with a bunch of white flowers with red pistils. He came over and sat down on a rock, showing us what he had while rambling on and on about how nice they looked and smelled. They weren't half as nice-smelling as the purple-and-red flowers which got me, once again looking around the compound, wondering where he may have picked them from. I even asked the group if they had seen any red-and-purple flowers. They said no.

Catarina was practical as well as nurturing. She was the only one of us who had children of her own—two boys and a girl, now healthy adults with good jobs and "tolerable relationships," she'd told me. Her husband had died three years ago. Since then, she had been flying down to the orphanage to spend her Canadian winters there. I trusted her judgment on how to deal with the kids and saw others asking her for advice too— even if Jack would have liked us to come only to him. She sat Albert down next to her and put her arm around him, then chatted gently with him about letting the adults know where he was going, so he wouldn't worry them. He just smiled back.

With the sun rapidly setting before us, we needed to get the children out of their bathing suits and get them into dry clothes for dinner. But then the dinner gong reverberated down the slope and throughout the tepid evening air, and we all realized we had messed up on the timing. It pained Jack to think we had miscalculated dinner. He then smiled and said, "There must be a reason for our misstep."

Chuckling, I asked, "And what will you call this chapter?"

With a furrowed brow, he rubbed his chin and replied, "Lack of Attention to Detail Causes Ineptness."

"Or Ineptness Causes Lack of Detail," I replied.

"I hope you're not thinking of writing anything serious. You're not very good at it," he said with a straight face, then turned abruptly and walked away.

Under my breath, I muttered, "Inept Jerk causes Orphans to Miss Dinner."

Gunther, who was standing next to me, said, "Wanker Starves Toddlers."

"*Pendejo* Ruins Evening—" I added.

We laughed, and then continued laughing as we created new chapter titles all the way to the *dormitorio*.

Chapter 20

The Scott

A few days later, we built the boxes for the bathroom toilets, which were a minor success with the kids. With one step up, they could either sit on the toilet or stand. The dilemma? When sitting without help, they often fell in, and without our help, they couldn't get out. To remedy this issue, we began giving toilet-sitting lessons. The children seemed to enjoy these lessons so much that they began holding their own classes. It wasn't unusual to walk into the bathroom and see three or four of them taking turns, practicing sitting on the toilet with their clothes on. Proud of ourselves and the kids for putting their best efforts into the task, we praised ourselves and the children at nightly meetings. But even though the boxes were a step in the right direction, the enjoyment of peeing outside seemed impossible to curb. Yet we felt that given time, the boxes and the toilets could win out—or so we hoped.

Harry being away, I had the room to myself. I liked the space, and without Harry to engage my libido, I felt freer and calmer, although part of me yearned for his return. Since the kids usually went to bed around ten o'clock, I began having nightcaps with Catarina and Gunther. We would hang out in the great room and then head down to the dock for a smoke. It was at the dock where Catarina would leave us. With a flashlight from her pocket, she would signal The Scott to come get her. She introduced Gunther and me to him, but it was always from a distance and in the shadows of the mangrove trees under cover of night. He'd mutter "Halloo" to Gunther and me, and we would say hi back, nothing more, nothing less. Sitting in his boat with his hat on, he would help Catarina get into the dinghy. His voice was sturdy and comfortable, his movements economical and precise. Then finally, out of frustration with not seeing what he looked like, I brought my own flashlight one night and shined the beam directly into his face. He sputtered and threw up his hands and shouted, "Hey, you! You're blinding me!" I didn't care. My suspicions about his identity were finally answered. It was him. His coral blue eyes and angled face were unique and distinguishing.

"Catarina," I had said with a concerned tone while taking hold of her skirt as she went to get into the boat. But I was too late. She pulled my hand away and sat. "You trying to make me trip?" She questioned.

"No. Nothing. I'll talk to you tomorrow." If he hadn't killed her yet, he most likely wasn't going to, or was he waiting for the right time? Then I backtracked and thought about what I'd read in the paper. His real name was Dan Scotchwick. He'd kidnapped a fifteen-year-old child, and even though he'd received the ransom, he'd killed the boy anyway. Something must have gone wrong, I thought. And then it occurred to me that he wouldn't kill or kidnap Catarina. She had money. They were a couple. He most likely wanted to marry her. I watched them motor off into the sparkling river, the moon cut in half surrounded by stars and chalky light. Then I told Gunther what I knew.

"Odd that he's back," he said, lighting another cigarette to keep the bugs at bay.

"Cheeky, don't you think? Yena could have him killed."

"Yup," Gunther remarked, looking at me. "I wonder what he did with his money. He's broke. I guess he needs more."

"He's found a gold mine with Catarina. She told me she's good at picking stocks. From what I gather, she has millions." I paused here to ponder something else that bothered me. "I thought you said the death of the boy bothered Harry?"

"He must not know it's The Scott that killed him," Gunther handed me one of his Marlboro cigarettes. They weren't' as tasty as the Gitanes, but nicotine is nicotine, and I felt calmed. We stood on the dock until we'd burnt our smokes to the nub, then walked slowly back up to the *dormitorio*. Neither of us wanted to talk. It was disconcerting to have such a man living just off our innocent shores.

Later, alone in my room and in bed and unable to sleep, I read until one or two in the morning. I had expected Harry to arrive back from his trip after a couple of days, but a week had gone by and no Harry yet. Concerned, the next day I asked other *nineras* what they thought of his disappearance, but no one thought it was strange. Gunther said, "It's just typical Harry." I decided not to worry, yet something ate at the back of my mind that all that money and land he was dealing with may have put him in danger. The other issue that bothered both Gunther and me was how to tell Catarina about The Scott. She was so happy and in love, and it all seemed so sad to tell her that her man was evil. But we did it anyway. It made her face droop at first, and her gaze went blank. Then she came back to us and said, "I don't think he did it. If he did, he would be in jail." She then told us to mind our own business.

"Love is blind," I said to Gunther.

"Love is blind," he said back to me. Then I thought hard about the orphanage and the life we all had created for ourselves and the children. "Do you think any of us have any common sense?"

"Doesn't matter as long as we have luck." I knew he'd say that, and it made me laugh.

"Luck is fickle," I added.

"Yes, it is."

"You know though, I have a bad feeling about The Scott. I mean, why is he here?" I said, looking at Gunther. He took a drag from his cigarette and exhaled a straight line of smoke, and replied, "Why would a murder come back to the scene of the crime?"

"I bet Harry knows."

"They're friends."

"I wonder why? Doesn't seem right. I also wonder why Harry isn't back?" We stood for a while smoking in silence. Then Gunther smacked his lips together and said, "That man has luck. He's up to something, but I bet he'll be back soon smiling and looking like a shiny button."

"Still doesn't explain his friendship with a killer."

"No, it doesn't, does it?"

Chapter 21

TOYS

During our nightly meeting, Molly and Golly wanted to know when the party would take place at Club de Bote. No one knew, but Alex grumbled something about the owners having it during the full moon because they were the type of people that liked full moons for parties. I suggested that a lot of people liked full moons for parties because it made them more fun, my comment received several, "Rights" and "Yes, yes'."

"But what's a Rabbit Moon?" I asked.

"Mayan," Jack replied. He then scratched his head and looked at Sarah. "Probably has something to do with fertility."

"I like '*abbits*," Golly said.

"I *don'*," Molly said.

Changing the subject, Catarina brought up the toys, "just rotting away" in the attic room.

"Legos and Barbies," I added.

"Let's bring them down tomorrow," Jack suggested. Then, looking at his notepad, he asked, "What do you all think of the chapter title "Plastic vs. Organic Toys?"

Catarina wanted to know if she would get an acknowledgment in his paper because she suggested we get the toys.

"You didn't suggest it, I brought the toys up the other day," Jack corrected her. Which was true. Not that it mattered, because Jack and the rest of us had forgotten about the toys.

"Maybe she should get an acknowledgment for reminding you," Gunther said. This made everyone snicker.

"Milla is coming tomorrow," Alex said, changing the subject. "It's too bad we have selfish people in this group." When he said this, he was looking at me, then continued, "I'll be in El Puente tomorrow morning greeting her. Do what you want with the toys. I'm all for the organic play, not plastic fake shit. Anybody have a tent?"

"Use the attic," Gunther said. There was a moment of silence, followed by giggles.

The next morning when the kids were in school, Gunther and I lugged the boxes down from the attic. It was a smelly job that made my arms itch, and we both spat a lot. Once all the toys were outside, Golly, Molly, Gunther, and I stood by them, examining the goods. There was a positive suppleness to the air, not a cloud in the sky, the blues palpable and the leaves shimmering like glinting fans. Although the offensive gases emitting from the boxes made us cringe, we were, as Gunther put it, "Chuffed to bits over the act of giving."

"What joy they'll aav," Molly said, admiring the baking oven.

"I wish I had a cam'ra to take their pictures," Golly mewled while snuffling at the hair of a blonde Barbie. "She smells like the backside of a dog." She tossed it back in, wiping her hands on her oversized T-shirt.

There was also a scent of sewage in the air. At first, we thought it was due to the boys peeing outside, but then Cadmael, who walked by us, stopped to admire the toys. He told us, partly in Spanish and English and using a few Mayan words, that the pipe carrying water from the river had cracked and upset the septic tank. In the same breath, he said, "But the water tanks are fixed, and now we have running water in the bathrooms."

"But not if the river water isn't coming in," Gunther said.

Cadmael had a shovel in his hand. We watched him walk into the back of the *dormitorio* where Eadrich and Aapo were digging a hole behind the washbasin.

"I always thought they piped all the waste into the river," I remarked, wondering if we should deal with the toys another day. We wanted to wash them off, but the washbasin seemed off-limits now.

"They do upriver. You know, use the river as their toilet," Gunther yawned, forgetting to cover his mouth; all his back molars had fillings.

The four of us stood in silence for a few minutes. It was something we did before embarking on a new subject or project or thinking of more ideas about the old ones. Someone sighed, and another made a strange yo-yo sound with their mouth. It was Golly. It was her warning signal that she had something brewing inside her that wanted to come out, but she wasn't sure how to voice it. We all stared at her, waiting for her to stop making yo-yo sounds. When she did, she declared that the kids wouldn't care about the toys. This announcement opened up a whole new point of view about "the plastic bits," which was how Golly now referred to the toys.

"It's because of what Jack said," Golly said, fumbling at her lower lip with her tongue. She had a bug bite there, and it was bothering her.

"What did Jack say?" I asked, standing as still as possible so as not to sweat excessively.

175

"What doesn't he say?" Molly jumped in.

"What did Jack say?" I asked again for no particular reason.

"I can't remember," Golly pouted.

"Well, I don't care what Jack said," Gunther remarked, his voice testy as he tossed as many toys as he could into a wheelbarrow he'd borrowed from the workmen. He was still miffed at Jack for not giving him acknowledgment for his ideas. Bristling with irritation, he barked, "Come on, we need to wash the toys." Long, squiggly dribbles of water ran down his face, as the day was exceptionally hot.

"Testy today," Molly said with perfect diction, causing us all to look at her.

"No, well, yes. But I really want to give the kids the toys," Gunther said. His tone was sincere.

"Fine," we all said.

Tossing more toys into the wheelbarrow until it was full, we strolled over the squishy ground to the washbasin. The smell of feces became stronger, which made us look at each other and frown. I had a small kids' wheelbarrow where I'd put the Barbies and G.I. Joes and began putting the plastic dolls into the sink. Molly and Golly each had a box full of Legos that made them cough and hack because it seemed some attic animal had made a mess on them.

The workmen had already dug a hole as deep as they were tall; all of them were inside of it. We listened to them chat in their native tongue, trying to understand what they were saying as we began washing the toys. Gunther thought they were talking about us. I felt they were talking about back home in the mountains because I kept hearing a word that sounded similar to "mountain." Molly and Golly said they were talking about girls' tits. Then we forgot about the men and watched the older kids walking up from the dock to their dorm. They were carrying knapsacks and pillowcases full of clothes, as they had used them as suitcases for their trip home. As usual, they were joking and poking each other. "Back to boarding school from being home for the holiday weekend," Gunther said.

"Long holiday weekend. It lasted a week," I said.

"I don't like them," Golly said.

A bird above the cafeteria screeched, and we stared at it, waiting for it to make another noise. We then discussed our made-up history of the youngsters. One day they would be the older kids, which seemed hard to fathom. "But what were their lives *befaw* coming here?'"

We determined that our children's first few months of life were most likely riddled with very dubious relationships or catastrophic endings like Charlotte's. After all, they were orphans. Their present life, we agreed, was solid and predictable. They walked the radius of what resembled a lumpy, non-regulated soccer field day after day, eating the same food morning, noon, and night, the weather hot and wet, humid-hot and not-so-wet, hottest and hotter, and constantly wet and humid. Nothing changed more than a nano-inch except for us. We were the only things that changed. We figured it was the reason the children's eyes appeared distant at times, which we diagnosed as tragic.

"But then, whose life isn't tragic?" Golly lamented while pulling her oversized shorts out of her butt-crack.

"Queen of England's life isn't tragic," Molly said with a look of triumph.

"Possibly if we talked to her, she would say it is—all those teas and the bloody hand wavings," Gunther replied while studying a toy cash machine, then added, "My life wasn't and isn't tragic at all. My parents are divorced, but they're happier. My mother has remarried three times. Drippy men with small wankers. My mother's swell, though, and I love her, especially her kidney pie. My father, his name's Pete. Pete's a fantastic fellow."

"Me mums makes meat pies that taste like paste; me dad's a truck driver. 'Hey r' all right," Molly said.

"I don't much like them," Golly said.

"I thought you said you weren't related," I remarked.

"Any idiot would know we are. Of course, we're from the same parents; we twins," Golly said, making the yo-yo sounds again. "But not identical. I'm prettier."

"Eleanor?" Gunther asked, then added. "What about your folks?"

"They're fine. Normal," I said.

"I don't think that's possible," Gunther remarked with a sigh.

"You're right, but why talk about it?" I said.

"Cuz it's good to talk about things," Molly said.

"These toys are making me sad," Golly said, picking up a truck and deciding to wash it.

Sarah and Jack spotted us from the quad area and came over. Sarah was upset that all the toys looked like humans or were replicas of human inventions. She wanted a bug doll. Jack bowed, circumspect, and had a few titles that he threw out at us: "Is Plastic Necessary?" and "Modernization and the Imagination: What to Make of It?"

He said his "toy chapter" for his dissertation would be filled with defamatory examples of bad biological parenting and how playing with fake stuff makes one greedy. More pertinent to this section of his dissertation would be a look at "how the modern world is destroying free will with cheap thrills," a substructure to his substructures.

Jack also appeared more jubilant than anyone else so far about the toys. I assumed his constant jumping up and down and frantic touching of each object were due to his dedication to his work—the information he would glean from the subject of children and toys. Molly and Golly were convinced he wanted to play with the stuff, and that that was the reason behind his recent constant smiling. They had seen him tuck a navy-blue Matchbox car, a Charlie Mack 1960 Corvette, into his pocket while shifting through the boxes. When Sarah and Jack walked away, Molly immediately said, "What kind of parents did he have?"

"Unfit," Gunther answered, "if they're anything like him."

"I can't believe he pinched a toy," Golly piped in, hands on her big hips.

Alex and Milla came over and rumbled through the pile of toys. Alex was in a good mood due to Milla's early morning arrival. I was elated to see Milla too and she me, until Alex kept whispering in her ear not very nice stuff about me. His whispers being loud, I could hear everything he was saying. He said I was a hoggish slut with tendencies to laugh at inappropriate times. I took offense because I wasn't hoggish, but then possibly he had meant selfish, and yes, I could be selfish. Slut? Not for a year, and laughter was healthy. It was one of Jack's four tenets for raising children in what he called his "Third Book", even though he did not have a first or second book. He just liked the sound of 'third book.'

The other three tenets were:

- Agree to disagree. (A difficult concept for three- and four-year-old children.)

- Avoid harsh discipline. (We did this by not particularly disciplining at all.)

- Adults should be good examples by keeping their behaviors normalized. (The problem was the word "normalized." No one could come up with a good example.)

The word "normal" frequently came up and was discussed ad nauseam. For example, during snack time, the word "normal" was brought up because of Alex and Milla's earlier behaviors. Alex had somehow gotten the key to the *oficina*. When he arrived back from El Puente with Milla, they spent their first two hours of togetherness in the little white building fornicating. When walking by, one could hear them panting and thumping. None of us thought highly of their choice of place to have sex. We were trying to get the older kids not to have sex, and the younger kids didn't need to know about it yet. Also, the building's backside was a favorite peeing place for several of the boys.

At one point, Milla and Alex were having a particularly loud sex session while little Henrik and Raymond were letting loose by the building. Before I could get to the boys and lead them away, they had already peed all over each other with wide eyes and open mouths, as the howling inside the *oficina* resembled the skinning of a live cat.

Alex and Milla's behavior was so absurd that the rest of us were rendered speechless at first. When we, meaning Gunther, Molly, Golly, Catarina, and myself, finally regained our composure, we agreed it was normal behavior because sex was a very normal act.

"All animals do it," Gunther had reminded us.

"Some animals shouldn't," Golly had pointed out. But we all agreed the place they had chosen wasn't normal or appropriate, even if the act bordered on normal.

Jack's response was to mutter, "What noise?" Golly seemed to think Jack, being a sex addict, rather liked the smutty noises.

At lunch, Alex and Milla were met with mumblings from the group such as "Maybe you could keep it down," and "I think there's a shed in the jungle that would be better." Alex snorted at our remarks and thought people were jealous. Alex's mouth was swollen from use; he fiddled with Milla's pink spandex tank top, her breasts and shoulders seeming of great interest to him, but inappropriate to touch at lunch. Occasionally he wandered down to her crotch and backside. Milla, cheeks flushed and her neck sporting a large red hickey, we were convinced had been screwed stupid. I had known her as a gregarious, kind, intelligent person, but at lunch, she giggled at our remarks, ignored our suggestions, and fanned herself with the scarf she had worn to cover the hickey. It was only when Mouse appeared at Alex's side that reality sank in.

Mouse, having grown sullen from the lack of attention from Alex, drew Alex away from Milla long enough to convince him that show-off sex wasn't popular with the kids. It wasn't anything that he said; it was merely his presence. We could see it in Alex's eyes. Mouse reminded Alex that he had a purpose here, and his purpose was to look after the children, especially Mouse. For the first time since I'd known Alex, he appeared sheepish and even blushed. Then coughing, because fake coughing can give a person time to think, he came up with a solution. Alex proposed a compromise. If he and Milla could move into the *oficina*, they wouldn't make any noise. "Silent sex."

"Really? That's a shame," Jack said, disquieted and grossing us all out.

"Ja, ja," Alex said.

"What about the woman who works in the office?" I asked. "The woman with very dark skin and light blue eyes."

"You mean the young girl with the tight jeans. Striped black-and-white tank top with the exposed lacy bra and the remarkably small stomach?" Jack asked.

"I hadn't noticed," I remarked, adding. "But—yeah."

"She doesn't work here. No, I take that back. She pretends to work here. She's Esmeralda's daughter or niece. Lives in a small northern village in the mountains. Visiting, that's all."

"She took my letter?"

"Why not?" Jack replied, stuffing a tortilla filled with rice and beans into his mouth.

"Why?"

"What?"

"Stop."

"You stop."

I got up and bussed my plate, helping Wooter and Bernarda with theirs. We had only washed a few toys due to procrastinating too much, so I thought I'd go out and get a head start. I also wondered if it mattered that I gave my letter of introduction, which wasn't a letter of introduction at all, but Harry's list of items for his garden project, to the wrong person. Then I wondered if it actually was a list of items for a garden project. What if it said something else? Blowing air out of my mouth, I grumbled, "It probably doesn't matter." I mean, why would it? It bothered me that although I wanted to think well of Harry, the crush I had on him pushing me to think the best, I couldn't help but think there was just something not right.

Chapter 22

Russian Bank

A week and two days after he had left, I was settled in bed with the overhead light on, along with my flashlight to read better. It was late, maybe midnight. Several of my clothes were unfolded and thrown on the floor. I had a rum and coke in the hand that wasn't holding the flashlight and an open book balanced on my knees. When Harry walked through the door, I was shocked to see him and a little embarrassed.

"Welcome back," I said, putting the book aside while running my eyes over the room and the mess.

He looked at me and the surrounding area and puckered his lips. He seemed to want to comment on my slovenly housekeeping skills but stopped himself. Instead, he sighed and smiled. Not wanting to seem too pathetic, I scrambled out of bed, gathered up my clothing and wet towel, and put it all in a pillowcase I was using for dirty laundry. Then I stammered, "I thought you were coming back a few days ago, but you didn't and well—" I paused to look at him. "I'm only neat if I have to be." This made him chuckle. I felt better.

He had a bag of food with him. He walked over to me and asked, "Hungry? If you are, pick one." He'd brought a veritable orchard of various fruits: apples, pears, oranges, and several packages of cookies. Shocked that he was willing to share his food, I said, "So, I guess it's just salsa and pencils you don't share." He laughed and nudged the bag toward me. I took an apple. I hadn't had an apple since leaving the States; even though apples grew in certain areas of the region, I never saw them. Also, we never had fruit at the orphanage, which I found odd since there was plenty of fruit growing in the area. I took a bite; it was crisp, the snap and sweetness like candy and autumn combined.

In the florid beam of the overhead light, I saw he was wearing a tie with little dogs that appeared to be terriers. His Old Spice deodorant, light yet distinctive and appealing, wafted its way toward me. "You're so dressed up," I commented.

"I had a meeting. An important meeting," he remarked while looking at my T-shirt. "Is that Tinker Bell?" He then read the words under her feet out loud. "Faith, Lust, and Pixie Dust."

"Variation of the Peter Pan saying," I said, then added, "I didn't buy it. When I was in Mexico, I had my laundry done in a group wash area. Somehow, I ended up with this T-shirt. It's good for sleeping in." Long and loose-necked, it fell to my knees. The armpits had holes; soft and worn, I liked it. I also wouldn't have worn it if I knew Harry was coming back. Tinker Bell had big boobs and lips.

He went over to his side of the room and changed in the shadows of the rafters, and I crawled back into bed. When he flipped the mosquito netting back to get into bed, I saw he was wearing boxer shorts with stripes, and he had dark bruises on the right side of his ribcage.

"Harry, did you hurt yourself?" I asked.

"Yes. But I don't want to talk about it."

"Okay." I assumed it had something to do with his delayed return and clandestine activities. And what about The Scott? "Harry, I met The Scott while you were gone." Then, trying to seem nonchalant, I said matter-of-factly, "I read about him in the papers before coming here. *La Noticia*." I paused to think how to word what I wanted to say next. "Harry."

"Yes."

"The paper said he kidnapped a ki—"

"—I know," he said cutting me off, and then as though reading my mind, he added, "I told Catarina to stay away from him. But she's crazy about men who wear fedoras. Now, I don't want to talk about any of this, except please believe me when I say I don't like him, and the situation is complicated, and, well... Let's just leave it at that."

I felt relieved that he didn't like The Scott. I didn't want to have a crush on a man who didn't mind having a kidnapper-murderer as a friend. And, although I wanted to ask him more questions like: why do you appear to be chummy with him? And how do you know the guy? And why do you think he is back in town? I didn't. Harry and I didn't know each other that well and it just didn't seem right to probe, at least for the time being.

So, the two of us remained prone under our mosquito netting, munching on our apples in silence.

"Eleanor," he eventually said. I loved the way he said my name. It resembled the serious note of an exotic trombone. I wanted him to say it again, so I didn't respond.

"Eleanor," he said, saying my name louder.

"Yes," I finally responded.

"I'm going to be home more. I know I told you otherwise. Just a few nights I might not be here."

"Why would I mind?" I asked. "It's your room too." I wasn't sure what I thought of him being around all the time. I knew I was going to have to be neater. And what if my crush on him got out of control? I sighed, resigning myself to good behavior, and asked, "What changed?"

He went on about the corruption in the city with its poorly paid police force and greedy government officials. He said it was "imperative" that he stay nearer to El Pueblito to protect certain interests. It was on the tip of my tongue to ask him about his bruises and the real estate deals, but it didn't feel right. If he wanted to tell me more, he would.

I watched him put his apple core in a plastic bag outside of his netting and tossed him mine to dispose of too. The last thing we wanted was more bugs. He talked for a little while longer, telling me about the indigenous people protesting in the streets. "It's always about land. But the lack of humanity is probably the biggest issue," he said. When he spoke, he seemed preoccupied with an oval gold locket that he wore around his neck. It was attached to a thin, gold chain. He kept rubbing the flat sides, as if it were a good luck charm. At one point, he went to take it off but then hesitated, patted it, and settled into sleep. I wondered if he noticed how much I was watching him.

"Can you not sleep?" he asked.

The overhead light had been turned off, but I still had my book on my lap and the flashlight on. "Does the light bother you?"

"No, but I'm, well, I'm not tired. I know it's late, but well, maybe I'll read too." He had a book under his pillow and a flashlight. When I inquired about the book, he told me the name: *Ardiente Paciencia*, or Burning Patience, by a Chilean writer named Antonio Skármeta of Croatian descent. Harry went on to tell me the story. "It's about a poor postman in Isla Negra who befriends Pablo Neruda. He asks for his help writing poems to the woman of his dreams."

Harry's words made me gush, "How romantic. Do you like poetry?"

"It can be useful." I thought of Jacquelina and what a lucky girl she was to have someone as adorable as Harry sending her love poems—or so I imagined he did.

That night, if only one of us had been a good sleeper, we would probably never have gotten to know each other as well as we did. As it went, Harry nor I could find much solace in our respective beds or our books. I don't know if it was a restlessness brought on by darkness—or the love of living that demanded staying awake. Or that our DNA was just never that tired. But whatever the cause of our insomnia happened to be, it became the catalyst to something deeper and life-changing—at least for me. It started with a very simple, unimaginative question.

"What's your favorite color?"

He said it was green.

I told him green was everywhere in the jungle; didn't he have another, more intriguing color?

"No, and lucky for me I don't have to go searching for it," he chuckled and then said, "Your turn."

I replied, "Blue." Which wasn't any better.

I asked him about Holland and his childhood. I also mentioned that Catarina said he wasn't Dutch. He reminded me that she liked The Scott and that her insights about people were a little off. I agreed. Then he told me, "I'm Dutch. But like many people, my ancestry is a mix."

At first, he stumbled about where to begin with his life as a child. Then he told a story. When he was a boy, he had a songbird the primary color of yellow. The bird had arrived as a gift from his grandmother. He called her Luri because the name meant "all good things." Luri being confined to a shoebox with holes, and his mother not allowing the bird to fly around the house, he built a cage at school during woodworking class and made it one hundred and fifty-two centimeters high, out of tall grasses and pine. "It was like a basket, only with larger holes. The cage was big enough for me to sit in. I sat with Luri and read," he said, his voice calm and reflective. "But she died one day. Just fell off her perch onto my lap." The story seemed to make him sad; I felt sad for him too.

As the night carried on, instead of lying in bed and staring at the ceiling while we talked, when Harry mentioned having a deck of cards, I told him I had a deck too. Two decks of cards were perfect for playing Russian Bank. It was a game of deceit and guile for which one needed a quick eye. And as it turned out, we were well matched, Harry had a keen eye for treachery, and I, for beguilement.

The idea was to catch the other person cheating. We brought the crooked lamp up from the kids' dressing room for better vision and used a small fan to keep the air in the room moving. He shuffled the deck, and I dealt the cards. His stealthy flicks of the deck appeared professional, but his covert duplicity was inanely obvious at times. My obsession with staring at his beautiful face was a downfall. We ate the fruit he had brought and sipped from juice glasses I found in the great room, tepid rum with a splash of warm coke. We kept having rematches. The hours ticked by without notice. We were both confused when up through the floorboards blared the raspy hip-hop song. It told me, *Move it, baby—move it.*

"The night went quick," I said.

"Leave the cards where they are. No touching, no tripping and scattering them. We'll continue tonight after I return from El Pueblito," he said with a crafty glint in his eye. I looked down at the cards and wondered what he saw that I didn't. Feeling too rushed to count what was there and what might be missing, I shook his hand in agreement. I was needed downstairs.

Harry went to bed with his earplugs, and I went to peel soiled onesies off toddlers. Tired and a little tipsy, I figured naptime was just around the corner.

"Are you drunk?" Catarina, at the foot of the stairs. She looked refreshed from her dingy ride over.

"Possibly, but nothing poo and urine can't cure," I replied, gulping down what was left in my water bottle.

With the pipes finally fixed, we could bathe the kids in the showers. All week, Catarina and I had been setting the kids free from their cribs and stripping them for their morning shower while the others slowly made their way downstairs. We never said much to each other during these wee hours. Since I found out she was in love with Dan Scotchwick, a wedge had become between us. I felt she knew deep down that the man wasn't any good, but superficially she adored him. I dealt with it by never bringing him up. Gunther and I still brought her to the dock after dinner for our evening meetings. We still smoked cigarettes and chatted together as we waited for his arrival. And even though Gunther nor I spoke of the man, she couldn't help herself. She was also funny about how she described the two of them. She always used food terminology— "buns to die for; scrumptious nuts to nibble on." She felt "poached" or "roasted" after sex, sometimes even "fried." She loved chewing on his mouth, equating it to a "platter of exquisite morsels." "Yummy," seemed to be her favorite word.

His pantry was filled with sumptuous, canned goods like sardines, pickles, asparagus, and Chef Boyardee ravioli. Her descriptions of these foods: "rich and saucy, like him" —always made Gunther and me hungry.

This morning, standing halfway down the steps looking at her yawning and dripping on the floor, I wanted to tell her about how much fun I'd had with Harry playing cards. I wanted to tell her about the yellow songbird he had as a child, and that he liked the color green. But I didn't. And I didn't tell her after dinner down by the dock either. Instead, I just wished her luck and sent her on her way. The dinghy swayed and zigzagged with the weight of two. The putt-putt sound disappeared into the dark.

I didn't tell her because I liked living at the orphanage. I liked the kids. The group of *niñeros* were fun. I liked the idea that Harry would play cards, night after night. My life was simple and uncomplicated, and I wanted to keep it that way. It seemed stupid to talk about a man who was taken and to make more out of something that wasn't or shouldn't be. She knew I had become judgmental of her relationship with The Scott, and I felt she would turn the tides and scold me for having fun with Harry, even if it was all innocent. Yes, it was much better to keep certain things quiet.

Chapter 23

Body Parts

The toys were still unwashed. Gunther, uncomfortable with our half-assed job, turned to me after lunch, a few days after we'd brought the toys down, and said, "Let's get these babies washed," and poked my arm, and tugged on my shirt, then pulled my hair. He was the type of person who liked to touch, nudge, roll against, and hug. Being less demonstrative, but someone who liked to play, I pushed him back with a little more force than I meant to. He tumbled into the pee mud while I stood aghast. "This is not a time for more procrastination," he protested. We wanted the kids to have the toys for their afternoon playtime.

Dumping the contents of the child's wheelbarrow into the washbasin, we doused the Barbies and G.I. Joes with the cheap, watery dishwashing liquid we'd borrowed from the kitchen, and scrubbed. Gunther, not able to resist bubbles, blew a clump at my face. I blew a clump into his. Our silliness made us laugh so hard we cried tears of laughter and gasped for air. When we finally regained control of our senses, there was a silence so quiet that I could hear myself breathing. Looking at Gunther, I wondered why I didn't have a crush on him.

He was fun, and I knew he liked me. But then maybe our relationship wouldn't be the same, its carefreeness gone, the fun turned into something more demanding. Thus I thought, and dismissed the wily nature of romance and began scrubbing the toys.

Gunther wiped the wheelbarrow out with a towel from the *dormitorio*'s towel stash. He then dried the toys. Watching him, I realized he was like having a fun brother. It was a wonderful feeling to have a brother like Gunther. Just like I didn't mind my obsession with Harry, although it worried me some, because it was fun to have a romantic interest even if it were to remain unrequited. I splashed water on Gunther. He splashed back. At the end of our water fight, we were drenched, and we still had a box and a large wheelbarrow of toys to wash.

When we finally finished, we dumped the clean toys into the middle of the quad's play area. Trucks, tugboats, motorboats, a play phone, Lego bricks, Matchbox cars, a toy hoe and rake, and a little oven for baking. The child's red wheelbarrow was now filled with washed Barbies and G.I. Joes. I placed it in the middle of the area so the kids could pick through its contents.

Frankie, the twins, and Mouse wanted nothing to do with the pile of toys; it was as though we had told them to play with garbage. They put their suits on, and Sarah volunteered to swim with them. Before departing for the beach, Sarah had also glared at the pile of toys with an expression of deep offense, her round, light-blue eyes now beaded and dark. She lectured us in her lilting voice that often bordered on the edge of crying. "Bugs can't eat plastic. Nothing can eat it. It's like a pile of rocks. Only rocks are pretty, and when they disintegrate, they make sand. Ants love sand." She dramatized her last words by letting out a wail of despair, clenched her hands into fists, and shook them at the toys.

"Go on," Golly said, picking at a scabby bug bite on her left thigh. "Git—"

Sarah didn't take offense to Golly. She was happy to leave with

Frankie, the twins, and Mouse.

Wooter, Albert, Charlotte, Penelope, Bernarda, El Gordo, Rosamond, and several others walked over to the pile of toys and began shuffling through them. There wasn't any running or whooping.
They did it because we told them to. El Gordo poked and prodded the
orange, fake phone with his fingers before selecting it. He immediately
pulled the receiver off and tossed the dial part aside. As he was walking
toward the beach with the receiver, I asked him where he was going.
He told me he was taking his boat to the *rio*.

"Boat?" I said, nudging Milla, who was sitting next to me. "El
Gordo thinks the phone is a boat."

Milla had decided to be friends with me since Alex and she had a
place to fuck—her word, not mine, only she pronounced fuck *frook*.
She was Swedish or maybe Norwegian, but then she was a Lapland-
er, which made her possibly Finnish. She spoke English with a heavy-
tongued accent. When describing her homeland, she would say *tune-
draw* instead of tundra, and she liked to have a good sweat in the
sownas. When I pointed out the crumpled flower Albert had stuffed
in his back pocket, she said, "*Bowtiful floower.*" It made me depressed
to think not only was I not speaking much Spanish, but that my English was being shortchanged too. I'd already picked up a little Cockney, and without noticing it I said stuff like, "Me bottom is wet from
the blimey humidity," and I referred to the kids at times as "Tom tits."

Albert had zeroed in on the red wheelbarrow full of Barbies and
G.I. Joes. He wheeled them over to Esmeralda, who was standing by
the outside wash area of the kitchen, watching us—it was something
she liked to do in the afternoons. When she grew tired of standing,
she would often sit in a dented, lopsided wrought-iron chair in front
of the sink. The pregnant kitchen lady was with her too. They looked
over the dolls Albert had in his wheelbarrow, and each took one. They
tucked them into their skirts, only the dolls didn't fit and their heads
and hands stuck out. Albert then took his goods around the quad,
walking in circles, visiting trees to pee on, and stopping to pick a few

of the yellow flowers scattered by the cafeteria.

Bernarda, Penelope, and Charlotte were playing with the cars and trucks, but not in the manner one would think. They were throwing them at the dirt, picking them up again and chucking them again and again. Molly went over and showed them another way to play with the cars and trucks, which was to move them over the ground like a boat. Molly made motor noises and honked a few times. The girls stuck their tongues out while running the cars all over the place, spitting and drooling, trying to make motor noises, while once in a while trying to honk like Molly.

Wooter and Rosamond were constructing a building with Gunther using the Lego bricks. It had lots of twists and turns that didn't make any sense. Henrik and Raymond grabbed the tugboat and a speedboat and went to the beach.

It was all very amicable and placid. There wasn't any fretting over who had what. It seemed the same as when they played with rocks and sticks. The kids were content.

Jack, who was sitting with his notepad observing the children, hadn't written much. His jaw and mouth were tightly pressed together. He looked frustrated. Eventually, he put his pen and notepad down and went over to the girls, Bernarda, Charlotte, and Penelope. They were over by the path that led to the pigs and the big kids' school. There were long planks that crossed over the mud. The girls were pushing their cars along the planks. Jack took his navy-blue Matchbox car out of his pocket. He had the girls tilt the boards up, and they began racing their cars into a puddle. I looked over at the open page of Jack's notes; it said: "If I never have any time to play, I don't want to live."

I showed the page to Milla, and she said, "Jack's okay, he *spocks* directly from the liver." Alex, who had just walked up from the beach to retrieve Milla because he wanted help with the little ones' swimming, corrected Milla's idiomatic expression by saying, "Jack's a sitzpinkler."

Gunther chimed in, "I think he could be a nancy."

"I knew it," Golly said, glancing up. "I knew *eeeh* never played as a child."

I kept my remarks to myself as I was very busy. I'd gone and gotten a bucket of water, using a toy bucket, and was building a sculpted mud road along a high mountaintop made of mud and sticks with Wooter and Rosamond. They had grown bored playing with the Lego bricks and left Gunther to build his mangled fort by himself. Another little girl named Luna joined us, too. Luna had wispy, thin black hair and was missing a front tooth. She was very good at packing the mud along the mountain walls. Her little hands scooped up the wet dirt and patted the sides with gentle swipes and patience. Rosamond was using tiny pebbles to decorate the side of the road. Wooter was making a moat.

We made a great team. We also created guardrails with Maya nuts; small, round, hard-shelled orbs. If the construction worked, I figured it would be fun, even thrilling, to see the 1947 purple Roadster and the 1965 yellow Citroën Matchbox cars I had put aside fly down our mountain.

Birds sang, a light breeze was present, soft and ethereal, and the afternoon heat folded around us like a thick, wet glove. The slightest movement caused profuse sweating. The kids' cheeks, flushed and wet with perspiration, were a signal that we needed a break. Molly had already fallen asleep with four kids pressed into her soft, pillow-like body. My three workmates eventually joined them. Under the upside-down canoes, the workmen were snoring. There seemed to be little choice in the matter. It was like a field of Wizard of Oz poppy dust had fallen upon us. Leaning up against the log, I dropped off too. Napping, I was happy to learn, was something we did every afternoon. It made playing cards all night then getting up at five doable.

When I awoke, Albert had reappeared with his wheelbarrow. Somewhere between giving away a few dolls, picking flowers, and our nap, all the arms, heads, and legs of the Barbies and G.I. Joes had been dismembered. Ripped from their torsos. Golly and I looked at each other, astounded. Why would he do that?

Gunther yawned, stretched, and stood up. He picked through the broken dolls and then asked Albert what he planned to do with the ruined dolls. Albert told us he wanted to sell the parts. This made us laugh.

"I bet he was a Chicle' vendor," Golly said, adding, "Blimey!"

"Brilliant. A true entrepreneur. From Chiclet seller to body part peddler," Gunther said.

"Sick in the head," Molly interjected.

"It's what happens when you *don'* have *paren's,*" Golly remarked.

We beat the subject of selling body parts up into a pulp. It eventually became a moral mess and our new pastime. Similar to the game of Telephone, our imaginations took words and replaced them with thoughts best left untouched. By dinner, we were talking about the orphanage's side business of selling body parts by harvesting them from the young bodies of its clientele. Because it wasn't true and because it was so ill-minded, we thought it was funny. We talked about fattening the kids up. I even overheard Milla say to Esmeralda, "Lot a of food for the kids. We're rendering *laaard.*"

Chapter 24

Routine and Consistency

As the days passed by, the daytime hours, minutes, and seconds seemed caught in a circular, repetitive motion of perpetual sameness. Even my nights playing cards with Harry, although splendid—and no matter how tired I was, I made myself stay up—had a sameness to them. Either he won or I won. It made it hard to distinguish one day or night from another. It caused me, all of us, to believe we'd been at the orphanage longer than we had. A minute was more like an hour, an hour an entire day, and a day a whole week, a week a month, and so on. It didn't mean life was boring, just predictable and unremarkable —and I didn't mind it. I thought this was how the world should be. No rushing, working together within the confines of a remote space filled with overgrown trees, water, sand, and the laughter of children. It was calming and pleasant. I also finally understood my mother's contentment with her institutional living. Never a day out of place; bingo mid-day; Scrabble after dinner; meals served at the same time; the menu predictable and with only slight variations.

When the workmen killed a pig, a giant, pink pig that fed us large, luscious chunks of pork, we ate it until it became thin pieces of strapping. Then we received a donation of cabbage. We had cabbage with beans and rice for a week. But these fluctuations in our diet didn't seem to mark time, any more than Wooter losing a tooth or Penelope learning the doggy paddle. Mere memories, but when did they happen? Entry and exit points to the day always were the same. Did an incident happen a week ago or a month ago? It was hard to tell. Since the sun was always bright and the birds constantly sang, none of us knew if today's happenings happened yesterday, today, or the day before.

While sitting next to Jack on a log one day during snack time, I mentioned the disorientation of time at the orphanage.

He replied, "Einstein. I gather you've heard of him?"

"Yes," I replied, ignoring his derogatory insinuation. It was the only way to deal with Jack. He was socially inept, and the group forgave him for it for the most part.

He then pulled a notepad from his back pocket and scribbled down a few sentences. He looked up at me, then wrote some more, and finally said, "Has to do with Einstein's theory of special relativity. Time speeds up or slows down depending on how fast a person moves. We move very slowly here—and therefore, so does time." He then scratched his chest and said, "Excellent. Raising children in a time warp situation. I can use that."

I smiled because I thought of asking him for an acknowledgment. Instead I said, "I have no idea how long I've been here."

"No one does," he remarked, looking around for his wife. She was by a puddle that had been heavily peed into. It looked like she was collecting water bugs. Agitated by her activity, he left to bring her into the *dormitorio*.

Later that night, I told Harry about Einstein, Special Relativity, and the orphanage's time warp issue. He agreed that time was strange here, but he also had a watch that told him the day. But he still couldn't tell me how long he'd been in the country, let alone working at the orphanage.

"Maybe it's a country issue," I said.

"A Central American time warp," he joked. We both laughed, and since he was distracted, I flipped a card, threw another down, and won the game.

"I don't like cheats," Harry objected, taking a sip of his rum and a splash of Coke.

"Harry, this entire game is about cheating," I said, pouring myself another beverage.

While dealing out the cards for another game, I told Harry about Jack's hypothetical theory of child-rearing. "He likens this place to a commune. Doesn't approve of parents, especially biological parents. Thinks they're dodo brains." Then, seeing Harry trying to cheat, I remarked. "You can't play that card."

"Yes, I can."

"No, you can't."

"You're right."

"I caught you, so it's my turn. Now back to Jack," I said, and moved a card, then another, until I was stopped too. "Jack has this dissertation he's writing," I said, sitting back, eyes narrowed as Harry shifted his cards. "For instance, Chapter Twelve, 'Routine and Consistency.' The thing is—the orphanage has already been set up as a model for this equation. But we have reinforced it with other stuff."

"Really? Like what?" Harry asked, leaning back with his drink in his hand, waiting for me to put down a card. His eyes were steamy from the heat and the booze. Their intensity caused me to stumble just for a moment as their blueness briefly took my breath away. Taking a sip from my cup, I put an ace of diamonds by a queen of spades.

"I don't think so. Nice try," he said, raising his left eyebrow.

I took the card back and threw another that worked, but if caught again, I'd lose. Continuing my line of thought, I said, "As I mentioned before, the orphanage is pretty much a straight line from the dorm to the caf, to the school, to the quad, to the—"

"I get it."

"Yup, everything is routine and consistent. But we've added stuff like—we don't keep the clothes in the bins anymore. We've divvied them up and given each kid a cubby hole. Henrik's and Raymond's cubby holes are at the bottom of the rung so they can easily get to their clothing. Shoes are put on the floor under a bench for safekeeping. We insist the children fold their clothing when the laundry returns, and that they neatly put it away. Dirty clothes are put into a hamper, no throwing them onto the floor anymore. What we're doing is taking routine and consistency and coupling it with gradual responsibility."

"You haven't been doing this all along?" he asked with a smirk.

"Kind of, but not consistently. Why are you smirking?"

"Nothing. I mean, it's just that. Have you thought of applying, what is it? Routine and Consistency in this room?"

"Funny," I said and laughed. "Now there's nothing wrong with my side of the room." And there wasn't. All my clothes were folded and neatly placed on the floor. Dirty clothes were in the pillowcase, although out of the corner of my eye, I saw a rogue sock. It had a hole, and the bottom of it was black-brown.

"I'm just playing," he said, his tone sincere. After a minute's pause, he said, "It's hard to always keep everything in order. All it takes is one day. An hour of something going wrong, and *poof*." I felt he was talking about something that may have happened recently and waited for him to continue with the thread, but he stopped talking. A shadow had swept over his face. He seemed lost in a distant thought.

Changing the subject, I asked, "How's El Pueblito and all those dinners you have there?"

Glancing up from the cards, his expression hard to read, he ignored my question and asked, "What did you get your diploma in?"

I smiled. He didn't want to talk about his present life. He never did, except for Jacquelina. He brought her up whimsically almost every night, like a note on a calendar to remind me she existed.

"Political science," I said, half-lying; I hadn't graduated yet. But I would graduate once I arrived back home again and took the language test. Something I felt wasn't going to happen for a while, but it was my secret. He had his, I had mine. Harry also didn't need to know that my need-to-know Spanish was also a need to understand who I was and what I wanted out of life. He didn't seem like the type of person who had the need or even the desire to spend time figuring himself out. At thirty-five, he had an air of wisdom, as though he had been born knowing more than most. Yes, an old soul, I thought. My soul felt immature and silly around him, but I wasn't going to let him know that either.

As the night grew into the early morning, Harry talked about his childhood. I felt that Catarina was right in saying Harry wasn't Dutch. He did like licorice, and smoked Gouda was his favorite cheese, but that's like saying I like apple pie, so I must be an American. Although the songbird was a pleasant story, most of his childhood had been spent in a place of unrest. He had to leave school when he was seven for an entire year because the entrance to the building had been bombed. He made toys out of shrapnel and once stole a gun from a sleeping rebel.

"I didn't know Holland had rebels."

He said there were a lot of bad rules in his "village," which he corrected to "town." As a youth, he spent most of his time stealing gum and cigarettes from kiosks in a square that had several abandoned buildings, too many pigeons, and old ladies wearing colorful hats and shawls. "Harry, that doesn't sound like Holland to me," I said. "Who was bombing the people? What rules didn't you like?"

"Did I say bombings? Strange. I didn't mean that at all. Oh, and rules? Like many, as a child, rules were to be challenged." I knew it was the rum making him slip up. His stories were half-truths because when he strayed too far, he brought up the Hague or getting high in Amsterdam, clichés he could have left alone, as they were a dead give-away to his ruse. At times, his stories were also strange and creepy, like the one about the rat that lived in his house when he was five and pissed on all the flour. Or the one-armed maid from the mountains with a big nose and a sloppy lower lip that wiggled when she became angry. Then there was the boarding school he was sent away to, due to troubled times. "I also wasn't behaving the way my parents thought I should. I had an unhealthy intelligence."

"What does that mean, Harry?"

"It was something my father used to say. They sent me to Spain during my teenage years, and then I went to England for more schooling. College."

"Yes, you use *vosotros*, and your accent is British, and well, something else too." I was beginning to see Harry as a complicated man, as none of his youth was ordinary. But no matter what fact or fiction was, I found him fascinating. I knew my stories didn't quite have the same flair. I grew up as an only child in a country that, although at battle with a Far East nation, Vietnam, America wasn't the one being bombed.

We had lived in the woods in a house that had ten rooms. We weren't rich, but we weren't poor either. No rats, but we had mice. We had money for basics and comfortable furniture. My father painted, my mother knitted and made delicious soups. Between the ages of four and five, I pretended to be a woodland elf. I called myself Siofra and wouldn't answer to any other name.

"The woods are a perfect place for fantasies," Harry had said while peeling an orange. Several locks of his hair came loose and fell over his eyes, a frequent occurrence that always gave me pause. It took a lot of restraint not to push it back for him.

"Look out the window at the moon. It's pretty, like a painting by Manuel De la Cruz," he said.

"Who?"

"He's a Spanish painter. Gothic, old."

We were in the middle of a very intense game, and I was winning, but I got up anyway to look at the moon. Behind my back, I could hear him shifting his cards. "What are you doing?" I said, glancing back around.

"Nothing," he chuckled. A smart player got away with it, but he was clumsy and noisy. I waved my index finger at him, letting him know I was on to his tricks.

Standing at the window, breathing in the damp night air, I looked at the moon, keeping one eye on the game, and said, "It's been growing." Surrounding its curves were deep black lines matted with stars. It rested in the middle of a tree nook and looked like something out of a storybook. A big grin in the sky, I thought, feeling enchanted.

"When you arrived there wasn't a moon, just the shadow of one."

"How do you know?" It puzzled me that he would even remember that night.

"I had been in El Pueblito. When I arrived back, the sun was just below the canopy. I saw you on the beach."

"You did?" I said and turned around to look at him. He was sitting cross-legged with his elbows resting on his knees, studying the cards.

"Your thick hair," he said, rearranging the cards, not noticing I was watching him. "Dark and wavy. It framed your face. A face that looked like a porcelain doll in the dim light of the rising sun." His words caused him to glance up at me. Our eyes caught each other and remained there. Swept up in his mythical-sounding tale of "Eleanor" on the beach, I listened intensely to each consonant and vowel as his voice grew distant, hesitant, and soft. "There was a nest of sand and leaves around you like you'd made a bed. You were sleeping so soundly and not moving that, I thought, maybe you were actually a doll, but then you stirred."

"Did I wake up?"

"No. But I knew you were real and left."

"Don't you think you should have woken me up?"

"Why?"

"I don't know, the crocodiles. And the manatee." For some reason this made us laugh. It was the type of laughter that poked at our silly bones and tickled our ribs. Still standing by the window, unwilling to pull my eyes away from his, even though they were tearing with laughter, I all of a sudden stopped and looked away, then back at him again, only I wasn't laughing anymore. He looked so happy. He was trying to stop laughing but couldn't. The rum and gorgeous, fun Harry held me tight. I wanted to kiss him. Just like that, I wanted to walk over and take his face into my hands and kiss him. But then, biting my lower lip, an uneasiness crept over me. My thoughts of kissing him were out of place. I couldn't help but think he was thinking about kissing me, too. I could see it in his expression.

I sat back down and dismissed the idea as foolish and said, "Now let's see how you've cheated." But as I was having a hard time focusing, I asked, "How did you meet Jacquelina?"

As it went, he spent the next half hour talking about her, and I won the game. Small victories, I thought.

Chapter 25

Lies, Lies, Lies

Enhanced "routine and consistency" had us, the *niñeros,* realizing that what we had earlier perceived as subdued tranquility in our daily lives was merely a lack of knowing various levels of contentment. This had Jack pondering, "What you don't see, you don't know."

Gunther pointed out that the expression wasn't new, and that Jack had it wrong. "It's what you don't know you have to live with," Gunther corrected.

Alex said, "No, it's *nur bahnhof verstehen.*"

"In English, please," Catarina demanded.

"Absolutely no clue," Alex translated.

"Inn'it wha' ew don' know won' hur' yah," Golly said.

Whatever it was? Life was better, easier. The children truly seemed happier, so how could we not think our world had improved? The marches over to meals were much more pleasant. Going to school became less whiny. The boxes we built for independence in the bathroom had finally curbed the peeing outside. Only Henrik and Raymond remained stubborn about this, randomly peeing on ants, beetles, and worms. The kids were also learning how to balance themselves on the toilets, and there was less falling in.

At night, the children all knew to put their shoes in a row under the bench. Even tough guy Frankie, who was used to throwing his shoes into a corner, now laid them nicely down to rest at night. Crazy Mouse followed through too. Mouse rarely knew what he should be doing. When we, more like Alex, got him to stop shaking, he would look around, smile, and nod, then mimic his fellow orphans. It helped that it was a group task.

"Individuality can produce a persecuted feeling," Jack liked to toss in here and there, his hollow eyes revealing a tortured soul.

"Don' worry Jack, we like ya," Golly would say when she saw he looked blue. We were convinced Jack had been bullied as a kid.

The conventional plastic toys, lost or broken, were also no longer used. The jungle elements such as twigs, mud, and rocks had regained their status, lending once again an organic element to their playtime. Albert had grown bored with his ruined dolls—the arms, legs, heads, and bodies of the Barbies and G.I. Joes. He had abandoned them to the small wheelbarrow which he had left by the trash bin near the back door of the kitchen.

At night, we still danced but shooed everyone out early—that is, the kitchen ladies and the older kids—in order to read to our little ones. This allowed the little kids to fall asleep early without a fuss. During our nightly meetings, we congratulated each other on doing a good job. They were learning. We were proud. We were also learning.

Yet there was something unsettling or, should I say, brewing among the *nineras*. It was hard to put my finger on it, but the signs were there. It was as though we couldn't take the silence, the lack of conflict. Possibly it was a malignant pathos within us, an eruption of a dominant gene that opposed calm. With our minds and bodies relaxed, our fight-or-flight instinct annihilated by harmony and serenity, we needed an outlet. Our need for disruption was like a primordial hubris—subtle and nondescript. This need for trickery and strife had always been there, hence the made-up stories and the pathetic joshing of selling body parts. But now, like a faucet drip, it had grown louder and louder. The *nineras* had begun to unravel. It had been slow, like the time warp we were living in.

We just couldn't shut up. We felt the children and the local staff didn't understand what we said. Or did they? If they did, they pretended not to hear. I did feel they were listening. Cadmael knew some English. Possibly the others, too.

One day, while I was talking to Milla about selling the children's body parts and wondering what other countries took place in such diabolical deeds, I caught the workmen staring at me, wide-eyed, resting under the canoes. They didn't usually watch us from their lairs. Their expressions, typically blank, had turned mystified with a pinch of horror.

Another time, when the subject of body parts came up, I was with Molly and Golly. They wanted new stomachs. They felt if they replaced their bad metabolisms with fast metabolisms, life would be grand. They giggled like misfit hyenas at the idea of having the stomach of a three-year-old. During this conversation, Esmeralda and the two other kitchen ladies inched their ratty-looking plastic chairs over to us from their normal perch by the outdoor kitchen. I assumed they were trying to understand what we were saying.

"They caan't understand us," Molly said.

"Don't be so sure," I replied, then added. "Language isn't just words, it's facial cues and tones that are the dead giveaway. Well, that's what I read somewhere." While I spoke, the ladies shuffled their chairs back to the sink. "Interesting," I whispered. "I bet they know more than they let on. I mean, they hear English all the time. For Christ's sake, they're linguists. They already speak two or three languages."

"I don' know their language. Not one word," Molly said.

"Do you ever listen to it?" Golly asked, nudging Molly like she was a dummy.

"No blimey, no."

"I bet," I said, still speaking in a hushed tone, "they're picking up words here and there. Piecing them together. Bodies, parts, children."

Then we all laughed because it sounded sinister, and sinister seemed funny.

We remained silent for a good minute. The kids played while a light breeze fluffed at their matted, damp hair. It was insufferably hot. I wiped my face with my shirt and yawned because it was almost naptime, and said, "So what do you think the kitchen ladies do when they go home?"

Golly made up a story. It was a perverse, mischievous account of warlocks and witches. When I turned my head to see if the workmen were still awake under the canoes, all three had their eyes wide open. They crawled out and walked briskly away.

Witches were real in this country. *La Noticia* printed daily stories of people putting spells on their neighbors for revenge. "Being a witch can get you hung or put in jail in this country," I said, watching Eadrich, Aapo, and Cadmael disappear into the jungle.

Golly's imagination didn't end with *brujas* and *brujos*. She insinuated the local people were savages, living wild, naked lives full of debauchery in the backwoods. It was a dark tale of sex, sodomy, and bestiality. With her Cockney accent, subdued, I could understand every word. "I bet they sell baby parts too."

When Gunther joined us, he corrected the story and said, "The men aren't warlocks, but guerrillas. Using the orphanage as a cover-up." His words made me think about my bus ride to El Puente. All those men told to get off the bus at gunpoint. They were being accused of being guerrillas. Quiet and unassuming, clothes tattered, faces drawn, it was my understanding they only wanted a good paycheck, food, shelter, and a happy family to come home to. I didn't agree with Gunther. I didn't agree with anything that was being said. But that didn't mean I didn't join in. The lies, the gossip was like opium to our bored souls.

As the days passed, we added more details to the business of selling body parts, babies, *brujas* and *brujos*, guerrillas undercover, and the unquenchable sexual appetites of the villagers. The lies began to make us feel paranoid. We thought the locals were talking about us too.

Hamit, who liked to come into the *dormitorio* before breakfast to tell us the news, said his head had received radio frequencies that told him that the guerrillas in the north were thinking of coming south, but we told him they were already here. He smiled, proud his head had been correct, and grumbled, "That's too bad."

When Hamit picked his teeth and told us El Gordo was an undercover dwarf sent to spy on us, we agreed. When Hamit said, "You all better keep an eye on him. Don't let him near a machete," we shook with fear and disgust.

Molly whimpered, "What a horrible way to die."

When Hamit said, "Esmeralda has put a spell on my wife to make her mean."

We said, "So that's what's wrong with her."

No one liked her. She was a skinny, straight-backed, stuffy woman from Panama City who wore pencil skirts and cotton blouses that she kept buttoned up to her chin. Her hair, cropped short and slicked down on top of her head, made it look painted on. Now since Hamit was talking about her in a not-so-nice tone, we added her to our afternoon fables. We gossiped that Hamit's wife was a reptile similar to a crocodile, but more like a vampire monster type. Until she left, we all agreed we needed to keep the youngsters away from her or she'd eat them.

And more absurdly, when a group of outsiders arrived, a tour boat with a shallow draft going up and down the shores of the river visiting different sights—lunch at Club de Bote, tortilla making at an authentic Mayan village, and birdwatching—not only did we the volunteers act weird, but the kids didn't help.

The group of tourists pulled right up to our beach and threw down a gangplank. They brought platters of brownies for the kids. It was a humanitarian visit, they told us. They wore floppy hats and white deck shoes. Their shorts and shirts were the colors of peppermint and pistachio ice cream. Their visit caused a few of the older kids to revert to their days on the streets. They stood before our rich guests, looking depraved and sad. They told them they were sick and poor, and that we mistreated them. "I need money for food. We must buy food. We starve." Some kids even crawled around on the ground pretending to be too weak to stand.

This unsightly behavior caused our visitors to look at us aghast. Then when Milla thanked them for the brownies, she added, "We're fattening them up to sell."

Molly and Golly showed a group of stout ladies with sunglasses to prevent glaucoma the broken doll parts, and said, "Need any body parts?"

When I said, "These kids are the biological children of the president of the country," the group walked back up the gangplank, pockets empty of money, befuddled and shaking their heads. We could hear them muttering stuff like, "Odd group. Do you think the kids don't have food? What was that about body parts?"

It made us laugh. They also gave us something new to talk about for days. We talked about their dour mouths and untarnished sneakers and started rumors that they had stolen a few kids.

What was astounding was that no one brought up the true evils that lurked within our shores: there was a man living on a boat only yards away who had kidnapped and killed a child: the Minister of the Interior was trying to steal land from the locals: the oil companies planned to ruin the lake and the river—a lake and river that fed, washed, and created a livelihood for thousands: Harry was never around during the day anymore and when he came back at night, it was with a sack of money. The money never stayed around long. The next day it would disappear. Did he bury it? I had no idea. He never wanted to talk about it.

Chapter 26

Love

I don't know how many times I went to El Pueblito before deciding I didn't want to make the drive anymore. It unnerved me. My emotions made little sense because the week before I had enjoyed the trip. Gunther had gone with me and the workmen, but then Gunther always went with us. It had become a weekly or maybe bi-weekly ritual. We ate carne asada and napped in the park while waiting for parts—the kitchen stove, the launch engine, tools, paint. There was always something needed.

But then I woke up one morning and dreaded the idea of driving the beaten-up, stinky car. Was it the pressure of not crashing? Of keeping it on the road and everyone safe? Had I become a wimp due to the easy, relaxed living at the orphanage?

One night I complained to Harry while playing cards, "I think being here is making me soft."

"You don't seem it," he said, adding, "your nerve at playing this game—is like steel."

Then I thought about my life. My travels in my head. It caused me to lose a game. Hell, before coming to the orphanage, I'd been very free and fluid. Riding buses, hitting various cities, and staying in places only for a short while, then leaving. Here, it seemed, I 'd become stagnant, and it scared me, but I also liked it.

Sitting back on my heels and squeezing a juicy lime into a half-filled glass of rum, I told Harry about my travels. "When I was in San Cristobal de las Casas, I rode horses every day, up to Chamula and over to the river with crocodiles. In Lago Atitlan, I walked on hot coals and fought off banditos by telling them I was a *bruja*. In Oaxaca, I spent my days weathering the doldrums of language school by going to the ruins in the afternoon. I hung out with the women, the Zapotec vendors. I liked talking to them. They swore a lot. When the turistas didn't buy anything, we would say, *'Por que estos pendejas turistas no compran, lo por que son mierde!'* I also ran up and down the ruins like a billy goat. The women kept saying I would fall, but I never did."

Tucking a clump of hair behind my right ear, I wondered, "What's happened to me? Now I don't even want to go into El Pueblito."

"I don't blame you. The town's a flea-bitten sore."

"I don't even think I can speak Spanish anymore. My mind has become mush." I was rambling. It caused me to throw the wrong card down, but he didn't notice, which made me think I should tell him more stories.

"Do you want to leave?" he asked, his voice thin like something had been ripped away from it.

Looking up at him, I thought, *No, I can't. I'm in love with you.* But I said, "I could. It would be better for my Spanish. But not yet, I like it here. Why leave a place I like?"

"Why don't we speak Spanish together?" he said. His face brightened.

"Yes, we should. I haven't been speaking very much Spanish lately. I'm rusty. But sure."

My mind felt slow. My retention was watered down with drink. It was as though I had been lapping up warm milk with sedatives, and I stumbled around with even the most rudimentary words. I couldn't even remember the name of the book I was reading—but then, I laughed to myself, the book didn't even have a name.

Harry rattled off a series of stories in crisp, rapid Spanish about his father, Don Ricardo Unias, and one about a sister named Soledad. They had Spanish names, which I found peculiar. He was slipping again, but his voice was clear and smooth, and I found delight in listening to him. His accent was still a mystery. He wasn't a foreigner speaking Spanish, but a native. He neither spoke like a Spaniard nor anyone local. What country was he from? "Are you from a country in the south?" I whispered, as though my thoughts had escaped.

"Remember, I lived in Spain."

"Yes, but your accent is different."

He looked away at the wall and drank his drink, lost in thought. I stopped questioning him about it. He didn't want me to know. I kicked his foot with mine, and he came back to life. "It's your turn," I said, and he rejoined the game.

At one point, when all we could hear were the inhales and exhales of the hammock room (louder than normal) he began a story about Jacquelina. Something to do with her snoring, but he never finished it. His last words about her nasal sleep just dribbled away and ended. He looked sad.

"What's wrong, Harry?" I asked in English. I decided to give up on speaking Spanish because it was too tiring.

"You're not trying."

"It's late. Not tonight." I felt embarrassed and poured myself another drink. "They don't use *vosotros* here. It confuses me when you use it," I said, and then gave him a wily look. "Why don't you live with

Jacquelina?" Most nights, I tempered my drinking. Nursing a beverage, and only having two or three, but the last drink I had poured was my fifth. It made me braver and pushier. Since he wasn't answering me, I added. "You seem to love her a lot. I mean, you are to be married. Why are you here, Harry?"

Silence. How odd he wouldn't or couldn't answer, so I changed the subject. "Why are you at the orphanage? You seem too talented to be living such an obscure life."

"Why not?" A twinkle had entered his eyes, and he seemed happy with the compliment. Glancing at his glass, I noticed he too was drinking more than usual. His mouth wet, his eyes shiny, he continued. "One job is as good as another."

"Is it a front to allow you to do other stuff? To stay in the country to buy and sell land?" It wasn't exactly what Gunther had told me, but I had a hunch.

My guess as to what he was up to had him looking at me strangely. His brow twisted inward, his mouth opened and shut without a sound. Leaning back onto his hands, his legs bent to the side to allow for the card game, he gave me an amused, penetrating stare. I looked away and saw the moon had leveled itself and was peering in through the window like a meddlesome neighbor catching wind of something good. Then, looking around the room, a certain heat took over me. The bad lighting gave a sultry, film noir effect to the place. Harry's silence caused the whirring of the fan to become louder. I would wait for a reply before saying another word. Although what I really wanted to do was lean across the spread of cards and smother him with my body. Instead, I scooped the cards up and shuffled, pleased at my willpower.

"We weren't done with that game," he said.

"We weren't?"

Then Harry laughed.

"What's so funny?"

"You." But his bewilderment was palpable. Possibly laughing was the only answer he could give me. Handing me a packet of cookies, he said, "Here, munch on these. And please tell me, what is this all about?"

"It's time for me to go to bed," I said, stuffing a cookie into my mouth. I suddenly felt very woozy. "How about an orange too?" Instead of tossing me the orange, he handed it to me by taking hold of my hand and placing the orange in it. Leaning in close, his breath colored with rum, frankincense, and myrrh, he said, "Don't go to bed yet."

I said nothing back. His touch melted my obstinacy and will to stay chaste. I weakened and let him cradle my hand in his. He then pushed my hair away from my face with his free hand and said, "Eleanor, you're right. I am selling land. It's complicated. I do like teaching."

"But you rarely teach," I interrupted, laughing, which woke me up, and I took back my hand. "Didn't you go sailing with The Scott today?"

He frowned. "True."

"Why would you go sailing with The Scott?" My tone was judgmental. He had said he disliked the man, yet he spent time with him. I ate the orange while staring at the floor, then sighed. "I don't care what you do, Harry. It's your life." Which was a lie. I cared deeply about his life and his happiness. I also cared about mine. I rolled over onto my knees and stumbled to get up. "I've had too much to drink." He reached out and grabbed my hand again, and I weakened and sat.

"I should go to bed," I said, letting my eyes roam over his face. We were in a room lit by a soggy lamp and a moon. It was warm and sultry, with only a light breeze from the fan to cool us off. We were drunk. It was an ambiance made for a fiery romance novel. But I wasn't drunk enough to be fooled by it, not when there was an elephant in the room, and not only one, but two: Jacquelina being one, and my fear of kissing him the other. I was already crazy about him. If I kissed him? If I slept with him? Nothing would be the same. Being Harry's hapless lap dog—his concubine, his pet—wasn't the issue. I had resigned myself to the possibility. But it seemed inevitable that it wouldn't end well. So I smiled. Not tonight, I said in my head. It pleased me that I could be so mature. Maybe I was growing up? "Harry," I said and gave him a sheepish tilt of the head, "What about your fiancé? You haven't told me why you live apart."

Letting my hand go, he replied in a mottled tone, "It's better we don't live together. She has her life; I have mine. Eventually we'll join." He didn't look at me the way he usually did when speaking of the river, the sun, books, or tales of his youth. He looked confused, downtrodden. Hemmed in as though masking some regret, or maybe it was just wishful thinking on my part. Stuffing orange pieces into my mouth, I once again got up to go to bed.

"Stay for another game," he said, in a childish tone.

"Tomorrow, Harry." And I stumbled back onto my squeaky raft, alone.

Chapter 27

The Monkey

The next day I had a hangover. The morning hours were dreadful. During snack time, I added a three-count pour of rum into my green drink. It was delicious and helped my equilibrium. After lunch, the dull throb in my head finally disappeared. I spent most of the afternoon playtime in the water with the five- to eight-year-old kids. They loved it when I tossed them from my knees over my head into the deeper waters. Most of them could swim to stay afloat by either using the doggy paddle, breaststroke, or a mangled crawl. Occasionally I threw a kid behind into the dark blue, and they would sink. Nothing too worrisome. I would just strut over, reach down, pull him or her up, and bring the child over to where their feet could touch. What always surprised me was how they wanted to be tossed again. Brave or foolish? I couldn't decide.

Another few days went by, then came the day before we were all to go to the Club de Bote for the party. I awoke, gasping for air. It was as though I'd been holding my breath. Taking in big gulps and wheeze as though I had a sock stuck in my throat, I soon calmed down, but then an eerie, perplexing wave of fear crept in like a heavy fog of gloom. I'm not sure the cause of what I deemed a panic attack. I had no recollection of dreaming. But I must have been. The taste in my mouth, bitter. Sipping on the water I had by my bed, I turned to look at Harry.

Although dark, I could usually make out the form of his body, and when I quieted my heart and breath, I could hear his. But he wasn't there. Turning my flashlight on, I threw the beam over his bed and to his corner of stuff. Was he dressing? No, he'd gone off somewhere, which I found strange. He had been in the room last night. We had played cards and bickered over a rule that allowed for a second chance; he wanted one, but I didn't because I didn't need it that night. It put him in a foul mood, and he went to bed shortly after our disagreement. But then, I think he had begun the night ill-tempered because he wasn't laughing a lot, and Harry was the type of person who laughed a lot.

Since he never got up before me, the only explanation was that he didn't feel well. Scrambling out of bed, I dressed and went downstairs to see if he was in the bathroom. He wasn't there. I shrugged and went into the nursery to take the kids out of their cribs, they were awake and reaching for me. Then Catarina appeared in the doorway, and I asked, "Have you seen Harry?"

"He's a man of many mysteries," she said. "But I know he had words with my dumpling last night?"

"Dumpling?"

"Scotty. Not sure what about. I don't think it was good."

"What hour?"

"I don't know, I was half asleep—but late."

"You mean early morning. I was playing cards with him until 12:00 or possibly 1:00. He didn't seem like he wanted to leave."

While the kids were showering, Mouse ate some soap and threw up. Albert declared flowers were evil because one had pricked him. Penelope and Bernard had decided they preferred being naked. We finally got them dressed. When the kids went peacefully to breakfast, I was convinced the world had inverted itself.

As usual, Hamit came into the *dormitorio* to tell us the morning news, and we smiled; his comical reporting and cynical nature made him funny. This morning he looked unhappy, which made us feel unhappy too. He had crumbs on his chin and a white film on his lips, as though he'd been eating toothpaste. The handle was missing from his mug with the neon pink lady, and when he belched, he didn't do what he often did—blame it on one of the kids. Instead, he complained about the rot and the mud. Standing with the sun to his back, his cowlick looked like feathers, and his wide girth seemed flatter, like a wilted sheet.

"The rainy season's here. And the moon will be full *toomorra*. Rabbit Moon," he announced, slurping his coffee, then looked up into the sky as though the radio waves had spoken to him. But he seemed sluggish and not into it. His dejected mood ruined the godly effect. He let his arms drop with a thump to his side. His attempts at smiling, fake. He did have all of our attention, and we waited for him to speak.

I had been reading *The Gashlycrumb Tinies* to Bernarda and Penelope. Looking at Hamit, I said, "H is for Hamit, hoodwinked by hooligans."

Gunther, who was standing by a wall fiddling with his nose and staring at Hamit, said, "Yup, rained last night. And that's about right—a full moon, making my bug bites itch. What again is a Rabbit Moon? Never mind, I don't care. What else you got?"

Hamit puckered his lower lip while playing with the broken edges of his mug, and finally spoke, "Guerrillas blew up the utilities north of here. And—and my wife has finally left me to go live with her sister in Honduras."

Someone whispered, "Good riddance." This made Hamit's eyes open wide, then he began to cry. It shut our sour thoughts about the woman down, and we waited for him to stop. He finally quit weeping and rubbed his chin and chuckled, "She liked things to be orderly. It's hard to have order in a jungle." He then babbled on about heading out tonight to wipe the "stench of despair away" in Puerto Punto and its' *La Callejón de Putas*. Puerto Punto was a whore town that was about an hour's bus ride away. The streets were lined with kiosks filled with made-up ladies wearing spandex and stiletto heels—very inappropriate footwear because the streets were often muddy. No one discouraged him. We all mumbled that it was a good idea, unless he contracted a venereal disease, which would be unfortunate. When he left, he picked up a small suitcase that had been by the screen door. We listened to him walk down the path toward the dock, the dirt and pebbles crunching under his feet.

At snack time, there was another unforeseeable occurrence. Alex and Milla were in their house, the *oficina*. The door was open. They were naked and arguing. It was very wrong of them to have the door open because we could see them clearly: white skin pocked with bug bites, and thick, black pubic hair that was much too long. They were yelling at each other in their native tongues. "An argument truly going nowhere," Gunther commented. Molly went over and shut the door, but not before a backpack went flying out.

Milla was leaving too.

"Oh, good. I get my drinking buddy back," Gunther remarked while staring at the fuming Alex, standing in the *oficina*'s doorway. Lips swallowed up by anger, he was giving Milla the finger. She was dressing in front of everyone. Once she slipped her sandals on, she ran off to the dock to wave down a water taxi. Not even a goodbye.

"Rude," Molly said.

"Their scene was rude," Golly said.

"Speaking of rude—there goes Alex's good mood," I said, flicking a beetle off my arm. He had been almost pleasant since she arrived.

The worst of the day happened during afternoon playtime.

I missed my nap because Albert had quietly slipped away from the group. He went into the trees to the south side of the dock. But before doing so, he had looked around the way a person does when they don't want anybody to follow them. I was sure he was going to get one of his sweet-smelling red-and-purple flowers, even if he'd sworn off flowers for good. I'd had my eye on him for weeks, just waiting for this moment. This afternoon, his covert turn of the head was my cue to move. Forcing myself up off the ground, I stealthily wound my way toward the dock, hiding behind thickets and trees. The river bristling with sunshine caught my attention for a brief moment, and I paused to stare off at paradise. As I made my way over to the dock, I stood on the edge of the mangroves where Albert had gone. Moving a heavy branch aside, I peeked in. Albert was standing several yards away by two large brown birds that were picking at something.

I walked a few feet across the mangled roots of the mangrove trees. A waft of thick, foul air struck me. It was the smell of a rotting animal. I put my shirt up over my mouth and nose, and said, "Albert, *venga*." He needed to get away from whatever it was.

Albert looked over at me, then back to the birds. A blackbird with a red-striped beak joined them. I walked nearer. "Albert, *por favor*." Whatever it was, it fascinated him. His arms hung by his side, his hands bent and reaching out, his mouth edged open. He was wearing bright plaid shorts and a striped, collared Guess shirt, and his hair was slicked back. An impressive-looking little boy.

One of the brown birds hopped up and jumped onto the dead thing. Its head bounced up. It was a small skull with sunken eyes and a jaw with several long, oily teeth. The face was half-eaten and had chunks of hair and skin hanging from it. "Dammit, Albert!" I was angry that he wouldn't listen, as danger seemed imminent.

Squinting, with my hand over my nose and mouth, I saw it was a dead monkey. And then it occurred to me that Albert couldn't move. He was stuck in place, frozen by the vileness of the image. I made my way over the thick roots, gagging with every breath, and finally reached Albert and picked him up. He was a heavy, solid little boy, and the walk back over the roots was difficult. When I reached the dock area, he clung to my neck and wouldn't let go. I carried him back to the group sitting in the quad and sat with him on my lap. He rested his head on my chest and stayed that way for quite a while. It was the first time he had ever wanted to be by anyone. He was a loner who only occasionally played with Wooter. Most of the time, he wandered around the compound searching for pretty flowers by himself. While I sat with Albert on my lap, I couldn't help but think there was some vibe in the air that was messing us all up. Was this a prelude to something bigger and more catastrophic to come?

Chapter 28

Doc

The day of the party, everyone—staff, kids, *niñeros*, workmen, the birds, and the bugs—all seemed more out of sorts than the day before. It was like a catastrophic storm was brewing on the horizon, and we had neglected to batten down the hatches. The party had us all buzzing, but I felt there was something else beyond the excitement of tasty, free food and booze. To the unobservant eye, not a hair looked out of place, but something was amiss. Whatever it was, I felt it wouldn't take much to unleash.

Harry still hadn't come back, but once again, Catarina and Gunther assured me, his behavior wasn't unusual. It still had me chewing the side of my mouth and pouting. I had imagined us together, eating and drinking at the club, like a date. Then it occurred to me that he may have gone to fetch his fiancé to bring her to the party. This realization crushed my fanciful dream, and I didn't want to go. It was stupid and foolish, but I was gaga over the man, even though it wasn't right. I'd even begun hoping, wishing his fiancé, the infamous Jacqueline, would drop dead, be hit by a car, or just go away, never to come back.

All just silly, fanciful, and ugly thoughts.

"But you have to go. If you don't, you'll feel left out because we'll tell stories about the scrummy food for a long time afterwards," Gunther said, poking me, then nudging. Then he tried to hug me. I pushed him away. I was helping Doc with her rounds, and she looked miffed that I wasn't by her side. "I don't know. I'll think about it." How truly pathetic to not go, I said to myself.

I caught Doc's eye, and she waved me over. It was mid-morning during snack time, and she was inspecting her kids. My duty was to carry her bag. With her malaria dormant, she had walked up to the main compound from the *clínica* to inspect the kids for lice, worms, and overall health. In the past it was something she did every week, and Catarina or Alex usually helped her. However, Catarina had gone into El Pueblito with The Scott to buy a non-gunked up shirt for the party and wouldn't be back until after lunch. Alex, who was her deputized assistant, was at the *clínica* cleaning up spit cups and bloody snot-gauze and keeping the place in order while she was away. Golly, Molly, and I felt it was an excellent distraction for him since Milla had left. For the most part, he had become insufferable. He wouldn't stop constantly insulting everyone in German. *The coward*, I thought. *He knew English, use your English.* According to Golly, who somehow knew German, or at least claimed to know German, Alex was calling us slappable idiots, along with fuck-heads, snot-eaters, and the females, slut-cunts. We females especially found slut-cunts to be the most offensive and wished he would leave and go back to Germany. But according to Gunther, he had no plans to do so. "Trust fund kid. No need to work."

Now in the quad with all twenty-four kids, I was the temporary assistant. It was easy, since all I did was follow Doc around. The kids were talking and drinking the green drink while waiting for their turn to be inspected. They were used to it. Some even made up maladies just for attention. Doc was good with them. She would pat the ones with the dramatized symptoms on the head and say, "All better now," even though she did nothing except touch them. What I did find interesting was Cadmael lurking in the shrubs by the *clínica* path. I gathered they were a item, and he couldn't take his eyes off her. He kept looking over at Doc and winking: sometimes he waved, and she would wave back. I never mentioned my observations of Cadmael and Doc to any of the others because we didn't gossip about real stuff, only made-up crap. But if I remembered, I planned to consult with Molly and Golly about the lovebirds. My curiosity had gotten the better of me.

"Eleanor. Earth to Eleanor." I had been staring at Cadmael when Doc's voice refocused my attention on her. "Dat dead monkey you found with Albert? Be more likely to produce salmonella or trichinosis, not cholera," she clarified. "The toxigenic bacterium serogroup Vibrio cholerae has contaminated dah river," she continued as she meandered, stopping at each child with me at her heels. "But it be farther up where the population is dense and many of the outhouses are directly over dah water. The river runs north, thanx God." Glancing at me, she paused for a moment, then looked away to rummage through her worn leather bag that I held in my arms. She paused to look toward Cadmael. Eadrich had come over, and they were both heading toward the little kids' schoolhouse. As they passed by, Cadmael blew Doc a kiss. I smiled. Doc sighed but ignored Cadmael's cute flirtation, and pulled out a brown bottle of deworming medicine, mebendazole, from her bag. The bottle had a skull with crossbones. Beneath the warning label it read, "Candy-flavored."

"Mon, cholera is a diarrheal illness caused by infection of dah intestine." She continued to prattle on as though talking about a warm summer breeze. She pulled on the kids' ears, put drops on their tongues, and sifted through their hair looking for lice.

"It be a horrible death. It's like your body is melting and coming out your ass. Some people have just mild symptoms, but most have dah blue skin, sunken eyes, lots of watery diarrhea, vomiting, leg cramps. Rapid loss of body fluids causes dehydration and shock. Without treatment, death can occur within hours. We had one case here a couple of months ago. Make sure you drink from dah left tank, not dah right."

I looked over at the water tanks; I had been drinking from

the right tank because it tasted better. "Maybe the tanks should be marked," I commented.

"Threadworms, hookworms, tapeworms, roundworms," she said, rambling on. The nasty worm names sounded like a grocery list. "The kids, dayh eat the dirt, dayh drink the river water when dayh swim, dayh poop in their bedding, which is washed with cold water, not hot. These worms are everywhere. We can never really rid them of the parasites because dayh constantly get re-infect themselves. It's what makes dayh stomachs puffy."

Most of the kids had the type of stomach seen on thin old men who drank too much beer. I had thought their round bellies were due to them being kids. Malnutrition had occurred to me, but they were well fed. So it was worms.

Standing next to her with her bag cradled in my arms, I couldn't help but wonder about my gastrointestinal tract and the ugly possibilities of what might be there. "What about us? The adults?"

"It's dah principal reason why life expectancy on dah river is only forty years. Worms don't kill immediately. It's a slow death. You bite your nails?"

When she said this, I was in mid-bite.

"Well, don't."

In her bag, she also had some fizzy tablets for giardia, paregoric for diarrhea, cream for scabies, and a bottle of Pedialyte for cholera. By a warped-looking mahogany tree, she had placed a giant bottle of lice prevention shampoo. At swim time today, she told us to shampoo the kids' hair with the stuff.

Dabbing Charlotte's bug bites with Tiger Balm, Doc sighed. "The jungle is a tough place to raise kids, but also a fun place. Dayh swim, dayh play. Buiti—all good."

I dug my fingernails into my scalp because it itched, and then I handed her the bottle of mebendazole. She put a couple of drops on

Charlotte's extended tongue. Charlotte smacked her lips and made an "umm" noise.

Then out of the blue Doc asked, "How's living with Harry?"

Not giving me time to answer, she continued. "Harry's smooth, you know. A real Casanova. Watch yourself." Her melodious accent had an edge to it. I wondered if she liked him, but then she was with Cadmael. Or so I assumed.

She leaned down and sifted through El Gordo's thick, black hair. "Mon, he got loads of them eating away at his scalp." She cupped his cheeks in her hands and cooed, "My poor baby. We'll wash your hair good and clean today."

"He's got a fiancé," I said, taking the empty bottle of worm killer out of her hand and giving her a new one.

"Harry has a fiancé?"

"Yeah," I said, staring at the bottle of lice shampoo, thinking I would like to use it today too.

"Yah, he does," she said, smiling without showing teeth.

"So that's that," I said, staring at her back, feeling depressed over the reality of it.

Doc was crouched down, looking at a cut on Frankie's right pinky. "Just a scratch," she said. He then stuck out his tongue, and she gave him a few candied drops. "He likes the stuff," she mused. "They all do."

"They burned the monkey," I said, changing the subject.

"Good thing."

A few clouds had moved in, blocking the sun, and the birds momentarily stopped singing. The small voices of the kids chatting, broken up by laughter, became louder and then quieted down. Finishing up, Doc turned toward me, standing very close. Her heavy-lidded eyes moved slyly around and latched onto mine. She then reached over and pinched my arm hard. I flinched. She had long nails and had pierced the skin.

"Oh, sorry, you had a bug, but I got your skin," she said, the corners of her mouth turned up into a smile.

I didn't buy her line. Staring at her for a few minutes, trying to think what might have come over her, blood dripping from the cut, I put her bag down and walked over to the *dormitorio*. I needed a Band-Aid. One of my own Band-Aids from my own kit, not from hers.

The *dormitorio* was silent and free of people. A light fluttering of leaves from a jacaranda tree brushed the screens of the back windows. Warm air blew in lazily, flapping the pages of the open books lying on the great room's floor. It was calming, and my anger subsided, but not my disbelief.

Walking into my room, I saw Harry sitting on the floor by his bed. My first desire was to run over and hug him, but I went with the second impulse, which was much less demonstrative. "Harry, where have you been?" I said matter-of-factly and went over to my backpack. Then, because he said nothing in return, I added, "Did you hear about the monkey?" He let me tell him certain poignant events that had taken place over the past few days without interrupting me. As I talked, I rummaged through my bag, head down, searching for my Bacitracin and a Band-Aid. Once found, I took them out and doctored my cut while going into detail about the kids and all their lice. It was good to be talking to Harry again, yet he stopped me when I ragged on Doc.

"She did what?"

I walked over and showed him the growing blue bruise and the small but deep slice on my arm, which was when I noticed Harry was filthy. There was dirt all over his clothing, and his bare feet were chafed and smeared with mud. He had a puffy, red lump on the left side of his forehead. His hair was out of sorts and wet, his blue eyes were touched with gray, and his olive skin was pasty.

"Mangroves can be tricky," he said, his tone fragile, something new in his repertoire of emotions.

"What do you mean?"

"What I mean is, don't try walking in the dark in these woods. Serves me right, I suppose." He laughed and grabbed my hand. Then he gazed at me with eyes that now twinkled. He squeezed my hand lightly while asking me to get a pot of boiling water from Esmeralda. He wanted to boil the germs out of his damaged forehead.

"What happened, Harry?" I asked, removing my hand. "Which mangroves?" He was a mess, and it tore at my heart. Yet I found myself angry at his secrecy.

"I—don't——can't. Not now. Please, just get me some water."

"Harry?" I stood in front of him and waited for some sort of explanation. His lower lip shook. I believed he was about to cry, but then he stopped himself. He looked at the floor and then cleared his throat and looked at me the way one of the four-year-olds might after stubbing a toe or falling. I thought of Albert after he discovered the monkey and his fear and shock. It made me want to cry too, but instead I sat on Harry's bed, the squeak making us both laugh briefly. Then I put my arm around his shoulders and drew him into me. I'd never hugged him before. He was strong, and I could smell the essence of myrrh through his musty sweat and the swampish mud.

"Love is hard. I'm not sure if I'm cut out for it," Harry said into my shoulder, his voice muffled. Then he sat up straight and brushed his hair back, as though slightly embarrassed. I let my hands fall to my sides and we sat for a few minutes side-by-side.

"What does that have to do with mud and bruises?" I sighed.

"Everything and nothing."

I got up and went to the cafeteria via the back door. Doc was still in the quad, and I wanted to avoid her. Molly had Doc's bag in her arms. They were chatting about the kids. Thankfully, Esmeralda was happy to boil water for Harry.

Walking back into the *dormitorio* with the hot water, I heard Harry singing in the shower. The song had a lovely, sonorous tune; he was singing in Spanish. It was a song about mountains and love. Heading toward the melody, I hummed the tune, my mood buoyant and my gait light. I was glad he was back and that he hadn't broken anything, except maybe his heart. But then that was doubtful. It was probably a spat with his girl, but then where had they met? Gunther said Harry liked to stay at the La Vista Hotel in Pueblito, but then Catarina told me earlier he had been on The Scott's boat at some odd hour the other morning, arguing. And as for the mangroves? They were everywhere. I knew I would never get a straight answer out of him, but his admission that "love was hard" I could agree with.

In the bathroom, the humid air was flushed with the scent of minty soap. He was in the second stall, naked and all lathered with foam. I had glimpsed Harry naked as he slept. I rarely saw him dress, and when I did, he was shy and turned away from me as I looked the other way too. We always tried to be respectful of each other's space, but we lived together, which made it difficult.

As it went, privacy was nearly impossible at the orphanage. Since the kids showered in the morning, we all had to shower later. There weren't any curtains. We all had seen each other naked. We all had seen each other on the toilet. We talked to each other about our day sitting on the toilet and in the shower. The kids came in while we were sitting on the toilet and in the shower. They were always curious if we were peeing or pooping, or they wanted to get into the shower with us, to which we all said, "No." It was all very natural and open. It would have been impossible any other way.

"Harry, you have a lovely singing voice," I said, adding, "I'll leave the hot water on the counter by the sinks."

"Thank you," he said, then blurted out, "Wait! I want to tell you something."

I leaned up against the wall by the sinks and waited. He finally came over with a terrycloth towel wrapped around his waist. He looked scrubbed and healthy, although the knock on his head had turned an awful mix of red, blue, and purple. There were scratches on his legs and arms too. I handed him the cloth I had gotten from Esmeralda and leaned back once again and waited for him to speak. The minty scent emanating from his tan, firm body and the small, curly black hairs on his chest made me want to move closer, to hug him, kiss him, but I stayed put. In silence, I watched him dip the cloth into the hot water and place it on his forehead.

"While I was in the shower, I was thinking about everything that's been happening here. You know, about the excessive gossiping and people seeming itchy for some excitement. And the monkey, Hamit's wife, and Milla leaving. Now, don't think I'm foolish." Harry said, wincing when he pressed too hard on his head.

"A little late for that," I teased.

"It's the moon," he said, glancing at me briefly to catch my reaction.

"It's always the moon," I said. Then I sighed. "Hamit said it's your Rabbit Moon tonight."

"Not my moon, but yup, the Rabbit Moon begins tonight," he said.

"I guess it has to do with fertility. Mayan."

"Fertility? No, that's not it. The locals were discussing it this week," he said. "I don't think much about hocus pocus, but I had a terrible morning, and the week hasn't been good either. And, well, I think this moon is making everything worse. According to the locals—"

"—According to legend," I laughed. "Is this going to be a creepy campfire story?"

He laughed, and it made me smile to see him happy. Not thinking, I blurted out, "I love the way you laugh, Harry."

This caused him to pause and study my face for a moment. Then he smiled and said, "Thank you, but you still have to listen to my boogie-moon tale. Now the locals in El Pueblito said this moon—this Rabbit Moon, so craven and disastrous; so disruptive and insane that darkness will fall upon the world for an entire month."

"Sounds awful," I interrupted.

"Now listen. No one's safe. It's mischievous and mean. Aapo is leaving to go protect his relatives in the north. It's got everyone jumpy."

"A whole month?"

"The words of the locals," he remarked.

"This seems so unlike you." I played with a loose clump of hair on my shoulder, keeping my eyes on Harry's every move. Then I said, "There are so many moons. So many to choose from: Wolf moons, Super moons, Blue moons, Pink moons, Harvest moons, Half-moons, now Rabbit moons. Rabbits and moons—makes a good title for a children's book."

"Well, this children's book isn't cute, more like a Brothers Grimm fairy tale. When the moon appears tonight, it will unleash tiny little rabbits, if it hasn't already. These rabbits will run around the earth, causing chaos for a month."

"Wonderful. I don't suppose the rabbits have names like Frankie, Penelope, Wooter?" I chuckled.

"Sounds about right."

We both then fell quiet. He looked me in the eye, and I looked back at him. We just stood there in silence, staring at each other for a few moments, listening to the rustling of the trees. He then leaned in and gently drew my pinched arm toward him. Taking my hand into his, he held it tenderly, weaving his fingers into mine. I let him do this. I had missed him the way a flower missed its petals and the ocean its water. From the look in his eyes, the tone of his voice, he missed me too. It was as though he kept looking at me as if I might leave or as if he wanted to say something more. But he didn't, so I said it: "Did you have fight with Jacquelina?"

Silence. I could see him digesting what I said.

"Maybe," he said. "But more importantly, are you going to the party at the club tonight?" When I didn't answer him immediately, he lightly squeezed my fingers, then played with the palm of my hand reluctantly, releasing it while keeping his gaze latched onto mine. Such a strange dance, I thought. I wondered who this Harry Van Cleef really was? The answer was not simple, and possibly unknowable. Leaning coyly against the wall, I said, "Sure. Are you going?" There was also something different about Harry on this bright, sunny morning. It was the first time he had held my hand during the day. Possibly the bump on his head made him forget he was attached to another. A giddiness rose up inside of me as the thought of a date, a quasi-date, a fake date, but a date with Harry, could be a reality, and I smiled.

"Good—good. I wouldn't miss it," he said, suddenly upbeat. "The owners of the club do this every so often. I think it makes them feel better, since they usually cater to the rich."

Bernarda, Charlotte, and Penelope came into the bathroom and wrapped their arms around my legs. Hugging me, they asked if I would come help them with the fort we were building in the great room. We had been working on it forever because it was always being wrecked by too much roughhousing. We had gotten the cardboard from the cabbage shipment that had come eons ago which gave it a soggy vegetable smell. None of us minded the odor.

I left with the girls, and Harry began to sing his lovely song in Spanish again. Then I chuckled. Were relationships like our game of Russian Bank? Each player had to rid themselves of their fifty-two cards before the other caught them cheating or misplaying in order to win.

Chapter 29

The Rabbit Moon

The day of the party, Henrik was sick. He had thrown up on me three times. I'd tossed almost all of my clothing outside in a bin to be washed at some point. But I had a clothing dilemma. Besides the trashy Tinker Bell shirt, nothing else was clean. I wanted to look better than I normally did for the party now that Harry was going (I believed) alone. If he did bring Jacquelina, it would be disturbing and well, a wake-up call to possibly stop my daydreaming about Harry, me, and a lusty, love-filled future. My smelly hair was a clotted mess of undigested black beans, spittle, and I don't know what. The best I could do was take a shower, and if she didn't mind, borrow some clothes from Catarina. As for make-up? I didn't have any, and no one else probably did either.

The laundry ladies, barely five feet tall and almost as wide, were to be the babysitters. Their arrival allowed us to get ready for the party. But Henrik, little Henrick, clung to me because of his bad health. When I handed him over to the babysitters, he made a weak crying noise, then dropped his crankiness when one of the more bodacious ladies hugged him tightly against her breasts. The guilt I'd felt at leaving him since he was so ill receded.

I ran toward the bathroom to shower. Catarina, who disliked showering on The Scott's boat because the head smelled like dead mice and there was no room to turn around, was already soaping up. I jumped into the stall next to her. The cold water was always an issue for everyone at first. In the mornings, we had to fool the kids to get them to shower. We did this by having a group of seven or eight children step into a stall without the water on. Once in, we would turn the water on, and they would wail and stamp their feet. Some might say we were cruel to fool them like this, but they wouldn't get in if the water was already on. There were always a few attempts to bolt. We met this rebellion by blocking the exit with our bodies and arms. Trapped under the cold spray, the briskness eventually turned tepid and enjoyable. Their transition from horror to contentment was visible in their faces. Lots of smiles and laughter. When we handed them washcloths and soap, they giggled, splashing their feet in the puddled water. They liked to wash the stall walls and each other. When it came time to get them out, we had to turn the water off. This was just as upsetting as turning it on.

"These kids and their lice," Catarina said to me as I slowly put one shoulder into the spray, then my head, then the rest of my body. We decided to use the delousing shampoo. The warning label said overuse could cause neurological damage.

"I wonder if it's better to just be bald," I replied. The shampoo smelled like cookie dough, which was nauseating when mixed with the vomit. "Did you bring your Dr. Bronner's Lavender with you?"

"Here." She reached around and handed it to me. Her nails had been filed and polished.

"Fuchsia, nice," I commented. I'd given up trying to convince her to dump The Scott.

"I want you to check my hair," Catarina said. Standing in front of me, naked, she bent down so I could see her hair and scalp. The bad lighting made her strawberry blonde hair blur into a mesh of tangles. I saw a few twitching things in her hair that looked like tiny pieces of paper. "You might want to use the nit comb," I said.

"I've got them?"

"I don't know. Maybe." The Scott had thick tufts of sandy brown hair, which meant he probably had lice too, which made me smile.

Catarina checked my scalp and said she didn't see anything, but I believe her eyesight was bad because she always squinted when trying to see well, and the lighting didn't help. We both shrugged and dismissed the inconvenience of having "freeloaders" in our hair as part of jungle living and went upstairs. She lent me a billowy white cotton blouse speckled with pink roses and green leaves and gave me a pair of blue jeans she said she didn't like anymore. For herself, she put on a floor-length sundress and left. The Scott was waiting for her at the dock with his dinghy. She was full of bubbles and lustful thoughts and kept saying, "Yummy."

Outside in the quad, under the rays of the cafeteria floodlight, the group waited. We all looked touched up, but that was all. Sarah had on an adult-sized Lilly Pulitzer sundress that had ended up in a delivery of clothing for the kids. With her flat, short hair pulled from her face by a bumblebee clip, her thin, shapeless body stood motionless while her eyes bounced along the ground, looking for bugs. She was a larger version of our children and possibly completely insane, but also friendly and sweet. Her knees were dirty because she had been looking for dung beetles earlier in the day. Jack had pants on, khakis with a frayed hem. They were too big around the waist. He was using a purple bandana as a belt. His shirt was missing a button, but his hair was combed. We all thought he may have washed it. Alex had the same thin pair of striped balloon pants on that showed his penis wobbling across his upper thighs when he walked. He swore they were new. He had braided his flaming red hair instead of tying it in a knot on top of his head. The braids made him look like a spooky girl, although this was more due to his black pinprick eyes.

Gunther looked rosy, but that was because the sun had burned his cheeks earlier in the day. He was wearing his hair in pigtails instead of pom-poms, but no one could see the difference. Molly and Golly wore matching yellow-and-orange floral dresses that buttoned down their fronts; the orange matched their hair. They must have gained weight since buying the dresses because the strained buttons exposed lumps of white, bulging flesh around their midriffs and heavy, freckled cleavage. All it would take was one button to pop and everything would burst out. As for myself? The borrowed blouse was more like a short dress, the blue jeans more like blue leggings; they were tight, but the stretchy material made them comfortable. I felt different in the clothes—somewhat more sophisticated, even fashionable, since everything I had was threadbare and loose. My hair was clean, fluffy, and heavy. I had rolled it into a French knot and secured it with a stick.

We walked down to the dock where Manolo was waiting for us with the launch. We were seven people who most likely back in our hometowns would have had nothing to do with each other, but we made light, easy chatter about the children and the day. When we arrived at the launch, we squabbled over seating and foot placement. I ended up sitting between Molly and Golly, which was not my first choice, but because one of my flip-flops' toeholds had snapped, delaying me, I lost the seat by Gunther to Alex. Sitting between the girls was like being squashed between two sweaty cushions. Leaning forward, I rested my elbows on my knees, which allowed me to breathe. The two of them used my back as an armrest.

Kicking the launch into gear, Manolo headed swiftly across the river. Spray spit up into our faces, and the multicolored lights emanating from the club drew us in like a beacon of civility. The Scott's boat was dark except for a lone light over the bulkhead. One of Catarina's skirts was hanging from the boom, drying. Then I looked at the moon. It was full and bright, a giant sphere of marigolds and apricots. Resting mere inches above the rainforest canopy, its magnetic powers were alluring.

"Heaven's best jewel," Gunther said. Then he added with a snicker, "Does anyone see the big rabbit ears?"

We had been talking about the Mayan myth earlier in the day and decided anything that went wrong we would blame on the Rabbit Moon and the unleashing of the little rabbits, at least for a month. Then we realized we might not know when the month was up, so Molly put a notch on one of the wooden sides of the cubbyholes, declaring, "Day one." We found the solution very satisfying and, once again, we were proud of our resourcefulness.

"I see its sniffing nose and unblinking eyes," Jack mused.

"Ew, it's looking right at us. Bad 'abbit. Go away." Golly fussed, waving her fist at it while digging her resting elbow into my back.

Haphazardly listening to my cohorts, I found myself glued to the moon. Whether it was because of its rich colors or a desire to see something fantastical, I saw the image of a giant hare sitting with its legs crossed. The rabbit, or rather hare because it was big and long, was smoking a cigar, and he or she was staring right at me. It had a devilish grin, as though to say, "I've got you now. Just try to escape." I knew it couldn't be real. I was hungry, and for the second day in a row I'd missed my nap by the dugout canoes; Henrik being ill; the day before it was Albert and the monkey. Possibly I was hallucinating. But when I blinked, the image didn't go away. Sitting up, I poked Gunther's back as he was sitting in front of me and said, "That damn rabbit is looking at me."

"Gone daffy on us. Well, nothing a good drink can't cure," he remarked, tweaking my chin and turning back around. Then the engine cut out and we glided into the club's dock.

Standing up, once again we all fussed with each other about who would get out first and shouldn't someone grab the rope and why wasn't the dock higher. Golly and Molly both ripped a hole in the back seams of their dresses. They didn't care. We didn't care. I was also sharply told by Manolo that if I didn't take my broken flip-flops with me, I wouldn't be allowed back in the boat. "Fine, Manolo." Thinking

I could glue the broken pieces back together, I left them on the dock to gather back up again when it was time to leave.

Chapter 30

The Party

It was a party for the club's boaters too. I overheard someone say they had to pay to attend. Tall and skinny, fat and round, cocktail guzzlers—the air thick with smoke and gin. The crowd, already drunk, cigarettes between their fingers and lips, spilled their drinks when they spoke. It seemed they had an abundance of hyperbole for their seafaring tales; loud and crass, too much time in the sun; unhealthy complexions, wrinkled, and red—this group of outsiders gave us pause at the entrance. The world beyond the orphanage of money and small talk seemed deformed and unfamiliar. "Maybe we should go back," Golly mumbled. But as our eyes weaved their way through the crowd, we caught sight of the buffet table. Our jaws dropped, our bored taste buds enlivened, I said, "We've gone to heaven." A whole pig, grouper, potato salad, slabs of beef, ribs, sandwiches, tamales, pizza, soup, bread, watermelon, even asparagus, we became like bumper cars and pushed and shoved our way through the crowd, tactless and determined.

Hearing Catarina shout my name, I stopped inches away from

a ham-and-cheese sandwich and glanced around. She was at the bar with The Scott. She had one arm around his neck and was waving to me with the other. It was the first time I got a really good look at him since the village, then there was flashing my light into his face when he picked up Catarina. Usually when he dropped her off, he was a shrouded in dark sunglasses and his hat, which I found odd. He was a handsome fellow with thick brown hair and an angled, rugged face. When he placed his hat on, a beige fedora that he pulled down to dip over his left eye—his eyes the color of a coral blue sea and as penetrating as daggers—it was more apparent to me than ever that there was something not right with him. Evil oozed from his aura, along with a hidden but overt mean streak that given the right circumstances could be fatal to others. His presence made me cringe, and I turned back to the sandwich plate.

Las Noticias had said Dan Scotchwick (a.k.a. The Scott) was from Indiana, USA, and that he had been living in various countries in Central America for a decade. His occupation? He sold high-end rare sailboats for a living. Then I thought, that isn't his only occupation; kidnapping was another, and then murder. But he obviously wasn't good at any of his trades because rumor had it that he was penniless. I was still amazed that Yena, if she had the money Gunther said she had, why she hadn't hired a hitman to knock The Scott off yet? It was puzzling. Families sought revenge for their loved ones in these parts, usually with impunity, and even if she didn't have much money, an assassin could be hired for only a dollar. I took a bite of the ham-and-cheese sandwich. It was delicious. It was on actual bread and not a tortilla and lathered with mayonnaise. Chewing, I thought about all the people I knew who had been touched by the boy's death. The murder had taken place in El Puente, a town I had now grown quite familiar with. Yena and Harry, Albert who had found the boy's body, and now Catarina were all mixed up with the creepy guy. Something seemed very out of sorts, but it wasn't something Harry ever wanted to talk about, and although I'd asked Gunther, he knew nothing except that Harry was helping Yena sell her land. I also thought of my conversation with Hamit: "Ceeement blocks float," he had said. It was all enough to stop me from eating, but I hadn't had flavor in so long, it was impossible to stop myself from gorging.

I put the sandwich on a plate and picked up a cheesy piece of pizza. "Come say hello!" Catarina shouted. Once again, I looked over at them. Dan Scotchwick, his eyes dead centered on mine, gave a few arched waves as though *I'd be foolish not to join them.*

"I want to eat! I'll come over later!" I took a bite of the pizza. The tomato sauce was spicy. Going down the buffet, I piled big chunks of everything onto my plate.

Golly was sitting at a back table with a mound of food in front of her. Beside her was Hamit, and beside him was a boxy, big-eyed woman. She looked worn out and had too much makeup on and wore spandex that was too small for her busty figure. I gathered she was a souvenir from his trip to *la callejón de putas.* I joined them. Hamit made introductions. Her name was Matilda. Every time Hamit squeezed her thick waist, which was often, she laughed, showing a mouth missing two front teeth and back molars encased in gold. Hamit, who was sweating in his leisure suit, kept leaning in to smell her hair and neck until they finally got up and left. They were staying at the club. Hamit wasn't sure if he wanted to come back to the orphanage— "too many memories," he had said. I thought they made a pleasant couple. But before they walked away, I asked, "Who's going to teach the kids English?"

"One of the hag dorm biddies," he growled.

"They don't speak English."

"You don't have to."

"What about the news?" I blurted.

"Easy, never changes."

"Yes, it does. It's been raining. It didn't rain when I first got here."

"Rain and hot. Hot and rain. No big diff."

So that was that—no big diff. But I was going to miss his morning news briefs. Golly thought it was better that he left. "Hee a bit David."

"What?"

"Crazy."

When the waiter came by, I ordered a fruit punch and so did Golly. We ate in silence. I ate most of my sandwich, then went back to the pizza, ribs, fish, salad, and mushroom caps until there were only a few bites of tamale left. My drink in front of me, a bright orange-red concoction with an umbrella, was sweet and like having dessert. I gulped it down and ordered another. Then for better comfort, I undid the buttons at my waist and leaned back, the chair pressed against the rail. Stuffed and relaxed, I played with the umbrella in my second drink and looked around, wondering where Harry might be. He was late.

Looking over at Catarina and The Scott, they looked sloppy drunk, as I had hoped. Backs to the restaurant, they took turns nibbling on each other's ears.

To my left, two tables away, I caught sight of Molly and Gunther sitting almost on top of each other. Molly was feeding Gunther with her fingers. She would dip a piece of food into his mouth and rapidly pull it away. Then, after teasing him for a while in this manner, she would feed him by stuffing the morsel into his mouth.

"That's disturbing," I said to Golly.

"She's besotted with him," Golly said, giggling while putting her putty fingers over her tittering, red mouth.

"Golly, you have lipstick on."

"Found it me pocket," she giggled.

"What's so funny?" She wouldn't stop giggling. "Golly, how can you be drunk already? You just got here."

"I don' 'old me liquor well," she said, breaking out into hyena-hysterical laughter, then snorting.

Out of the crowd, Doc swayed toward us with a plate of food and a drink. She sat down with a thud, spilling a little of everything. I hadn't spoken to her since she'd pinched me.

"Sorry," she said, her jaw slack. "I don' mean it. Dah bug I killed on your arm. I hurt you." Wearing a tight yellow shirt that accentuated her large breasts and small waist, she looked like a poster pinup slated for a male locker room. Even with her drooling drunk mouth and lopsided eyes, she was a babe. Sitting next to her, I felt like a child, or more like my body had forgotten it was supposed to be female. "Sorry I hurt you," she slurred, again and again, then leaned in and kissed me on the cheek, hugged and smothered me in her flesh. Her breath was pasty and boozy, with a hint of cherry.

"It's okay," I said, pushing her away. She started eating but didn't seem to get much food into her mouth. Her ability to chew was off-balance. Frustrated, she slid her head down on top of her breasts and went to sleep.

"Doc been here all afternoon," Golly said, still giggling.

"I can tell."

I belched and immediately felt better, so I put the last few pieces of the tamale into my mouth. I realized I was eating for taste more than need. When I tongued something hard and undesirable in the tamale, I immediately spat it out over the railing into the water. Golly and I watched in silence as giant carp rose up from the murky depths with puckered mouths. They fought unmercifully over the small tidbit. Once devoured, they slunk back into the deep, tails first, their eyes staring at us as they disappeared.

"Don't wanna fall in 'ere. Stodgy fish— may ea' me. Yoo-hoo... Yoo-hoo, look at meee!" Golly shouted, waving to the fish and snorting so hard she forced mucus out of her nose. Then, calming herself, she began stuffing a ham-and-cheese sandwich into her mouth.

"You know, Golly," I said, watching her. "When you travel, you represent your country."

Swallowing her food, she looked at me and said, "Yeah, Americans are a bunch of Neanderthal cunts, but you're all right." Then she burst into a fresh round of giggles and snorts while trying to take another bite of the sandwich. I was shocked by how clearly she pronounced "Neanderthal."

Wiping my mouth, I took a long swig off of Doc's fruity drink, since mine was empty and Doc was snoring. Her head snuggled on top of her breasts, her plate of food pushed aside, she looked at peace. It occurred to me to pinch her, but what if she woke up? I gave Golly a deadpan stare and let out a burp that turned a few heads. It was one of those belches that came from deep down in the belly and felt great. So as not to seem unrefined to the other boozing boaters and their aghast stares, I pointed at Golly. Golly began swallowing air to retaliate. When she finally burped, it was a tiny little hiccup, but she grinned as though it were a masterpiece. Picking up one of Doc's chips, I dipped it into the guacamole on her plate, crunched down on it, and chewed extra loudly, exposing the chewed food. Golly took the chips and began chewing loudly with her mouth open. Then we tired of our bad manners game, and tossed a few chips into the water and waited for the carp to reappear. They came in wiggling their tails and nabbed the food. We threw a few more pieces at them. They ate and left. Bored, Golly and I sat back and looked over the crowd.

"He looks lonely," Golly said, nodding toward Alex, who was sitting at the bar downing shots of rum. She rose to join him, knocking her chair over. Her dress bunched, stuck in the crack of her bottom, and the seam on her left shoulder displayed another tear. Golly took unsteady steps over to Alex and bumped into him, then poked him in the shoulder as though he didn't know she was there. He put his hand on her rump. Golly showed her appreciation by swishing her rear around in snuggly circles. When did they start getting along? I wondered.

As I sat in the seat by the railing, Doc snoring beside me, I felt like I'd been stood up. Disappointed? Or was it more like disenchanted? I ordered another punch. Harry had said he would be here, but he wasn't. Through the haze of smoke and bodies, I could see Catarina and The Scott smooching at the bar. Gunther and Molly were still playing games with their food, Gunther biting at the air as Molly teased him with pieces of pizza. Golly and Alex had disappeared somewhere. The image of Golly making out with Alex was nauseating. Finishing my third (or was it my fourth?) drink, I ordered another. The beverage was just the right mixture of sweet and sour; the toxicity bordering on flammable.

Glancing across the oily inlet at several Bertrams and a sailboat lined up along the dock by the shore, I gazed for a while at the flames of the tiki torches illuminating it all. Then a man came into view. He was walking toward the sailboat, then walked onto it. I watched him take a bottle out of a box on the deck. Standing at the stern of the boat, he lit a cigarette and stood, sipping his beverage. We made eye contact. Blond, he looked to be in decent shape and around my age. He waved at me. I waved back. He then waved for me to come over, but I shook my head, no.

A man standing next to me interrupted my exchange with the blond by introducing himself as Rubin. He sat down at my table without asking. Bald with a pug nose, he owned one of the Bertrams, along with a sesame seed farm in Chile. His friend Enrique joined us. Enrique had a patch over his eye and a mustache with a slice through the upper right half. The men were older, possibly sixty. Gray and weathered, they smoked cigars and drank Bourbon on the rocks with their pinkies extended, salaciously licking the booze off their lips with each sip. Rubin told me in English that he and Enrique were vacationing at the club, and that they planned to go fishing. "Would you like to join us?" he asked.

"No, thanks. I'm busy," I said. When another man came over, the men mumbled something to each other, shook my hand, and left. The man who'd shooed the men away introduced himself as the Minister of the Interior. I was about to tell him to go talk to The Scott because he was a criminal too, but he was called away by a thin brunette wearing lots of jewelry.

Having imbibed what seemed like a gallon of booze, I got up to go to the bathroom. It was then that I realized I'd overdone the drinking. Drunk but not wanting to look it, I re-buttoned my pants. The action caused me to sway, but that didn't deter me from picking up my replenished drink from the table. A roady, I thought. A sign by the hotel entrance had an arrow pointing down a wooden walkway that said, *Banos*.

Holding the railing, I wobbled down the walkway. My world was spinning, so I shut one eye. "Bad me," I mumbled to myself, thinking life was going to be hell with the kids tomorrow. I was mesmerized by the green Christmas lights wrapped around the pilings at the end of the dock and stared at them for a while. Feeling queasy, I was happy to see a water bubbler at the base of the steps going up to the bathroom. Before making the ascent, I stood by the bubbler filling and refilling a Dixie cup over and over again with water. The chatter and laughter from the party was dreamlike and made me want to throw up. Then another sound appeared, a low moan like someone was hurt and trying to speak but couldn't. Queasy more than having to piss, I dismissed both, thinking someone might need help. I took a right down the dock that went to the lagoon, the low, rhythmic groan acting like a string pulling me along.

Chapter 31

The Blond

The dock jetted out into the middle of the club's lagoon. With my drink in hand, I reached the end of the dock. Standing under a single light attached to a piling, I took in my surroundings. The scene was beautiful and eerie. The moaning, louder now, was coming from the shore across a small lagoon filled with soupy, green water that was illuminated by the piling light. The light had attracted small and big fish, swishing around trying to eat water bugs. Then, life suddenly grew dark. A cloud had moved across the moon, and it began to rain, light sprinkles that thickened, then disappeared.

I concentrated again on the moaning sound. Since I was behind the club, the forest surrounding the cove was black, with only a few shiny leaves flickering in the moonlight. A thick white line glistened down the middle of the river. I forgot why I was there and watched the clouds float away, and the rain stopped. The moaning which had grown louder reminded me that I was there to help save someone. The shore had a burnished, ashen color to it, and as my eyes separated shadows from light, I could see a strip of land across from me, gray where it met the dark river. "Hello!" I yelled, thinking I saw a movement. There was no response. There seemed to be two different moaning sounds, one high and one low. Squinting, I saw a couple of large white maggots slithering around on top of each other in the mud under a loping, demented-looking tree. I rubbed my eyes and blinked a few times; giant maggots seemed an impossibility, but then so did a giant hare sitting on the moon.

Then I grew disgusted and said, "Gross. Maggots." It was also disturbing to think that maggots moaned. Belching from my diaphragm, I grimaced. The queasiness that had been bothering me was now hitting my upper gut and edging toward my throat. I breathed in deep and tried to keep the food and booze down while still fixating on the slimy movements of the grubs. They were making sucking, muddy sounds coupled with low grunts. It was all fantastically weird. Then a maggot laughed. It was Jack. What the—?

Sitting down because of my weakening knees and gurgling stomach, I made out Jack's pointy nose bobbing up and down. His legs erect, his feet leveraged against a rock, he was pounding down hard on the maggot under him—whose legs were flapping in the air. I had been wondering where they had gone off to. Yup, sex addicts, I thought, and chuckled.

Then, it just happened. I threw up. My dinner came out like a blasting firehose. My entire meal was hurling itself into the river with such force that I had to hold on to the clapboards to avoid falling in. On my knees in the child's pose, staring down at the fish, blurry-eyed, gasping for air, retching sounds echoing, I thought it would never end. When it briefly subsided, it was my turn to moan. I wiped my runny nose and gooey mouth, only to fall forward and vomit the last of the pink froth into the greedy mouths of the fish. "Dear God!" I said to the sky and laid down on my back, the cup of punch upright and full by my head. I closed my eyes and went to sleep.

"*Estás bien?*"

Confused, I snapped my eyes open. A man was staring down at

me, just a few feet from my face, nose exaggerated, his cheeks pushing his mouth into a puckered circle. I looked him over. It was the blond fellow with the sailboat who I'd waved to earlier. He was lithe, tan, and wore cargo shorts that fit him well. "Thanks, I'm fine," I said, shutting my eyes again and willing him to go away.

"Are there people over there?" he asked. I opened my eyes again and saw he was standing upright with his nose in the air. He was looking at the beach.

"Maggots," I said and sat up, my head throbbing. Thirsty, I took a sip of my drink. The fresh fruity flavor had a replenishing effect and washed away the hideous taste I had in my mouth.

Glancing at the blond man, I watched his expression as he tried to make out what was going on in the mud. He chuckled, "That's not very sanitary."

I laughed, which hurt my head, so I stopped and the pain subsided.

"Spank me again! Harder!" It was Jack's voice. A resounding slap, then another—slap-slap-slap.

"That's new," I commented.

The blond gave me a hand to help me up, and I took it. I was better, much better, but possibly still a little drunk.

"You do realize feeding the wildlife isn't a good idea," he teased, looking down at the water.

"Funny... American?" I could tell my words weren't coming out as smoothly as I wished.

"Canadian—Halifax."

"Nev—never been. I was on my way to the bath—room," I said, picking a thread of hair off my clammy, damp face. I smelled like liquor and soaked garbage, and wondered if I would throw up again, but then thought not.

"The club dumps their sewage in this lagoon," he said.

"That's *gross*," I replied, and stared at the murky water.

He waved his hand for me to follow him, but his steps were too long and energetic for me. He stopped and waited. "Maybe you should leave the drink?" he suggested. I took a sip and poured the rest into the water.

"I'll carry you." Before I could protest, he walked over and picked me up. I didn't mind. I was very tired and wanted to go back to sleep. I even rested my head on his shoulder. He smelled of cigarettes, camphor, and salty sweat. Not a combination I would have thought calming, but it was.

"Raspberries? I detect oranges and pineapples too."

"You forgot rum." I chuckled.

"I'm Dorian. Dorian Titlemen. And you are?"

"Eleanor. Elle... an... or."

"Eleanor, Elle... anor?"

"Eleanor."

"So, your first and last are the same?"

"No, Eleanor Abernathy, from Boston." I needed water, and badly. I let him carry me down the dock to the bubbler, where we stopped. I drank half the container. When I finished, he picked me back up, which I found funny because I was now perfectly capable of walking. He continued to carry me up the steep ascent. It was made of uneven rocks, which he stepped up with ease. Once at the bathroom, he gently put me down and said, "I'll wait for you."

"No. I'll be fine," I said, then added, "Thank you for your help."

"My pleasure. All right, Eleanor Abernathy. Come see me afterward. I'll be on my sailboat." He pointed to his boat and paused for me to maybe comment on its size or something like that, but I said nothing, so he turned and made his way down the steps. I found sailboats beautiful to look at, but I could take or leave sailing; the seating was always uncomfortable and the going slow.

The water I'd drunk made me feel much better and nearly sober. The women's bathroom doors had a picture of a chicken. Its breasts were exaggerated and held up by a lacy brassiere, and the men's room doors featured a rooster wearing a cowboy hat; it seemed tacky for such a fancy place. When I flipped the light on in the women's room, several geckos ran for cover; a cockroach was crawling up the wall by a cobalt blue sink. The light was a dim single bulb hanging from a wire directly over my head. It looked as though it may at one time have been encased in a decorative lamp, but someone had helped themselves to it. The shellacked tile floor was swept clean, and to my delight there was a toilet seat and toilet paper. The hand soap was in a bottle labeled "chamomile-citrus." I picked it up and smelled it. Delightful.

Sitting down on the toilet, I luxuriated in the seat's thoughtful curves long enough to create dents in my thighs. When finished, I splashed around in the sink and washed my face, armpits, and legs. Luckily, I was able to scrub the pink splatters out of Catarina's blouse. There were paper hand towels piled up on a little table that also had a bottle of jasmine-scented lotion. I couldn't stop smelling the lotion and was tempted to take it but didn't. I used more than half of it on my face, neck, arms, and legs, then immediately regretted my overindulgence because the bugs seemed to be attracted to the scent too. I doused myself again with water, splashing around, and wiped off as much of the lotion as I could. Then, I once again dried off with the paper hand towels, using them all up. Feeling refreshed, I walked out, sat down on the steps, leaned into the wall, and took a nap.

When I awoke, a breeze was lapping my face; it felt like the fur of a soft puppy. I was feeling exceptionally well for losing my dinner. In fact, I felt terrific, refreshed. The earlier mayhem seemed to have scattered somewhere into the night, and I sensed the party was over. Melodious ranchero music played from the restaurant as I walked back down the hill—the words to the song, *"Your love is bursting in my veins,"* or something to that effect. I hummed and sang along.

At the bottom of the steps, I glanced over toward Dorian's boat and saw he had a light on in his cabin, and he was standing next to a flickering tiki torch, smoking a cigarette. He waved. I waved back but immediately regretted it as he started to move down the dock toward me. I knew he wanted something from me, which I had no desire to give. He had a pleasant, almost beautiful face, like one of those Roman statues in a museum, only with eyes that moved, and he was bronzed from the sun. I'd been traveling long enough to know northern girls from the Western Hemisphere were rare and hard to grab hold of in these parts. Here, I was a novelty; nothing more, nothing less. I didn't take his persistence and advances as a monumental compliment. Yet, if I wasn't so hung up on Harry, I might have found him "yummy."

"Can I buy you a drink?" he asked, his voice smooth and direct.

"No, but you've been sweet." My words sounded stupid, canned. If he'd said them to me, I'd know he was just playing me. I thanked him again and went to leave. He touched my arm, then held it. His hands were rough and firm but gentle. I affably removed his hand. "Bye, Dorian from Halifax."

He took a drag from his cigarette and blew a straight line of smoke into the air. I could tell he was annoyed, but that was his issue, not mine. As I walked down the ramp to the restaurant, I felt his eyes following me. I had a feeling I would hear from him again. I hadn't mentioned the orphanage, but he seemed like the type of guy who would figure it out.

The restaurant had cleared out. The bar seats were empty, and the table occupants had thinned down to only a passed-out drunk and a man and woman, probably yachters, talking closely at a corner table. There was a faded, relaxed hue to the restaurant's emptiness. Dumbfounded about how I was going to get back to the orphanage, I went over to the bar and sat down on a stool. I asked the bartender when the party had ended. He told me an hour ago. His name was Max. Max poured me a gin and tonic with lime and placed a bowl of chips on the counter.

"I don't suppose there are any water taxis at this hour?" I asked.

"Where have you been?" a voice boomed from the river entrance to the restaurant.

"Harry," I said, beaming. It was on the tip of my tongue to tell him he'd just made my night, but instead I said, "How unexpected."

He walked over and sat down next to me, a scowl on his face. Grabbing hold of my shoulders, he tenderly turned me toward him and looked into my eyes and over my face as if to make sure I was all right. "You had the whole place looking for you," he said.

"Who's everyone, Harry?" I asked, thrilled he'd been worried, then added, "I have a feeling all my peeps were too drunk to know I wasn't present."

He smelled like cigars and whiskey. I wanted to kiss him and give him a great big hug, but instead I sat staring back at him sheepishly as he scolded, "Going off without telling people—well, you had us. Golly was beside herself. She thought the fish ate you."

I laughed lightly, then leaned in toward him and said, "You must have arrived late."

He had on a button-down white shirt, which he had rolled up at the sleeves and untucked from his dark-green cargo pants. He looked lovely. Unable to resist touching him, I pushed his hair away from his face and studied his forehead. "It doesn't look good. How do you feel?" His bump had turned an ugly purple, and the gash had grown a black scab.

"Fine. I forget it's there unless I rub my head."

"How come you arrived so late?" I asked, nudging his wet sneakers. "Your feet are sopping wet. Splashing in water again?"

This made him laugh; then he cleared his throat and said, "I was sitting in the dinghy out on the dock. I was going to leave, but then I heard your voice and stumbled a little trying to get out."

His words made me smile. Not knowing how to respond because I found it adorable that I had made him stumble—and it wouldn't have been a nice thing to brag about—I remained silent, staring at his face and letting him talk.

"I arrived late to avoid a government official," he said, and asked Max for a neat whiskey.

"I think I met your government official. Minister of the Interior."

"Yeah, crooked as the day is long." Max delivered his drink, and Harry gulped half of it down. He then turned toward me, his eyes reflecting the bar lights. "Okay, your turn. Explain yourself."

"Bathroom."

"What?"

"I took a nap on the steps."

He smiled, "A nap? Uh." And touched my cheek letting his hand linger for a few moments. I wanted to put it back on my cheek but thought *not*. He seemed in good spirits and told a funny story about his day. He'd had lunch with a fellow from Chile and another man whose glass eye fell out on the floor when he took his eyepatch off to rub his brow, causing a ruckus in the restaurant. "Scared the staff stiff." Before I could tell Harry, I had met Rubin and Enrique earlier, Harry said, "It seems everything is coming to an end."

The phrase hit me wrong. It didn't sound right; it had no future. "What does that mean? Coming to an end?" I asked.

"I don't know," he said, and cupped his hand to my cheek, looked me in the eye, and let go. "I don't know," he repeated.

I didn't want to be too serious because I felt that would be a terrible way to be on our first time away from the orphanage together. Besides, if I got too sad about him going away, which I wasn't too sure he was, I might cry, so I nudged his knee with mine and told him a few stories of my own, such as Hamit not wanting to teach anymore, and Molly and Gunther's food teasing.

Harry didn't think Hamit was serious, and as for Molly and Gunther, he was glad he missed the show.

Max, who had been putting glassware and condiments away, now leaned against the back wall of the bar with his arms folded and looked like he wanted to go home.

"We should get going," Harry said.

"I gather we're taking your dinghy?" I asked, then turned toward Max. I asked him for two bottles of water and a bag of chips to go.

"Yeah, The Scott's skiff."

Hearing The Scott's name, I drummed the counter with my left index finger, wondering if I should say anything. It had been wonderful sitting at the bar with Harry, and I had no desire to ruin the rest of the evening by bringing up an uncomfortable situation. It was already bad enough that he had a fiancé. As it went, morality wasn't on my side, and as for Harry, I wasn't sure if it ever had been. But then, because I couldn't help myself I said, "Dan Scotchwick. The Scott. I just don't get your relationship."

"I know, you've mentioned it before." Harry shifted in his seat and looked at me with that peculiar way he had when trying to read my mind. Away from the light, his eyes were the color of the ocean on a cold winter's day, growing darker. "We shouldn't talk about him here," he said, finishing his drink, but then added in a whisper, "I've told you, I don't like the man. In fact, I hate him. The whole issue is complicated on so many levels that—" He stopped talking and stared at his empty drink. It wasn't like Harry to say he hated anything. He then sat up straight and snapped out of whatever had overcome him. Smiling, he leaned over and pulled a clump of something indescribable from my hair while saying, "What's this? Why do you smell like raspberries and jasmine, or is it chamomile?" Getting up, he tossed the gooey pink clump into the water, then walked back and sat down again. The abrupt movement jarred the locket he had hidden in his shirt to appear.

"Don't know what that was—pizza, possibly," I said, then changed the subject. "What's in the locket?"

"My parents."

"How precious." I was glad he didn't say *fiancé*.

He showed me their picture. A handsome couple. He looked like his father but had his mother's eyes.

"Shall we go?" he asked and touched my arm.

When we stood up to leave, he looked me up and down. "You're all wet, but you look different. You bought clothes."

"Borrowed."

This made him laugh. He then pulled my broken flip-flops from his back pocket. "They were on the dock. I thought you might have swum back to the orphanage."

He handed the flip-flops to Max, and Max threw them out. I was going to protest, but then fixing flip-flops was most likely impossible.

My mood upbeat, a wave of giddiness filled my throat and heart because what fun it was to be with Harry. Tossing a water bottle over to him, I unscrewed the top of another and drank a hefty swig and joined him.

Chapter 32

The River

Its diminutive size made it look more like a child's toy than a practical, usable boat. The motor looked weak; a tiny turtle's head stuck to a stick. Harry's broadness and height dwarfed it even more.

Hesitant to get in, I untied the boat and stood on the dock with the line in my hand and wondered out loud if it would be better to stay the night at the club, but Harry wouldn't hear of it. He pulled on the engine cord. With each pull, the boat violently rocked. When the engine started, it made putt-putt noises, and oily smoke roiled up into a noxious cloud behind Harry's head. It was a pathetic display of bluster, like a sick dog having a fit.

"Come on, get in," he said.

What the hell, I thought. If Harry made it here okay, we should be able to make it back to the orphanage. Sliding in, I kept my weight centered in the middle and sat down.

"Why are you facing me?" Harry asked as I settled in on the seat in front of him.

"It seemed like a good place to sit. We can talk this way," I said, pushing us away from the dock with an oar.

"I don't have any legroom."

"Well, I don't either. Move your legs left, and I'll go right." Instead, we weaved our legs together, our inner thighs touching each other's knees. It was cozy. The heat emerging from his body was comforting since the night air had chilled me, and I was damp from my soiree in the bathroom. The moon was blue and crisp, and I could see that the rabbit (or hare?) had curled into a ball with its eyes open. "What an eerie sight," I said.

"What? The moon?" Harry asked.

I was about to tell him about the hare-rabbit but thought better of it and looked to the left of his head and watched the club shut itself down. First, the lights above the tables went off; then the bar lights disappeared. The tiki torches were snuffed out, and the green Christmas lights gone. Only the lights at the end of each dock were left on. Dorian's cabin light was off. The Bertram that had been docked next to him was gone. Possibly Rubin's and Enrique's boat; maybe they'd gone fishing.

I looked up at the stars. "It's pretty out," I said.

Neither one of us talkative, we sat in silence as we wended our way across the vast river. The current tugged us north, a cinching pull, small waves lapping with eager jabs, as if the water was playing a game of tug-of-war with us. Harry diverged south toward the *peligroso* sign, so as not to overrun the beach.

"Jack and Sarah had sex on lagoon beach," I muttered to Harry, breaking our silence.

I told him how I had thought they were maggots. "White, slimy maggots acting like horny bunnies under the rays of the Rabbit Moon." My story made him laugh and laugh, a deep, light laugh that sounded like walking on silky sand. When he stopped laughing, we both remained quiet, listening to the gurgling, putt-putts of the engine. At one point, Harry knocked my right knee with his; our eyes met, then floated away again.

When we hit the middle of the river where the currents pulled the strongest, the boat began rearing up as eddies and churning waters batted its sides. I thought the worst of it was over because we were on the verge of cutting out into calmer waters, but then something large clunked into the side of the boat. I assumed it was a log, but Harry swore it was a "damn dead animal." Whatever it was made me lurch forward into Harry while letting out a muted yelp. Harry grabbed me with his free hand. Holding my waist while grasping the tiller with the other, he tried to keep on course. "Sit back down," he kept insisting. "Now!"

The stern was taking on water. Buckets of it. The gravity of the situation was dire. But my legs had fallen under his seat, and my knees were stuck. Twisting my body, trying to pull one leg out at a time, tipped the boat even more. The water damage was irreparable; the tiny craft had become swamped, and we floated out. Treading water above the dinghy, we watched, stupefied, as it disappeared into blackness.

We then shot a concerned glance at each other. The situation was dicey, as the current's overpowering strength had our bodies floating and bouncing north. Yet when our eyes met, we each gave a comical smirk. I'm not sure why we found it funny. Maybe we thought it was all silly and stupid, because how pathetic to have sunk the boat.

"Can you swim well?" Harry said, reaching over and tugging my arm.

"Yes, Harry, I can swim well." I'd been swimming all my life. I competed in high school. Nothing fantastic, but good enough.

We swam toward the shore using the breaststroke. Harry stopped to kick off his sneakers and said something about them dragging him down. His feet free, we began again, this time swimming the crawl.

We swam across the current and not against it, and since we had been dumped on the south side of the orphanage's shore near the *peligroso* sign, by the time we broke through into placid waters, we were only off track by about a few feet to the north.

Angling back, we touched ground on the slimy, leaf-rotting river floor by the mangroves next to the schoolhouse. Then, with a little more effort, we lugged our exhausted bodies up onto the sandy orphanage's beach. We flopped down on the sand and giggled at our success, then lay in silence for a while to catch our breath, along with being amazed that we made it (or at least, I was). Looking up into the sky, we listened to the roll of the small waves upon the shore. I stared at the stars and watched a few blinking as though an SOS signal; yet the Milky Way a swath of glorious colors, its beauty of it mesmerizing. But once the chilled night air ate through the sweat of exhaustion, I began to shiver. Harry reached over and put his arm around me and hugged me against him, his chin resting on the top of my head. For a few brief seconds, I thought there was no better feeling in the world.

"I'm famished," he said, and squeezed me closer.

"I can't believe the boat sank," I replied and pressed my face into his chest, his dampness giving off a steamy warmth.

He sucked in some air and blew it out. "I know." He then seemed to have a burst of energy and sat up. "Meet me in the bathroom. I'm going to go get our towels. And an apple. I think I have an apple. Banana, too, and an orange—which would you like?"

As my mindset was always a little off-balance around Harry, I thought asking for the banana would be too presumptuous, so I said, "Apple."

"Apple it is." He took off up the hill.

I stayed put a few moments, breathing and missing his body and feeling giddy and happy to be alive. Then I jumped up and ran up the hill to the *dormitorio* as though I were in a race, a race with myself to the unknown.

Chapter 33

The Shower

The *dormitorio* was quiet except for a few grumblings from the children in their cribs. The two laundry ladies were asleep on the floor, huddled together like pudgy balls of colorful cloth and loosely bound hair, children's books scattered by their sides. I tiptoed carefully into the bathroom. Harry was by the sink, naked except for a towel wrapped around his waist. He was eating a freshly peeled orange and handed me an apple. The overhead light was off, and my flashlight was on and resting on the top of the middle shower stall, pointing up and giving the room a soft, yellow hue instead of its usual gray, fuzzy haze. Shadows dark and light molded our bodies, presenting an intangible yet romantic aura. We stood together eating for a while, munching, and looked at the floor with an occasional glance toward each other. Harry had brought water, too, which we drank.

It was awkward to have him with me in the bathroom with us both about to take a shower. I'd never felt shy around him before, or for that matter, around anyone at the orphanage. Out of place, at times. Definitely, questionable parenting skills and poor word choices, but never shy like I did standing there with him. I found myself second-guessing not only my movements but my thoughts. I couldn't decide if I should just whip my clothes off in front of him and get into the shower or wait for him to get into the shower first. He didn't seem to be in any rush. I then decided it was better to clean the sand off myself and my clothes, along with the river from my body (although the shower water was river water) than be bashful. Picking up the generic minty soap he had brought, I walked to the farthest shower from the door, turned the water on, and got in with my clothes on. It was perfect; I was washing my clothes and myself at the same time. First, I took my blouse off and scrubbed it, then my bra, pants, etcetera.

Harry got into the shower next to me. He turned the water on and began humming a light, fanciful tune. There it was, settled. Nothing but good friends. I felt relieved and disappointed at the same time.

Then Harry stopped humming to say, "Can you hand me the soap?" He was looking over the stall at me. He was tall enough that his eyes were several inches above the rim. I didn't think it was very good of him to be standing there staring at me with only my underpants on.

"Why do you have your underwear on?" he asked.

"I'm washing my clothes. I haven't gotten to the underwear yet."

I handed him the soap, then took my underwear off and threw them on top of the rest of the wet clothes. Harry kept humming his merry tune, then stopped and asked, "Could you wash my back? I can never reach my back, and I think it must need cleaning very badly."

His request gave me pause at first because I knew it would be a dangerous presumption on his part to think I could just wash his back, without any other type of hanky-panky going on. But then I thought, *Of course I can behave*, and walked over to his stall. I took the soap out of his hand and stood behind him and made small, foamy circles all over his very firm, strong back. "Harry," I said. "You have two moles along your vertebrae and another below your left shoulder. Have you ever had them checked out?" With my fingers, I made circles from one small mole to the next one.

"Moles? Let's see what's on your back." I turned around, and he inspected my back by taking his fingers and drawing lines across my shoulder blades and above my bottom. "I see bathing suit marks. One across your rib cage and the other just above—"

I muffled a laugh so as not to wake the laundry ladies. I turned back around and leaned against the stall wall and faced him. The water was splashing off his shoulders and in between us. It made me feel weak in the knees and petulant and confused. His handsome face, his hair wet all slicked back and slightly sudsy, brought on a profound seriousness that he seemed to feel too. The coloring in his face was flushed, his eyes dazzled with a subtle torment of some sort. I'd seen that look on his face before when we laughed too hard over a joke, or had the same sentiments about a peculiar idea, or when we touched each other by accident because I had grabbed a card he wanted, or when he was going left and I was going right, when in actuality we were going the same way.

This seriousness that had come over us struck a note in me that was both fearful and rhapsodic. I had a great urge to cry, but not because I was sad. It seemed all my pent-up desires for him had become unhinged. Gone without even a whisper. The present world surrounding us, empty. It was just Harry and me, and no one else existed. We stared at each other. The water cascaded down upon us; a waterfall and the sound of rain. Then Harry reached over and put his hand on my cheek. The barrier splintered, he bent down, I moved forward, and we kissed. His lips were gentle, soft, and wet, and he tasted like fruit and whiskey and sweet water. Our arms around each other, our lips roamed. I kissed his ears, his cheeks, his neck.

He lifted me up, and I wrapped my legs around his waist, the cold, smooth tile at my back, the heat of his chest enveloping me. We hit a symbiotic note, and for a few abandoned moments, we were both rendered unearthly and bound only to each other.

Then something went wrong.

There was a squawking sound like a crazed bird stuck inside the room. Wherever it was, it was very, very angry.

"Ehebrecher! Ehebrecher!"

The noise grew louder until it was in the shower with us. Pulling away from Harry's lips, I looked to the right of his head. My vision was blurred by the dancing water on his back, my body still rhythmically heaving up and down. Blinking, I opened only my right eye to see Alex's angry face twisted into a snarl, barely a foot away. He was shaking his fist. I winked at him and went back to kissing Harry. Then I panicked at my audacity and dropped to the shower floor. Harry let out a groan.

Alex was yelling all sorts of stuff in German. It made everything seem like a mad dream. But it wasn't a dream. I was awake and Harry was standing in front of me, his wonderful taste still on my lips. I kept catching the word *Schlampe*. Most likely something very derogatory.

"Go away, Alex," Harry said. Then he looked back at me. He had a distant, frozen expression on his face, his olive skin, off-white. He then looked up at the ceiling and bit his lower lip, as though cursing the gods. Alex had moved over to the toilet area. He then came back over and again yelled, *"Schlampe!"* and ran out of the room. His bare feet slapped against the cement floor, and the screen door slammed shut, shaking the foundation.

"Where's he going?" I said, my voice raspy.

The water, still splattering down on our quieted bodies, seemed cold and pointless. The deadweight of fatigue gripped us like a heavy, waterlogged blanket. And to make matters even worse, our morning wake-up song had begun blasting its pushy, demanding words *"Muévelo—Bebé."*

Flashing panicked looks at each other, we grabbed our towels and swiftly made our way through the kid's dressing room to the stairway. The laundry ladies were up and patting down their skirts. They said, *"Buenas."* We nodded back.

Molly and Gunther were on their way down the stairs as we were going up. Sleepy and entangled in their need to study their footing, they both mumbled, "Good morning." I had left my clothes and flashlight in the bathroom. A feeling of dread seeped into my mind. It was a botched crime with irrefutable evidence left behind. Then came the awareness of there being no return; life as I had known it had changed. It wasn't remorse I felt, but I did almost prefer the unobtained prize than losing a friend to the insanity of sex. But what was done, was done. My steps became small, and I fell behind. Why rush? Harry didn't seem to notice as he plowed into the room with his beautiful body and strutting confidence. His inner pool of mystical strength produced in me a sudden weakness and the uncertainty of doubt.

When I reached the room, I walked in and shut the door. Harry had turned the overhead light on and was standing in the middle of the room with his towel still wrapped around his waist. His hands were on his hips, his head tilted sideways, his eyes dark and unreadable. My hair felt wet and heavy on my shoulders. I pushed it back and met his stare and smiled. Letting go of the apprehension of losing myself to another, I stifled the need to laugh. I was giddy. Giddy with my life. Nothing mattered but this moment—and at this moment, life was perfect.

Harry threw me the same comical smirk he expressed when the tiny toy boat had sunk. With my eyes attached to his, I turned the light off and made my way over to him in the dark. Tripping on his toes, I wrapped my arms around his waist. We crawled under the mosquito netting of his king-size bed. The rubber squeaking, we moved to the floor.

Chapter 34

The Aftermath

That morning, I helped with washing the kids, but arrived late. It didn't seem to matter, since everyone (that is, the adults), except for Alex (who wasn't present), were too out of it to notice. No one was smiling. Their expressions were flat and cadaverous from too much booze and not enough sleep. But we had a routine to follow, which we did, quietly and with some embarrassment. No one spoke. No one knew what the other might have seen. Catarina handed me my clothes with an expression on her face that said, "Is there something you need to tell me?"

Golly mentioned the Rabbit Moon at snack time, which reminded us that the craziness of the night was the "Rabbit's fault." This casting off of blame helped all our spirits, and by dinner we were joking about the night, light-hearted and at times spilling over with laughter.

As the days rolled on, it was apparent that the fallout from the party had some residual effects. Molly and Gunther had become an item, an annoyingly loving item. Gunther nicknamed Molly "Minnie;" when scolding, "Minnie Mouse;" and sometimes just, "Mouse", which confused our littlest Mouse. Molly called Gunther "Gunthy" and occasionally, while licking her lips, "Gun Boy." When sitting with them during meals and playtime, I found their references to wedding plans to be "flapdoodle," to use one of Hamit's words; Hamit had returned. Gunther and Molly wanted a black-tie affair on the cliffs of Cornwall, a tent with flowers strung from the ceiling, Queen Elizabeth and "stodgy" Philip as guests (even though they didn't know them), and the food to be an extravaganza of New England lobsters, oysters, and beef Wellington for those with seafood allergies. They were to leave in a carriage drawn by four white Clydesdales. Their children were to be named Fionnula and Primrose, if daughters, and if sons, Tiberius and Ptolemy. Gunther had become unrecognizable. He had been swallowed whole. He went from being a blustering thespian who found comical fault in everything, to become a spat-out a "gooey-eyed, harlequin ninny" (Hamit's words again). Hamit, who had adamantly declared he wasn't returning to the orphanage, did so after spending three days at the club, bringing his new gal with him. She helped him out in the classroom. They never left each other's side. She even helped him with his news briefs in the morning. She claimed to be clairvoyant.

I missed Gunther's friendship, and Golly missed Molly's. Molly and Gunther were never apart, and Golly, having chosen to hang around with them, had become the third wheel—melancholy, glum, and lost.

Jack and Sarah had to have all sorts of painful shots due to developing a prickly rash on their genitals and strange oozing abscesses on their lips and thighs. They also were abstaining from sex because of other ailments that they kept hushed. Flummoxed and tetchy over the situation, Jack became extra bent and pointy. He had taken up a constipated gait and snapped at clothing not folded with neat corners, shoes that weren't perfectly aligned, and children remaining in the shower seconds too long. It wasn't until Catarina started feeding him cigarettes and thimbles of rum with his morning, lunch, and evening rice and beans that his mood became airy and jaunty again. The liquor's cheery effects caused Jack to come up with a new chapter for his dissertation: "The Dangers of Boredom." Through tiny sips of rum, he downgraded his chapter on "Routine and Consistency" by adding a subtitle: "Too Much of a Good Thing Smacks of Hell," and emphasized the dangers of monotony when raising children. He then punctuated his new chapter with an addendum titled, "Kids Kill Your Sex Life."

"You mean contaminated mud." He had it all wrong. The kids had hardly 'killed' his sex drive or life. In fact, it hadn't been killed at all; just disabled. But it wasn't worth arguing my point of view. Jack, bleary-eyed but happy over finding a justification for his mud rolling with Sarah, could finally enjoy life again, even if blaming children was pretty lame. Sarah, on the other hand, had become more obsessed with bugs, if that was possible. She was convinced that as a couple, they were now incubating a cluster of sarcoptic itch scabies within the skin of their bodies, which caused her to assume the affect of a proud mother. I often caught her looking at her limbs lovingly.

And then there was Catarina. Before the party, Catarina had a lover who she was crazy about. As far as we all knew, her lover was crazy about her too (and a kidnapping murder.) Then it all fell apart that fateful Rabbit Moon night.

While Catarina and I stood on the dock having our evening cigarettes (Gunther preoccupied now) she told me what had taken place with The Scott and two other "unsavory fellows." She lamented, "We'd left the party. It's hard to know what time, I'd had too many of those punches, but, well, I think it was late. A man who owned a sesame seed plantation somewhere, I think it was Chile, was here on a fishing trip. He spent a long time talking to Scotty. When we left, the man took his big boat over to Scotty's boat to have a nightcap with us. Him and this other fellow who had a patch over his eye. But then they didn't want a nightcap. They wanted Scotty to come with them. He wouldn't go at first, then said he wanted to take his dinghy and would meet them in El Puente. The fellows laughed, then said sure, we'll motor alongside you. And he went. He got in his little boat and took off toward El

Puente. I tried to tell him to go in the morning, but he said business comes first, love." She paused here to take a long, pensive drag, then continued. "Hell, I was famished for sex and felt yummy inside, but then The Scott told the man, I think his name was Rubin, to drop me off at the orphanage dock. Scotty kept telling me, 'Business, business, business.' He gave me a big, juicy kiss goodbye. I stood on the dock for a while and watched that big boat roar off into the night with my love beside it in his little dinghy. It so late, I kept thinking. What could they possibly be doing in El Puente?" She bit her lower lip, stubbed her cigarette out and quickly lit another.

I wonder what those fellows would have wanted with him. Why did Harry have The Scott's dinghy? I kept my thoughts to myself. Then, gazing over the river, I said. "Hey, his sailboat's gone."

"Yup, gone." Catarina frowned. "He went away. Why? Didn't even say good-bye."

"Did you see him take off?"

"No. This afternoon I noticed it was gone."

Her pain made the lines around her mouth more prominent, and her fun-loving spirit to be sad. I was at a loss on how to cheer her up. I refrained from telling her she was lucky that he was out of her life, but then maybe I had him all wrong. Maybe he hadn't killed the kid. Maybe it was all lies by a muckraking newspaper. I gave her a hug and we went back up to the *dormitorio* to hang out with the kids. Walking up the hill she said, "Maybe he came back and brought his boat to El Puente. Or maybe he docked it at the club." This speculation seemed to cheer her up. "I have only two more weeks here," she said, which had us laughing because we both felt it was like two months.

We stopped walking. She lit another cigarette and stared out over the river. Puffing and blowing smoke all over our arms and legs, she said, "I'm looking forward to the Canadian spring air. I'll write a letter. If the salami shows up, will you give it to him?" Then she laughed while shedding a few tears. "You know, Harry warned me to stay away.

I just couldn't resist the surprise. Swimming over to his boat and all."

We both laughed, and then she smiled. "Let's keep in touch. Write to each other. Hey, if you're still here when I come back next year—won't that be fun?" Thinking a year ahead was too much of a leap forward, but I said, "Sure. Sounds like fun." Then, out of curiosity, I asked, "What did Harry say about The Scott?"

"That it wouldn't last long. He was right."

Before walking into the *dormitorio*, we both glanced up at the moon. A speck was missing from the left side, as it was in a waxing mode. Neither one of us saw a picture of a rabbit or hare, but possibly a human face when we squinted.

"What do you think? That Rabbit Moon is gone?" Catarina asked.

"Looks like it. But I think its' bad vibes last a month. We have to wait until the new moon."

"Shame."

Catarina checked the club and had Manolo check El Puente for The Scott's boat, but he wasn't in either place. As for me and Harry, Alex told everyone and anyone who would listen, including the kids (in German), about Harry's and my shower episode: "*Knallen—so eine schweinerei!*" No one actually cared because it was understood that no one had been on their best behavior that Rabbit Moon night.

I also found out through Golly that Alex had gone off that fateful morning to Doc's place. Since we didn't see him at breakfast, I assumed he'd stayed and eaten with Doc. Golly thought Alex had a crush on Doc, which upset her because she had a crush on Alex. "Life can be very miserable," she fretted, making yo-yo sounds.

Golly was my interpreter when it came to Alex. This was strange because she was the last person I'd consider a linguist. She liked to tell me what Alex was saying about me. Although we'd all doubted her abilities at first, she really could understand German. She had spent a summer as a nanny for a German couple in Wachtberg, North Rhine-Westphalia. I was surprised how well she understood the language with only three months of study under her belt. Her ability to speak was a different issue. Her English was nearly incomprehensible; her Spanish never had any r sounds nor t's. I often wondered if she was making up what Alex was saying, but it sounded like his vernacular. If I had to speak to him, which I tried desperately not to, he would reply back, "*Leck mich arsh*"—"Kiss my arse," Golly said—or, "*Geh-zum Teufel ficken mopse*,"—"Go to hell, boob!" she sagely translated. Luckily, the little kids didn't understand. The kitchen ladies laughed at Alex. Aapo, Cadmael, and Eadrich wondered why he was so agitated and shook their heads while giving Harry the thumbs-up.

With help from Golly, I learned to say, "*Sich verpissen, Alex!*" (Fuck off!)

As for Harry and I, we lived the way we always had lived together: staying up late, playing cards, and sipping rum, only I slept in Harry's bed now, not mine. Often at night, the fan whirring, the bugs slapping and picking at the screen, the air thick with humidity, rum, and fruit, during a hot game of Russian Bank our legs, arms, and torsos would become entwined, scattering the cards and matting them to our bodies. It was blissful.

Harry had also stopped bringing up his fiancé's name, Jacquelina, and I stopped mentioning her name too. I also knew Harry's fiancé couldn't have just disappeared. She was there in his head, but what had he done with her? I never asked, because I didn't want to know. The future wasn't spoken about. We were living in the moment. It was a perfect place to be with him. However, during the day, when walking the kids to school, splashing in the river, tossing the five- and six-year-olds over my shoulder into the deeper waters, helping Henrik and Raymond carry their plates of food, nudging the kids in and out of the showers, dressing, building forts, I would often gasp at the air for a brief moment over the reality that nothing lasts forever.

Chapter 35

The Sandcastle

A week and a half went by, according to Harry's watch, backed up by Molly's daily notches, when a day came around that was hotter than any other day we'd had since my arrival. The rains had begun to beat down on the ground every night. It created muddy messes everywhere. A stream now flowed around the washbasin behind the *dormitorio*. Once the sun took to baking the earth, the air became thick and heavy. By mid-afternoon, we felt waterlogged from just breathing.

Putting the discomfort of weather aside, on this incredibly hot day, Bernarda, Penelope, Charlotte, and I built a sandcastle on the beach. A light breeze made the beach the only place to be during the afternoon playtime. The sandcastle was a massive structure. We constructed it by pouring buckets of sand, on top of each other, one after another. This flurry of activity made a mound taller than the girls, which thrilled them to bits, and their determination to finish was admirable. We smoothed down the sides and created turrets, a moat, and a courtyard. We collected rocks, sticks, and pebbles, and made windows and doorways. Charlotte filled the moat up with water, and Bernarda helped. Albert came over for a while and placed yellow flowers all around the castle walls.

By late afternoon, we were still busy with the details: straightening out crooked edging, filling the interior with ants and beetles; Penelope found a worm, Bernarda a caterpillar, Charlotte a frog. The birds were singing, and the bright, languid sun had dipped west. It was around this time that I saw something lurking near us on the embankment, in the bushes. The visceral, uneasy sense that someone was there. Then suddenly, with only the warning of a breaking stick, Frankie rushed in. His stout body bundled and pitched, his limbs tight then straightening as he flew through the air, head arched as he landed flat on top of the castle. With limbs and legs, he scrambled the sand beneath him into an unrecognizable mess. It was a surprise attack. We were dumbfounded, briefly immobilized.

Shaking myself to move, I stumbled to get up and grab him. But it was Bernarda—my Chiclet-toothed, dimple-faced Bernarda—who got to him first. She grabbed the back of his shirt and flipped him around. She was strong, her anger mighty. She pounded punches into his face and kicked his stomach. I pulled her off, still swinging. She hit the empty air with vengeance; mouth gnarled and teeth bared, her body hot and tense. I gripped her in a basket hold, trying to calm her down. "Hush. It's okay. We can build another." She trembled and cried great sobs of frustration. It was then that Penelope picked up a big rock and threw it at Frankie, hitting the back of his head. It was the first and only time I heard a sound from Charlotte. She screamed.

Grabbing hold of the three girls, afraid they'd torture the boy further, I huddled them together on my lap, holding pieces of clothing and arms so they couldn't get away. Slumping into me, they gave up the struggle, wailing and mumbling, "*Malo, Frankie—malo.*"

Frankie lay on the ground, not moving or speaking. Eyes open, he looked dazed as he searched the trees and the sky. What was unusual was that he wasn't shedding a tear. His round face seemed calm. Golly and Eadrich, who were nearby, came running over. Golly took the girls; Eadrich picked up Frankie. Golly hugged each girl to her full breasts and cooed, "Pudd'n pies, me chocolate nuggets. Don' cry." Then scrunching her mouth up into her nose, she looked at the castle and Frankie, and said, "Barmy Frankie, dodgy sod."

The back of Frankie's head was red and wet with blood. Crawling from Eadrich's arms to mine, his body sweaty, his weight like lead, he was malleable and clung to my neck with his hands. I hugged him. The girls had punished him enough. Eadrich dabbed his wound with a bandana he had taken from his neck, then wrapped it tightly around Frankie's head. He looked like a ninja. For the first time, because he was such a troublemaker, I felt sad for him being an orphan with all his energy and no parents to coddle him.

The three of us quickly decided I should immediately take him to see Doc.

The pathway to the *clínica* was a long web of overhanging shrubs, branches, swampish puddles, and roots. It was laborious, carrying Frankie for the fifteen minutes or so it took to get down the path. I almost tripped a few times. The new footwear I'd bought in El Pueblito, a fake pair of Tevas, were helpful. Flip-flops would have been unmerciful.

As we broke out of the jungle, I saw that Doc's clinic was a combination of residence and hospital—a gray, wooden, three-room structure on the edge of the river shore where the land jetted out. The peninsula made a fold of swiftly running water that gushed around the spiked curve. The power of the water was in the air and underfoot. It gave me the feeling of being overpowered, crushed under its weight. It was an eerie, crazy feeling that made an unrealistic paranoia to creep up under my shoulder blades and up the back of my neck. Frankie seemed happy, yet I wished Alex had been around to take him. I still wasn't too keen on being around Doc, even though she had been apologetic at the party, but I hadn't seen her since.

Profusely sweating, I put Frankie down once we reached the door. For a kid with a bad bump on his head, he seemed frisky, desiring to run around. Stomping his feet like a bull about to take off, he made tough-guy, growly sounds and showed his teeth. I grabbed his hand. "Frankie, what's up?" I asked in Spanish. He said something about wanting to smash the ant mound over by a nearby tree stump. I picked him up again.

To the side of the front door was a sign painted in big black letters: "CLÍNICA." Attached to the right of the house on stilts was a screened-in porch. Above the door to the porch was a sign that said "ENTRADA." I opened the creaky screen door and walked in with Frankie and put him down on the floor. He hugged my legs, shyly looking around at the people. Sitting on the benches along the walls were indigenous women, men, and children. The stench of sour corn made my eyes water. It was too small and hot in the room, even if the windows were open. The people were quiet and solemn, stoically cradling their ailments. Their eyes displayed the reasons for their visit— red-rimmed, sunken, lifeless, speaking of pain and forsaken hopes, a silent listlessness. I found it hard to breathe, yet the birds were singing up a storm.

"Dah birds are singing their asses off today," Doc said, walking onto the porch from the interior of the house. Her aura beamed light and sunshine until she looked at me and darkened. "Oh, from the back, I thought you were someone different. A new volunteer. Why are you here?"

"I brought Frankie. He hurt his head." I stood motionless. Her dislike of me was odd. I had never spent much time with her, except that day that I helped and she'd pinched me.

Frankie went running over to Doc. She kneeled down and removed the bandana. "Nasty," Doc said. "What you do to yourself?"

A woman grunted, her skirt bunched up around her waist displaying bony knees. I turned and looked at her. She had a flat face with saggy, dark skin; she smiled. All her upper front teeth were missing. Poverty was raw in the room. I held her gaze for a moment before averting my eyes.

"Come on in," Doc said, waving for us to follow. We went into the examination room. It was basic, with a metal table covered with a green, plastic cushion. A large, white cabinet stood against the wall, the open doors exposing medicines and bandages. There was also a wooden school chair in a corner next to a large open window. Looking out the window, I could see the beginnings of a garden. Someone had half-built a large wooden frame and placed a mound of dirt beside it. The earth was rich and dark.

"Is that the garden Harry's building?" I asked.

There was a long pause before she answered. "Was building," she corrected, her voice distant, flat.

Doc seated Frankie on the table, his short, robust legs barely dangling over the edge. She then asked me to fetch the iodine and the butterfly Band-Aids from the cabinet. I did as I was told. When I gave her the stuff, she leaned forward and stepped on my right foot; this was exceptionally painful because Tevas are sandals. I flinched, but she didn't seem to notice or care.

"You stepped on my foot," I said, but she neither looked at me nor said anything back. She hugged Frankie to her breasts, and he nuzzled his little head into the solid plumpness of her flesh. I stood looking at her. The desire to leave was immense.

"Have you been well?" I said, thinking her malaria might be back, making her mean.

"Busy," she said.

Frankie nuzzled and pawed like a lecherous, minuscule old man at her chest. She didn't seem to mind. Her body was the shape of an upside-down violin, her glossy, coal-colored arms glistening as the sun sparkled through the palm fronds into the room. I wondered if Frankie truly knew what he was doing.

"He seems to like you," I said, wishing I had let Golly or Eadrich bring Frankie to the clinic. She turned and sneered at my remark, sheer hate embedded in her eyes. *What had I done?* I asked myself again while watching her use a penlight to peer into Frankie's pupils. "He doesn't have a concussion. What happened?"

I explained to her about the castle and the girls and the crazy violence that it had brought on. She sucked in air through her teeth and whistled. "My, my, Frankie, such a little pest you can be. Well, I'll clean the cut, and—why don't you have a seat in the chair." Not wanting to anger her further, I sat down, although I didn't feel like sitting; I was jumpy and really wanted to leave.

"What's up with you?" I asked as I sat. She turned and walked over, leaving Frankie on the table, swinging his legs. Her height towered over me like an ogre observing its prey. Had she planned this, me sitting beneath her? Fed up with her nonsense, I sat back, relaxed, and gazed directly into her hooded stare. The blackness of her pupils, tense yet luminous in the indifferent afternoon sunlight; light that ebbed and flowed into the room through the lethargic fluttering of the foliage outside. Sweat trickled crookedly down my armpits and along my spine. I forced a smile. "So, what do I do with Frankie? Should he stay here, or should I take him back? And why do you dislike me so much?"

She ignored me and turned back to her patient to put a butterfly bandage on his wound, then placing him on the floor. Frankie touched the bandage on his head and looked over at me, then to the door. The door was shut, and I knew he wanted out. He was fine. Being sick didn't have any purpose for him. Doc, seeing what he wanted, opened the door, and he ran out. The kids in the waiting room stopped with whatever they were doing to look up. Doc walked out and said something to the sitting children in one of the indigenous languages. Then those who could jumped up and ran outside with Frankie to play. Doc walked back into the exam room.

"He'll be fine," she said, clearing her throat. "I want to keep an eye on him. Why don't you help me?"

"Really?" Shocked, I asked, "Where's Alex? I thought he'd be with you."

"He's shacking up with one of the laundry lady's daughters. Don't see him much."

"Must have just happened."

She laughed and threw me a wild-eyed look. "Lots of things just happen—right?"

I concluded she might be crazy. Hesitant to stay, I too looked at the door.

"Don' worry, I won't be nasty anymore," she said, smiling. So she was aware of her behavior. How strange.

Getting up, I looked out the window at Frankie playing. He was running around in circles with kids chasing him. "It's late, and I don't want to walk back in the dark."

"You got a good half-hour," she said and winked at me.

A middle-aged woman with thin shoulders and an extended belly was Doc's next patient; her face drooped, pulling her eyes and mouth down toward her neck. Under five feet tall, she sat on the table, dangling her legs, her skin dry and marred. She wore a tattered bib over her huipil and a thick, woven skirt. Her hair, like the rest of the women in the waiting room, was pulled back into a tight a bun. Doc listened to her lungs, examined her eyes, and looked into her mouth and throat, then stood straight and sighed. Turning to me, she said, "This woman is tired. She most likely is anemic and suffers from a poor diet. I will tell her to eat better and get some rest, but it won't do any good. Well, vitamins could help, but they may make her sick to her stomach if she isn't eating."

Then she spoke to the woman in an indigenous language. The woman nodded and got up. When she left, she said to both of us, "*Vaya con dios.*"

"I told her not to sell all her fruits and vegetables at the market for money. Keep some for herself. It won't help her family if she dies."

Several more patients came and went. Doc's ability to navigate the different languages was impressive. She spoke Mam, Q'eqchi, Spanish, Creole, Garifuna and deciphered the issues in English to me.

The last patient was a woman who looked more like a child than an adult, with large, inconsolable eyes that darted about when she spoke. She also kept scratching her arms and legs, which seemed more out of habit than need.

"She is ill because even though it didn't rain last month, water got in her house, taking her pots and pans away, but what she really means is that there wasn't enough food because her husband used his entire paycheck to get so stinking drunk he passed out, and then when he woke up, he beat her." Doc wiped her hands on her T-shirt, pausing before she continued. "They often speak in rhymes because the truth is too painful. It can also be dangerous. The laws here favor those who have money, and those that don't, well, they're often punished for complaining." Then she asked me to fetch an icepack from the cooler on the floor, saying something about the Club de Bote being a big donor.

I went over to the cooler and opened it. Several blue ice packs were piled on top of each other. "The club," Doc said, turning to look at me. "You know the club? The one we all went to. They donate a lot of medical supplies to me. The owners, the workers come here too for small stuff."

"The owners seem like nice people," I said, thinking I should get going because it was getting late. The sun was now directly level with the window.

"Nice enough," she said back. But Doc wasn't through lecturing me about the local population. It was annoying because it all seemed very condescending. She went on and on about stuff that was obvious—the war, the state of affairs in the country. "I know, I know," I said, then randomly added. "Aapo left recently to go back to his village to save them from the Rabbit Moon."

She laughed, folded her arms over her chest and stared at me. I wasn't sure what she wanted, so I waited. The silence was fatiguing; I'd missed my nap. I couldn't tell if it was the injustice that was aggravating her, or me—possibly both. Interrupting the silence, I said, "Okay. I'm going. If you need me to help again, I will." I turned to leave.

"Your Harry isn't a good man," she blurted out. "He's selling their land."

Is that what this was about? What had been bothering her? I thought, then said, "He's not mine."

Puzzled by her words, I leaned back against the wall and let my eyes roam up and down Doc's statuesque physique, and said, "I heard that the land he was dealing with belongs to Yena."

Fiddling with items in her cabinet, she remained silent. Listening to the kids shouting and laughing, I thought hard and long about the situation. Was I ignoring the bad acts of a man because I liked him? Catarina and The Scott came to mind, and I bit my thumb nail, then said, "I thought everyone was selling because of the oil company coming in?" I added.

She laughed. "What do you want from Harry?"

"I'm confused," I said, finding the question out of place. Then something occurred to me. An epiphany, like when I'd be playing Russian Bank and for several plays, I'd only been concentrating on one half of the game, when I should have been looking at all of it.

"Doc," I said.

"Yah?"

"What's your real name?"

"You don't know?"

"No, I don't."

"Jacquelina."

"*Que mierda*," I muttered, shaking my head in disbelief. Then anger swept over me. "Why didn't you tell me you are Harry's fiancé? I mean, the day I helped you with your rounds. When I told you Harry had a fiancé, you could have told me it was you."

"You knew I existed. Why should I tell you?" Her voice was haughty and cavalier, her eyes unblinking and mean.

"Because you want people to know...because you're happy." But then, maybe happiness wasn't the issue here. I added, "To be open and friendly." But that didn't seem to be it either. It was obvious their relationship had issues, if Harry was spending all his non-work time with me. I was about to ask her if she was still Harry's fiancé, but then she did something unnerving. She took a machete off a shelf and held it up over her head as though she were going to hit me with it. I know there are some rough and tough people out there that may have stood their ground, but I wasn't one of them. I was also disgusted by the situation; the secrecy and what I perceived to be high-school theatrics. I said flippantly, "You can have him," and walked out to fetch Frankie.

With Frankie in my arms, I stormed down the path to the orphanage. Her words *You knew I existed* kept running through my head. For what seemed like months, Harry's stories had been filled with her name. He loved her—*la amaba*. The Spanish verb "to love", when spoken in the past tense was always in the imperfect. An action with no definite beginning or end, because love didn't have definitive lines. With my stomach in my throat, my mind churning, I wished I'd never come to the orphanage—or if I had, instead of living with Harry, I'd cleaned the third floor and made it mine or tucked a hammock in the corner of the hammock room. I knew better. Hell, I'd had been chaste for a year, and then ignored my own advice. I was furious with myself, with Jacquelina, with Harry.

Chapter 35

Ants

Frankie immediately fell asleep in my arms. My long, aggressive strides over roots and muddy ditches caused me to stumble, but the jolts didn't affect his sleep. A few times when I tripped, I twirled and nearly fell into the soupy mangrove swamp that hemmed in the path. The ground snagged and tore at my feet, yet I was blind to physical pain. My emotions had spiraled into a muddled, confused mess and were like the clattering of a poorly tuned instrument in my head. The noise, the mayhem, all made me want to scream. When I mindlessly pushed a palm frond away, and it snapped back and hit me in the face, I stopped. It stung. The physical and the emotional had melded together. The slap was also a wake-up call that shut down the accusations toward others and myself, lifting the glaze of self-defense. It burned into my cheek a dismal shout of reality, bit at my ego, and triggered a descent into self-pity. I felt sad for myself. I loved Harry.

The jungle heat steamed around my head along with the whine of the beetles, the yapping of the birds, and the darkness slowly strangling the light. I coughed and broke into a sobbing mess. My tears dripped onto Frankie, and he briefly opened his eyes then shut them again. I stopped walking and took a deep, shuddering breath of the earthy forest air. To waste time brooding wasn't a good idea. The incoming night had made the pathway less visible and the jungle shadows deceptive. An eerie feeling of danger circled around us.

I shifted Frankie onto my other hip. He awoke and let out a light cry, then rolled his head back onto my shoulder to sleep. A twig cracked behind us. I jerked around, thinking Doc (or rather Jacquelina) may have followed us. I jerked my head around and gazed down the path toward the *clinica*. There didn't seem to be anything or anyone there, but then again, it was hard to see. Above, a bird fluttered leaves upon the ground. Another twig snapped. A chill flooded through my veins, and whatever thoughts I had of *love lost* were devoured by what might be lurking around us.

I took a step back to see the thicket more clearly. In the shadows about fifteen feet away, under a loping willow, was a silhouette of a howler monkey. In the gray light behind him, I could see he was upright and holding onto a branch. He was tall. His genitalia, long and pink between his legs; it dangled and swayed as he was moving one foot, then the next in a fixed march. His dark mane framed his large, black eyes, which gave him the appearance of being human. I stopped breathing. The boogeyman couldn't have been a more frightening sight. Grinning, his lipless mouth exposed yellow teeth. The birds that seemed to have quieted began to chatter again. I stayed still and kept my breathing low, not wanting to give him a reason to chase.

He shook the branch he was holding and appeared to be laughing. He then puffed up his chest and opened his mouth wide. The howl that came out was icy and deafening. My stomach tensed and knotted, and I whispered, "Please go away."

Then Frankie's eyes popped open, and he began to cry. "No... no...no," I said, fearing his crying would inflame the monkey even more. I hugged him tightly and shut my eyes, and whispered, "Shut your eyes, Frankie. Shut your eyes." The horrific sound stopped, and the wind of swift movements brushed my face. I opened my eyes to see the howler above us in a craggy tree, looking down. Then he took off. He swung from one branch to a vine and back to a branch. "He's flying away," I said in a low tone to Frankie. Taking a deep breath, I shifted him onto my other hip, and we resumed our trip back. I was exhausted mentally and physically. When I tripped over a root, this time I stumbled and dropped Frankie into a puddle of roots and mud and fell onto the ground. My hip and elbow fell hard against a root, but I was fine. Getting up, I looked for Frankie. He had crawled out of the puddle and was stomping around. He picked up a rock and threw it at me, hitting my knee. "Ouch!"

Frankie was wide awake. He went back to the muddy puddle, jumped in it, and made lots of slurpy, splashing noises as he kicked the water. I groaned at his behavior. To tell Frankie not to do something just made him want to do it more, but I told him to please stop anyway. He ignored me. Too exhausted to pluck him out of the mud, I sat down on a large, round log to rest and think.

With my chin in my hands and my elbows on my thighs, I pouted. I didn't want to break up with Harry. I loved the silly world we had created, but now it seemed ruined. I then began to imagine the conversation we would have when I got back. It didn't go well. It unfolded as a battle of who's right and who's wrong. Possibly I could just leave, I thought. Leave the orphanage and the whole mess behind. I had been wanting to check out the Bay Islands off of Honduras, and now was as good a time as any to do just that. I smiled at the idea. It was such a simple solution. The thought of doing something new seemed refreshing. I then imagined traveling around the Bay Islands and bumping into Harry because he had dumped Jacquelina after quickly realizing he loved me—like some Harlequin romance novel, I mused. Then I grew sullen. "Shut up, Eleanor," I said out loud to myself.

Looking over at Frankie, I saw he had uprooted a large rock, and with great strength he tossed it into swamp like water, then jumped into the muck after it clapping his hands. "Frankie, we need to go," I said. He crawled out of the soup, walked over to me, and leaned on my knees. I patted his back and said in Spanish, "Good boy." He smiled and climbed onto my lap and leaned back against my chest. He was wet and muddy and smelled like rot. A grackle whistled from afar, followed by a guttural, high-pitched honk. The sound spooked me at first, but I knew the sound. It was just a bird. "Just a bird," I repeated out loud.

I sat for a few more moments because it was already pitch black, and the rush to get back while light was gone; besides, confronting Harry wasn't something I wanted to do now. It seemed too final. Back to feeling sorry for myself, I gently rocked Frankie back and forth in my arms while taking deep breaths and sighing. But then I felt something crawling between my thighs and within the folds of my crotch. At first, I noted the sensation as just a tickle. Then something stung, then a hundred more stings and it became like an elastic band's continuous zap. I let Frankie slide to the ground and jumped up. The sensation of a small torch sizzling my flesh came to mind.

The biting prevalent and rapid, I looked at my limbs but in the dark I couldn't see a thing. But I could feel them with my hands and crushed them with my fingers. Ants were everywhere on my body. My arms and legs were covered in them. I yelped, swatted, and brushed them off, but there were too many. I rushed over to the side of the path and found a puddle. Splashing the foul water over my legs and arms, I then took my shorts off and used them to help me thrash at the ants, but they were fast and hid behind my knees and dug deep into my crotch. The only solution was to sit in the puddle and drown them.

The attack was over almost as fast as it had started. I stood up. Dripping wet, my crotch and thighs were searing, my fingers already swollen. I breathed deep and long, clenched my teeth, and then picked Frankie up, who had been ripping up leaves. I carefully put my shorts back on and stormed down the last five minutes of the blackened path to the compound, ignoring the fact that every inch of my body was aflame with pain. The light over the cafeteria was cluttered with bugs and moths. Everyone was in the dining hall eating. A low hum of laughter crusted the air.

"It's dinner time, Frankie," I said keeping my voice steady. I put him down and winced. The sting of my inner thighs felt like a peeled blister. Frankie wiggled away from my hands and ran across the spotty grass and dirt into the cafeteria. Alex, who was standing by one of the tables, saw him and called him over. He then picked up Frankie and examined his head. His inspection complete, Alex tweaked his chin and placed him back down. They walked over to the buffet together. It was a wonderful sight, a solid homecoming for the little guy. As for myself, I wasn't hungry. The only thing I wanted to do was lie down. As I made my way to the *dormitorio*, each step was agonizing. I felt all beaten up, physically, and spiritually. I was a mess.

When I limped in through the bedroom door, the light was on, and Harry was on his bed counting money. Piles of money. How apropos, I thought. He was wearing brown linen slacks, and his long legs were crossed and jutted out across the floor. His white shirt, unbuttoned, was flung open. His chest and smooth stomach were exposed; he only had a slight ripple where he slouched. He looked sexy, delicious, "yummy", and despite my throbbing, itching inner thighs and crotch, feverish haze, and my agitation about my situation, I thought of sex.

He glanced up, startled at first, and went to cover the piles of money with a towel that was on his bed, but then changed his mind and tossed the towel aside. What was the point? I supposed filling in what his mind with thinking. He again looked at me, this time with a great, big, welcoming smile that made me feel like I was the only person in the world who meant anything to him. I mistakenly smiled back, but then dropped the grin and frowned. I didn't think I should be friendly. Not because I was angry; I was in too much pain to be angry. I just wished the day hadn't happened. Again, I wished I'd never become his roommate. I wished I liked sleeping in hammocks.

Hobbling over to my bed, I said, "What is the verb 'to pretend' in Spanish?" My voice was raspy; my throat felt as though it was closing in on me.

"That's easy. It's *fingir*."

"Right." I was going someplace with the word but was too miserable to think.

"Give us a kiss."

"I can't," I groaned, flopping down on my bed. The mattress squeaked and bounced me up and down. "I wish I had some ice to sit on. Do you have any ice?" I asked, looking at the ceiling.

"Ice? No?"

I glanced at him. His lips were moving as he divided the money into stacks. He was hyper-focused but also seemed calm. But then, he was usually calm, even though his whole body was full of energy. He looked happy. It made me mad and sad at the same time to see him so happy. I looked away. The air in the room was dusty and hot, and my body was sweating and itched to the point of madness. My need to throw up was imminent, but it hurt too much to move.

"You know what the problem with only one temperature is?" I asked, choking down bile and wishing I had a gun. Not to shoot Harry with, but myself.

"No. What is it?" He looked up and stared at me. I stared back. His intense eyes were curious and full of expectation.

"There's no contrast. A person constantly feels the same temperature, and it becomes unnerving. Do you think it is something innate in humans that makes us unhappy when everything is the same? Do you think that's the way we ruin things?" The wooden rafters had several knots of various colors. I began to count how many knots I saw to distract my mind. I was also thinking if I had ice, I might live, but without ice, the desire wasn't there.

"Well, I don't think anything stays the same. With each minute, we get older and think differently."

"Maybe some people get older. I don't think it's a collective thing." Then, changing the subject because I couldn't seem to follow a thread, I asked, "The money? What's with the money?"

"What's wrong with your hands? They're red. And puffy. Did something bite you?"

"No. Maybe." I could no longer move without every fiber of my body twitching. "Are you stealing?"

"What are you talking about?" He put his money into the brown leather bag on the bed. "What's going on?" He put the last of the money into the bag and stood up, then began to button his shirt. An amoral character, I thought. I never would have fallen for him if I hadn't starved myself of sex, I bitterly fumed. I fell for a dissolute man because I had deprived myself of the joys of carnality for a year. "Never again am I going a year without sex," I said out loud to the ceiling. "Shame on me."

"What?" He fluffed his shirt, something we all often did to bring cooler air in; a scent of Old Spice blew my way. The scent of Harry, although he was sometimes minty too. "You haven't seen my locket, have you?" he asked.

"You keep asking me that. It's been gone for a while."

His shirt buttoned, he began to put his shoes on.

"Where are you going?"

"I'll be back later," he said, distracted.

To me, his remark was more depressing than anything else, because what did "later" mean? I watched in silence as he sat on his bed and put his leather shoes on. I then found myself leaning forward and vomiting up part of my lunch into a cup by my bed.

"Good grief," he said, grabbing a bowl he had been eating beans from. He handed me the bowl, took the cup, and placed it outside the door.

"Ants' nest. I sat on, I think, a red ants' nest," I said, coughing, my throat raw. The need to throw up again made it hard to say anything else.

He laughed. It irked me that he laughed, but then I would have laughed if he'd told me the same thing. It was a ridiculous thing to do. The stupidity of it made me chuckle, although it was painful and caused me to throw up again, this time into the bowl.

"I see you ate rice and beans again today." The joke wasn't funny. He crouched next to me and ran his eyes over my body. "This isn't good. Your neck is all swollen." His tone was concerned.

Harry gave me his full water bottle. I drank half of it. The tepid liquid was soothing. He then retrieved a jar of Tiger Balm from his dressing table. Unscrewing the top, he kneeled by my side and gently rubbed the balm onto my swollen hands, neck, thighs, legs, and arms. I watched him and wished he wasn't so caring. I wished he was being mean and evil to me, but he wasn't. His breath smelled sweet, and I realized he had been eating licorice, something he never ate when I was around. Catarina had been right; it was the one thing he truly didn't like to share. A few tears dripped from my eyes, which caused him to pause. He kissed my forehead and used the tail of his shirt to wipe my cheeks. His lips compassionate, the camphor soothing, I allowed myself a deep breath and gained control—only momentarily, because the tears kept flooding out. They dripped down the side of my head and into my ears and made me lightly shake.

Harry kissed my forehead again. "This isn't good. But the balm should help." He rubbed it on my arms and stomach. When the Tiger Balm jar was empty, he got up and threw it into the trash bin then, opened his toilet kit and brought out a bar of licorice. "Here," he said, "chew on this. It will help settle your stomach."

I smiled and tried to make a joke, "Sharing licor—" But I couldn't finish the sentence.

I touched my tongue to the candy but couldn't chew. The Tiger Balm was working. It countered the itch, almost nullifying it. My body immediately felt relief. My emotions, however, were convoluted, but somewhat rational. To me the issue wasn't that he had a fiancé because I knew that. It was more about her living next door, and Harry not mentioning it. It was a peculiar way to behave. If you loved someone and wanted to marry them, why was he sleeping with me and right in front of her. I needed clarity, but more than that, I was hoping he didn't love her anymore.

"I brought Frankie to see Jacquelina this afternoon," I said, staring at him. He was standing by his table, sifting through items, looking for more salve. "Don't you want to know how Jacquelina is?" I asked.

He turned around and looked at me. "How is she?" he said nonchalantly. He then stopped fiddling with the items and stared down at me. He looked puzzled, and all I could think was, *You've been caught.* He walked back over to me, picked up the throw-up bowl and placed it outside the room. He then put an empty cup from the side of his bed next to me. "The balm should make you feel better. I just wish I had more."

"Why didn't you tell me Doc is your fiancé?" I asked, nibbling on the licorice; the anise flavor had become pleasant, almost refreshing. He remained silent. Why wasn't he answering? "Why are you here with me and not at the *clínica*?"

Standing in the middle of the floor, his shoulders stooped, he cocked his head and met my gaze. He started to say something, but then stopped and looked off at the wall. I had put him on the spot. Not an ultimatum, just answers. Was it fair? Yes, of course, it was. I knew the reality of the situation, so why not be honest? Clearing his throat, he looked down at the floor and whispered, "I did at one time."

I needed to throw up again and picked up the cup and spit into it, then continued, my voice slowed by my constant swallows. "I thought your fiancé... lived in the city. But she has been here all along. It makes no sense to me... Please say something that makes sense."

His hands on his hips, his eyes searched the cracks on the floor, then the ceiling; his silence made me want to throw something at him. And then I felt childish. I second-guessed myself about what I had been saying, was my tantrum warranted? I also wanted to hate him but couldn't.

The dense, hot air had built up around my neck and ears, clogging them and making me shiver even more. I wanted to scream and kick my feet in frustration, but I had neither the strength nor stomach for such behavior. Instead I muttered, "I feel so awful. I just feel so awful."

He straightened and twisted sideways to look at me briefly. His eyes displayed thought and torment. Ruffling his hair, he pinched the tip of his nose. We could hear the group coming back from dinner. Jack was talking, but it was too hard to hear what he said. Then the tape was placed into the cassette player. The lyrics, loud and boisterous, seeped through the floorboards: '*The golden woman covered in saliva and stars, on the bedroom floor—*'

"I guess they're skipping the evening meeting," I said. It made me smile, thinking about how unproductive the meetings often were.

"Manolo is waiting for me," Harry spoke over the music. His words were cold and void of emotion. He went over to his bag of money, picked it up, and walked to the door. He was wearing shoes with leather soles that made *clip-clop* sounds. His sneakers had been lost that fateful night of lust.

"I'll let the others know about the ants. I'm sorry I have to leave, but it's urgent that I go tonight. You'll be okay." His expression was inflicted with worry, or was it? I was having a hard time reading him. Possibly his concerned appearance was nothing more than a furtive mask for his desire to leave. Yet he was twisting once again, stepping out, then back into the room. "When I get back tonight, I'll go over everything with you. I promise. It's not what you think." His voice was smooth but tinted with panic. His bag was slung over his shoulder, and he paused once more in the open space of the door. "I'm going to get you some more Tiger Balm. They sell it in El Pueblito." And then he was gone.

I wanted to shout for him to come back, but I couldn't shout. Instead, I lay prone on the raft listening to him *clip-clop* down the hall. Then the only sound left was the music and its lyrics: *'Staring straight into the abyss, naked moon bathed in sweat, climbing his body, never stop— please—'*

Chapter 37

Recuperating

I spent a good part of the following week in bed with a fever. It had been brought on by the insidious red ant poison. "Insoluble piperidine alkaloids," Sarah had explained. "Can be fatal. Anaphylactic reactions are tricky. You're lucky to be alive."

There had been grumblings among my fellow *niñeros* about getting Doc. I begged them not to, as I was convinced the only item in her doctor's bag would be the ominous machete. Sarah didn't push the matter. Being the in-house authority on insects, she gave me a handful of the local allergy medication, which made me sleep better and brought the swelling down. However, she felt the only way to assure my recovery was to make amends with the illness's creators. The screwball went down the *clínica*'s path to the red fire ant log and brought back a jar full of the nasty, venomous creatures. She brought them to my room mere days after my injury, when I was in the midst of having fits and turns, when delirious fetishes were causing me to see red, mean manatees in my room.

She put the jar of frantic ants, scaling the glass, in front of my face. I screamed, a gut-wrenching, soul-purging sound, and swatted at the air, thinking she was going to put them on me. Instead, she left the jar of ants by the door inside the room, suggesting, "When you're less hostile, tell the ants you're sorry for sitting on their house." She also gave me a lecture: "Ants are the backbone of the earth. Without them, we would starve, trees wouldn't grow, and disease would be rampant. They eat the dead and poop life-giving substances. Always watch where you sit and walk because you've probably already killed millions." Her tone was very accusatory and unforgiving.

Four days later, when I awoke, Golly was standing by my bed with a bowl of black bean soup and a packet of cards, along with a baby she introduced as Ptolemy. I asked her to remove the jar of red ants from my room. They were still over by the door, crawling on the glass and trying to get out. The lid was nothing more than a piece of paper tied with a string, escape was imminent, even if they had been there for days.

She did as I asked and left me with the soup and baby Ptolemy, saying, "He's a good baby. Won't cause you trouble."

He was round and chewed on his hands. Snot dripped down his nose, and the diaper he wore was a makeshift, ill-fitting sheet tied on with a strip of ripped, frayed cloth. I ate my soup and watched Ptolemy suck on his fingers. He seemed happy, kicking his legs out and giggling, but then he fell over. Putting the soup down, I reached out and picked the baby up because he had turtled and didn't seem to be able to right himself on his own. The movement made me dizzy. It was then that I noticed Ptolemy's diaper was wet, and he'd stained the floor. Crawling onto my knees, I stood up slowly. It was good to be up. My arms and legs were still swollen and red, and there were dark scabs where I'd scratched, but I was better. I could walk, and I didn't feel nauseous anymore.

I slowly crept over to Harry's side of the room and looked inside his clothing bag. I pulled out one of his T-shirts. It smelled like him, and I kept it up to my face for far too long. Walking back over to the baby, I took his diaper off and wrapped his bottom in Harry's T-shirt.

"He won't mind," I said.

Harry hadn't been back since he left that fateful day with his money. It was disturbing to think he had left me half-dead and hadn't returned to see if I was still alive. I figured Harry, the pseudo-Dutchman and greedy land shark, had taken his money and run. Where to? Probably his fake country, Holland. Yet no matter how angry or hurt I felt about his disappearance, I missed him.

"How's Ptolemy?" Golly said, coming back into the room. "Molly named him. We've got twelve of these little marshmallows now. We all gav'm names because they didn't have any." Molly went over to Harry's bed, pulled the top sheet off, and placed it on the floor to sit on.

"Where did the babies come from?" I asked.

"Rosario brought them two nights ago. In the middle of the night! A bit potty of her. Waffled on about us doing such a crack'n job with the kids, then left. They've messed our routine. Spend all our time looking after the babies now. The kids have stopped lining their shoes up and walk around all stroppy. We have no consistency anymore. It's all goo and random diapering."

"I gather Jack has a new chapter to add to his dissertation now."

"No, he says it's just fine the way it is."

I laughed, "The babies stumped him. Interesting."

I had Ptolemy up on the bed with me. When he smiled, his round cheeks made his brown, bright eyes disappear. I gave him a piece of mushed-up beans, which he ate, then spat back out, making his mouth black.

"We don't have any bottles or baby food. We've been smashing up the beans and rice and giv'n them milk in cups. More milk gets on their chests than inside their mouths. They poop a lot, so they're getting something inside them. We've started a nappy tally. Drew it on the wall. I've changed over one hundred nappies since they've arrived." Golly tossed me the packet of cards, bent down, and picked up Ptolemy. "I'm going to put a proper nappy on him; when I come back, let's have a go at Old Maid."

"Old Maid?"

"Eat your soup. I'll bring you some water when I return." She wiped the drool from Ptolemy's mouth. Sitting with little effort on her full hips, he leaned into her breasts. Before leaving, Golly glanced back at me and said, "Glad to see you sitting up. You look better. Not narky anymore."

"Thanks." I was better. Weak, but better. Once she shut the door, the room looked blue and dusty. A disquieting feeling of emptiness set in. I let my eyes roam over the walls and floor, thinking I didn't like the room anymore. Harry's bed still had the mosquito netting flipped up. The creases in the bottom sheets where he had been sitting were still there. His toothbrush, toothpaste, deodorant, hairbrush, and nail clippers, all untouched, like ancient statues in a grim landscape. It all made me feel lonely and sad. I shut my eyes. The kids playing in the great room echoed up through the craggy boards, along with the sound of babies mewling; one was outright crying. I fell asleep.

When Golly came back in, she had Ptolemy and another baby with her, along with balancing a cup of water. She handed me the cup and said, "This is Marley." Marley had a ribbon wrapped around her head, tied into a bow. Her shirt was too big, and someone had rolled up the sleeves. It was pink with Benetton written in alligator figures on the front.

"I named her," Golly smiled. "Marley's me auntie's name. I like me auntie." She placed both babies down on the floor, letting them crawl around. Picking up the deck of cards, she shuffled, then dealt. "Now sit up and keep those eyes open. And drink up," she said.

I did my best to look awake and toss my despair away. It was wonderful that she was bringing me food and water. The room that had grown melancholy while she was away, now full of life, and the babies were funny to watch; quiet but clever, they'd crawled over to the door and were trying to get out. Luckily, it was shut. Looking at my left hand and the scabs on my fingers, I asked, "Have you seen Harry?"

"No, but there's been a Harry sighting."

"Yeah, who saw him?" The news was uplifting, although I wasn't sure what I should do with it.

"Catarina saw him. She drove the workmen into town two days ago. I think she was looking for that Scotty fellow." Golly picked up a card and frowned. "I never win at this game. I need to win. Don't want to be an Old Maid."

"It's just a game," I said, amused that she took it so seriously.

"Catarina said Harry's stay'n at the La Vista."

"Without his clothes?"

"I guess? She didn't talk to him. When she came back from town, she wasn't happy. She was all brassed off. Gutted, you know. She left yesterday for Canada and didn't get to say goodbye to that fellow. I don't know. What did you think of him? A bit smarmy, don't you think?" Picking another card, she added, "She left you her address. Wants you to write. Tried to talk to you, but you being all dicky, she couldn't."

When the deck was almost spent, I realized Golly had the Old Maid card. I tried to figure out which it was in her hand so I could pick it, but her expression was always the same; no matter what card she was looking at, she appeared worried. We played two sets, and she was the Old Maid both times. She left with the babies in a huff, insisting on a rematch.

"Fair enough," I replied, happy to have something to look forward to. When she shut the door, I felt sad again and picked up my book that was next to my bed and tried to read, but my mind kept floating off. I kept seeing Harry lying on his bed, fiddling with his toilet kit or sitting on the floor sipping rum. I also replayed various scenes in my head like Doc's behavior and what Harry might have meant when he said, "It's not what it seems." As much as I had been trying to hate him, I couldn't. When the afternoon heat arrived and sleep finally took hold, I welcomed it, grateful for its peace.

Golly returned after dinner balancing a bowl of bean soup, along with Clive and Jubilee in her arms. "Jack named them. We also have a Fido and a Gremlin—Alex's kids. Fionnula, Tiberius, and Ptolemy, well, you know who named those three. Catarina named an absolutely adorable feather-headed girl, Peaches. Sarah named a little boy with a narrow chin *Escarabajo*—I guess it means beetle."

"More like a nickname."

"We put a baby aside for you to name. But we got bored and named it ourselves. Another go at the cards?"

"What did you name the baby?"

"Eleanor."

"Really—kinda crazy to have a child here named after me."

"It's a solid name. We all like it. Well, Alex had a problem."

It made me happy that they had named a child after me. For a brief few moments, I couldn't stop smiling. We played a couple more hands of Old Maid. Again and again, she lost. I found it puzzling that Golly kept losing. But she was determined to win and would be back.

As the days passed by, Golly became more and more obsessed with the game of Old Maid. When the kids were in school, she'd come up to my room with various babies, plop them down on the floor and let them crawl around while we played a hand. Baby Eleanor was a fat little girl with a tiny mouth that was stuck in between two giant cheeks which made her very kissable.

During snack time, under the pretense of bringing me a green drink, Golly and I would play a quick game. Late at night, she'd often unexpectedly burst in through the door, insisting on a hand before going to bed.

She'd put on weight since Molly had started seeing Gunther. To get down onto the floor she'd bend down, then fall onto her bottom. To put one ankle over the other or to sit cross-legged, she had to help her legs go where she wanted them to go. She often kicked me by accident because her knees didn't want to bend. She had stopped wearing shorts and now wore a pair of light cotton balloon pants, which were no longer ballooning because they were full. I felt bad for her. She had bright, kind blue eyes. All she wanted was not to be an old maid. She was kind and giving. "Someday you'll meet someone," I often said to her. She always replied with a smile. We were the only two single people left in the compound—Cadmael was officially shacking up with Doc, and Aapo was still in the mountains. I had this uncanny feeling Golly felt we were bound together in some sort of single sisterhood. I didn't mind. It was nice to have a sister.

"Doc and Cadmael?" I questioned.

"Yup, they been on and off for a long time."

"What's a long time?"

"Don't know."

I let the subject go. I didn't want to talk about Doc, Harry, or Cadmael.

After a few more days of hanging out in my bed, playing cards, and moping, I began getting up and helping with the morning washing of the children. Between Catarina being gone and me being sick and the new babies, the kids weren't being bathed in the same manner. Some even got away without showering.

Their clothes weren't being folded correctly, and they were now walking themselves to school. The pooping, peeing, and feeding of the babies had the *nineras* strapped. I also began swimming in the afternoons with the little kids; they liked the attention, but I could tell it wasn't enough. I wore a pair of Harry's boxer shorts and my bathing suit top. The mid-afternoon dip doused what was left of my blistering bites with a refreshing coolness. I had also started wearing Harry's T-shirts while sleeping and around the place. I liked how they fluffed easily to let the hot air out and the cooler air in. And although I was active like the little kids, now left primarily on their own, nothing was the same.

One evening after dinner, Golly came into my room. She had Clive and Jubilee and insisted on a hand of Old Maid. "Okay," I said, sitting up, still depressed and feeling moody. I didn't find anything amusing about the orphanage anymore. The whole place seemed sad. I didn't like that the babies had messed up the consistency and routine. The place had fallen apart, and I needed a change.

"New volunteers have arrived," she informed me. "French. Two stinky, scrawny, long-haired boys. They smell like rotten pickles. And the girl? She's jabby. Her name's Noya. Like annoying."

"'No ya' means 'not ready' in Spanish. Her name will confuse the kids," I said, dealing the cards.

"They stay'n in the attic urine room, fixing it up."

I was happy to hear new arrivals had come. It would make it easier to leave. But like Catarina, I needed to go into town. I needed some answers, closure. I wanted to say goodbye.

Chapter 38

Milla

I walked down the solitary, muddy street of El Puente to where the dirt road and the rutty paved road met. No one had told me, but Catarina had smashed the orphanage's car into Yena's house. A barely functioning vehicle was now a pile of scrap metal. Waiting for the bus wasn't so bad; it was even nostalgic. It was a beautiful morning, the air fresh from a recent downpour. The early-hour temperatures made it the most comfortable part of the day. Once the sun began to bake the puddles and the water-saturated trees, the air would turn to dense steam.

The school bus appeared, grinding its gears, painted with a colorful red-and-blue face of a dragon on the front. I stepped up and paid the bus driver's young assistant and sat down in a seat near the door. The bus was nearly empty. Ranchero music was blasting, the dashboard was cluttered with religious pamphlets, and the windshield was plastered with Christian slogans such as "*Dios es mi guia*" and "*Jesús me ama*." I was in a good mood. The anticipation of seeing Harry made me smile, and I chatted up a storm with the assistant. He was from the area and had eight brothers and two sisters.

The trip to El Pueblito was like a crazy amusement park ride, tossing me into the air and throwing me up against the window. I was all tuckered out when the bus pulled into town. Getting off in the center, I straightened my clothing and hair, went inside a small tienda, and bought a Coca-Cola. Standing on the front steps, I drank it looking around the street. It was still early, and the place hadn't woken up yet. A few dogs were roaming around, and one was sleeping. The La Vista Hotel was just a block away, and I stared at the entrance while gulping down large, gasping slurps of the fizzy beverage. I imagined myself walking down the sidewalk toward the hotel and Harry walking out. We'd both stop and look at each other. I wondered what the look on his face would be when he saw me. I thought he'd be surprised, and I was hoping in a good way. Then a man with a lumpy face and pig-like nose stumbled by. He was drunk and was scratching his armpits with a spatula. I sighed, thinking what a horrible town this place was.

Giving the empty soda bottle back to the tienda owner, I made my way to the hotel. A couple of men with glossy, tired, droopy eyes sat under the tattered green awning of the caged liquor store, drinking beer. The kook was sitting on a chair in the cage. He was looking out, a beer in his hand, and several empties were on the table next to him. He hadn't started playing music yet and seemed sullen, almost morose.

On the front wall of the hotel, which was next door, someone had placed a sign that said, *No soy un baño.* A woman in a bib wearing a straw hat was sweeping the steps. She looked like she was dancing with her broom. I walked by her into the lobby.

The lobby had harsh yellow walls and a rust-colored tile floor. A gangly spider plant hung from the ceiling, and two giant hibiscus plants stood in the corners by the stairs to the second floor. The place was clean and generic-looking. With no one tending the register, I took the liberty of glancing through the guest booklet. Not one name looked familiar. Shutting the book, I leisurely strolled out into the yard. A swath of overgrown vegetation lined the stucco walls. The air was wet and had a rotting, all too familiar odor. A bluestone patio with a glass table and cobalt blue wrought-iron chairs took up the right side of the grounds; the rest of the courtyard was made up of flowers, some grass, and a scattering of recliners. There was a man with dark wavy hair sitting on one near the back fence. A sparse-looking banana tree stood by his elbow, giving him a wisp of shade. He was reading a newspaper. Facing the sun away from me, his moppish dark hair and how he held his paper making me think of Harry. My stomach fluttered, and I could hear my heart beating. My head also felt light, like it might fall off me. Taking a deep breath, I steadied myself and walked over to the man. Stopping a foot away from him, I stared at the back of his head and cleared my throat.

The man turned and looked at me while folding his paper shut. "*Sí.*"

"I thought you were someone else," I said, feeling immediately depressed. He was an older man with a thin face and small features. On his nose he wore round silver wire-rimmed glasses. His most distinctive feature was his eyebrows; they met over his nose and were much too bushy for his face.

"Do you know a man named Harry? Harry Van Cleef?" I asked, my insides gripped with hope. The man looked at me, puzzled, so I said it all again in Spanish.

"No," he replied and then shook his paper in the air as if a pesky fly were bothering him and went back to reading.

The front page caught my attention. There was a photo that took up almost the entire page of two young, pretty women, smiling. One was a blonde girl with straight, white teeth, and the other was a brunette with sunglasses on. I moved closer and leaned in to see the caption.

"Please. Go away," he said in Spanish. I could tell he was from Spain; he spoke quickly and with a lisp.

I didn't leave. Instead, I kneeled to read. '*Mujer golpeada hasta la muerte en la aldea de la montaña... para vender los partes del cuerpo.'* The words were disturbing; I tried to read the story but couldn't because the lettering was too small.

Standing up, I asked for the paper. "Just for a minute." Frustrated, he got up, bunched the paper into a ball, thrust it into my hands, and walked away. His hard leather soles slapped the tiles as he went back into the hotel. From the back he did look like Harry, although his demeanor was all wrong.

I sat down on one of the lounge chairs and stretched out. Unfolding the pages, I began to read. The blonde girl's name was Milla Borja. She was from Finland. The other girl was from Italy. Two days ago, Milla and the Italian had been traveling in the mountains. They went into a village to visit a market famous for rugs and baskets. After leaving the market, they went into the center of the town and were met by a crowd of locals. The locals swarmed around them, shouting accusations that the girls were there to kidnap their children to sell them to rich Americans for body parts. The girls were kicked down to the ground and beaten to death with clubs, feet, and fists. The village elder said he had been told from relatives living by a river in the south about atrocities being committed by foreign whites. He gave the police a piece of paper proving the accusations true. There were six words written on the paper: hacksaw, wood, bags, machete, rope, and nails.

Putting the paper down, I realized I'd been holding my breath while reading and gasped for air. I sat for a few moments, digesting the article. The whole thing at first seemed incomprehensible. Then a very uncomfortable feeling welled up inside me, coupled with disgust. I imagined them, Milla and her friend, trapped by the angry crowd. The smell of unwashed clothing and madness similar to the stench of hundreds of sickly, underfed chickens, and rabid dogs. The pain of each kick. The raking of skin as choleric, angry hands grabbed at them, everyone wanting a piece. The horror of it was unfathomable, the list of items and accusations unconscionable.

A mountain village, I thought. Aapo had gone back home to the mountains nearly a month ago to help protect his relatives and friends from the Rabbit Moon. He knew Milla, and he knew we weren't harvesting body parts. It was a joke—nothing more than stupid babbling to pass the time. And the list of items? It had to be the letter I gave to Blue-Eyes—it was the items Harry wanted from the hardware store to build a garden at the *clinica*. Nothing more, nothing less. Did they really believe our inane, made-up blather? Our cynical, bored minds giving way to playful jests? There had been nothing sinister about it at all, just idiocy and our own amusement. I bit my nails. I felt guilty and horrified. But more than the unforgiving feeling of guilt, I was enraged over the senselessness of it all. Who beats someone to death over a list of hardware store items? My mind swirled, and I thought about what Doc had said about the people being angry due to so much having been taken from them. Then I thought of what Gunther had mentioned about our volunteer positions: "They used to be jobs. Paying jobs."

Reading the last paragraph of the article, the paper brushed off their deaths as "fatalism." It had a disquieting sound and kept me seated, my mind churning with the viciousness and the backward simple-mindedness of it all. Then, not wanting to think about it anymore because I was already sad enough, I tried to push the incident down deep where I couldn't retrieve it readily, but it kept popping back up. The images. Poor Milla. I found myself silently weeping, but for only a brief moment. Wiping my face with my shirt, I folded the paper and tucked it into my daypack for the others back at the orphanage to read. They would all be so sad—horrified, I thought.

In front of me was a door in the fence that led to the main road. It wasn't enough to keep out an insane mob, I thought. Did this rundown town think the same way as the people in the mountain village? Then, crinkling my nose, I got up. I'd had enough of the town and felt it was best to leave. Besides, Harry wasn't here, just a Spaniard.

When I walked by the liquor store cage, the kook had finally put ranchero music on. It was blasting into the street, while in the cage he gyrated his body to the tune. Spotting me, he howled a wild catcall.

When I didn't respond he called me a "*pinche cula.*" Disgust flared inside of me, followed by hate. I hated this place. The rot, the drinking, the poverty, the rich fruit owners, the oil, the lumpy roads. A skinny dog came over to me to see if I had anything for him. I swatted at the air, shooing him away. The sun, already baking the land, made everything putty and moldy. I thought about going back to the States. Was it time?

Grateful to see a bus waiting by the tienda, I ran over to it and got on. The assistant was eating a tortilla while collecting money. I paid and sat down by the door. I didn't feel like talking on the trip back, even though the young helper stood by me the whole way to El Puente. He kept asking me questions about where I was from, was I traveling alone. I told him I didn't speak Spanish.

Remaining in my head, I made future plans. Fanciful daydreams of images of better days to come, but none of my thoughts had me returning home. No, I wanted a different country. Not the USA, and not here.

Once in El Puente, the sun directly overhead, I decided to try one other way to find Harry. Walking over to Yena's house, I knocked on the door. The thin, ragged man who had been at the house that night so long ago opened the door. When I inquired about Yena, he shrugged and at first told me to go away. When I gave him the history of how I had met her, declaring I wanted to say hello, he became friendlier. He told me she had sold the house and had gone south with her grandson and nephew. Looking behind him, I saw the room was completely bare, not that it ever had much. He must have noticed my curiosity because he added that he was just cleaning up and leaving too. I then asked him if he knew Harry Van Cleef. He laughed and shut the door.

All my means to find Harry used up, my mood dispirited and blue, I went back to the main road, bought a hot dog from a vendor, took one bite, and threw the rest away. I then secured a water taxi to take me back to the orphanage. It was a smallish canoe with a zippy engine, and we flew over the water. Rounding the bend by the *peligroso* sign, we saw the waters off the orphanage were ablaze with small crafts. It was the *policia de la marina* in their hard-bottomed rubber Zodiacs. I told the driver to check it out. Joining several other onlookers, we idled in the water by the mangroves on the north side of the schoolhouse. There were several policemen, guns on their hips, faces serious, and caps with gold trimming pulled on tight. They were standing in the water and searching through the mangroves. Then several more appeared coming out of a thicket of mangled roots, branches, and reeds. They were carrying a stretcher with what appeared to be a body zipped up in a black bag. They put the body into one of their boats. It was a gruesome sight. The anxiety and nausea I felt over the butchery of Milla and her friend was now drenched with the death of another. Frozen in place, I once again forgot to breathe.

Chapter 39

Leaving

I sat cross-legged on the dock with all my possessions, which were not many: a backpack, a daypack, a book, and a water bottle. I had left my bed and all its drapings for the next person. Too cumbersome to carry around. It hadn't been as difficult as I had thought to say good-bye to the kids. It was as though they expected it. No sadness, just a small wave of the hand, then aloofness and off to play. Volunteers came and went. In a three-to-four-year-old's brain, how was the change comprehended? No big deal? Or was it a loss that would cause great stress to their lives later in life? Both, I thought, because it's usually both.

I got the answer I was looking for that day I went into El Pueblito. It was Harry in the body bag, and now a hollowness rested inside me like a giant drum empty of life. We had a vigil at the orphanage for Milla and Harry, the disruption of "routine and consistency," and the rabbits who were supposedly gone now, according to Molly's wall chart.

Golly finally won at Old Maid. She was also very obnoxious about it. It was as though I had never won a game. She kept going on and on about me being the old maid and how she was now "Ge'tin a China plate for a husband," and I was only to have "Barnies and Porkies." When she hugged me good-bye, she wouldn't let go.

Now morning, I sat for the last time on the dock listening to the lapping of the waves on the shore while reading the last few pages of my book. It had turned out to be a poetic book that didn't help me with Spanish fluency; the words were too literary. Yet, I did chuckle over the psychiatrist in the novel describing the male protagonist to be like a twitchy woman who sleeps around looking for an "authentic" orgasm.

Putting the book in my backpack, I looked up to take in the morning light of the river one last time from the dock. It was mysteriously calm. The middle turbulence had quieted down. Breathing in the splendor of nature, my eyes rested upon the sun rising above the trees, a light orange color visible and beautiful and so spectacular I figured the day could hold nothing but good tidings, or at least I hoped so. I was emotionally spent. It was a tiredness that only time could cure, not sleep.

Across the water, a sailboat was winding its way from the Club de Bote. It was heading toward me, its bow sleek and narrow. It was a sloop-rigged L. Francis Herreshoff H-28. I knew this because I had been told in detail about every inch of it through notes passed from Manolo to Golly to me when I was ill. A twenty-eight-foot boat wasn't large for a seafaring sailboat, but this one was long enough, wide, and sported a shallow draft for comfortable shoreline sailing and sleeping, or so I was told. It was the color of night and had a white pinstripe outlining the lacquered mahogany railing, which was dappled with shiny brass cleats. There were three off-white sails, and the mast flew a blue-and-red Belizean flag because he'd purchased the boat there from a fellow named Dan in Belize City. The sails were furled, as the present direction of the boat required the precision of a motor.

"Ahoy, Eleanor!" Dorian yelled, waving an arm while holding the brass helm with the other. He wore a ratty-looking straw hat that shrouded his eyes. With only the tip of his nose, mouth, and chin showing, he looked comical. He was standing upright and appeared robust, his smile kind. Maybe he would grow on me, I thought, sniffing the air. Taking a deep breath, I stood up.

He threw me a line, and I tied it to the left front piling. Leaning into the sailboat, I handed Dorian my bags, undid the line, and jumped in while pushing us away. Dorian kicked the throttle into gear, motoring us back into the outer waters. We planned to go up the river to the mouth of the ocean, then head to the Bay Islands off of Honduras. They were my plans, and since Dorian did nothing but wander from one shore to the next, they were his plans too.

Passing around a bend, we saw the *clínica* tucked behind mangroves and willowy vines. A broad opening appeared, and I saw Doc outside standing by the half-made garden talking to Cadmael. "Doc was Harry's fiancé," I said, more to myself than to Dorian.

"Horrible tragedy," he said.

I remained silent and began to look through my bag for a Spanish dictionary and a notepad. I wanted to look up words and write them into sentences. I needed to do something, anything to preoccupy my mind. For some reason seeing Doc brought back a searing rawness to Harry's death.

"They say the body was nearly decomposed," Dorian remarked. He had one hand on the wheel and the other in his front pocket. "If it weren't for the locket tucked inside the sneakers bouncing by his bloated blue head, they never would have been able to identify him. The *policia* seemed to think he had been there for weeks being torn up by the fish, crocs too. Did you know him well?"

When I didn't reply, he continued. "I guess one of the little kids found him. Alfred?"

"Albert," I whispered, wishing he would just shut up.

"The body was trapped by the mangrove roots that had a bunch of purple and red flowers growing on them. Interesting. That kid Alfred likes flowers. I like flowers, too—must have been horrible for him to see something like that. You know, in the papers, his name wasn't Van Cleef. It was some long name—lots of names. Possibly French?"

Glancing up, I said, "Chilean. He was Chilean. That's what the police said when they came to get his stuff. He had several different passports, though." I glanced over at Dorian. I hadn't wanted to think or talk about Harry but doing so actually felt good. It made the incident more distant, as though I were reciting a story in *La Noticias*. "It's all so strange," I continued. "I kept asking the police, what was his name? I mean, what was his real name? And you're right. It's long. They knew for sure he was Chilean. I wonder how they knew that with all those different passports."

"Yes, that's right, Chilean. Well, he had cement blocks attached to his feet. It never ceases to amaze me how the locals kill people and put cement blocks on the victim when everyone knows they float." He then chuckled, took his hat off, and wiped his brow. His blond hair was matted to his head. He ran his fingers through it, making it spiky, then put the hat back on again— but the rim was bent back, and he looked goofy. Still looking at his face, I found I didn't find him attractive anymore. He had become irritating and plain-looking. But then my whole reason for being with him had to do with the idea of a pet. Harry's idea, and then again, it was a lot of people's idea too. When a pet dies, people like to go out and get another one, so they feel better. But this wasn't working. It was all going terribly wrong.

"Do you want some water?" I asked, getting up and going down into the galley.

"Sure, luv." It also bothered me that he called me "luv."

The living area was cluttered with old rags hanging off the cushions; pieces of paper and other knick-knacks were scattered over the floor and in the corners. The air smelled like old shoes and cleaning fluids. I began opening and shutting drawers to see what he had: flares, a flashlight, a bottle of gin, gum, sleeping pills, more dirty rags.

A guidebook on Central America was on the counter by a sink full of filthy dishes that had attracted flies. I picked it up, flipped the pages, and randomly landed on Panama. I read down through the different sections on how to get there, half-listening to Dorian babbling in the background.

Scuba diving was described as pleasurable and exotic, and there were surf schools on the Atlantic coast. Scuba diving seemed attractive to me. There was a scuba-diving language school that had language classes in the morning and diving in the afternoon. Now that would suit me well, I thought; I still needed to improve my Spanish. I also read that I could either take the mailboat or a small plane from the town at the mouth of the river that we were motoring to, to Panama. Yup, Panama could be a better choice than the Bay Islands, I thought. Then, for a brief moment, I was taken aback by a visceral sadness. I would go alone because I needed to start anew.

Realizing Dorian was still talking, I began to listen to him again. His voice was shallow and tinny. How boring and dull, I thought, pushing my hair away from my face. Standing among the clutter, I huffed, wishing I'd gone to El Puente and taken a bus.

"I was talking to the bartender at the club. Max, great guy. You know what he said?" He was shouting now, most likely because I hadn't been saying anything back. Climbing up the ladder with a couple of waters from the mini-refrigerator, I handed one to Dorian.

"He said Harry had relatives here. I guess an aunt. An Indian woman named Yenara, but he called her Yena. She was from the Muppet tribe in, in—"

"Chile. I think they're called Mapuche." That's what the boy who drove me to the orphanage in his motorized canoe had said. So, I muttered again, "Yena and her family are Mapuche." I then thought of another time, an era gone by, and said, "I went to Chile once. Years ago, as a kid. My parents and I went to the Atacama Desert. My father wanted to paint it. Beautiful place." Taking a sip of water, I said, "Before it all fell apart."

"What fell apart?"

"My family."

"They do that sometimes," he replied. I then sat down on the seat next to him and asked, "What did you say about Harry's indigenous aunt?"

But instead of answering me, he was stuck on the word "muppet". "He's part Muppet. Didn't look it. I used to see him with the clinic doctor having drinks at the bar. They fought like crazy. Don't think they liked each other."

"I think he loved her," I said, not particularly happy to hear about them drinking together at the bar, but glad they fought. Then, reflecting back over the months, I thought about conversations, words that had meant little then, but that now appeared important. "The aunt from Chile. The bartender said her name was Yena?" I asked.

"I believe it was Yenara or Yena or both. I wonder whose side of the family she was on. I guess she was wealthy. Moved here with a few family members when Pinochet took over the government. Bought up cheap land, built shit. Smart lady. Max said he helped the family with maintenance stuff. Sometimes ate dinner with them. I guess that's how he know's so much. Oh, he said that Yena had to leave quickly. Gosh, real cloak-and-dagger stuff going on. Some ministry fellow trying to mess with her deeds. She had sold all her properties and that official fellow, the...the Minister of the Interior wanted all her money. Said it was his. There was a gunfight. Must have been when that Harry was killed. Do you know, that minister guy and his pack of goons chased Yena and her family clear across the border in the middle of the night?"

I chuckled. How silly of me not to have picked up on all of this until now. Harry had been a teen when Pinochet came into power. No wonder there were rebels and guns in his stories. His stories made sense now; I just had the wrong country. "So they had to leave in a hurry," I said, then fell gloomy, again. "Sad Harry didn't make it."

"Why be sad, he's a criminal."

"Doesn't sound it. Seems the authorities are the criminals." I looked down the river with a heavy heart, took a deep breath, and refocused on Dorian. "Max knows a lot. Did he say anything about a man named The Scott, Dan Scotchwick?"

"Mean to the help. Disappeared and never paid his bar bill. But get this: They found his sailboat down a swampy estuary. The club owners claim it's their boat now—it's their payment."

"His boat was found. I wonder where he went?" I paused to think. "Doesn't make sense. Did Max say what happened to him?"

"He had a theory."

"And..."

Dorian rubbed his chin and bit his lower lip as though wondering if he wanted to tell me, then he looked off to the side and sighed. "Well, ummm...Max thought it was The Scott's body and not Harry's they found."

"The sneakers and the locket," I said thinking out loud while having a moment of clarity. "He lost them in the water. My god, I think Max is on to something." And giggled as blueness, depressing, defeating thoughts that had been plaguing me for days began to melt away.

"What do you mean?" Dorian asked. His tone was skeptical.

"Harry had lost his locket. He wasn't wearing it when they so called killed him. Nor his sneakers because he had lost those in the water weeks before, too. Those two items were how they identified him. What Max said makes sense. It's The Scott they found all decomposed. Yes, that must be it!" I began to laugh. The shock of Harry being alive. "Why, that handsome devil," I mumbled, then gulped back my joy. "I wonder who killed The Scott?"

"What are you saying? And what's so funny?"

"Nothing." I had no idea who killed The Scott and didn't want to speculate. But I did have my suspicions with The Scott going off with the fellows on the Bertram, and why did Harry have The Scott's dinghy? There was no point in saying these thoughts out loud. Harry being alive was thrilling and I didn't want to muddle it. "Life. It's so full of surprises," I said and laughed, and laughed.

"A man's dead and you're laughing. This is scary." He took his hat off and wiped his brow, cocked his head at me, and asked, "Are you not right in the head? Tell me, do you miss the children?"

"Of course," I said. "If I were more together, settled, I'd have taken a few home with me."

"I thought you said most weren't adoptable."

"Most isn't all of them. Albert's adoptable. Wonderful, curious, flower-loving Albert. I wonder what will happen to him?"

"Grow up, get a job, get married, have kids. What do you think?"

"I don't know."

"Eleanor, you're not going home. Right? We're going sailing," he said insistently. I didn't have the energy to tell him that I would be leaving him. So I merely replied, "I said if I had it together, but I don't. Anyway, they're in good hands; the French have arrived."

Sitting back, I looked out over the river; a blue macaw sat in a tree as a pelican dove down into the water. In the lazy sunbeams, swaths of flies clouded the air and butterflies flitted in between dark and light. The air smelled of greenish water and sweet linden trees. I relished time and life, the enjoyment of wallowing in a second, making it an eternity. The orphanage had been wonderful at making time stand still, I thought, thinking how interesting life was. Human quandaries and their daily existence, and how at the bat of an eye a leaf falls or a hungry bird finds a fish.

Giggling again, I said, "If my friend Gunther were here, he'd say I'm lucky."

"Of course, you're with me," he remarked.

"Well, yes, of course, but also because I have options in life." I paused and bit one of my nails. "But I don't know about my common sense. I did sit on an ants' nest. But if you're lucky, you just end up with a few scars. What do you think?"

"Why, I have a boat and a beautiful girl on it. I'm a very lucky man."

I watched Dorian steer the boat and found myself glad to be with him. It was temporary, as I had other things to do, like work on my Spanish and scuba dive. But he had become tolerable now, even pleasant to be with; most of all, I was grateful not to be alone. My heart felt like it had been peeled thin. It ached. Even though I was convinced Harry was alive and the body they found was The Scott's, I knew I'd probably never see Harry again.

"I wonder how many Harrys there are in the world," I pondered. "Or rather, Heraldos. That was his real name. Well, that's what they say his real name was."

"Whose?"

"Harry's."

"Hundreds, thousands. But I don't think you'll find a lot of Dorians." Dorian removed his hat and tossed it onto the deck. He looked annoyed.

"Harry doesn't know my last name," I pouted.

"I know your last name. Abernathy."

"I never told Harry. I wonder why?" I said as though talking to myself.

"I don't think we should talk about Harry anymore. It's getting boring," he snapped.

Ignoring him and lost in thought, I sat back against the gunwale.

Even if he knew my last name, I doubted that he would look for me—much too complicated. Then I blurted out, "Serendipitous encounters! Dorian, have you ever lost something only to find it again?"

"A dog."

"One day. Someplace fun like a mountain top or surfing or scuba diving, or a cafe sipping coffee in a city—maybe I'll run into him." And I laughed. It was so fantastic to have hope.

"I doubt it. The people who are looking for him don't want him alive. If he is alive. They'll get him sooner or later," Dorian lit a cigarette and took a long draw.

"How do you know this?" Was Harry's past so wayward that certain people wanted him dead?

"Why...why...Max told me."

"That's awful. Did Max say why they are looking for him?" I had a feeling Dorian was making it all up.

"No."

"Harry's resourceful. Hopefully he'll be fine," I said, and added, "Don't be jealous of him."

He laughed, "I guess I'm being a bit of an idiot."

His remark made me smile. Although I would be leaving him, he wasn't a bad fellow and, as far as I knew, kind. Yet my heart belonged to another, at least for now. This didn't mean we couldn't have fun. Running my eyes over his face and body, he had become handsome again. "Dorian," I said coyly. "Would you like to stop for a while and rest?"

Acknowledgement

I would like to thank the members of the Westport Rivers Writers Guild: Corey, Paul, Jerome, and Dwayne. They patiently, and at times, not so patiently, listened to the first draft and some of the second draft of this novel. Ugh! No one should have to listen to or read a first draft; the Guild was instrumental in keeping me writing. Thank you to my partner, Paul Andonian, for letting me read bits and pieces to him at breakfast, lunch, and dinner. A great big thank you to all the Beta Readers and proofreaders, and to editors.

L. Wendell Vaughan has written for various magazines and newspapers. Rabbits and Moons is her first full length novel. She wrote a children's book in 2001 called "Andy Ant, *What Could possibly Be On The Other Side to See?*' The book has been noted for its lessons on diversity and making new friends, and was made into a play by the Circle Nursery School. Vaughan, a world traveler, has spent a vast amount of time in Mexico, Central and South America. She taught high school history and English for 21 years. She lives in the southeast area of Massachusetts with her partner, Paul, and her horse, Pages.

Made in the USA
Middletown, DE
10 March 2023

26392083R00194